Rev...
"Ribbons and Salt

I enjoyed reading this enchanting book and I was intrigued by its unusual title: "Ribbons and Salt". The vivid description of the magnificent banquet in Bordeaux transports the reader to a subtle battleground where secret machinations trigger a tumultuous cascade of emotions and intrigues against Alienor and her impoverished family. This book swept me into a bygone era with articulate, ebullient strokes of a fascinating and seemingly tragic love story set during the French Renaissance. I loved Alienor's grit and determination to enhance her condition, and the way the entire storyline has been interwoven with elements from European Medieval literature. I highly recommend this poignant romantic narrative!

Hemma Myers Sood, author of Tijara's Mystery Codes

The bygone era of the French Renaissance comes alive in Klara Wilde's debut novel "Ribbons and Salt". From the beginning, you can sense that Alienor is going to be a strong and occasionally feisty character. It is clear that the author has put a lot of research into her book and that she herself enjoys historical fiction and loves the Renaissance era.

Rebecca Lange, author of Her Hand in Marriage

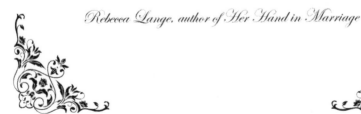

Reviews for "Ribbons and Salt"

"Ribbons and Salt" is a magnificent family saga steeped in tragedy, classism, and courtly love, wrapped beautifully with a ribbon. Klara's storytelling is unique and, I believe, will keep the readers on their toes as she weaves through different perspectives and timelines. While not written chronologically, the transitions with each chapter are seamless and had me eager to flip each page. I found myself intrigued to further educate myself on the French Renaissance, in love with the headstrong Alienor, and swooning over the romance.

Chelsea Lauren, publishing editor and author of
Theodore's Work in Progress

From its very first pages, "Ribbons and Salt" captivated me with its fascinating story and immersed me in the richly detailed world of sixteenth century France. I often found myself holding my breath at all the unexpected twists and turns in the plot, and had a hard time putting down the novel, hungry to discover more about its enthralling characters and their secrets.

Victoria Diaconasu, Beta Reader

ISBN 979-8-9864995-2-9

Cover Design by Brittany Evans

Edited by Represent Publishing

RIBBONS
AND
SALT

RIBBONS
AND
SALT

KLARA WILDE

Represent Publishing

First Part

Tokens of Fin 'amor

Chapter One
Alienor

"All we need is one day. One day and our lives can change forever. Fate does not need more to alter its course. One day is enough. It was enough then. It shall be enough now. And that day is upon us," Alienor whispered in Catarina's ear.

They had been the first to descend from the borrowed carriage, which had taken their family to the banquet. They were waiting for the others by the gates of the Ombriere Palace.

Her sister said nothing in return. She just stared ahead at the high, grey walls.

The sun was setting over the city of Bordeaux. The ancient fortress was lit by so many torches that it appeared to shine with the brightness of a hundred moons. It was a good sign. Light was needed to chase away darkness to the chasms that birthed it and to dispel any trace of bad luck from her path. Alienor was only sixteen years old, but she knew that the time was ripe. She had a tryst with fate, and she was not going to keep her waiting. She

1

gazed at the magnificent building that had housed, once upon a time, the wedding banquet of Alienor of Aquitaine. That, too, was an excellent omen. The great queen was her namesake, and just like her, she was determined to forge her own path in life. Alienor told herself that it was like stepping into her own territory and that she shall triumph that evening, come what may.

Once her father sent away the carriage, they all joined the stream of richly clad guests and soon found themselves in the palace's courtyard. Neither Alienor nor any of her sisters had been to a banquet in Bordeaux before, nor visited any of the other great cities of the Kingdom of France. Filled with awe and self-consciousness, she did her best to look poised and distinguished. The gown she was wearing was made of blue brocade and had seen better days, having once been her mother's. It was one of the few items of value to have survived her family's sudden fall from grace, and Alienor had had to work hard over the past weeks to improve and revive it. She was content with the results. Her gown was embellished with a fashionable gauze partlet, which covered her shoulders and cleavage, and with new sleeves which matched the silver-coloured underskirt. She knew she was no match for the beautifully adorned, rich ladies of Bordeaux, but she felt confident she could hold her own in grace and elegance. However, she knew that, more than anything else, it was her astuteness she should rely on that evening.

"Oh, to be in Bordeaux at the mayor's banquet! I do not know how to still my heart..." her eldest sister, Elisea, exclaimed, coming to a stop in front of the palace doors.

"Please, Elisea, try to gather yourself. Remember that it is of the utmost importance to look dignified tonight!" her other sister, Catarina, whispered in an alarmed tone of voice while passing Elisea by and lifting her black gown to step over the high threshold.

Alienor walked alone behind them, since she was the youngest. Their parents had walked in first and were already leaving their hats and capes with the servants. Once she and her sisters did the same, they all stepped into the banquet hall. It was enormous compared to the one they had at home, and it was filled to the brim with guests. Lavish tapestries adorned the walls, servants rushed from side to side carrying jugs of wine and trays of fruit, and the minstrels' music rose above the humming of the voices of those lucky enough to have been invited to attend the banquet that evening.

A few moments later, Alienor was standing with her back pressed against one of the hall's high walls, a goblet of mead in her hand. She took a sip of the sweet liquor and stole a side glance at her sisters, who were standing by her side. Elisea and Catarina were still engrossed in a hushed and tense exchange of words. She loved them both dearly, but she knew she could not rely on their help that evening. The power to change her fortune lay with her and her alone. She had to distance herself from her family and go in search of a certain gentleman. For good or for worse, her fate was in his hands, and there was no turning back.

Alienor took another sip of the sweet mead for courage and left her sisters behind without a word of farewell. She passed by her parents, who were surrounded by a small circle of their acquaintances, clearly enjoying themselves if one was to judge by the smiles on their faces. She crossed the long banquet hall, gliding between the couples dancing the minuet and the groups of lords and ladies engaged in lively conversations. Her eyes searched the crowd for his unforgettable face, but he was nowhere to be seen. She reached the large doors that opened into the inner courtyard, and she took a deep breath of fresh air. Her eyes moved with purpose over the noble guests assembled in the courtyard to admire the games of the acrobats employed for the occasion by Monsieur de Montaigne, the mayor of Bordeaux. Their juggling torches created a dramatic display of dancing lights and shadows, thwarting Alienor's attempts at distinguishing the faces in the audience. The music of the minstrels was spilling out of the banquet hall. She felt the mead warming her from the inside. But she reminded herself of her duty. She couldn't afford to waste precious time. The announcements were to be read soon. Alienor looked at the setting sun and estimated that she most likely had only about two hours left.

She searched through the crowd with renewed urgency, presenting her excuses right and left as she forced her way across the courtyard. She caught sight of him, at last. He was a few steps away, but had not noticed her presence. Her heart beat faster and faster. The gentleman appeared to be enthralled by the acrobats' performance. She stared at his profile, at his long chin, sharp nose, scarred cheek and took in his black cape and long feathered hat. There was no mistake. It was him. Alienor took a generous gulp of mead and took a step towards him.

"Oh, here you were, dear Éléonore! We have been looking for you."

Catarina appeared behind her as if out of nowhere, closed her fingers around her upper arm, and pulled her back. Caught in mid-stride, Alienor had to stop, but she did not turn to face her sister at once. Though they were still several steps away from him, her sister's exclamations accomplished the feat of drawing the attention of the gentleman in black. And, for a moment, their eyes locked in a lingering gaze.

"I was coming to you..." Alienor willed her eyes to say the words her lips could not whisper. Then she turned, with a sigh, towards her sister: "Ie suis venue icy chercher de l'air frois[1]. The air was hot in the banquet hall, and I could hardly breathe."

And with that, she followed her sister back inside. But, as she was about to step through the doors, she cast one last glance over her shoulder and saw that he was still standing there, looking at her.

Chapter Two
Armand

Bordeaux, Easter Monday,
early evening

"We have been looking for you." A woman's voice carried above the minstrels' music and the occasional cheer from the surrounding crowd.

Armand shifted his gaze from the spectacle in front of him towards the source of those exclamations. He was almost startled to find a lovely young lady staring right at him, mere steps away from where he stood. Then he saw another young lady was standing right behind her, holding her by the arm, in an elegant, almost statuesque pose. And then, with the inevitable clarity of the first lightning in a calm summer sky, he recognised her. She held his stare. He found it rather bold of her and could not help but feel embarrassed by it. He came to understand that she might have been on her way to talk to him when the other lady must have caught up with her. Armand hoped the blood did not rise to his cheeks in apprehension. He tore his gaze away from them. It was best to feign indifference.

It might have been a coincidence that she was there, but either way, Armand had no wish to talk to her yet. From the corner of his eye, he stole a long glance at the two young ladies as they walked away from him. The one who had appeared to be headed his way was, beyond a doubt, the same young lady he had met at the tournament. Her hair was black and coiled in an elaborate coiffure of braids enlaced with shining red ribbons. A long translucent veil covered it and fell on her back and shoulders. And Armand would have recognised those bright brown eyes anywhere. He saw her reach the palace doors and then turn her head to look straight at him. He hurried to look away, but not before he glimpsed a hint of a smile on her lips.

She does not seem embarrassed at all to seek a gentleman out in that manner! Yet she is very young. Who is she? Armand wondered. He had never before met a girl, a lady from a well-off family, judging from her clothes and jewels, who showed such direct manners in front of a man to whom she had not been properly introduced. His sister Anne, who was not much older than that lady, was a true master in the art of decorum and would not be seen displaying anything else but graceful self-restraint at all times. Though, in all honesty, she did so a little too well and too often, even in the privacy of their home. Armand was left wondering at times whether his sister had any feelings beneath her impeccable countenance or whether there was any chance that Anne might not turn into a younger version of their strict, cold mother. That young lady, on the other hand, moved around freely, without a chaperone, and she did not find it difficult, it seemed, to speak her own mind. At least, she had not seemed to do so that morning. The two of them had ample opportunity to talk during the tournament, since they had sat next to each other. Her astute remarks still echoed in his mind. She even succeeded in bringing about a smile on his face on one or two occasions. And then there was the ribbon...

The tournament had been a part of the elaborate celebrations organised on Easter Monday by the retiring mayor of Bordeaux,

Pierre Eyquem de Montaigne. His estate neighboured that of Armand's family, and they had socialised on many an occasion. It had been impossible to ignore his invitation. Armand was there because he had been selected to accompany his father at the festivities given in honour of the newly elected mayor, Louis de Saint Gelais. It was said that he had yielded great power at the Court in Paris and that he had been entrusted with the education of the royal princes by Queen Catherine[1] herself. Armand, and the whole of France with him, knew that he was, furthermore, a natural son of the former King, François I. That made him a half-brother to His Majesty, King Henri II. Armand understood he was but a pawn in his parents' game, whose sole intention in attending that banquet was to ingratiate themselves with such a powerful and illustrious character. His family had enjoyed such a close acquaintance with the de Montaignes they were sure to want to continue the tradition. Power and connections were all they liked to talk about, especially his mother. She held, after all, such high hopes for his younger siblings', Anne's and Aimery's, futures...

Armand took another sip of wine to chase away the bitter taste that filled his mouth whenever he thought of his mother and her stratagems. They had thought that his presence at the festivities that day, alongside his father, would be enough to promote his family's interests. But what if he were to go a step further? After all, they had not prohibited him from participating in the games...

Armand had to admit that he had done little else than thinking of that lovely young lady over and over throughout the day. He found her pretty, with her fair skin and upturned nose. And she was candid and self-assured. It seemed as though she could see beyond the shallow appearance of men and circumstances and grasp their hidden meaning. He had not met a girl like that before. He remembered the warmth of her body pressed against his on the crowded stone bench of the old Roman amphitheatre and the sweet perfume of her hair. He could still feel it in his nostrils, a subtle scent of lavender and camphor oil. Those were expensive luxuries, which meant that she had to belong to a family of means...

Armand took another sip of wine to clear his head. He had expected to see her at the banquet, of course. Yet he had dreaded that moment. A sigh left his lips. He had to talk to her. It had to be done.

His reflections were interrupted by the loud exclamations of a group of ladies standing next to him. The acrobats' bold jumps made them laugh and applaud. That reminded him of the young lady's refreshing laughter earlier that morning. It had sounded genuine and almost wild, different from the restrained laughter of the other noble ladies he had met. And her pointy remarks had been most entertaining. It had been impossible to desist from smiling once or twice. He had to admit that he rarely smiled these days... since his return from Italy. Armand found it difficult to laugh without a care at some silly joke or at the exaggerated, shameless behaviour of a jester after witnessing the atrocities, the hunger, the misery...

His nostrils filled, as if by magic, with the raw stench of death, of burning human flesh, and he felt a familiar cramp in his stomach. Like fog rising from the warm earth, the memories rushed forth, taking shape in front of his eyes. He saw once again the hundreds of half-rotten corpses piled up high on top of each other on the streets of Sienna, waiting for the soldiers to come and light them up. And then the flames consumed them, as quickly and eagerly as they were wood, making the hot summer air, already infested with disease and despair, impossible to breathe. His stomach churned as he relived the terrible moments that had almost cost him his life.

Armand shook his head and pushed away those memories. He looked again towards the entrance to the banquet hall. It was getting late. The announcements were bound to start soon, and he was yet unprepared.

Chapter Three
Catarina

"Are you feeling unwell, cara sor[1]?" Catarina whispered in her sister Alienor's ear as they were braving, hand in hand, the sea of noble guests gathered in the main hall. "Was that your mysterious gentleman?"

Her sister looked her in the eye and nodded, but did not say a word. She didn't have to either. They understood each other well enough without words.

"Alienor, why did you stop?" Catarina asked as they both came to an abrupt halt, and she bumped into her sister's shoulder.

Alienor did not answer. Catarina looked up and then she saw it... she saw him... the reason her sister had come to a stop. Her hand sprung to her mouth, and she stifled a scream.

"Is that who I think it is?" she heard Alienor whisper as she grabbed her by the arm.

"Yes, it is him. The monster..." Catarina whispered back.

The person in question turned around, perhaps alerted by

one of the other gentlemen around him. He locked eyes with Catarina. She wondered if there was a glimpse of recognition in his eyes, if the sight of her and her sister reminded him of his past crimes. They were standing before him, hand in hand, just like they had back then, facing him and his soldiers in their castle's grand hall, with tears trickling down their little girls' cheeks. But to him, those cruel deeds might have been nothing but a trifle. Death, pain, misery... they must amount to nothing in the eyes of such a powerful and wicked man who did not shy away from harming innocent children. He was there, in front of them, after all those years, but did not appear to remember a thing. He looked them up and down with an arrogant air.

Catarina felt her composure crumble. All those years, all those prayers, all those songs she played on the lute at night trying to forget it all, to make peace with what had passed... and yet, there he was, alive and well. No, not just well, thriving! He looked healthier, richer, and more celebrated than ever before after his return from captivity in Spain. He was receiving honours from His Majesty the King, taking part in tournaments, enjoying himself at banquets...

"My ladies," she heard him say, slightly dipping his head in their direction.

He had a smile on his lips as he did so. He was once again attempting to humiliate them, to show that he was their superior in one and all regards. Catarina felt righteous outrage surge, unstoppable, from the very depths of her being. She could no longer repress it. All that her family had endured those past eight years, all the suffering, the deprivations... It had all been because of him and his accursed companions.

"Meu Deu...!"[2] she heard Alienor whisper.

She must have realised, too, that he did not know who they were, that he did not remember what he had done to them. But Catarina did. The memory was edged into her soul, and she could not fight it any longer. Two tears left the corners of her eyes. They ran along her cheeks, leaving them wet and cold.

That day, too, had been wet and cold. There had been water everywhere... freezing, unforgiving water that would not stop pouring down on them from above. Water was supposed to be holy and purifying, or so she had been taught in church. But water had come like a calamity that day, like a vengeful, heavy, implacable wave that swept through their lives... And in its wake, like the survivors from a wreckage, hungrily seeking for their loved ones among the debris brought to shore by the waves, Catarina and her family were left to live with the knowledge that the lives of those they loved had been swept away forever...

She had kept silent when that gentleman and his soldiers had barged into their home. She had neither spoken nor screamed. But she will not be silenced any longer.

Catarina wiped her tears and took a step forward. She said, perhaps a tad too loud, just as he was about to turn back to his peers: "Mon seigneur de Montmorency!"[3]

Called out, the man stopped in his tracks. Several other noble guests turned around to look at them. Catarina felt their eyes on her, their stares burning into her arms and shoulders. She was breaching all rules of decorum by addressing a knight, a scion of one of France's most powerful families, in that direct manner, without a proper introduction.

"Yes, Mademoiselle de...?" she heard him say, his voice resplendent with the confidence that only wealth and power can bestow on one so young.

"My name is of little consequence, monsieur," she said as she boldly took another step towards him. "But know that your hateful actions are not forgotten."

"My hateful actions? Are you quite well, mademoiselle? I am afraid that the heat of the mead must have climbed to your head..." she heard François de Montmorency say to the men at his side with a snort.

They all laughed. Catarina felt her neck and face burn. She knew that she was being foolish, that she was embarrassing herself in front of all those noble lords and ladies. But she couldn't bear to keep silent... not after all those years... not anymore...

She took a deep breath and was about to retort, but Alienor proved faster.

"Monsieur, I congratulate you for your performance in the tournament," she heard her sister say, then pause.

Catarina drew a deep breath in. The Chevalier de Montmorency raised an eyebrow, but bowed his head nevertheless to accept the praise.

"Some might even say that it was incredibly brave of you to come here today. But while your presence here is... unavoidable, it would only be unwise of you to mock us in this manner. We are of the noble blood of old Aquitaine. This is our home," Alienor continued.

Catarina was surprised to hear her younger sister deliver those lines with perfect confidence as she faced François de Montmorency, without turning her eyes away, without fear or weakness... She felt her heart soar with pride and stole a glance at her sister. Alienor swept the crowd with her gaze.

Catarina looked around them, too, and saw that some were nodding in approval. And none of them had said a word to interrupt or contradict her. In truth, none of the other noble guests could afford to attract the wrath of the de Montmorencys, and by extension of the new mayor and the king, by taking the side of two young girls. But she realised that few, if any of them, appeared to sympathise with François de Montmorency at that moment. She saw it in their glaring eyes and furrowed foreheads that, although eight years had passed, the cruelty of the de Montmorencys had not been forgotten in Bordeaux.

The chevalier shifted his weight, obviously uncomfortable and at a loss for words, and that unbearable arrogant smile of his was gone.

"En fin, mademoiselle... I do not know you..."

"Si ell dur, yo fort!⁴ We stand strong and proud, my lord. And we are not afraid. Bordeaux remembers. The whole of Aquitaine remembers!" she said, her voice loud and stable.

Catarina forced herself to look the man who had destroyed their lives in the eye. After two more heartbeats, something changed in the way the chevalier looked at her. And then he raised his right hand as if to protect his upper left arm. He had remembered, at last! In the stunned silence that followed, the sisters nodded to each other. Then, in silent understanding, they turned their backs on François de Montmorency and his retinue. They walked away, arms entwined, one dignified step after the other. The crowd opened to make way for them to pass. The guests stared and whispered. But the heads that bowed before them and the voices that murmured their approval were far from few...

Chapter Four
Armand

Armand de Ségur de Montazeau was sweeping through the crowd of assembled ladies and gentlemen in search of the young lady he had met at the tournament. It was his second turn about the vast banquet hall. So far, he had only managed to locate Philippe de l'Isle, his friend and companion in arms, but he had preferred to not approach him. He was standing in a corner, surrounded by several young ladies. Armand saw him mimic a sword fight or the manoeuvring of a harquebus, and he knew from experience that the Chevalier de l'Isle was telling them a highly exaggerated story about his military exploits. The ladies seemed to love it. They usually did. Their laughter and exclamations were so high pitched they rose above the music and the general clamour of the hall. Armand could not get away from them fast enough.

After a little, he stopped to catch his breath and replenish his goblet with more wine from the pitcher of a passing page. It was then he caught sight of a lady who could very well be the one he sought. He was not entirely sure it was her, because she was standing with her back to him. She was talking to an older lady. He tried to get a better look. It had to be her. She was wearing red ribbons in her dark hair, covered by a translucent veil trimmed with silver thread. If only he could have a better look at her, and see her face... then he would know for sure. The older lady's eyes rested on him, and she had the same reaction of petrified terror that he was used to seeing his appearance entice in others. It occurred to him he must have been staring at them in an indecorous manner, and he shifted his gaze. He was, however, still unsure of what to do next.

After a moment's reflection, Armand concluded that the older lady must have been her mother. But if her frightened reaction to his scar was any indication, she was not going to allow him anywhere near her daughter. In that, she was not alone. He smiled bitterly as he watched her hand move across her voluminous chest. Only a select few crossed themselves openly, as if they had seen the Devil himself. It was probably best for him to turn around and make himself scarce...

But before he could make up his mind, the young lady turned around, a dash too swiftly. He was both relieved and embarrassed to see that he had been right. It was her. He could not forget those lovely eyes... The lady stopped short when she came face to face with him. The long, gauze fabric attached to her elaborately coiffed hair became loose in the process and fell down. It trailed in the air gracefully for a moment before landing on the floor in the space between them. Perhaps in an attempt to retrieve her veil, the lady bent her knees but then stopped in mid-air and turned the movement into an as elegant as possible reverence. She then stood and faced him with a very straight back, her hands folded with poise in front of her. And she smiled at him.

Startled for a moment by the young lady's rather amusing movements, Armand was slow in picking up her fallen veil from the floor. "Mademoiselle, vostre voilette!"[1]

15

He swiped the floor with the long black feathers of his hat, bowing in a deep reverence, before standing tall again and presenting to her the veil with his outstretched hands.

"Ie vous remercy, monsieur.[2] You are very obliging," she answered, with composure, receiving her voilette.

They stood there facing each other in silence for a moment. He felt at a loss for words. She looked so dignified and noble, quite unlike the talkative, even irreverent girl who had sat on the same bench with him earlier that day at the Roman ruins known as the Galien Palace. It was there that the tournament had been held. Armand's determination wavered again. He did not doubt it was the same lady; he had even recognised her dark blue dress, but she was showing him no sign of encouragement.

"Are you enjoying the banquet, monsieur?" she asked.

"Yes, my lady. Are you?" he replied, grateful for the question.

"Yes, monsieur, very much," she said with the faintest smile.

Armand noticed that her lovely complexion acquired a light, rosy glow. He was not sure, but he thought he saw a hint of a blush on her cheeks. It made her complexion look even lovelier...

"Would you do me the honour of dancing with me, my lady?" He had, at last, mustered the courage to ask her.

"I would, my lord," she said, curtsied and then added, in a hushed tone of voice: "Gladly."

Armand bowed into a long reverence to better hide his embarrassment. His neck was burning. As he rose to his full height again, he stole a quick glance around him to reassure himself that no one else had heard those words. He then looked back at her and noticed that the young lady had turned around and spoke in hushed tones to her mother. It occurred to him he had forgotten to take off his cape and hat upon entering the hall. He dashed away to search the crowd for his page.

Chapter Five
Alienor

Bordeaux, Easter Monday,
early evening

Alienor's proper name was Éléonore de Durfort de Civrac. Her mother liked to remind her to use the French version of her name when out in society. But Alienor was her true name. It was more beautiful and genuine. It was the Occitan name of the greatest Occitan queen, and she was proud to wear it.

"Catherine, you must try a bit harder, dear," her mother, the baroness of Civrac, told her second eldest daughter.

They were standing near one of the corners of the hall, listening to their mother's animated words. Catherine was what she liked to call Catarina. Elisea was the eldest daughter and had inherited their mother's name, Élisabeth. Their father, whose title was François de Durfort, le Seigneur de Civrac, Rauzan et Pujols[1], was engaged in conversation with Monsieur de Rémy, a few steps away from where she stood. The subject must have been a very captivating one, judging by their ample gestures.

From the corner of her eye, Alienor became aware of the

glances that Monsieur de Rémy's eldest son Louis was casting in their direction. She stifled a giggle.

"Éléonore, my hopes lie with you. It seems a bit too late for your sisters..." her mother whispered, trying her best to pretend she did not notice the smiles and long glances her eldest daughter was, in her turn, directing towards the said Louis de Rémy.

Alienor understood her mother's thinking. Madame de Civrac had brought her three eldest daughters to Bordeaux in an attempt to secure a better future for each and every one of them. Madame de Montaigne's games of chivalry were a God-sent opportunity that neither of them could afford to miss. The banquet had just begun; the possibilities were endless. Alienor knew she was going to remember that day for as long as she lived. A lot was at stake, and she had to succeed.

She and Elisea had promised each other the night before they left Rauzan that come what may, they would do everything in their power to save their family from certain ruin. They were both practical, and they understood one another. Catarina, on the other hand, was shy and stubborn. She liked books, music and philosophical questions more than she liked people. And her lack of interest in the day's games kept attracting their mother's reprimands. It was to be expected, but it did not make it any less unnerving. Truth be told, Alienor found that their mother was ill-disposed towards her sister. She was harsh and unfair, and she kept hurting Catarina's feelings. Like so many times before, her sister had turned to face the wall and was sobbing in her handkerchief. Alienor put an arm around her shuddering shoulders.

"It is quite alright, cara sor!" she whispered.

"Oh no, this will not do, Catherine! Élisabeth, dear, quickly, your sister is not feeling well. Please escort her outside. She is in dire need of some fresh air!"

Madame de Civrac manoeuvred Catarina out of Alienor's embrace and into the arms of her eldest sister, who was thus forced to interrupt her flirtations with Louis de Rémy.

"Chere mere!"[2] Alienor protested, but was silenced by a cutting look of her mother's.

She knew it was a lost cause, yet her heart ached for Catarina. Elisea took her sister by the arm, and the two of them disappeared into the crowd. Her mother had a satisfied smile on her lips. It was clear that she was pleased to have found the perfect solution to both her problems. While Catarina was too shy, Elisea was too flirtatious. And Alienor knew that deep inside, Madame de Civrac did not approve of an alliance between her eldest daughter, the family heiress, and Louis de Rémy. Her suspicions were soon confirmed.

"That girl is determined to undermine her own mother's best efforts and remain a spinster for the rest of her life! While the other will settle for an unequal marriage and tie our fates to this family of newly enriched opportunists..." her mother whispered in her ear.

"They are both trying their best, Mother..." she said and then stopped.

Alienor noticed that her mother was not listening to her. She appeared to stare in shock at something past her daughter's shoulder as if she had seen a spectre standing right behind her. The terrified look in her mother's eyes sent shivers down her spine. She hoped she was not going to have another episode... The only person she could think capable of inciting such a strong reaction was the Chevalier de Montmorency. She prayed she was mistaken.

Alienor turned around with a swift movement, her heart threatening to tear her ribcage apart. But it was not him. It was none other than the gentleman she had been looking for since arriving at the banquet. She thanked the Lord and let out a breath she did not know she had been holding. But her relief was brief. In turning, the veil covering her hair became loose and fell at her feet, which made her blush with embarrassment. But he picked it up and returned it to her. They stared at each other in silence.

Alienor felt very uncomfortable standing under the glaring

glow of a mural torch with the veil in her hand. She prayed that her appearance did not betray her feelings. It was the moment she had been waiting for, and she was overjoyed that he was seeking her out. But that was not how she had envisioned their reunion. The heat from the torch was becoming more and more insufferable, and she could feel her armpits grow wet. She was anxious to cover her head again. Standing without a veil just two steps away from a young man made her uneasy. She knew the scene would look scandalous to any onlooker. Her mother must have been outraged, although she thankfully kept her silence. The mere sight of that mysterious gentleman had already produced a strong reaction from Madame de Civrac. Alienor could almost feel her mother's disapproval burning between her shoulder blades. But she fought the urge to turn away.

Instead, she engaged the gentleman standing before her in a respectful exchange of empty pleasantries. At length, he invited her to dance, and she accepted. The chevalier then took his leave. Alienor hurried to turn around and enlist her mother's assistance in securing her veil back in place. She was naturally grateful for her mother's help, but she felt less so once she started whispering about the chevalier's appearance.

"Oh, Good Heavens, Éléonore, how do you know this ghastly gentleman? Do not tell me that he is..."

"Maman, please make haste. The dance is now ending, and the next one is about to begin!"

Several couples took their positions in the middle of the banquet hall, the place reserved for the dancing. Alienor joined them at the arm of the gentleman in black. It took all her strength to not blush when she looked the noble chevalier in the eye. He was standing right in front of her, without a cape, clad in a rather stylish suit made from the purest, shiniest black velvet. Many years had passed since she had seen such a luscious, expensive fabric up close. It occurred to her that he might be very rich. Gone was the hat with black, long feathers, and she saw, for the first time, the long, curled locks of brown hair falling over his broad shoulders. The scar on his left cheek looked rather striking. She realised she had been staring at him, and that he was staring at her in return...

The minstrels stroke the first chords, and Alienor lowered herself into a slow reverence. She gripped the folds of her blue dress and lowered her eyes. With a bit of luck, he had not noticed the blood rising to her cheeks. She stole a glance at him from under her lashes just as he strode towards her. Even if he had noticed, he was not betraying that knowledge in any visible way.

You have come this far, Alienor. You cannot act shy now and ruin everything! she thought while graciously taking her turn around her dance partner.

"You are a mystery, my lady," he said to her, raising his voice over the music and the voices of the other couples crowding the middle of the banquet hall, trying to strike a conversation, just like they were while following the intricate steps of the minuet.

"What might you mean, my lord?" she replied, trying to still the mad beatings of her heart, yet smile and move graciously in accordance with the cadence of the dance.

"Am I mistaken, my lady, or did we sit side by side this morning at the old ruins while we watched the games of chivalry?" he asked, raising his arm in a gracious arch in the space between them, waiting for her hand to join his.

"We might have, indeed, my lord," she answered, wondering where that was leading.

She raised her hand to meet his, following the prescribed dance movements. And then their hands touched for the first time.

He continued with a smile while they each took a step forth, towards one another: "And yet, you somehow do not seem to be the same person, mademoiselle."

They were standing very close. Her face was just a breath away from the chevalier's. She stared into his blue eyes and said, in a half-whisper: "It was me, I assure you, my lord..."

His nod was almost imperceptible.

"And were you, by any chance, searching for me in the court-yard earlier this evening, my lady?" he continued.

They both took a step back and let go of their hands, as required by the dance.

She took a deep breath and said: "I was. I wanted to talk to you, my lord."

He nodded gravely and took another turn around her. Then their arms reached upwards in unison, and they, once again, stepped towards one another. He kept looking into her eyes as they danced. She kept his gaze, trying not to blink.

"About your ribbon, my lady?" he asked her.

"Yes, my lord."

She felt her cheeks glow even warmer, but she willed her eyes to not look away from his. She prayed he would somehow understand.

The dance steps required them both to step back now and disengage their hands. She took a step back and tried to free her hand. But he did not let go. Instead, he tightened his hold on her fingers. She looked into his eyes again with a startle. And it became clear, then and there, that they understood each other.

Chapter Six
Catarina

Bordeaux, Easter Monday,
early evening

"We are only as strong as our fortress. It is written in our very name. The family of Durfort. We build strong walls to protect ourselves and those we love. We do everything in our power to hold the castle, to hold the gate and not let those who might not wish us well inside. The problem is we almost never know whether someone might or might not wish us well. Not at the very beginning. So it is safest to assume that they do not and talk to them from the distance of the high tower. We do not let the bridge down and invite them in until after we know their declared intentions to be true. But eight years ago, my father did lower our bridge, and opened our gates... too soon, much too soon... We are only as strong as our fortress. Once it falls down, we are sure to fall along with it."

Catarina liked her own company. And she enjoyed having conversations with herself, in her head, or even by whispering to the winds on occasion. Especially if it was from a great height and there was no one around. The winds muffled and carried away her words. Like in that very instant. After sending her elder sister back into the banquet hall, she had climbed the stairs leading to the rooftop of the palace's great tower. Leaning with both her elbows on the edge of the parapet, she watched the setting sun. Her thoughts wandered, as was their habit. The dreaded encounter with the Chevalier de Montmorency had made them spin, and her mind was busy at work in yet another futile attempt to make sense of her and her family's fate. She was alone but for the sentinel standing at his post. It was quiet there, and she liked it. She needed a respite, away from the tumult of the banquet, the pressure of the game and the antics of her family. The memory of what had passed was still with her, permeating her thoughts, reminding her of the importance of the choices one makes, at each and every step, in life.

"Si ell dur, yo fort," she whispered to the wind.

Those were the words she had thrown at the man who had caused their ruin. They were her family's motto, la devise des Durforts.

"As long as my fortress is standing, I shall be strong," she told herself, like Aunt Isabeau used to when she put her to sleep.

They had lost so much, but Catarina still had her parents and her sisters. And Rauzan was still standing. Unlike their castle at Pujols, which had burned down, Rauzan endured. It had been pillaged, impoverished, forgotten... yet its sturdy walls and towers still stood high and proud. There was no telling what the future would bring for her, but Catarina vowed to stand high and proud, like her ancestral castle.

She let out a long sigh. In truth, she had known for a while that her participation in Madame de Montaigne's game of fin'amor[1] had been pointless. They might just as well have given that ribbon to another young lady who was not bound to let her parents down like her. It was no secret that she lacked most of the qualities that would have enabled her success that evening or helped her sparkle in society with grace and beauty, like her sisters.

With a sigh, Catarina pulled away from the parapet and climbed down the stairs. It was time to join the chaos of the banquet hall once more. Her family must have been wondering where she was.

She found her parents where she had left them, standing by the side of the hall. She made her way to them. They were watching the dance. Her sisters were among the couples dancing the minuet. The glare her mother sent her way in lieu of a greeting made her look down at the hem of her gown. Catarina saw her apprehensions confirmed. She had grown accustomed to disappointing her parents. Yet that seemed even more painful than before.

She stole a wilful glance at her sisters, who were dancing in the middle of the hall. Catarina knew she could not be like them. She was neither as pleasing as Elisea nor as bright as Alienor. And then there was her youngest sister, Elina... a girl of fourteen springs, too young to be introduced to society yet. She was the prettiest of them all. Catarina wondered where that left her. She was the second daughter, seventeen years of age, and with every prospect of remaining an old maid...

Catarina asked a passing page for a cup of mead. Once she received it, she took a sip and let out a sigh. It tasted sweet and enticing, just like honey. The music streaming through the hall was divine. She closed her eyes to hear it better, fading out the clamour of the guests. The minstrels played the lute with so much more mastery than she ever hoped to achieve, despite practising every day. She knew that such extravagant banquets came into the path of those like her once in a blue moon. More important than some silly game of the imagination was to enjoy oneself and create beautiful memories to last a lifetime.

All of a sudden, Elisea, all smiles and chatter as usual, tripped over the hem of her dress and nearly fell over Catarina, spilling the contents of her goblet on the floor. The dance had ended, and the pairs dispersed from the dance floor towards the edges of the enormous banquet hall. Catarina shot out an arm to steady her sister and then promptly took away her goblet.

"You have had quite enough of mead for one evening, it seems, cara sor," she told her in confidence before Louis de Rémy joined them.

And so did this gentleman! Catarina thought, but kept the notion to herself. To him, she said: "Monsieur de Rémy, how did you enjoy the dancing?"

Elisea and Catarina were standing arm in arm. They did not see eye to eye on most subjects, which was to be expected since they had very different dispositions. The manner in which her eldest sister carried herself at the banquet that evening had made Catarina want to roll her eyes more than once. What she saw in Louis de Rémy remained a mystery to her.

"Very much... Of course, my lady."

And Louis de Rémy's cheeks turned even rosier as he raised his cup towards Elisea, and they both smiled at each other. In the uncomfortable silence that followed, Catarina was shocked to notice that her sister was throwing meaningful glances between her and Louis de Rémy in a very untactful manner.

Suspecting that her sister meant to force the gentleman to invite her to dance, she protested: "Élisabeth, ie vous en pry[2]..." but she was interrupted as the gentleman finally took a step forth and cleared his throat loudly.

"Mademoiselle Catherine de Durfort de Civrac, would you do me the honour of the next dance?" He bowed with elegance, if somehow unsteadily.

Catarina felt her cheeks grow warm. She found herself in an impossible position. She did not have any good reason to reject the first and potentially the last invitation to dance that she would receive that evening. And yet, she felt uncomfortable that her sister had to insist in that unbecoming manner for Louis de Rémy to feel obliged to invite her to dance.

"A vec plaisir, monsieur,[3]" she answered with the most pleasant voice she could sum up, bowing into a curtsy.

Catarina offered him her hand and then followed him to the centre of the hall. She looked back at Elisea over her shoulder and hoped her intense glare would let her sister know how she really felt about her meddling. But her sister raised her goblet and smiled at them wholeheartedly.

Catarina's attention was soon drawn to the pair right next to them. It was none other than Alienor and that mysterious gentleman of hers.

"How many dances have you danced with him tonight, sister?" she whispered once she reached her sister's side.

Alienor smiled, and so did she.

They aligned with the rest of the ladies on the dancing floor, standing in one row. The minstrels stroke the first accords of the dance, and they all curtsied in perfect synchronicity to the gentlemen who stood in their own line across from them.

Catarina recognised the notes. It was an old minuet, one of her grandmother's favourites. Unable to afford a dance teacher, it had been her mother and grandmother who had taught her and her sisters to dance. Catarina could play on her Italian lute most of the songs she had heard so far at the banquet. It was as if she could see the notes in front of her eyes. Music was dependable and soothing. The notes of a song were predictable, unwavering from their tempo, regardless of where, when, or who was playing them. She felt safe in their company. Gentlemen, however, scared her.

Alienor's partner looked like a sinister character with that striking scar of his. She swallowed hard and forced herself to look at Louis de Rémy instead. He was not that handsome either, but Catarina could not avoid looking at him since he was her dance partner. At least, there was comfort in knowing she didn't have to pursue the affections of any gentleman that evening.

Chapter Seven
Alienor

Bordeaux, Easter Monday,
after sunset

Late on the evening of the banquet, Alienor was crossing the stone courtyard of the Ombriere Palace in the company of her mysterious gentleman, whose true name was Armand de Ségur. She knew it because they had been introduced.

The two of them had danced together several times. She had lost track of the dances. As far as she could remember, there had been minuets, allemandes and even a danse basse. Her feet ached. Gliding hand in hand across the dance floor for the whole length of the dance basse had brought the heat to her cheeks more than once. But the smiles they had exchanged, the manner in which he had looked her up and down when he thought she was not looking, gave her hope. After a while, they parted ways, and she joined her sisters by the side of the hall.

Alienor and Catarina spoke at length about the unfortunate encounter and their ensuing confrontation with François de Montmorency. They congratulated each other for their courage and esprit[1]. But they agreed to conceal their encounter and the presence of that man at the banquet from their parents and their talkative sister. There was no point in darkening their evening with painful memories... Besides, it had become clear that Elisea was not interested in anything other than enjoying herself at the banquet and the attentions that Louis de Rémy was lavishing upon her. An engagement was imminent.

As the three of them stood in a corner of the hall, sharing whispered observations, Elisea remarked now and then upon the jewels and the gowns of the noble ladies. Catarina, on the other hand, was a keen observer of the human mind and its working, just like Alienor. They enjoyed pointing out to each other the comic mannerisms of the various members of the illustrious assembly. Some of them were mere strangers. Others, like the Lamothes and the Rémys, were close acquaintances. But being familiar with their mannerisms did not make them any less entertaining.

The evening had advanced. The sisters had danced, talked and made new acquaintances, like any of the other young ladies present at the banquet. They had not allowed the unpleasant encounter with the Chevalier de Montmorency ruin their evening. The past was the past, and they all needed to look towards the future.

And then, just as Alienor was exiting the hall together with Catarina, she had bumped into the Chevalier de Ségur at the door. They had both tried to exit the stuffy banquet hall at the same time. He had seemed preoccupied but had gallantly greeted her and her sister, offering them precedence out of the door. Out in the courtyard, he had asked to speak to her in private, and she had found it impossible to refuse his invitation. They had unfinished business, after all.

When Catarina took her leave, the two of them looked at each other in uncomfortable silence at first. Alienor kept glancing at the chevalier in the hope of encouraging him to speak, but his mind must have been busy because she noticed the shadows of several emotions reflected upon his scar-crested, long face.

At long last, he asked her whether she would do him the honour of accompanying him to a more private place where they could talk undisturbed. He suggested the rooftop of one of the towers guarding the old fortress. She agreed, despite the little voice in her head which warned her against such a breach of decorum. Time was running out. She was not going to put in jeopardy the victory she coveted, nor allow one whole day's painstaking work to go to bits for such an insignificant detail. It would have been pure folly to decline a tryst of fin'amor on that day, of all days.

They climbed the narrow steps leading to the tower's rooftop in silence. The stairs twisted and twisted, and her long skirts kept gliding out of her grasp. Alienor felt rather self-conscious. One wrong step, and she could fall, making a fool of herself in front of that gentleman who was climbing the spiralling staircase right behind her. Once she reached the top of the stairs and emerged into the chilly air of the evening, she walked to the crenulated parapet. She had to strain her eyes, for night had already descended upon the city. She looked in the distance, beyond the roofs of the nearest houses, inside which the good citizens of Bordeaux must have started to ready themselves for bedtime. The high tower of Porte Cailhau was visible, but nothing much beyond it. The moon was yet to rise.

Alienor reminded herself that she needed to focus on looking graceful and dignified, and hold back her emotions. Truth be told, she was growing tired, but she could not give up when she was that close. She had to continue on the path she had chosen and answer the call of duty... for her family... and perhaps even for herself.

She stole a side glance at the Chevalier de Ségur, and she was startled to see he was staring at her. She could not help but blush. But she did not look away. Her dignity, her pride, was her best weapon.

"I am glad that we have been formally introduced at last,

Mademoiselle de Durfort," he said, breaking the increasingly uncomfortable silence between them.

"Yes, indeed, monsieur."

For a moment, they both looked at each other as if to measure one another anew. Alienor knew she should not be the one talking. Not anymore. She had pursued him all day. To encourage him, she had taken enough daring steps to make half of the ladies in attendance blush. The words of her mother and her nurse, repeated to her and her sisters day after day, year after year, were imprinted in her memory: "La dignitet et la patiente sont les plus belles vertutes d'une noble demoiselle."[2] It was time for her to be that. A dignified young lady. And to be patient. The chevalier was taking his time. They were alone on the keep's rooftop, except for one sentinel standing still, like a marble statue at its post.

A delicate perfume climbed up from the courtyard below, and Alienor recognised it at once. It was the sweet scent of blooming lilac. Faded echoes of the minstrels' music streamed out of the hall below. Even the occasional laughter or exclamation reached them as if coming from a great distance. She was aware that she was alone with a young gentleman whom she had not met before. It was, in fact, the first time in her life that she found herself in such intimate circumstances with a gentleman, and her heart was pounding hard. But above all else, she was longing to hear what more he had to say.

"I understand that you are the niece of the Lord of Monluc, my lord commander," he observed after a while.

She smiled. "Yes, my lord. He is my uncle on my lady mother's side. And I was glad to notice that he held you in high regard, monsieur!"

"Thank you, my lady. It is a privilege to serve with the Lord of Monluc," he replied with a nod and asked after a pause: "If I may inquire, my lady, are you close to your cousins, the Chevalier or the Captain of Monluc?"

She took a moment to think her answer through. "I am close to my cousin Marguerite de Monluc, yes. We write to each other, but I am afraid I have not met any of them in a long time, monsieur. Have you served together with my elder cousins, the Chevalier and the Captain of Monluc, my lord?"

"Yes, mademoiselle, with the Chevalier de Monluc in particular. I heard that his health is improving."

"Yes, my lord, it is what Cousin Marguerite wrote to us, too. We hope he will recover soon. But, as you must surely know it yourself, mon chevalier, certain wounds take a long time to heal..." Alienor said and stole a glance to catch his reaction.

Armand de Ségur flinched, but did not turn to look at her. He seemed to stare at the night sky.

"You are right, mademoiselle. Such is our fate. But we are men of arms, and we do not shy in front of danger. We cannot. And when the king and the country need us, we answer the call of duty without wavering."

The depth of his words surprised Alienor. She almost blushed at hearing him speak of duty in that manner. It resonated with everything she believed in.

"Yes, my lord, you speak the truth, and I commend you for your bravery and sense of duty," she said with a smile. "Ladies do not carry arms and do not fight for king and country, like you gentlemen. But we, too, must value our duty above all else and face life with courage, as best we can."

The Chevalier de Ségur appeared shocked by her words, just as she knew he would be. He looked at her for a while, and she held his gaze. It was, after all, his turn to come to a decision and tell her what that was.

He nodded. "If I may take the liberty of saying so, you are most unusual, Mademoiselle de Durfort! Has anyone else told you that before, my lady?"

Her mind could have been playing tricks on her, but she thought she saw something akin to a glimpse of admiration in his eyes.

"Not by many, my lord... I must confess that until tonight, I have scarcely ever left my father's domains in Bazadois."

"And yet you seem to have many an opinion at hand, my lady..."

"One does not need to travel the world to keep oneself informed, my lord," she offered.

"Indeed not, my lady," the chevalier of Ségur replied and added, after a short pause: "May I be so bold as to inquire whether you and your family share the religious convictions of your relation, le Seigneur de Duras?"

Alienor took a deep breath in. She had expected religion to be brought up, and she had an answer at the ready. Yet explaining the peculiarities of her family when it came to this subject was not easy. And as far as she could remember, the de Ségurs were devoted Catholics, so she had to mind what she was saying. It was not worth losing her best chance at forging an alliance that evening for the sake of her faith.

"Not entirely, monsieur. The Lord of Duras is indeed my father's cousin and the head of the Durfort family. But my mother has endeavoured to raise all of her children in the Catholic faith," she answered.

"And how about your lord father, mademoiselle?"

"My father was raised in the Protestant faith, in Navarre, where my grandmother was a lady-in-waiting to Queen Marguerite. Truth be told, religion has always been a topic of controversy in our family, monsieur."

Candour was the best choice. He nodded. She was aware of the unusual circumstances of her family when it came to matters of faith. Like her sisters, she had been baptised in the Reformed church, since they were de Durforts, but prayed most often with her mother at the Catholic chapel at Rauzan. She had been taught both doctrines and did not see them as incompatible.

After a while, the Chevalier de Ségur spoke again: "It occurs to me, my lady, that I should have guessed your noble lineage from the very beginning by the colours of your dress. Blue, silver, red... like your family crest. If I am not mistaken, the first and fourth quarters are argent[3] with a bend azure, and the second and the third are gules with a lion rampant of argent?"

"Indeed, monsieur," she replied, beaming.

He nodded in response. Alienor felt proud and glad at the same time. Proud that she had had the good thought to plan her apparel to reflect the Durfort colours, according to medieval customs, which had been revived for the day's festivities. And glad that her efforts had not gone completely unnoticed.

They looked at each other in the ensuing silence, some sort of tacit understanding passing between them. He smiled at her, and she smiled in return. And then they conversed for a long time... about the day's games, the code of chivalry and the beautiful works of Michelangelo Buonarroti, which he had been able to witness first-hand while in Tuscany, until they arrived at the subject of Monsieur de Ronsard's[4] latest book of poems, "La continuation des amours".

"If I may be so bold as to confess, monsieur," Alienor said with a smile, glad to see that the Chevalier de Ségur was, like her, an avid reader of poetry, "my favourite poem from this book is the following:

> "*Mes souspirs mes amis vous m'estes agréables,*
> *D'autant que vous sortez pour vn lieu qui le vaut:*
> *Ie porte dans le cueur des flammes incurables,*
> *Le feu pourtant m'agrée et du mal ne me chaut.*
>
> *Autant me plaist sentir le froid comme le chaud:*
> *Plaisir et desplaisir me sont bien incroyables.*
> *Bien heureux ie m'estime aymant en lieu si haut,*
> *Bien que mon sort me mette au rang des*
>   *misérables.*"

The Chevalier de Ségur interceded, with the faintest hint of eagerness in his voice, and continued reciting the final tercets of the sonnet:

"Des misérables? non, mais au rang des heureux.
Un homme ne pourroit sans se voir amoureux
Cognoystre par le mal que valent les liesses.

Non, ie ne voudrois pas pour l'or de l'Univers
N'avoir souffert les maux qu'en aymant i'ay
    soufferts
Pour l'attente d'un bien qui vaut mille tristesses."[5]

Alienor felt her heart skip a beat as they stopped in their tracks and their eyes met.

At long last, the bells from the nearby churches started ringing through the evening air. Only half an hour left before the announcements.

"Perhaps we should head back to the banquet hall, my lord..." Alienor said and turned as if to head back towards the staircase, hoping that he would stop her.

Chapter Eight
Armand

Bordeaux, Easter Monday,
after sunset

"Please wait, my lady," Armand exclaimed, putting a hand on her upper arm.

He had to prevent her from leaving. She could not go, not yet...

Mademoiselle de Durfort turned her head in surprise. His fingers had but grazed her sleeve, yet he could not help but feel embarrassed by his bold gesture. He withdrew his hand.

"Excuse me, I did not mean to..." His words trailed off, and he suddenly felt very hot. He looked away and tucked his hands behind him.

The moment when he had held her in his arms that morning flashed before his eyes, adding to his embarrassment. Time and again, he failed to take his intentions to completion in an elegant manner. Unlike his friend Philippe de l'Isle or the Captain of Monluc, his lord commander's son, Armand was not used to the company of ladies and lacked the charm and lustre to please them.

Although strangely enough, this particular lady seemed to turn a blind eye to his blunders...

She turned to face him once more, abandoning her plans to return to the banquet hall. "You are excused, my lord," she said with a mischievous smile.

For a moment, he saw in her again, the irreverent girl who had entertained him with her witty observations at the Roman amphitheatre that morning. The ease with which she could change her countenance was disconcerting. Mademoiselle de Durfort was much better at talking than he was. That much was clear to him. She had the natural gift of sparkling in conversation. If only he could be like that, too...

He swallowed hard, unable to muster a smile at a time like that. "Let us stay a little bit more, my lady," he said with a calm voice. "I have a matter of certain importance to discuss with you..."

"Very well, my lord," she replied.

He was becoming more and more aware of the swift passing of time. He had to make waste, come what may. It had to be done, and it had to be done that evening...

He straightened his shoulders. It was unbecoming, after all, to trifle with that young girl's feelings. For she was just a girl, despite her brave and, he had to admit, successful efforts to look calm and composed that evening. It was a long cry from the irreverence of some of the statements she had made that morning at the Galien Palace.

"Monsieur de Ségur?"

Lost in his thoughts, he had forgotten that she was standing there, waiting for him to speak.

He took a deep breath and spoke at last: "My lady de Durfort, you have been candid with me earlier today... at the tournament... and while we danced..."

She nodded in agreement but did not respond.

He looked at her and willed himself to show as much bravery

at that moment as he had on countless occasions before on the field of battle.

"And I, in turn, would like to speak with candour. We both know what the purpose of that strange game is, my lady."

He saw her neck turn a darker shade of rose. His words had made her blush. Although it might have been due to the unforgiving glow of the torches peppering the parapet... His resolution wavered, and he halted his discourse.

He then hurried to add, taking her hand in his, in a moment of unchecked forwardness: "Please excuse my frank manners, my lady. I am, after all, a man of arms, unaccustomed to the intricacies of courtly love. But I will endeavour to speak from the heart, as the poets say..."

Chapter Nine
Madame de Montazeau

Montazeau, early March

"This Easter Banquet is nothing but a complete waste of time, if you ask me, my dear. The mayor's wife must be unbearably bored if she has time to muster such inventions. No one has ever heard the like of it in the whole of Aquitaine, I can assure you, madame!" Claude de Ségur, countess of Montazeau, said to her close friend and confidante, Françoise de Foix, countess of Candale, who was visiting her, as she always did that time of the year.

The two of them had been friends since before they were married, and they were called Mademoiselle de Rochechouart and Mademoiselle de la Rochefoucauld. They had maintained a close relation even after they both entered excellent marriage alliances, though they met far less often these days. Claude devoted her time to her children, her beloved Anne and Aimery, and to her active social life, as befitted her rank. It was a great disappointment that she did not have more neighbours of impeccable breeding and character, like the countess of Candale. The latter lived a sheltered life on her estate at Benauge, which was a day's travel away from Montazeau. Her husband and eldest son, being almost constantly engaged in one war or the other, she led a secluded life with no one but her daughter Charlotte for company.

Since Frédéric de Foix, the Count of Candale, became a Protestant some years ago, he had become obsessed with furthering the cause of his new religion and embarked on a personal quest to defeat Catholic Spain. He was a celebrated knight and war hero, but Madame de Montazeau knew he had been mortgaging his domains in secret to finance his campaigns, and that her friend and her daughter lived in penury as a result. She also knew that the count had strong objections to their friendship. He thought that his wife, who also had to convert, as did their children, was fraternising with the enemy by spending too much time in the company of Madame de Montazeau, a devout Catholic.

"Quite right, dear friend. I was rather scandalised myself when I first heard of it. In our time, no one could have possibly thought of anything like this... No respectable family is likely to attend such a banquet, in any case. Though she is the mayor's wife..." Madame de Candale said but was promptly interrupted by her friend:

"The soon to be former mayor's wife!"

"Yes, of course, but then she has the support of the new mayor as well, my dear. He will be announced and introduced at the banquet, after all. Despite his undesirable... background, he has been entrusted with the education of the princes of France, and rumour has it that he has the ear of Queen Catherine. In fact, I heard that she and the king are quite taken with this manner of medieval... festivities. You are not thinking of refusing the invitation, are you, chere amye[1]?"

Her friend looked at her with eyes alight with interest. She lowered in her lap the embroidery that had been occupying her so far. Claude cursed herself for not having an answer at the ready. In truth, she had yet to make up her mind about her family's participation in the festivities. She was torn between her own convictions on the matter and her deep curiosity to meet the new mayor, freshly arrived from Court. A bastard though he well was, he was of royal blood and very close to the power circles in Paris, and she was well aware of the many possibilities that a closer acquaintance with him would open for her family. And then there was, of course, her husband's close relation with Pierre de Montaigne, the soon to be former mayor, to consider. He and his family were, furthermore, their neighbours. No, she could not, as much as she would have liked to, downright refuse that woman's invitation. She had to find an appropriate excuse for her and her beloved Anne. She would never endanger her only daughter's reputation in such a careless manner. At the same time, the family of Ségur de Montazeau had to be suitably represented at the banquet. Otherwise, it would be a social blunder unworthy of their rank.

"Of course not, chere madame. We will do no such thing. My beloved husband will attend, of course. You know very well how much the mayor holds him in his esteem. As for my dear Anne and I, you will agree, surely, that she has been looking remarkably pale and weak as of late..." she told her friend in a hushed tone of voice, making an ample gesture with her hand towards her daughter, who was seated by the window together with Mademoiselle de Candale, engrossed in her own needlework. "I am afraid her frail health will not allow her to attend the medieval festivities in Bordeaux. As for me, being the devoted mother that I have always been, I cannot bear to even think of enjoying such frivolities when my dear angel is feeling unwell," she said.

Madame de Montazeau could not help but feel proud. She had mustered that unassailable argumentation at a moment's notice, and without lifting her eyes from her embroidery even once.

"Mais bien cert, ma chere[2]. Understandably, our dear Anne's health and well-being must take precedence," Madame de Candale hastened to reassure her with a smile of her own. "And how about your sons? Might they not benefit from attending the festivities, too? Armand and Aimery could represent their family in Madame de Montaigne's... what was it that she called them... 'magnificent games'?"

To better mask her true intentions, her friend had kept her eyes trained on her embroidery while speaking. She even brought it closer to her eyes as if to inspect some mistake in the sewing. Madame de Montazeau took advantage of the distraction to cast a poisoned glance in Madame de Candale's direction. One moment it was there, and in the next, it vanished. Claude smiled again and took her attention back to her tablecloth, giving the fabric a good pierce with her needle. Madame de Candale could not help herself. She was jealous of Claude's wealth and of her many sons. She had always been. It was petty of her friend to try to persuade her to send her two unmarried sons to that lunacy concocted by Madame de Montaigne. But although she understood her friend's game, she knew better than to voice her thoughts.

Instead, she exclaimed: "Oh, my dear Françoise, you must have forgotten! Aimery is my youngest son, and he is only twenty years of age. He is much too young to attend such frivolities...."

"Yes, indeed, my dear. Then that leaves Armand..." Madame de Candale replied while she bent to retrieve her sewing scissors from the little basket at her side.

She is looking away in order to hide her vicious, Protestant smile, Claude thought, stung by her old friend's insistence.

She cut off some loose threads that were hanging from the backside of the little tablecloth that she was embroidering with an intricate pattern of dark red roses. She paused her sewing to look out of the window at the grey clouds gathering on the horizon.

Spring had already arrived at Montazeau and had brought with it no dearth of rain. Madame de Candale had come on her annual visit to celebrate the Quaresme Prennant[3] with Claude and her family. It was a tradition they had followed since they were girls, and they had been unwilling to abandon it, despite the Count of Candale's religious objections. Protestants did not keep

Lent, and they did nothing special to celebrate The Holy Mother, Virgin Mary's Ascension to Heaven, either, which was when Madame de Montazeau and her daughter would make their annual visit to Benauge. She would look forward to those visits every year and then count the days until she was absolved of her old friend's company. Only a few more days were left of that visit.

Claude's eyes rested on the two girls seated by the window, sewing, just like their mothers. They looked so much like she and Madame de Candale used to when they were girls... Much had changed since then. They had husbands to worry about and children whose futures had to be secured.

"Yes, indeed. Armand..." the countess of Montazeau said and stifled a sigh.

He could just as well go. There was hardly any danger for her middle son in those ridiculous games. And the old, as well as the new mayor, will then be satisfied, perhaps even impressed with their family's contribution. The mayor's wife, she could not bear to call her Madame de Montaigne, given her undesirable family background, might even overlook her and Anne's absence from the banquet.

"But, dearest friend, you must tell me, who is to represent la famille de Foix de Candale at these festivities? Is our dearest Charlotte to attend?" Claude asked, eager to return the blow.

"Oh no, perish the thought. We are still in mourning, after all..." came the reply.

Her friend's family had a strong reason to not attend the medieval games since the dowager countess of Candale had passed away around Christmas. But Claude was not one to admit defeat so easily.

"But surely, our dear Henri ought to partake in the tournament... He is such an accomplished knight, and he would be sure to win it!"

Henri was her friend's only surviving son. Besides his military talents, he was notorious for his gambling and drinking, squandering thus, not unlike his father, the family's fortune.

"You flatter him excessively, dear friend. Perhaps he and Armand could join these knightly games together?" Madame de Candale suggested, ever the snake.

Claude flashed her most convincing false smile. She had to think the thing over. Armand was a safe alternative, and if he felt like joining the tournament, she saw no harm in it. The best would have been for Antoine, her eldest son, and that sickly wife of his, to attend, but they had declined the invitation already. No doubt, her cumbersome daughter-in-law had forced her husband to abide by her wishes, yet again. She disliked distractions and imagined that she was tormented by a never-ending list of ailments. The countess of Montazeau, however, would have liked for nothing more than to have her daughter-in-law out of her house, even if only for a short while. She had, therefore, no intention of letting that go, and was sure to press the issue of their attendance to both Antoine and her husband. But if it failed, Armand would have to go to Bordeaux. The count had to be consulted, too, of course. But he was sure to present little, if any, opposition to her plans. He seldom did.

Chapter Ten
Alienor

"I am so proud of you, Élisabeth!" Madame de Civrac exclaimed, looking at her eldest daughter and taking her hand in hers.

The announcements were well underway, and her eldest sister's name had just been read out loud by the Lord of Montaigne. But Alienor knew that her mother was merely willing herself to sound sincere in her congratulations. The baroness was far from being delighted with that arrangement. Although none of them could claim the engagement came as a surprise. They had been given some time to adjust to the idea, since the Baronet of Civrac had first suggested the match between Elisea and Seigneur de Rémy's son, Louis, some months ago. Alienor suspected her mother had hoped, against all odds, that the game of fin'amor might provide a more desirable alternative for Elisea, who was, one had to admit it, the prettiest of her three daughters and the heiress to her fathers' lands. What

Madame de Civrac hadn't understood was that the girl had already made up her mind about marrying Louis de Rémy. Her sister was not wise, but she knew how to pursue her own interest, and she could be as stubborn as a mule. In that particular case, it was fortunate for them all that Elisea's interest coincided with the interest of their family as a whole. That marriage was sure to save them from certain ruin.

Alienor stepped forth to enfold her eldest sister in a fierce embrace. "Congratulations, cara Elisea! I am very, very happy for you. You will save us all, but I dare say that you shall have everything you wanted, too!" she whispered in her ear before releasing her.

"Oh, yes, cara sor, I most certainly will!" Elisea replied, laughing, and Alienor moved to the side to make space for Madalena de Lamothe.

Madalena was her childhood friend, and their families were close to each other. Her friend had appeared, as if out of nowhere, by Madame de Lamothe's side right before the announcements began. Their mothers had spent most of the banquet together, keeping to the sides of the hall, drinking and gossiping. Alienor had been surprised to see Madalena since she had made herself scarce during most of the evening, but the two of them had not been able to exchange more than frowns and glares behind their parents' backs. They had a lot to talk about, but it would have to wait.

She observed her friend. Mademoiselle de Lamothe seemed to radiate with joy and was nowhere near as nervous as she was. Deep down, Alienor wished just as much for Madalena's name to not be on those lists as she wished for her own to have found its way there.

The announcements continued. Her father put his hand on her mother's shoulder. They smiled at each other with affection and understanding. Alienor knew they loved each other still. Perhaps one day, she will have that, too. She looked away from their group, towards the place where she had last seen the Chevalier de Ségur. She was surprised to not find him there anymore. Her eyes searched the assembled crowd.

After a while, she caught sight of him, standing in the middle of a group of gentlemen. He appeared to be listening to Monsieur de Montaigne, who had stepped away from the table of honour, leaving the Count of Saint Gelais to proceed with the announcements. Three more gentlemen were by their side, one older and two as young as the chevalier. Their heads were bent in confidence. The mayor and the other older gentleman kept whispering in each other's ears. Alienor noticed that Armand de Ségur's hand was resting on the shoulder of one of the other young men, who was clad in a stylish blue suit. It was made of luscious light blue velvet, and it contrasted with the austere black of Armand's clothes. The two of them seemed very familiar. Next to the mayor stood the other young chevalier in elegant yet less flamboyant clothes of dark blue velvet. He bore a strange resemblance to the Seigneur de Montaigne himself, and Alienor guessed he was probably his eldest son, the Chevalier de Montaigne. Behind them, she caught a glimpse of Madame de Montaigne comforting a young lady dressed in red. Something was amiss, but she could not tell what it was.

Alienor was startled from her thoughts upon hearing her mother's laughter rising above the general clamour. She was talking to the de Rémys and other lords and ladies of their acquaintance with a big smile on her face. But she knew her own mother well enough to not be fooled by her display. Madame de Civrac had hoped for a better alliance for her eldest daughter. Having had her wishes thwarted, she had put her hopes on Alienor to succeed that evening.

She felt very, very tired. She remembered all the events of that memorable day, from the games of chivalry at the amphitheatre in the morning to the afternoon spent with the de Lamothes in Bordeaux and the banquet in the evening. The pressure to look elegant and poised, to stay calm and clear-headed at all times, has been difficult to bear. And as the evening grew late, she felt utterly exhausted. The responsibility she had towards her family felt suffocating, and she was perspiring in excess. Alienor longed to know that all her efforts had not been in vain, that she had succeeded where so many others had already failed. The moment of truth was near. If her calculations were correct, there were only a few unread names left on the list.

She felt Catarina's arm slip through hers. Alienor rested her forehead on her sister's shoulder for a fleeting moment. Words were not needed. Her sister understood her, and she took strength from her soothing presence. She looked at Armand de Ségur again. He, at long last, raised his head and looked at her, too. An intensity that she had not seen there before darkened his gaze. It was as if he was trying to tell her something. But she could not grasp the meaning of it.

Chapter Eleven
Elina

Rauzan, Maundy Thursday

"Tomorrow we are leaving for Bordeaux," Catarina started but was interrupted by her sister, Elisea:

"Oh, Catarina, please... You do not need to remind us. We have not talked about anything else in this house since that invitation arrived! I don't like it. All this talk is making me nervous. And I have to say that I dread this journey as much as I look forward to it..." she said, sitting on the bed.

She started to braid her long hair and get ready for what was, in all likelihood, a sleepless night, heavy with anticipation, for all of them. There was not one soul in their home that evening who did not feel dizzy about the incumbent trip to Bordeaux.

Elina was no exception, although her excitement was clouded by sorrow. Her family hardly ever travelled anywhere since they had had to sell their carriage years ago. They only left their castle at Rauzan twice a year. There was the annual visit to their relatives at Duras, when their rich aunt, Barbe de Durfort, would be gracious enough to send one of her carriages to fetch them. The

49

visits usually lasted three days, but were the highlight of Elina's summers. There she could play at her heart's will with her younger cousins. The Durforts' ancestral home was a grand castle built on solid rock, with many towers and secret passages to explore. The other occasion on which they travelled was her family's visits to Cambes, where the Baronet of Lamothe had his summer house. To travel there, Elina's family would be given the use of the Lamothes' spare carriage. The exact same one that had arrived that evening at Rauzan and was to carry her parents and sisters to Bordeaux.

"Well, we have a duty towards our family." Alienor nodded towards Catarina, then continued: "But we can also try to enjoy ourselves. Banquets like this one do not come our way easily. And who knows if there will be another invitation."

While still talking, she sat on the edge of Elisea's bed, arranging her nightgown around her. She gave her eldest sister a smile, and Elisea returned it, her lovely head inclined to the side while her fingers were occupied with the long process of braiding her tresses, which bore the colour of dark honey.

All of a sudden, Alienor turned her head to where Elina was hiding. Someone had, at long last, become aware of her presence. She had been lingering on the threshold of her eldest sister's chamber, hiding behind the half-closed door.

Feeling her sister's eyes on her, Elina took a step forth into the light, stifling a sob.

"Oh, hurry up and close that door! I am freezing," Elisea shouted from her bed, and Elina obeyed with slow movements.

Elisea was the most insufferable of her sisters, even more insufferable than Alienor, with whom she had to share a room. She was insensitive, arrogant, and liked to order her around for no good reason.

"Elina, ven!¹ Why are you crying, cara sor?" Catarina asked, taking her youngest sister by the hand and guiding her towards her side of the bed.

Alienor and Elisea exchanged a long glance. It was not a kind glance, thought their youngest sister. She had seen them roll their eyes. Catarina wiped away the tears from Elina's cheeks.

"If there will never be a next time, then I will never, ever be able to go to a banquet!" she exclaimed.

Elina was sobbing even harder. She felt Catarina's arms enfold her as they both kneeled on the soft mattress of her elder sisters' shared bed.

"We cannot know what the future holds. But I am sure there will be other banquets, cara Elina! Just wait a year or two..." Catarina said with kindness.

Her words reassured Elina, but she was tired of waiting to grow up.

"Yes, there will always be plenty of banquets in Aquitaine. But whether our family will be invited to attend... well, that remains to be seen," said Alienor, and Elina showed her the tongue.

No one needed her gloomy reflections at a time like that. And Elina would not forgive her anytime soon for having been allowed to accompany the rest of their family to Bordeaux while she had to stay at home. Alienor flinched.

"You little..." she exclaimed, but was interrupted by Catarina:

"Surely, cara Alienor, it shan't be long until we'll celebrate Elisea's wedding, and then yours, as well..."

Catarina started to braid her hair for the night. Her sister's fingers passing through her hair felt nice and soothing. At least Catarina cared for her. She wondered if she, too, shall find a dashing gentleman to dance with at the banquet. Tears flooded her eyes once more. Elina wanted that, too... very, very much...

"As well as yours, cara Catarina!" Alienor added.

"And soon, my little Elina, we shall be dancing at your wedding! I know that you will have the most handsome groom, for you are so, so pretty, and honestly, only the most dashing knight would do for you! But he should not be just handsome... He should also be..." Catarina said, kissing the top of her head.

"Brave and elegant!" Elina exclaimed, her words at the ready.

"He shall have to be fearless even when facing the fiercest of dragons, and he shall treat me like a princess, with the most refined manners..."

"That he shall, my dear. And he shall also be learned and cultivated. For we shall not settle for anything less..." Catarina added, making her little sister shift her position so that she may start braiding the other half of her hair.

Elina smiled up at her. Catarina was her favourite sister because she was kind and gentle and always took good care of her.

After tying a white ribbon in her hair, Elisea stretched and yawned. She looked satisfied to have completed her task and was quite ready to close her eyes.

"But you must grow up first, Elina!" she said. "And you must start to behave like a lady. Ladies do not sneak like that into other people's bedchambers!"

The youngest mademoiselle de Durfort felt her spirits sink again. If she got a penny every time someone told her that she had to grow up! It was not her fault that growing up took such a long, long time. In truth, Elina would have given anything to be older and, therefore, able to attend the festivities in Bordeaux with her sisters. To prove that she knew how to behave like a lady, she fought the urge to show her eldest sister her tongue and contented herself to send her a burning glare instead.

"Come now, Elina, let us retire to our room and bid our sisters good night," Alienor said, yawning.

Elina nodded. Catarina had finished braiding all her hair. She thanked and hugged her.

Alienor got up from the bed, picked up their candle and lit it again from the one burning in her sisters' room.

"Bona noitz[2], Catarina. Bon noit, Elisea."

Alienor took her little sister by the hand, and together, they stepped into the freezing corridor.

"Bona noitz," her elder sisters said in unison before Elina pulled with all her strength at the door, closing it shut behind them.

The sound bounced from wall to wall, across their family's medieval castle at Rauzan, sending chills down Elina's spine. She hurried to hold her sister by the hand.

Together, they climbed down the spiral staircase, one step at a time, careful lest they made a sudden movement, and the candle died, leaving them in complete darkness. The candle had little life left in it as it was, and it kept flickering, casting grotesque shadows on the wall beside them. Elina trained her eyes to look at nothing but the floor in front of her feet. The ancient stone floor was cold and uneven. Their bare feet made barely any sound at all as they walked on their toes.

Just like cats! thought Elina, and stifled a giggle.

"Shhh!" her sister admonished and then came to a halt.

Elina tightened the grip on her hand.

She did not think the ghosts were here, waiting for them tonight, was she? Elina wondered, looking up at her elder sister.

She noticed Alienor had tears in her eyes.

"Alienor, what is it?" she asked, her voice a mere whisper, trying hard to listen for any strange sounds piercing the silence that reigned over the castle at that late hour.

In truth, she wished for nothing more than for her sister to hurry away from that place. In their bedchamber, behind the heavy lock, they would be safe. For they were standing in the narrow passage connecting the new wing of the castle, called the ladies' wing, with the central staircase, and that was where the whispers of the dead were most often heard.

"Hold this!" Alienor called and thrust the candleholder towards her. "Take it!" she repeated, raising her voice because her little sister did not stretch out her hand.

Elina did not want to let go of her sister's hand. Once someone raised their voice in the passage, who knew what might happen...

Alienor put the candleholder directly on the stone floor. The sound of the metal frame scratching the stone floor echoed through the hollowness of the passage and the tall staircase tower next to it. She then bent down next to it and started pressing her fingers into her teary eyes.

"Alienor, anem!³ I am scared," Elina whispered, sitting on her haunches next to her sister.

That was certainly the worst place to linger at that hour of the night. Her sister was behaving very strangely.

"Elina! There is nothing to be scared about."

"Then why are you crying?"

"I am not crying because I am scared!" she said with indignation and rose while sweeping, with a swift movement, the candleholder from the floor.

As a result, the flame flickered one last time and vanished into thin air. Elina gasped and jumped to her feet. Then they both froze where they were, holding their breaths. They were surrounded by nothing but darkness and silence. Their eyes were still trying to adjust to the dim light cast by the clouded moon, and their ears struggled to detect any sounds. An owl sent its lonely cry in the night outside and its muffled echo resonated through the walls of their ancient castle. A screeching sound, almost imperceptible, could be heard from the attic above them.

Is it just a mouse? Another pebble falling apart from the old castle walls? Or... is it something else... someone else? Elina wondered, but did not dare utter a single whisper. *Which one of them is up tonight? Isabeau? Lois?*

She soon realised that her sister had dashed down the corridor towards their bedchamber, leaving her behind.

"Alienor, esper!"⁴ Elina cried, running after her like a blind mole in the darkness, her heart beating so hard that it threatened to deafen her.

Alienor's laughter came out of nowhere. It was creepy and malicious and entirely inappropriate. Elina cursed her sister for teasing her. She vowed to give her a good boxing once they reached their chamber.

Chapter Twelve
Alienor

"Oh, have you heard, madame? Someone has asked for the hand of one of the mayor's nieces tonight!" Alienor heard Madame de Lamothe tell her mother.

She looked around her and saw that many of the guests were whispering in a state of agitation. The news was spreading throughout the hall, although the match was yet to be announced.

"No, madame. How extraordinary!" her mother exclaimed.

"Madame de Montaigne will be very pleased indeed!" said Madame de Rémy with a meaningful smile.

"Yes, who wouldn't in her stead, my dear madame?" Madame de Lamothe chimed in, all smiles. "We all know that has been her purpose all long..."

"Well, I am glad to hear it. Does anyone know the name of the fortunate gentleman in question?" her mother asked.

Alienor shifted her gaze straight ahead towards the high platform at the end of the hall, where the Lord of Montaigne and the Count of Saint Gelais were reading the lists. She tried to not pay attention to the frivolous discussion unfolding right next to her. Loath to admit it even to herself, but she was growing more and more anxious. She cast a quick glance at the Chevalier de Ségur, who appeared to be having an argument with the good-looking young man dressed in light blue by the side of the long banquet table. Alienor was not sure what to believe anymore. He had not as much as cast another glance at her after that one time, when he had looked at her with pleading eyes from across the hall. Monsieur de Montaigne had resumed his place at the honour table while his wife and the young lady in red were talking to the other elderly gentleman who, it occurred to her, looked a lot like Armand de...

"De Ségur," she heard all of a sudden.

Alienor flinched and turned her head as if in a daze. She saw that it had been Madame de Rémy who had spoken. She then heard the name whispered time and again by the other guests around them. Her heart skipped a beat. It made no sense at all. She laid her hand on top of the delicate gauze fabric of the partlet covering the deep décolletage of her gown. Maybe she was mistaken. Maybe she did not hear well...

"Escusez moy, madame[1], did you mention the name of the Count of Ségur?" she asked as soon as she had a moment to steady herself.

"Oh non[2], of course not, Catherine," Madame de Rémy started, mistaking her for her elder sister. "Not the count himself, mind you."

And having said that, she almost choked with laughter, so Madame de Lamothe took over: "My dear Éléonore," she started, using her correct name. "What Madame de Rémy meant to say was that it was not the Count of Ségur, but his son, the Chevalier de Ségur who will be shortly announced..."

"De Montazeau," her mother corrected. "The gentleman's correct title is the Count of Montazeau, not Ségur!"

Her mother grabbed her hand under the cover of their skirts. Stunned, Alienor did not react. She let out the breath she had been holding. The Count of Saint Gelais made another announcement, and a tumultuous round of applause engulfed the hall. Alienor felt her arms become very stiff, and she was unable to raise and clap them. A shiver passed through her whole body, numbing it. She could hardly hear the applauses anymore, and she could only see the vague silhouettes of the ladies around her. It was strange. She felt as if she was falling from a great height, yet at the same time, she was unable to move a limb. Perhaps she was just dreaming, and none of it was real.

"Oh no, I do not see my other daughters! My dear Éléonore, you must come with me at once and help me find your sisters," her mother said out loud, so the other ladies would hear them once the clamouring applause decreased in intensity.

Madame de Civrac seized her daughter's arm and dragged her through the tightly woven crowd. Alienor was grateful for her mother's intervention and allowed her to carry her away. It seemed to her that she was floating through the crowded hall, as if on a boat that was taking her far, far away, across a vast expanse of water that was rocking it from side to side and made her sleepy. She wondered if that feeling was what they called "stupor". She had heard the word before but never understood its meaning. Before they reached the doors, Alienor felt the hall spin, and she leaned against her mother, who caught her in her arms.

When she opened her eyes again, she was sitting on a stone bench in the corridor outside the banquet hall. She tried to sit straight. Her mother sent a page to bring her something to drink.

"Le Cheualier de Ségur." The words were lingering in her mind, like an echo whispering back with one's own voice in the forest on a clear summer day. The Chevalier de Ségur and the mayor's niece. But what if Madame de Rémy was mistaken? Surely, there must be some misunderstanding...

"And now comes the moment we have all been waiting for, esteemed guests..." a voice rose from the hall.

It was the thundering voice of Louis de Saint Gelais. That was to be the last announcement.

Her mother sat next to her and put an arm around her shoulders.

"Not many blessed unions, the fruits of the day's trysts of fin'amor remain scribbled on this list. I feel honoured that it falls to me to announce, with great pleasure, Madame de Montaigne, the engagement of your niece, Mademoiselle de Louppes, and the Chevalier de Ségur!"

The hall ignited in applause. And all Alienor could do in that fateful moment was to force herself to stand up and walk, slowly, out into the cold air of the night...

Chapter Thirteen

Madame de Civrac

"An invitation has arrived this morning, cher mary[1]," Élisabeth de Durfort said to her husband while they were in their sleeping quarters, preparing to go to bed one evening in early spring.

She was sitting on a chair in front of her little table, facing the blurry mirror, in which she could hardly recognise her own reflection anymore. Her trusted lady's maid, Marie, was brushing her long, black hair with even strokes. She took a closer look and saw that yet another strand of her hair had turned grey.

Her husband had finished changing into his nightshirt and emerged from behind the folding screen, his nightcap in his hands. Whispering some further instructions, he bid farewell to his valet de chambre, Jean-Pierre.

"Chere Elise, you know I am very glad for you. And for our daughters. Invitations have been rather scarce of late... But still, I am at a loss for words... How could we possibly afford to attend a social event now? What with you and our daughters... young

59

ladies... well, I am sure you don't need me to explain... But the costs involved are simply outrageous..." he went on, struggling to find the appropriate words, while he climbed into the bed they were sharing as husband and wife.

The Lord of Civrac sat straight, leaning against the highly stacked pillows, and fiddled with the duvet. She did not like it when he did that. Duvets were expensive, and they all had to do everything in their power to keep their prized possessions in good condition, for they had no means to buy new ones. She thought of her evening gowns, which were amongst those treasured items. With some hard work and minimal purchases, they could be altered to fit her daughters.

"Cher François, you will like this invitation!" his wife said with a smile, interrupting him. She passed the instruction, with a mere movement of her eyes, to Marie.

The maid nodded, took a step towards the vanity table and picked up the pleasantly scented piece of paper, which bore the crest of arms of the Montaigne family. She then crossed the room to hand it over to the Lord of Civrac.

"That would be all, Marie, merci.[2] Don't forget to drink some mint brew for your stomach before you go to bed. Bonne nuict!"[3] she said and watched her go.

Marie was more than a maid to her. She was her trusted ally at Rauzan, where the household affairs were taken care of most of the time by her mother-in-law and her sister Yolanda, who was also their housekeeper. She and Marie had been through so much together. She had remained by their side when all the other servants had deserted them, and she had taken good care of her daughters for years, when they were little. In fact, she was in that woman's debt. It was her firm belief that Catherine and Éléonore might not have been alive were it not for Marie. Women could depend upon each other when they worked together for the same goal. Men, on the other hand, were less trustworthy...

Once they were all alone in their sleeping chamber, Madame de Civrac stood up from her chair and went to join her husband in bed. As she approached, she noticed an expression of incredulity spreading over her husband's face.

"Chere Elise, what on earth could be the meaning of this? This is unheard of..."

"Oh yes, it is. But think what this can mean for us. For. Our. Daughters," she whispered each word slowly, with a pause, looking him in the eye.

"Surely, you do not mean to..."

Élisabeth had already made up her mind. She was determined to attend the festivities with her daughters. She stood by the side of the bed, her spine erect and her jaws tightly clenched, staring at her husband. Surely, by now, he ought to recognise that expression on her face and understand that there was little he could do to dissuade her. However, she could see that her husband had his misapprehensions. He must have been thinking about preserving their good name intact, fearing that their daughters shall stain their reputations by joining Madame de Montaigne's game of fin'amor. She knew her husband well. He was in the habit of saying that their noble name was the only dowry he could still pass on to his beloved daughters...

"Elise, cecy est scandaleus![4] You cannot mean to throw our daughters into a scandal..." he said at last, patting the white, worn sheet with his palm, inviting her to climb into bed beside him.

She obeyed with reluctance.

"We have lost everything already, my dearest. Our good, old, noble name is everything we have left..." the Lord of Civrac added.

"I know, dearest. But as noble and old as it is, a name will not feed us. Not now and not in our old age. And it will not feed our daughters," she paused and then continued: "We need to secure our daughters' futures. If at least one of them can make a good marriage, there might yet be hope for us. Three of them are of a marriageable age already. Élisabeth is going to be too old soon. And Catherine, well... you know how she is. We cannot afford to cling to our name at the expense of our children's future."

"Elisea is already as good as engaged to Louis de Rémy, and if that wedding does not save us from penury, I don't know what will! My dear, at least, the other girls should be spared this embarrassment..." her husband exclaimed.

"There is no embarrassment, dear! The most respectable families of Aquitaine will be there, the Lamothes included. As for our daughters... Élisabeth, you know I dislike it when you encourage them to use those backwards Occitan names; she is eager to participate in the game, and Louis de Rémy can be easily persuaded to do so, too. If no other suitable gentleman happens to take an interest in her, all that Louis de Rémy will have to do is to offer his token to her, and she shall offer him hers. Our other daughters, on the other hand, have nothing to their name, and I highly doubt that we will be able to muster some decent dowry for them. So whoever marries them, today, tomorrow, in a year or five, they will have to take them without a dowry, regardless... But you know as well as I do that such gentlemen do not grow on trees, my dear! At these festivities, there will be plenty of young gentlemen from good families willing to turn a blind eye to these matters. It is the premise of the game, after all..."

"But to parade our daughters in this manner, as if they were..."

Seeing that he was about to insist, Madame de Civrac picked up the invitation letter, which was lying on her husband's lap, on top of the covers.

She held it up rather dramatically and declared: "This is a sign from God! God wants our daughters to have a good life. God wants to save this family from ruin. And we will be thankful and follow his guidance."

In the silence that followed, Élisabeth neatly folded the letter and then placed it carefully on the little night table next to her side of the bed. She then blew out the candle.

"Think about it, my dearest. Bonne nuict!"

Chapter Fourteen
Alienor

"Mademoiselle de Durfort, I have been looking for you. The announcements..."

Armand de Ségur's voice bounced from one wall of the courtyard to the other and startled Alienor. She had been staring down at her feet, listening to Catarina's comforting words, so she had not seen him come. She was standing by a bush of white lilacs in the spacious inner courtyard of the Palais de l'Ombriere.

The chevalier took a step towards her, and she became still. She felt so many emotions at once, surprise, relief, longing, pain, fear... And in truth, she did not know what more there was to say, so she just stared at him.

His words trailed, and they looked at each other in silence for a moment. Then he must have taken notice of her mother and sister, standing next to her, for she heard him say, with a bow: "Madame, mademoiselle..."

"Monsieur, as you must be aware, we have not been introduced yet..." her mother interjected in a stiff voice.

Alienor let out a sigh and offered the requested introductions: "Chere mere, allow me to introduce Armand de Ségur de Montazeau," she said with a steady voice that seemed to come from someone else. "Monsieur de Ségur, veuillez me permettre de vous présenter madame la baronne de Civrac, ma mere, et mademoiselle Catherine de Durfort, ma seur, " she continued.

Catarina and her mother curtsied and tilted their heads, as the etiquette required. He was, after all, the son of a count. But they did not utter a word. For a moment, they all stood there looking at each other under the night sky, the moon and the torches casting shifting shadows over their faces. Applauds and laughter could be heard clearly from the banquet hall nearby. The announcements must have given the noble audience a subject to talk about for weeks to come. The gentle breeze rustled the leaves of the lilac bushes.

Alienor was careful to avoid looking in the chevalier's direction. She stared ahead of her instead, towards the dimming flames of the torches on the wall. She had no idea what to do or say, so she just waited.

"Madame, I know this will sound like a very surprising request, given the fact that we have just met, but may I be allowed to talk to your daughter in confidence for a moment? We will be just a few steps away, within sight..." she heard him say.

His voice was grave, and Alienor wondered if he intended to apologise for misleading her throughout the entire evening.

"Chevalier, this is a most peculiar request. I cannot possibly..." her mother started, with a hint of indignation in her voice.

The chevalier appeared to be taken aback by her mother's words. She saw him flinch. He looked from the baroness to Alienor and back. She reined in the urge to bite her lower lip to stop it from quivering. The awkwardness of that conversation was stifling.

"Madame, mademoiselle, I see you are not pleased with the

announcements..." he said. "I should have... Of course, I should have spoken to you, mademoiselle, beforehand, but circumstances beyond my power prevented me from it. I most humbly request just a few moments of your time now, so we may talk alone."

"Very well, monsieur, I will listen to you. But only for a moment."

She would do it, although he was not worthy of her time anymore. Alienor could no longer avoid the gentleman or the fact that she had been defeated. She would be brave and allow his confession, no matter how much it will hurt her feelings. She had been strong and unwavering throughout the day, and she would not change that. But it was best to keep silent and not give herself away.

"Ne vous incquietez poinct, chere mere,"[1] she interceded, seeing that her mother was about to object once more.

Madame de Civrac gave her a curt nod, as did Catarina. Alienor could see that they were worried for her, but she would be fine on her own. She wished she could muster a smile to reassure them, but she just walked away without waiting for the Chevalier de Ségur. Her steps sounded hollow on the uneven stones paving the corridor that ran along the edges of the inner courtyard.

"Are you feeling well, my lady?" Armand de Ségur asked her once he reached her side.

His voice sounded concerned. He must have been very good at pretending, she thought. She had been mistaken about him from the very beginning.

Dignitet! Alienor thought, before she responded: "Yes, my lord."

She clenched her teeth to stop the other words from coming forth. She came to a halt once she reached a corner of the stone courtyard. That was far enough to be out of earshot from her mother and sister, yet close enough to still be under their chaperoning gaze. And then she waited.

The Chevalier de Ségur said nothing, and there was a long moment of silence between them. His contemplative attitude and his prolonged silence did not, alas, have a comforting effect on her state of mind. She had agreed to speak to him in confidence because he had insisted. She had hoped for a confession, for some insight that would aid her to better understand the events of the evening, his manner of acting and the announcement she had just witnessed.

Yet the time passed, and he was still standing in front of her in silence. Not uttering a single word. She felt anger rising from within her. She was angry at him and at herself. In fact, she had had no claim to him. It had all been nothing but a fantasy that she had carried in her head all day. They were but strangers to each other, after all... And, in the end, the chevalier had had no obligation to return her favour. She had wished to steady her racing heart with those words, but they only made the heaviness in her chest grow stronger...

"Mademoiselle Éléonore... it is true that I did not give you my ribbon before the announcements, but please believe that my intentions..." he said and tried to take her hand in his.

But Alienor took a quick step back. She could not allow him that familiarity, not anymore... not when he was engaged to be married to someone else. She felt tears welling at the corners of her eyes. All of a sudden, she felt tired... so, so tired. Disappointment clutched at her heart once more. She had tried hard to be brave, to be strong, and she had done everything in her power to win that game of fin'amor. And yet... it had all amounted to nothing. She had lost. And that Mademoiselle de Louppes, whoever she was, had won. She was no longer mistress of herself. Her tears were menacing to leave the corners of her eyes. That felt heavy on her eyelashes. And the Chevalier de Ségur kept his silence. Perhaps he was looking at her in that intent manner to better revel in her misery. Alienor did not know what to believe anymore. Anything seemed possible at that point. But she could not stand to be the object of his ridicule. With quick movements, she curtsied and hurried towards the castle.

"A Deu, monsieur,"[2] she said in a low voice as she passed him by.

Alienor felt tears roll down her cheeks. She wished she could have handled that last encounter with more grace and poise. There were other things she would have liked to say to him, but she had been unable to find the right words. Either way, she had to put an end to that uncomfortable farewell. And she willed herself to not look back.

What was certain was that the Chevalier de Ségur did not hurry after her. She passed by her mother and her sister without speaking to them. She could not have conjured a word to leave her throat, even if she had wanted it. It took all her strength to simply breathe. The choking sensation was growing stronger and stronger, and she did not know how much longer she could contain it. Alienor could hardly see where she walked through the mist of her own tears.

After a while, she heard the rustling of Catarina and her mother's gowns as they rushed behind her. When she reached the entrance doors, she told herself to show dignity and self-restraint and not look back towards the spot where she had left the Chevalier de Ségur in the corner of the courtyard.

Second Part

Games of Chivalry

Chapter Fifteen
Madame de Montaigne

A ntoinette de Louppes de Villeneuve became Madame de Montaigne upon her marriage, a long time ago. She was content with her lot in life and knew God had favoured her. She had a husband she could respect, and who respected her in return. The Lord had blessed them with five children and she was in good health. She had wealth, prestige and also power, since her husband, Pierre Eyquem de Montaigne, had been bestowed with the title of Mayor of Bordeaux two years ago. But it was her belief that, beyond one's duty to their family, king and country, one also had a duty to use the power entrusted to them by the Lord's good mercy to help those less fortunate.

She and her husband had always been generous contributors to the Church's coffers in Aquitaine. Why, through her husband's domains at Montaigne, they were direct vassals of the Archbishop of Bordeaux. She had a very close relation with the Archbishop himself, His Excellency, the Most Revered François de Mauny, who was also her confessor. Since her husband's ascension to power, Antoinette had closely supervised, and even taken part on occasion, in the charity work of the Church in Bordeaux. She had served soup to the poor every Friday outside the Cathedral of Saint André. She visited several orphanages and houses for the poor. Her old gowns and the garments that her daughters had outgrown were presented to their servants and their families. And she taught her children to give their toys away to the poor.

It went without saying that Madame de Montaigne attended church with her family every Sunday, as was expected of her, and she strove to inculcate the sternest Catholic values into her children and the others living in her household. Since she was a little girl, her family had always taken particular care in showing the most fervent support and belief in the Catholic Church. Her mother always told her she had to live her life like a true saint and prove that she was a devoted Catholic in every hour of her life. Her mother did not tell her why back then, but even as a child, she heard the rumours about her family's past. They were Sephardic Jews, expelled from Spain at the turn of the century, who had established themselves as merchants in Toulouse and later in Bordeaux. Upon arriving in France, her grandfather, Antonio Lopez de Villanueva, had converted to Catholicism and changed the family name to the French-sounding Louppes de Villeneuve.

Although she took no pleasure in being reminded of her family's humble origins, Antoinette had a strong fondness for those who, due to family circumstances beyond their control, had found themselves served a lower lot in life. And she knew full well that while it was, for the most part, the men who had the power to make and unmake their family's fortunes, women had to bear, more often than not, the direst consequences of their menfolk's actions. Life on Earth was hard, and not all men had the moral fortitude to live it, according to the precepts of God. Laxity of character was a sin that rarely went unpunished. And not everyone possessed the virtues that ensured one family's success in society, be it a perceptive flair for the power games of politics or an intuitive talent for trade and coin. Of course, in her experience, a combination of both was needed in order to ensure genuine, long-lasting success.

Her own family's fortunes were made with coins and quills in the accounting houses of Bordeaux and Toulouse. Having married into the de Montaigne family, she had considerably improved not only her own status, but that of her family as well. And she had made that successful alliance simply because her father had the insight and fortitude to use part of the wealth and influence gained through the hard work of generations of tradesmen to acquire a small property on the outskirts of Bordeaux, which in turn had enabled them to enter the ranks of small nobility. But not everyone in the Louppes family had had her good fortune. As a young girl, she had witnessed the terrible consequences her uncle Louis' bankruptcy had had on her beloved cousins' futures.

It was upon receiving an unexpected letter from the eldest daughter of her Uncle Louis, who was living the life of a merchant's wife in Toulouse, that Madame de Montaigne thought once more of the events that shook her girlhood. Antoinette and her sisters, Marie and Bourguigne, had married well. Cousin Catherine, on the other hand, was married off, rather late in life, to a cousin who traded candles in Toulouse. She had seen Simon de Louppes at the wedding. In addition to being poor and ugly, he had a limp of some sort and, all in all, had a frightening countenance. Yet Catherine had, at least, married. Her sister, Marie Madeleine, remained an old maid. She had taken care of her ageing parents and, after their passing, she had continued to live in the household of her elder brother, Pierre, where her status was slightly better than a servant's. And her other cousin, Jeanne, Catherine's youngest sister, became a nun at the convent of the Annunciates. Not because she felt any inclination, but because, aged twenty-eight, it became apparent that she would never receive an acceptable offer, and there was simply no place for two old maids in the family. At that time, the convent had but recently been established under the patronage of Jaquette de Lansac, the deceased mother of the most likely contender to the title of Mayor of Bordeaux, Louis de Saint Gelais. Madame de Montaigne could not help the smile that pulled at the corners of her mouth as the thought crossed her mind: the mistress of the deceased king, François I.

Truth be told, Antoinette de Montaigne did not like to be reminded of the impending loss of status that the change of mayors would entail for her and her husband, who had not been re-elected. But, praised be the Lord, her eldest son Michel's position as Counsellor at the Court of Aides de Perigueux had been secured. Though she was aware that it was not becoming of the devout Catholic that she was, Madame de Montaigne had relished the honours that were bestowed on a mayor's wife. She liked living in the city hall because of its central location and the large windows that gave into the Palace Square. But a true Christian had to be humble, and in order to appease her conscience, she liked to tell herself that, most of all, she had cherished leading the charity work of the Church and doing what was her duty by the poor and the needy of Bordeaux.

In any event, she could not help but feel sad that all of that would be lost to her in just a few months' time. She fretted over the fate of her charity work once Louis de Saint Gelais de Lansac was appointed mayor. His mother, who had, at least towards the end of her life, endeavoured to atone for her sinful youth through Christian charity, was long dead. And although a thriving man of forty and three, the count was still a bachelor, having led a lavish life of banquets and intrigues at the Court in Paris as the trusted confidant of Her Majesty, Queen Catherine. Her good work with the poor of Bordeaux would most likely not be continued once the new mayor took power into his own bastard hands.

Madame de Montaigne's attention was drawn back to the piece of paper in her lap. Her cousin Catherine was writing to ask for her help... or for money, to be more precise. Antoinette wondered whether it was not something short of a miracle that Catherine had not written to her before.

How did she manage to get by all these years? she thought and decided then and there that she would have to do more for her cousin than simply send her money.

It had not been in her power to save her cousins from their disgraceful fate since she was but a young girl herself at the time. But maybe there was something she could do for her nieces now, from the dwindling power of her position as the wife of the mayor of France's richest city... For her nieces and perhaps for others who shared their fate. It would be her most impressive act of Catholic charity as the leading lady of Bordeaux, the culmination of her mission as a benefactress towards all those in need, her magnum opus.

Illuminated with sudden inspiration, Antoinette de Montaigne fell to her knees in the middle of her reception room, startling her companions.

"Jeanne, Léonore, Henriette, pray with me!" she told her daughters and her lady's maid.

They hurried to put away their needlework and prayer books and kneeled next to her on the cold floor. She started to pray with fervour, asking for the Lord's help and guidance.

The name of Queen Alienor of Aquitaine came to her mind. That was, to be sure, a sign from none other than the Lord Himself! Because Antoinette was reminded that the queen had resided there during her time in Bordeaux. She might have knelt and prayed on the same old floor, in that exact same place as her. The Ombrière Palace, where the mayor's apartments were located, had been the residence of the dukes of Aquitaine for centuries. It was there that the legendary queen had held her Court of Love, that strange and fascinating notion that Alienor and her trusted ladies would pass judgment and solve the romantic grievances of her subjects.

A chill crawled down her spine, and she felt goosebumps blossom on her arms. Perhaps she could revive that tradition and organise an event that would mimic the great queen's court of love right there at the palace. Alienor of Aquitaine had been the one to take the Occitan tradition of fin'amor to the courts in Paris and London, where it became known as courtly love. She was, when Antoinette thought of it, the ideal patron for her project, a legendary lady who succeeded in marrying not one but two kings!

It was clear that the Lord sanctified her plans. He was entrusting her with a mission. Madame de Montaigne shall revive for one day the ideals of chivalry and fin'amor. She would organise the most magnificent celebrations Bordeaux had seen in years, with medieval games and lavish decorations, where young ladies and gentlemen of meagre means shall have the possibility to meet and talk and strike momentous alliances. It would all be done in a proper manner, with the families' blessings, of course. Yes, it was all coming to life in her mind... the vision sent from Heaven. Those prearranged meetings shall be called trysts of fin'amor, to honour the Occitan culture, the poetic tradition of the troubadours, and Queen Alienor herself. And the couples shall have to exchange tokens, like in the days of yore, and put down their names on a list. The Ombriere Palace shall become a Court of Love once more, and she, Antoinette, its reigning queen.

A smile flourished on her lips. She thanked the Lord for that enlightening vision and begged him to whisper in her ear the means to convince her husband to support her plans. Perhaps the festivities could be tied to some other incumbent public announcement or Catholic Holiday...

In the ensuing silence, she could hear the chilly winds of late winter howling at the windows. They were creatures of the ocean, born out at sea and brought to the doorsteps of Bordeaux by the powerful Garonne...

Or by the will of God Almighty, who sees and knows all! thought Antoinette de Montaigne before she made the sign of the cross and rose to her feet.

"Come, Henriette," she told her maid. "There is much work to do!"

Chapter Sixteen
Alienor

Bordeaux, Easter Monday,
mid morning

I t was the long-awaited Easter Monday, a sunny day in the middle of April in the year of the Lord 1556. The new mayor of Bordeaux was to be officially announced that evening, so it was an auspicious day twice over. Alienor knew that fate shall be on her side, if only she used her wits and stayed strong. She was not worried, for the word strong was embedded in her family name, and she was astute beyond her years... or so she had been told time and again.

She smiled and jumped out of the Lamothes' carriage. The sun was blinding, and she longed to reach the shade cast by the impressive ruins of the Galien Palace.

To mark the Holy Resurrection of the Lord and welcome the new mayor, the city of Bordeaux had organised a series of magnificent medieval games for everyone to enjoy at the ruins of the Roman amphitheatre, which was located just north of the city walls. A tournament, a fair, as well as spectacles with acrobats, jongleurs and mummers were to be expected. And in the evening, a banquet was to be hosted in Bordeaux at Palais de l'Ombriere, between the very same walls which had hosted the wedding celebrations of Alienor of Aquitaine and King Louis VII of France more than a hundred years ago. But the feast was reserved only for ladies and gentlemen of a certain rank, who had been lucky enough to receive the special invitations issued by Madame de Montaigne.

In the days leading up to the festivities, the soon-to-be former mayor had done his best to make the required preparations. Reparations were made to some of the ancient structures of the Roman amphitheatre so that the public might safely enjoy the medieval games. And the flags of the noble knights attending the tournament were displayed on the old walls to recreate the bygone era of the Arthurian legends. The tournament was the highlight of the festivities for most and had been suggested by the new mayor, Louis de Saint Gelais, freshly arrived from the Court in Paris. Or at least, that was what Alienor's friend Marie Madeleine de Lamothe had told her. She lived in the city, and her father was the Baronet François de Lamothe. He, too, had been the mayor of Bordeaux until some years ago.

Madalena, as she had called her friend since childhood, was Alienor's most trusted source of information. No hearsay escaped her ears, and she knew all about the latest whereabouts of every noble lady and gentleman in Aquitaine. In fact, Alienor suspected her friend played an important part in spreading out those rumours. But it had been delightful to spend Easter in the company of the de Lamothes in Bordeaux. Her family had arrived in the city on Good Friday. They lodged as guests with the Lamothe family, who maintained a big house in the city, in addition to their country home in Cambes. Their fathers had been friends their whole lives, and their families socialised on all the adequate occasions. They were one of the few families to not turn their backs on the Durforts de Civrac in the aftermath of the rebellion that ruined them. But even they did not know the full story of the tragic events that changed her family's fate forever, nor who were the ones responsible for it. To show repentance and to avoid further persecution, they buried the truth and made everyone else in their household, even the children, swear an oath of silence.

After sunset on Holy Saturday, they had attended the Easter Vigil together at the Saint André Cathedral, deep into the night. The next day, they had woken up late and had partaken in the traditional Easter feast. A whole roasted lamb had been served with a sauce made of red wine and several spices, some of which Alienor had not tasted before. Then the girls and their mothers had spent their Sunday evening in a feverish spree of preparing their apparel for the long-awaited celebrations on Easter Monday.

During her stay with the de Lamothes, Alienor had been sharing a room with Madalena and her little sister, Anaïs. Whilst the little girl slept beside them, the two friends had stayed up in close council until late into the night. Madalena had told her that the king, Henri II, had a taste for all things medieval and a true passion for tournaments. Louis de Saint Gelais, who was, in fact, his half-brother, seemed to share the king's enthusiasm and was planning on bringing the latest fashions from the Louvre to Bordeaux. And it was said that he had agreed to Madame de Montaigne's proposal of hosting the games of fin'amor, only upon making sure the celebrations would include a tournament. The mayor's wife had agreed on the condition that all barbaric conduct was to be avoided. In deference to her request, and to the two young ladies' relief, the tournament was, therefore, not to include a free fight.

"In conclusion, the men will parade themselves in medieval armours in the morning, and the women will parade themselves in colourful gowns in the evening," the lively Madalena had declared the night before, and they had both giggled with excitement at that daring notion.

Madalena... I wonder if she, too, shall strike a fateful alliance today... Alienor thought as she climbed up the stairs leading to the central seating area, which had been reserved for noble families.

It was hard to say which lady in her family was most excited about the day's festivities. Catarina was composed enough, and so was she, but Elisea and her mother could hardly conceal their excitement. Alienor could hear their laughter over the noise of the crowd and even over the minstrels' music. She knew that if she were to succeed in the game, she had to secure a tryst of fin'amor on her own. That meant that she had to distance herself from her family as soon as possible. She had to go out in search of her luck instead of waiting for it to find her. As daring as that sounded, she decided to sit somewhere else during the games, perhaps beside a dashing gentleman. She felt her heart beat faster in her chest as her mind settled on that strategy.

It has to be done. Remember to not lose your composure! Whatever else may happen today, carry yourself with dignity! she thought and took a deep breath.

Alienor took her hand to her hip to feel the small ball of ribbon resting in the hidden pocket of her skirt. Then she turned towards her mother, who was about to take a seat next to her father on a bench situated at the front, right behind the main gallery where the mayors and their families sat.

"I lost my handkerchief. I must go and look for it, chere mere," she lied.

Her mother looked at her with eyes opened wide at first. But after a moment, Madame de Civrac's eyes narrowed in a closer scrutiny of her daughter.

Alienor held her chin up and met her mother's gaze. She wondered if she could understand her intentions and if she would condone them. After two, three more heartbeats, the baroness of Civrac nodded to her daughter in silence and then sat down. But just as Alienor was turning to make her way back towards the passage between the tribunes, she felt her mother's hand take hold of her arm. Alienor turned back in surprise.

She looked down at her mother while bending slightly to better hear her whispered words.

"Prendez bien garde a vous, ma fille![1] This place is said to be visited by witches and all sorts of ruffians at night..."

Alienor nodded in understanding, then turned and walked away, leaving her family behind. She knew she had to go as far as possible from them, to a place where no one of her acquaintances sat. But for a young lady to walk around unattended, and to sit next to a stranger, was a blatant display of inappropriate behaviour in the eyes of the noble society present at the games. Alienor was exposing herself to plenty of risks, but she had to take that step nonetheless. While she loved her family, and she was certain that they loved her in return, it was true that spending the entire day in their vicinity would be a strategic mistake. Their presence would disempower her from adopting the daring, enticing conduct that was certain to attract victory. So she chased away any feelings of guilt and insecurity and focused on the task at hand.

"Coratge, Alienor. Et dignitet!"[2] she whispered to herself with an imperceptible nod.

Arriving at the narrow corridor which separated the left and the right side of the seating section reserved for the noble guests, Alienor stopped in her tracks. She looked for an empty seat on the other side as far back as possible. It was difficult to see past the steady stream of guests pushing their way downwards. The games were yet to begin, but she saw, casting a quick glance towards the tournament grounds, that the knights had started to take their places before the arrival of the mayors. She had but little time left at her disposal.

With fresh determination, she searched every row for an empty place. She had to squint to see something against the glaring sun, but she caught sight, at last, of an opening on the top row, next to a gentleman in black attire. He had to be a gentleman, for he carried a sword. An unusually wide-brimmed hat adorned with black feathers covered half of his face. She beamed.

The seat was as far away as possible from her family, and that suited her purpose well, as did the presence of an apparently unaccompanied gentleman. Fate was truly on her side that day.

Alienor took a deep breath and started to climb the stairs. Other guests were passing by her in a long stream, headed downwards in a futile attempt to find a seat nearer the old amphitheatre's arena. And there were also those who, like her, were trying to climb the stairs and were pushing from behind. She had a hard time keeping her balance and dignified posture. When a particularly corpulent lady passed her by, Alienor tipped dangerously to the side and almost fell on top of an old couple seated nearby. But a strong hand caught hold of her upper arm and pulled her in the opposite direction, restoring her balance. She was about to voice her gratitude when the stout gentleman, who had come to her aid, grabbed her by the waist and pressed her body hard against his.

"Aren't you a pretty one?" he asked, opening his grotesque mouth.

She realised, in quick succession, that, first, his breath stank of cheap wine, and second, he was about to bring his face even closer to hers. Revolt and nausea took hold of her at once. But Alienor had no time to waste and no intention to allow some uncouth character to take advantage of her. A forceful stomp delivered to the man's closest foot made him loosen his grip. A vulgar curse escaped his lips. While he was thus distracted, she pulled her arm out of his grasp and crouched to the floor for a quick moment. The man lost his balance, leaned in the suddenly empty space in front of him, stumbled on her crouching body and then fell with a thud on top of the elderly couple seated by the side of the stairs. There were cries, and an impetuous argument ensued. But Alienor was already running up the stairs, away from that dreadful man.

So much for my composure and dignity! Alienor thought a moment later when she reached the top row of seats.

There, she came to a halt. Flushed and breathless, she took one step to the side, away from the path of those who were climbing and descending along the corridor. She swept the dust off her beautiful blue gown with quick motions, and she was about to raise her hand to arrange her hair, but she stopped herself at the last minute. Her hand still in mid-air, she noticed that the gentleman with the black hat was looking at her. If her eyes were not mistaken, he had a smile on his lips. Alienor hurried to lower her hand, and she entered the row, advancing with small steps towards the empty seat. She glanced at her future neighbour and froze in place. He had turned his head, so his face was visible in its entirety. She gasped and held her breath. A long scar covered most of his left cheek, from the temple to the chin.

At that very moment, the trumpets of the heralds announced the arrival of the mayors in the covered gallery down below.

"Mademoiselle, assoyez vous!"[3]

"The tournament is about to begin!"

The noble spectators seated closest to Alienor were growing impatient. Some hands even tried to shove her to the side. She offered her apologies and continued to walk towards the end of the row. Reaching the empty seat, she took a deep breath in and sat on the stone bench next to the gentilhomme[4] in black.

At first, she sat perched on the edge of the hard wooden bench. But as he moved to the side to make more room for her, she decided to make herself more comfortable. It occurred to her that the ghastly scar must have been the reason why the seat next to him had remained unoccupied. No one else had wanted to sit so close to an unpleasant-looking stranger. Perhaps some even thought him dangerous.

Far from being scared, Alienor felt sad all of a sudden. She stole a side glance at him and saw he had his eyes fixed on the ceremony unfolding below, but that he swallowed hard a couple of times. She watched in fascination as his throat bone, prominent against his slender neck, moved up and down. She had, alas, no brothers.

Not anymore... she thought with sadness, but commanded herself to not dwell again on those painful memories.

In any event, she had not grown up in the vicinity of young men. Her father was a rather corpulent man, and she could not remember noticing his throat bone. Girls' and women's necks looked quite different. She wondered if she, too, had a bone in her neck, and before she thought it over, she raised her hand to look for it.

Her neighbour turned to look at her, his thick brow raised in a silent question. Alienor hurried to lower her hand. His eyes were blue, a peculiar shade of dark blue. It occurred to her that she must have been staring at his neck for an unbecomingly long time, long enough to make him uncomfortable...

"Oh, escusez moy, monsieur,"[5] she said, and looked away. Her cheeks burned, and she hurried to cover her mouth with her hand. But she was too late in censoring a loud giggle.

"May I ask what is the cause of your amusement, mademoiselle?" the gentleman asked.

One glance in his direction and Alienor understood he was quite displeased with her conduct. His thick eyebrows had knit in a deep frown, and he had narrowed his eyes. Seeing that his question remained unanswered, since Alienor had a very difficult time taking control of her breath and mustering a reply, he added in an impatient tone of voice: "Have you not been taught to not stare and laugh at strangers, mademoiselle?"

Chapter Seventeen
Elisea

Bordeaux, Easter Monday,
after sunset

Elisea's formal name was Élisabeth de Durfort, and her title was Mademoiselle de Civrac since she was her parents' eldest daughter. Her younger sisters all shared the title of Mademoiselle de Durfort. She cared for them, as was her due, but she knew that she was better than them. She was special, blessed with beauty and good luck. One day, she was going to inherit her father's lands, and then she shall be a baroness in her own right. What she lacked, on the other hand, was a fortune. But that was an error of destiny that she hoped to correct soon.

Truth be told, she had never enjoyed herself more in her entire life. The Easter Monday banquet at the palais de l'Ombriere was even more resplendent than she had expected. It was clear that banquets were her element, and she wanted to do nothing else for the rest of her days. It had been delightful to be able to dance side by side with the noble ladies from the high society of Bordeaux, to enjoy goblet after goblet of sweet mead and taste the exquisite

small fried fish and fruits de mer served to the guests on silver plat-
ters... But most of all, she had enjoyed basking in the gallant attentions of several young gentlemen, although none were more
arduous in his pursuit than Louis de Rémy.

The two of them had met before. His family owned a summer
residence not far from Rauzan, and their families had known each
other for years. They were one of the few neighbouring families of
rank who were generous enough to send their carriages to escort
the Durforts of Civrac when they were invited for a dinner or
other festive occasions. Elisea was aware that her father was eager
to pursue some sort of alliance with Thomas de Rémy, Louis'
father. She did not know the exact details and was not interested
in them either, but it had to be related to the fact that they were
dead poor, while the de Rémys were a very wealthy family of
merchants from Bordeaux. On the other hand, the Durforts were
of an old and noble lineage, while the others had only recently
been ennobled. Both families would achieve their ends if she
married Louis de Rémy. But Elisea's mother did not approve of
the match. She thought very highly of all those who had the blood
of old Aquitaine and not so much of everyone else. She knew
that, despite putting on a brave face to socialise with the de
Rémys, Madame de Civrac did not enjoy their company.

As for Elisea, she knew that Louis was neither handsome nor
bright. But he was a decent dancer, and he seemed genuinely
interested in pursuing her affections. And he was rich... very rich.
Or rather, his family was. Mademoiselle de Civrac knew it would
be years before Louis would inherit his father's prosperous trade
and his lands. But his family owned an imposing townhouse in
Bordeaux, in addition to their domains in Bazadois, several
carriages, an army of servants, and lots of coins. When it came to
titles and such, those bore little significance to her since she was
going to style herself as the lady of Rauzan and Pujols one day,
regardless of whom she married.

What she desired above all else was to live a lavish city life
away from Rauzan without ever having to worry about the cost of

things again. She wanted to own her own jewels, wear stylish gowns made of golden brocade, especially for her, drink only expensive wines, and attend banquets every week. She needed it, and she deserved it, too, after all the years of sorrow and deprivation she had had to endure at Rauzan. And she wanted to do it all while she was still young.

Elisea was aware that time was not on her side, what with her twentieth birthday around the corner. Louis de Rémy was about the same age and of a sweet nature. By marrying him, she could make all her dreams come true. When all was said and done, no other gentleman at the banquet that evening suited her as much as he did.

The one exception was, of course, the new mayor, Louis de Saint Gelais. Although quite old, he was vastly rich and yielded great power both in Paris and Bordeaux. Not to mention that he was the son of a king! He would have been, in truth, the perfect match for Elisea, if not for his superficial view of earthly possessions, of which she had none at the moment. That much had become crystal clear to her when the Lord of Saint Gelais had turned down her offer earlier that evening...

"Ancore vne danse, mademoiselle?"[1] Louis de Rémy emerged from the crowd and stretched out a hand to her.

His language was not very polished, his manners too frank, but she did not say a word about it. Language was, after all, not an important aspect of life. No married couple spent their whole days in each other's company, conversing. Indeed, once married, Elisea had no intention of spending her time at home with the de Rémys, not when she would have the entire city of Bordeaux at her feet. There would be plenty of banquets and social visits to occupy her, for Mademoiselle de Civrac was sure that, with her grace, beauty and noble lineage, she would charm in no time all the highly placed ladies and gentlemen of Bordeaux.

"Yes, monsieur. With pleasure," she said, smiling and falling into a deep curtsy.

Having perhaps realised that he had forgotten to bow to her

when he requested her to dance with him, Louis hurried to correct his mistake and inclined his head. It so happened that at that exact moment, Elisea, who was on her way up from her curtsy, stretched out her hand towards her suitor. In the ensuing confusion, Elisea's hand touched Louis' cheek, which, by that point in time, was already warm with embarrassment. She quickly withdrew her hand to cover her mouth as a rain of laughter escaped her lips.

"Escusez moy, monsieur," she said, between giggles.

"C'est moy quy devrois vous demander par don, mademoiselle!"[2] the Chevalier de Rémy said after regaining his composure.

Mademoiselle de Civrac was pleasantly surprised by his unexpected display of eloquence. He knew how to carry himself in a refined and elegant manner if he put his mind to it.

She tilted her head and gave him her sweetest smile. Elisea appraised him one last time, from head to toe. He had a strangely shaped nose and a very round face, but he was tall and not altogether unpleasant to look at. Louis smiled back at her, with adoration in his eyes, and she knew, beyond a doubt, that he would suit her very well. Her decision made, Elisea took out her reticule and searched for the piece of red ribbon hidden therein.

When she took it out, Louis de Rémy turned crimson with delight. He had, after all, already offered her his black ribbon twice that day.

"Mademoiselle!" he exclaimed, rushing to take her hand in his and to plant an ever-so-light kiss on top of it.

It was an elegant and chivalrous gesture, although his hand was trembling. His lips lingered there for a moment, and he raised his eyes to look at her. Their eyes met, and they smiled.

Chapter Eighteen
Alienor

Bordeaux, Easter Monday,
mid morning

"Have you not been taught to not stare and laugh at strangers, mademoiselle?" the gentleman next to her had said.

There was impatience in his voice. Alienor felt at first stung by the gentleman's direct, harsh words, and she reminded herself to sit straight and to behave with grace.

She tried her best to look serious and answer him in a dignified, polite manner.

"Oh non, monsieur. I quite assure you, my parents have taken great pains to impart upon me the strictest education..." she started, but after seeing the expression of righteous indignation on his face, she gave up.

Her hand darted to her mouth in an unsuccessful attempt to stifle the insufferable giggles pulling at the seams of her composure. Alienor thanked the Lord that neither her parents nor her elder sisters were there to see her. She imagined the outraged expressions they would have had on their faces, and that amused her even more. She pressed the back of her hand to her lips and closed her eyes while shaking with uncontrollable laughter. Visions of her stomping on that terrible man's foot and then running up the stairs with her skirts and farthingale[1] raised high in her arms flashed before her. To think that she had done such a thing, the dignified Mademoiselle de Durfort, in her beautiful gown sporting the colours of her family! And that poor elderly couple... Alienor started laughing in earnest, her head thrown backwards, fingers still pressed to her lips. She could no longer control her laughter, but somehow, at the same time, it became clear to her that her neighbour was feeling more and more offended by her unbecoming behaviour. His gaze became even sterner. The thought crossed her mind that he was, perhaps, thinking that she was laughing at him.

She would have liked to explain herself, but she could not utter a word. Every time her giggles abated, a new torrent of laughter emerged from her throat. But Alienor knew she had to, somehow, reassure him that he was mistaken... Noticing he was about to turn away, with a vexed expression on his face, she reached out her left hand and caught hold of his upper arm.

The gentleman stopped in his tracks and stared at her small hand, surprised by the familiarity of her gesture. The expression of utter shock that was imprinted on his face had an undesirable effect on Alienor's already strained composure, and she laughed out loud.

"Shhh..." several persons seated in their vicinity looked at them with scandalised expressions on their faces.

That, in turn, amused Alienor even more. Sensing a fresh wave of laughter surging in her throat, she pressed her right hand tightly over her mouth while her body tilted to the side in a spasm. She held tight to his arm to regain her balance. Her forehead came to rest on his velvet coat while her entire torso leaned into his arm.

The nobleman shot out his other hand to steady her, holding

her by the shoulder. Mademoiselle de Durfort became aware of the scent of his clothes. She sensed oranges, musk, and sweat. Somehow, that had a sobering effect on Alienor, and the giggles died in her throat. They were holding each other in an embrace. She looked up at him, blushing, and saw that he, too, was looking at her. The colour had risen to his face as well.

"Are you quite alright, mademoiselle?" His voice didn't sound angry or offended anymore.

Alienor pulled away, crossed her hands in her lap and sat with a very erect spine on the hard stone bench. She looked straight ahead at the Roman arena below, where the knights were engaged in their old-fashioned games. It was imperative she pulled herself together.

After a short while, she said in a serious tone of voice, without looking at him: "I apologise for my behaviour, monsieur. You might think me unworthy of being considered a noble lady."

He offered no reply, so she looked at him in all seriousness and added, hoping he would see the honesty in her words: "But I would like to reassure you that I did not laugh at you, my lord." Alienor paused to take in a deep breath. "Most certainly, I did not laugh at you because of your scar!"

The gentleman in black cringed when he heard her say the word "scar". And he looked positively perplexed. Unable to find his words, he blushed.

Alienor took courage and continued: "But your scandalised expression, monsieur, and the heat rising up to your cheeks, much as it does now, certainly did not come to my aid!"

Having finished talking, Mademoiselle de Durfort cast a broad smile in his direction. His face acquired even more colour, but he smiled back at her. It was the faintest of smiles, more a suggestion of a smile hanging by the corner of his full lips. The chevalier kept his silence and turned his attention to the spectacle of military prowess, which was by then well underway in the dusty arena of the Roman amphitheatre.

Alienor continued, undeterred: "I know that you saw me earlier, my lord. While I disgraced myself, tripping that gentleman and running up the stairs in that unbecoming manner..."

She stole a look at his profile and saw another smile pulling at the corners of his mouth, despite his best efforts to ignore her. From that angle, as she sat on his right side, the scar was not visible at all. *One could almost say that he looked handsome,* she thought, looking for a moment longer at his profile. *And the blue colour of his eyes was so...*

Her thoughts were interrupted by his even voice. He spoke without taking his eyes off the events unfolding on the tournament grounds below.

"You are staring at me again, my lady," the chevalier said and then hurried to add, casting a rather alarmed glance at her over his shoulder: "I beseech you. Do not start laughing again!"

But Alienor did laugh, only a little, and looked up at him with beaming eyes.

"Oh, my lord... You see it now, too. This has been your doing all along!"

She caught him smiling back at her, despite his best efforts to maintain a serious expression on his face.

"You, my lady, are most entertaining," he declared, and then they both sat in silence for a while, watching the tournament.

"If only the Chevalier de Candale[2] would have devoted more hours to preparing himself for the tournament instead of indulging in the gluttony of the bottle until late last night," she whispered, leaning towards him in confidence.

Mademoiselle de Durfort's gaze followed the said chevalier as he dragged his feet out of the arena. He had scored no points in the archery competition.

The gentleman turned to look at her in surprise. "And how is it that you are so closely acquainted with the Chevalier de Candale? Or the gluttony of the bottle, for that matter, mademoiselle?" he asked.

"I know that I am very young. And that I giggle a lot. Which is rather unbecoming. But I can assure you, my lord, that I am a lady of noble birth. And that there is more to me than meets the eye," she said with an enigmatic smile, keeping her eyes on the games. "Shh... Attendez, monsieur!"[3] Alienor warned, raising a finger to her lips as she noticed he was about to say something. "Here comes the Captain of Sansac[4]!" she exclaimed.

Her voice had sounded a tad too eager. And yet she could not contain her glee at having recognised the coat of arms of one of the most celebrated knights of France.

"I know he is a bit old nowadays..." she continued, to the increasing amusement of her neighbour. "But as you can see, his sight is still in perfect shape. I am quite persuaded that he will be crowned champion in the archery competition!"

The gentleman next to her tried hard not to laugh. Alienor could see the restrained movement of his lips.

"Vous auez peut estre reson, mademoiselle,"[5] he said.

It was her neighbour's turn to stare at her. He was a gentleman of few words, it seemed. But Mademoiselle de Durfort had noticed a certain hint of admiration in his voice.

A shudder climbed up her spine, and she felt self-conscious. Alienor swallowed hard but willed her eyes to remain fixed on the tournament grounds. It was a good thing that he was looking at her, after all. It meant that she had succeeded in making an impression. She wished it was as easy to control the colour rising in her cheeks, time and again...

Just then, a boy appeared next to her. He served the couple seated to her right two sugared apples. Her eyes were drawn at once towards the boy's fare. She had not seen such beautiful apples in her life. It was bright red and glazy, and Alienor bet it must have tasted sweeter than honey. But she checked herself and shifted her attention back to the games upon remembering that she had no coin in her purse.

"Come here, boy," the gentleman in black called out, raising his hand.

"Du cidre pour monsieur?"[6]

The boy was, in two steps, by Alienor's side.

"A goblet of cider for me. And a sugared apple for the lady," he ordered and then paid him.

Alienor felt her face grow even warmer. She was not sure if it was because she felt pleasure or embarrassment. But she took the shiny, red apple the boy held out to her. It must have meant that he was not entirely indifferent to her charms.

"You did not have to buy me the apple, my lord. But I thank you. You are most kind," she whispered towards him.

It was difficult to bite into the hard coat of melted sugar covering the apple. And she was not sure there was any elegant way to do it, either. As she studied the apple, turning it on all sides, Mademoiselle de Durfort found herself wondering about her neighbour's age. She stole a furtive glance at him. Seven and twenty? Thirty? She could hardly tell...

"It was my pleasure, my lady," he almost whispered his reply and then drank from his goblet of cider.

Alienor followed his gaze and saw that down in the arena, the field was being prepared for the final game of the tournament. It was the game she had been most looking forward to: the joust. The names of the eight knights were called out, and they paraded, one by one, on their armoured horses, with long lances in their hands. As they reached the main gallery, where the de Montaigne family and Louis de Saint Gelais were seated, together with the Lamothes and some other guests, the knights paused for a moment to bend their heads in respect.

From the corner of her eye, she saw Madalena jump up from her seat and, although she could not hear it, it appeared that she shouted something, perhaps an encouragement, to the knight bowing his head to them at that moment.

A chill passed along Alienor's spine, and she held her breath as she realised who that knight was...

"And who, may I ask, do you think will win the joust game, mademoiselle?" her neighbour asked, although she could not make sense of his words or the scene unfolding in front of her eyes.

In the next moment, the knight raised his lance until its tip reached the mayor's balcony. To her friend's dismay, Madalena de Lamothe took out a red ribbon and tied it to his lance. Alienor let out a long breath. It could not be true.

Chapter Nineteen
Armand

Bordeaux, Easter Monday,
late morning

"And who, may I ask, do you think will win the joust game, mademoiselle?" Armand de Ségur asked his neighbour with an amused expression.

But the lady seemed to not hear him. Her eyes were trained on the events unfolding in the arena. The knights were paying their homage to the officials seated in the gallery below or gathering tokens from the ladies of their choice on the tips of their long lances.

He curled his fingers into fists. Armand should have been there in the arena together with his companions in arms. Even Philippe de l'Isle was there, trotting around on his white steed. He caught sight of his father, the Count of Montazeau, joining in the general applause as a young lady seated next to him gave her token to the Chevalier de Montmorency. The Chevalier de Ségur did not uncurl his fists. He had no wish to cheer, for he found that medieval tradition of fin'amor rather ridiculous. To his surprise, his young neighbour did not applaud either. She seemed to be the type of girl who would enjoy such nonsense.

Armand turned his attention towards her. He had to look twice to make sure, but she appeared to have tears in her eyes. The lady kept surprising him with her intense reactions. It was hard to get the gist of her. But perhaps he had misjudged her, and she was not as interesting a character as he had previously thought if she allowed herself to be moved by such a silly gesture.

"I beg your pardon, my lord. Did you ask me something?" the lady said after a while.

He was, by then, in no particular mood to pursue a conversation with her, but he was a gentleman, so he repeated his question.

His neighbour took her time to answer, her eyes still glued to the tournament grounds, and the two knights who were readying themselves for their first clash at the opposite sides of the field. Armand had given away all hope that she was paying any attention to his question. She was probably regretting sitting next to him, so far away from the arena and the opportunity to give her token away to some knight or the other, like that young lady seated by his father in the main gallery. Her answer, therefore, surprised him all the more.

"It is hard to say, my lord. Le cappitaine de Sansac is wise to abstain from taking part in the joust. His eyes might yet have the acuity of an eagle, but his limbs are most likely... well, the way limbs are when one is over sixty years of age, I suppose..."

He felt a smile coming, but did his best to stifle it.

"Le comite de Noailles[1], on the other hand, is still an adversary to behold. And so is the Count of Candale[2]. I heard that he has recently mortgaged yet another one of his estates. So I think he might be a tad too eager to win this tournament. This, in turn, might cloud his better judgment and allow him to commit a foolish mistake," the young lady continued, then paused and asked him: "Do you know the young knight to the left of the

Count of Noailles, monsieur? Judging by his colours, I believe he must belong to the de l'Isle family?"

"Indeed, he is the chevalier Philippe de l'Isle," he offered, unable to fight a smile. "And this is, in fact, his first time to compete in a joust tournament."

Philippe was, after all, his closest friend and companion in arms. He rooted for him, although he was up against much more experienced knights.

"Are you acquainted with him, my lord?" she asked.

"Yes, indeed. We served together in the Royal Army."

"In the last war against Spain in Tuscany?" she wondered, surprising him with the eager tone of her voice, as well as her knowledge of martial matters.

"Yes," Armand de Ségur admitted, looking at the young girl seated next to him with fresh eyes.

He heard the lady draw in a sharp breath and turn to look him in the eyes.

"Not at Sienna, I hope!" There was surprise, but also a note of concern in her voice. Armand wondered if it was possible for such a young lady from Bordeaux to know of the plight he had had to endure last year in Italy...

"Yes, at Sienna!" he said after a while, letting out a breath he did not know he had been holding.

"I regret to hear it, my lord," she offered.

He nodded, and then they sat in silence for the duration of the first confrontation. But far from following the knights' movements in the arena, the Chevalier de Ségur had his gaze fixed on the horizon beyond the colourful flags sporting the participants' coats of arms. If it had not been for Sienna, his family crest would have been amongst them. And he would have been able to show his martial skills and prowess in the day's games.

He stole a glance at his neighbour. She appeared to be quite at ease, leaning back to rest the nape of her head on the wall behind them. To his surprise, she was not watching the games either. Her eyes were raised towards the sky as if to follow the slow passage of the round, white clouds above them. She was a most unusual young lady. But she was very sharp. He had to give her that. Her insight into the kingdom's military campaigns and the strengths and weaknesses of its bravest men of arms was commendable. Armand wondered if she was the daughter of one of them.

"And is it at Sienna that you got your formidable scar, monsieur?"

Armand flinched, taken aback by the lady's direct manner. His first thought was that she was mocking him. He was used to that. But when he turned to look at her, he saw no sign of jest or disgust on her face. The lady was still resting the back of her head on the wall and had tilted it to look up at him. Her expression was grave, devoid of any other emotion. After three more heartbeats, the corner of her mouth rose into a soft, reassuring smile.

It was seldom anyone would mention his scar to him. Well, men did, on occasion, to congratulate him, especially if they were fellow men of arms. But he had never seen a lady take an interest in his scar before. Most young ladies would avert their eyes upon catching sight of him. They even avoided talking to him, if they could. The few who had had to do so by force of being seated next to him at a dinner table had appeared to be cursing their misfortune throughout the entire evening. His neighbour, however, seemed to have walked away from her chaperones to sit beside him on purpose. When he came to think of it, Armand had never before sat so close to a beautiful young lady, not of his own blood. Their arms were touching, and he could feel the warmth of her body. For some strange reason, he felt neither awkward nor displeased by that. He could not remember the last time a young lady showed what seemed to be a genuine interest in his person and his military exploits. And he was most certain that none of them had shared with him such interesting, private thoughts or treated him as if they had known each other for a long time upon their first encounter. But that lovely young lady did, and it puzzled him. She had no qualms about speaking from the heart to an ugly stranger or smiling at him. She was unafraid to touch him, unafraid to ask him about his scar.

"Yes, at Sienna, my lady," he whispered after a long pause.

She nodded in understanding and looked away.

"I understood you were a man of arms, my lord. I wondered why you were not taking part in the tournament..." she confided, taking a bite of her apple.

"And you no longer wonder about this aspect, mademoiselle?" Armand wondered.

She did not look graceful, with her reclined posture and her bared teeth... less like a lady, more like a little girl. In truth, she must have been rather young... He stole another glance at her and tried to guess her age. The lady took another awkward bite. Armand thought better of it and allowed that. When all was said and done, no one looked graceful eating a sugared apple.

"Non, monsieur, I no longer wonder. For if you fought at the siege of Sienna together with the Lord of Monluc..." she paused and waited for him to confirm her supposition.

He nodded in agreement, and she continued: "Then I believe you must have either been hurt in battle, defending the city, or fallen ill during the long months of the siege, when the city was left without food or water... Or perhaps you had to endure them both..."

The lady took another big bite of the apple and chewed it with relish. She was not asking a question or making a suggestion. It sounded as if she was declaring facts that she was certain about without even looking at him. He did not answer. Instead, he looked away, trying to push away the images of death, malady and deprivation that were threatening to come forth. It was hard to imagine how she knew all that when she was a girl of... fourteen, perhaps fifteen. The only explanation was that she had a father or an elder brother in the military, but it was still impressive for a lady to show interest in such masculine pursuits.

"In conclusion, to answer your question, my lord... Since the

Count of Noailles just got eliminated by..." he heard the young lady say and then come to a halt, leaving her sentence unfinished.

Her body jolted forward, and she sat very straight and still. Armand followed her gaze and saw the knight wearing the yellow and blue colours of the house of Montmorency strutting victoriously out of the grounds to his retainers. He looked back at her in silence. To his surprise, he saw tears in her eyes. It was the second time he saw her on the verge of crying that morning, and both times, somehow, the Chevalier de Montmorency seemed to be involved. The sight of him seemed to have quite an effect on his neighbour. He had no clue what to believe or what to do in that situation. He wondered if he should offer her his handkerchief, but then saw her take out her own from the fold of her gown.

"Escusez moy, monsieur..." the lady said with a trembling voice, dabbing at the corners of her eyes with her lace handkerchief. "As I was saying, since the Count of Noailles lost to... the Chevalier de Montmorency, and your partner in arms, the Chevalier de l'Isle lost to the Count of Foix-Candale... I would say that, most likely, the champion of today's joust game will be your lord commander, le Seigneur de Monluc," she concluded and looked up at him with a smile.

Perhaps she was forcing a smile for his sake. There was still a sadness about her, but she seemed to wish to continue their conversation, and he gladly obliged.

"That is a most impressive reasoning, mademoiselle!" Armand exclaimed in awe, eager to come to her aid and distract her.

Her deep understanding of the strengths and weaknesses of the esteemed men of arms participating in the tournament was most extraordinary. And he commended her for regaining her composure in the blink of an eye. Yet, he could not help but wonder at the Chevalier de Montmorency's presence awakening such intense feelings in his neighbour. It was none of his concern, of course, but there seemed to be some sort of powerful connection between the two of them.

The young lady smiled again, and it looked genuine. She

nodded, and he could see a flicker of pride in her eyes. Armand could not help but be fascinated by that astute young lady and the overwhelming spectrum of passions he had seen reflected on her face in the short time he had become acquainted with her. Despite his better judgment, he felt more and more drawn to her in a strange and inexplicable manner.

"That remains to be seen, monsieur... I might be wrong, of course," she said, craning her neck towards him to better see the developments of the tournament through a breach between the heads of the spectators seated in front of them.

Armand de Ségur swallowed hard. She was so close to him. Her perfume filled his nostrils. He distinguished the scent of lavender, honey, and camphor. As he gazed at her profile, he caught himself thinking that she was not only bright but fair, too, with her beautiful brown eyes and long eyelashes, an upturned nose and small ears. She had a slender neck, with skin the colour of milk, and although it was in part covered by a veil, her body posture allowed him to catch a glimpse of the deep cleavage of her bodice.

"We just need the Count of Foix-Candale to make one impulsive faux pas..." the lady said, and he hastened to look away.

A burning sensation spread over his neck and cheeks. The Chevalier de Ségur urged his mind to let go of all those silly, unchristian thoughts and focus on the joust instead. They watched the game in silence for a while. When, with a thud, Frédéric de Foix, Seigneur de Candale, found himself thrown from his mount onto the dusty floor of the arena. They joined the rest of the audience in gleeful applause.

"Remarkable, indeed!" Armand whispered in admiration, stealing another glance at the mysterious young lady seated next to him.

He ached to ask her who she was, but did not dare do so.

"Thank you, my lord. I am honoured... and utterly unworthy of the praise of a hero who fought at Sienna!" she said, pulling away. "Perhaps I ought to congratulate you, my lord. I heard quite recently that your lord commander was made a Knight of France in the order of Saint-Michel by His Majesty the King. Were you in Paris to witness the ceremony?"

"No. I have never been to Paris, mademoiselle," he confessed.

The lady's honesty was contagious. He found himself sharing personal facts with a complete stranger...

"Yes, of course. It slipped my mind for a moment. Pray excuse me, monsieur," she hurried to say. "You were most likely still convalescing at the time."

Armand found her gaze fearless, even shameless, as she looked him over from head to toe. That lovely young lady seemed to enjoy staring at people... and, for some unfathomable reason, even at him. It was surprising that, far from finding it aggravating, the idea pleased him. Their eyes met, and she looked away. In any event, the lady had the decency to blush from time to time, which made her look all the lovelier.

"You look rather well now, my lord. I am glad to see you have recovered your strength," she said, and his breath caught in his throat.

No one had ever looked at him and declared that he looked well before. Not even his own mother.

Chapter Twenty
Alienor

Bordeaux, Easter Monday,
late morning

Alienor had no idea how the conversation had taken such a personal turn when she didn't even know that gentleman's name. Truth be told, she was crossing all boundaries of decorum. She knew it well. But she also knew that she had to succeed, come what may, in the day's game of fin'amor. By displaying only demure and polite manners, she was not going to get too far... Madalena's boldness inspired her, although her choice could not have been more disturbing...

As luck had it, her thoughts were interrupted by a loud gasp. She turned her head and saw her neighbour staring back at her. The colour of his cheek had turned to a deep crimson.

"Please excuse me, my lady," he offered, his voice shaking. "I am afraid that I am not at all accustomed to receiving compliments, least of all from fair young ladies such as yourself..."

He had called her fair. Maybe she was not altogether hopeless at that game. And maybe... maybe it was meant to be.

"I am sorry to hear it, my lord. It must surely be because you are a man of arms."

"How so, my lady?" came his stunned reply.

"Well, you prefer, perhaps, the clamour of the battlefield to the idle conversation of elegant dinner parties. And I imagine, my lord, that the opportunities for you to bask in young ladies' compliments must be somehow limited when one spends one's days knee-deep in the mud of the training grounds with a sword in his hand."

The gentleman smiled but did not say a word. They watched as her uncle, the Lord of Monluc, defeated his opponent in the joust game. Both of them joined their hands in applause. As it turned out, her uncle was his lord commander, so he must have shared her glee. They were not without connections to each other, after all. And her predictions were proving accurate, which was a relief. The last thing she needed was to make a complete fool of herself in front of that seasoned man of arms.

"If I may inquire, are you not concerned, mademoiselle, that the Chevalier de Montmorency will prove stronger and win the day? He is, after all, the younger gentleman of the two..." the gentleman asked her after a while.

The final confrontation, which was to determine the winner of the joust games, was about to begin. The two opponents mounted on their steeds and trotted to their agreed places, at the opposite ends of the arena. As she had predicted, one of them was her uncle, Blaise de Monluc. The other was, alas, François de Montmorency. Alienor was loath to have to set eyes upon him and his family crest again. She had known he would be there, and she had at once recognised his colours on the tournament grounds. But she could not have imagined that her best friend would willingly waste her token on him, of all men.

To further aggravate things, he had defeated knight after knight in the joust and made it to the final game. It was remarkable how, even after all those years, and from the great distance between his steed and her seat at the top of the Roman amphitheatre, he could still inflict pain. It was annoying that the mere sight of him could stir such emotions within her, making her eyes tear up in front of her neighbour. It was vexing that he should keep appearing out of nowhere as if to ruin her chances at forging a better future. And it was infuriating that he would dare show his face in Bordeaux at all...

And just like that, the memory she had tried to keep at bay all morning rushed forth, unbridled. Alienor saw a flash of lightning. It branched out over the expanse of the dark sky, casting its light upon the muddy plains of the Bazadois. It was raining, and it was cold. There were men, women, and children everywhere. They were running, and so was she. Her heart was beating very fast. They had fled Rauzan in terror, chased by the Royal Cavalry led by de Montmorency. She saw the riders in dark armours, imparting mortal blows to their right and to their left from the height of their saddles. The rain kept pouring down, soaking her to the bone. Alienor heard a thud, and then her hand slid out of the hold. She turned and saw that Lois had fallen to the ground. The frightened crowd pushed her, taking her further and further away from her brother. She saw her brother try to get up, but his feet kept gliding in the thick mud. A knight in black armour rode right at him. She cried out his name. She had to warn him. Breaking free of the push and pull of the crowd, Alienor landed on her back in the mud by the side of the road. She struggled to get back on her feet. The slippery mud was everywhere, covering her body, jumping into her open mouth. It tasted foul, but she kept screaming, hoping, against all odds, that her brother would hear her and save himself.

When she pulled herself up after crawling and then clinging to the side of an upturned cart, she saw the knight in black armour had reached Lois' side. His horse rose on its hind legs, and as another lightning flashed nearby, Alienor saw with clarity that the rider had a crest with tiny bluebirds against a yellow backdrop split by a thick red cross on his arm. It was the coat of arms of the de Montmorencys edged forever in her mind. In the next moment, hands grabbed her from behind. Her screams were drowned by the screams of the crowd rushing past, and by the thunders... those awful, loud thunders...

"My lady..." she heard a voice call out to her and felt a hand on her forearm.

The vision faded away, and she was back in the ancient amphitheatre, next to the gentleman with a scarred face. She noticed that he was holding her by the arm.

Alienor rushed to cover her face with both hands. Taking a deep breath to steady her racing heart, she willed herself to snap out of those dark memories. She could not afford to show weakness in that manner, over and over again.

"I beg your forgiveness, my lord. I feel very dizzy all of a sudden!" she said, trying to remember what he had asked her before, to push the conversation further.

"It is alright, my lady," he said, surprising her with the kindness of his voice. "It is almost noon, and the sun is too bright..."

"I remembered your question now, my lord!" she exclaimed. "No, I am not concerned. François de Montmorency may be a skilled knight, and he may have all the advantages of his youth. But he is also weakened by the time he spent in Spain as a prisoner of war. And he is overconfident... and evil..."

Alienor had barely whispered the last words. That was not the place and time to allow the past and its troubled memories to surge and cloud her mind. Yet, it was difficult to see him in the flesh, after all those years, trotting around on his steed, showcasing his success, his wealth, his fame... But she pushed her feelings aside and resolved to remain focused.

Mademoiselle de Durfort slipped her hand into the hidden pocket of her gown and clasped her fingers around the lean fabric of the ribbon. She held it tight, squeezing it in her fist until she could no longer bear the pain inflicted by her long nails pushing against the flesh of her palm. For the first time in her life, Alienor held the power to make things right. She had to do whatever it took to see it through. Her future, and perhaps even that of her loved ones, hangs in the balance. Her fate rested on that small piece of silk fabric. A decision had to be taken and fast. The tournament was nearing its end...

Chapter Twenty One
Armand

A rmand had to strain his ear to catch the young lady's last words, whispered under her breath.

"He is overconfident... and evil..." she had said.

Her words surprised him. It was clear to him that there was some painful, unresolved matter between her and the Chevalier de Montmorency. The Chevalier de Ségur knew that the Montmorencys were not altogether loved in Bordeaux because of the part played by the chevalier's father, the constable of France, in the bloody repression of the revolt of 1548. But the lady's grievance against François de Montmorency seemed more personal than that... To his knowledge, the chevalier was a celebrated man of arms and enjoyed an untarnished reputation. On the contrary, he had heard from his brother Antoine, who had highly placed friends at Court, that the king was planning to make him a knight of the Order of Saint Michel upon his return to Paris.

"But, more to the point, my lord, I believe that the chevalier is not swift enough when lowering his shield. His left arm has an old injury at the elbow..." the young lady continued. "And le Seigneur de Monluc knows about it. If he plays that knowledge to his advantage and strikes with speed, the victory shall be his!"

Armand hurried to close his mouth. The lady seemed to be on very familiar terms with both the Chevalier de Montmorency and his lord commander. He turned his eyes back to the confrontation unfolding before their eyes. He saw the two knights charge at each other. And, to his increasing dismay, he witnessed the following events in close succession, just as the young lady had predicted. He saw his lord commander charge forth, his lance aiming high at his opponent's helmet. François de Montmorency, noticing that, positioned his shield high up to protect his exposed neck. At the last moment, right before they were about to clash, the hero of Sienna lowered his lance and aimed it at his opponent's exposed side. The latter was too slow in lowering his shield, and he got hit, with the full force of the charge, in his left armpit, which was unprotected by neither armour nor shield. The chevalier's own lance had missed the Lord of Monluc, and his shield landed with a thud in the dust of the arena.

The result of the joust was unclear. Although harmed, François de Montmorency had not been unsaddled, and he still had the lance in his hand. Both knights rode to the centre of the grounds to convene with the master of the games. It was he who got to decide whether there was to be a second round, provided the chevalier did not yield. Montmorency was clutching his left arm.

While the entire tribune was holding its breath in anticipation, Armand turned to face the extraordinary young lady sitting next to him and asked: "Mademoiselle, how could a lovely young lady like yourself have knowledge of all this?"

She smiled and then tilted her head.

"I am afraid that is my secret, my lord!" she whispered with a radiant smile on her rosy lips. "I am just a lovely young lady... That is flattering and true, monsieur..."

He had called her "lovely". Armand came to realise, too late, that he had given himself away. The soft touch of her breath on his ear gave him goosebumps. He felt his face fluster again, quite against his will.

"But I do understand certain things, my lord," she continued, then paused to take a deep breath and added: "And I see that you are a brave, honourable knight..."

The tribunes exploded in tumultuous applause. The name "de Monluc" was on everybody's lips. Having had their eyes locked on each other, neither of them had noticed that, after careful consideration, the Chevalier de Montmorency had decided not to venture into a new confrontation. The master of the games announced that the victor was the Lord of Monluc.

As everyone around them jumped to their feet in joyful celebration, Armand followed suit. Blaise de Monluc rode towards the main tribune with a crown of flowers perched on the tip of his long lance. He offered it to Madame de Montaigne, who was thus crowned queen of the tournament, to more applause. Armand's chest swelled with pride. He was a lucky man to have served under such a brilliant commander, and he looked forward to meeting him again. He ought to stop by his tent later and congratulate him for his remarkable achievements.

While his gaze followed Blaise de Monluc, who was circling the tournament grounds with the victor's laurel crown on his head, Armand felt his lovely neighbour's hands tighten around his upper arm. He was a moment too late to turn his gaze towards her. Once he did, he saw her moving away from him, pushing her way through the standing crowd in the direction of the stairs.

Stunned by the lady's sudden departure, he stopped his hands from clapping. The Chevalier de Ségur stared after her, wondering why she had not bothered to say farewell. He tried to search his memory. The young lady had told him something as the crowd had burst into applause, but he had not heard her clearly. Try as he may, he could not remember hearing any words of farewell. Instead, he chanced upon a vague memory that made his heart skip a beat. It seemed almost phantasmagorical, but he thought he had heard the lady say that she admired him and that he was her choice.

Armand must have been mistaken. The words made no sense. Once the applauds died out, he followed in line behind his neighbours for his turn to leave the seating area and head towards the exit. A vague memory of the girl touching his arm right before she left flashed before him. He touched his right elbow and found, to his surprise, that a piece of fabric was hanging there. Armand looked down and saw a ribbon of red silk tied to his arm. Swallowing hard, he searched for a trace of the lovely young lady in the crowd, but she was nowhere to be seen.

He gave in to the flow of people pushing him down the dilapidated stairs of the amphitheatre. He descended the stairs, one step at a time, until he reached the bottom floor. And as he did so, he passed his fingers over the delicate silk of the ribbon adorning his sleeve, over and over.

Chapter Twenty Two
Aimery

Mortemart, early April

Aimery de Ségur could hardly master his anger. His mother had been adamant that he was not allowed to attend the magnificent Easter festivities organised by the mayor of Bordeaux. She refused to disclose her reasons... Instead, she simply sent him away to spend the Easter with his uncle in the Limosin. Le Baron de Mortemart was unbearably dreary, and his castle lay deep inside the Monts de Blond, far, far away from Bordeaux, Saint Émilion, and civilised society.

Aimery had raged and fumed, but his mother could not be moved. She had kept her calm while listening to him, yet she had remained extraordinarily determined to deny him his wishes time and again. She had stood still in her high chair, like a block of marble. That had left him bewildered, unaccustomed, as he was, to have her deny him any of his heart's desires. Madame de Montazeau had always turned a blind eye to all his misadventures before and had been in the habit of defending him in front of his father, who had shown much less patience for his youngest son's antics. Needless to say, the Lord of Montazeau had been more than glad to support his wife's stance on that rare occasion and prohibit him from joining the festivities.

His brothers, Antoine and Armand, had remained cold and silent, as usual, and had refused to involve themselves in the matter. They had shown little inclination to even lend a sympathetic ear to their younger brother's lamentations. His sister Anne's reaction had been even harsher. She had not even tried to dissimulate her glee upon hearing the news of Aimery's banishment. Not that her opinion mattered in the least. She was a harpy in the making, without the shadow of a doubt, and she was jealous of him whenever he was at the receiving end of their mother's attention.

After days of more or less furious persuasions, he had had to resign himself to his unjust fate. Two weeks before Easter, Aimery had taken his grim, half-hearted farewell from his parents, brothers and sister, and started, with a retinue of attendants, towards the Limosin. He arrived after a long and strenuous journey at Chasteau[1] de Mortemart, which was located — he was quite sure of it — at the end of the world, surrounded by mountains and forest as far as the eye could see...

His uncle, his aunt, and his cousins had received him warmly enough. But after spending several days, which had felt like months, in their company, he was ready to leave and to never look back. He was still bitter about having been forced to forego a delightful day of marvellous celebrations. There was even going to be a tournament. A tournament! And Aimery was going to miss it all... To think that sour mouth of Armand was going to attend the banquet in his stead... The injustice of it all tormented his every wakeful hour and haunted his dreams at night. In them, he was crowned the victor of the tournament, while beautiful ladies lavished their adoration at his feet.

He let out a deep sigh and took yet another gulp of wine from his goblet. Wine had been a most constant and trusted companion of his. He had taken a liking to the divine liquor since a rather early age. It never failed to comfort Aimery in his hour of need. That evening was no exception. The passage of time seemed painfully slow at Mortemart...

His cousin, René de Rochechouart de Mortemart, had recently returned, together with his father, from the north of France. René had made a name for himself while defending the city of Metz against the Habsburg Spaniards. He also took part in the re-conquest of Calais or some other port town. Aimery could not be bothered to burden his mind with such trifles. In any event, his cousin might have been a brave and skilled man of arms, but he was also utterly boring. He always had a frightful war story on his lips, and there was little else he enjoyed more than reminiscing about his great deeds of valour.

Aimery had tired of him soon enough, as he did of his uncle. Besides being a busy seigneur, François de Rochechouart was also a man of very few words. So when they did sit together at dinner, he hardly said anything at all. In fact, dinners at Mortemart were spent more often than not in utter silence. It was oppressive beyond endurance. Aimery was sure that his mother had sent him to Mortemart to punish him. But try as he may, he could not understand what he could have possibly done to deserve all that. The most patient of saints would have run away from there already, of that he was certain.

The youngest chevalier de Ségur had spent little time in the company of his other cousins, Madeleine and Gabrielle de Rochechouart. Though lively and pretty, especially Gabrielle, they were also very young.

Mere girls! If only they had been some three, four years older... Aimery thought with a sigh.

As a result, the young Chevalier de Ségur found himself, more often than not, sharing the company of his aunt. He knew full well that his mother would not have approved, and that made him want to stay by her side even more. Unfortunately, his mother was not there to witness his delicate attentions. Although Aimery did like to imagine her sitting in a dark corner of the sitting room with them, witnessing it all from the shadows, with tightly pursed lips, as was her habit whenever something displeased her. That thought always brought a sense of calm to his troubled mind and a smile to his lips. He wanted nothing more than to get back at his mother for the unjust treatment to which she had subjected him.

Madame de Montazeau had always disliked her sister-in-law. For as long as Aimery could remember, she had been complaining about one thing or another that she did or did not do. And she considered Renée de Rochechouart responsible for whatever misfortune had abated upon her brother's family throughout the years.

In truth, he did not have many memories of his uncle's family visiting them at Montazeau. But then again, Aimery was not one to give in to the alarming propensity displayed by certain members of his family, of spending one's days pondering or reminiscing... least of all, on such meaningless matters like childhood memories. He had never understood what the source of that animosity between his mother and his aunt was, and he had hardly bothered to think about it either... until now...

"And your lady mother forbade you, in no unequivocal terms, to attend that Easter banquet, my dear?" Madame de Mortemart exclaimed in surprise when her nephew revealed to her the true reason behind his unexpected visit.

They were in the baroness' sitting room, sometime after supper. Almost a week had passed since his arrival. His uncle and his cousin, René, had retired to the library to discuss something utterly boring, like what battle they could attend next or what repairs needed to be done to the stables. It was ridiculous what some gentlemen chose to spend their time doing! Aimery had followed his aunt to her private antechamber, enticed by her promise of a goblet of sweet wine. He would choose that over a tedious evening of listening to his cousin and uncle gloat about their many victories any day.

Madame de Mortemart's room was warm and cosy, and he had made himself comfortable in an armchair by the open fire, nursing his goblet. To his surprise, the wine was excellent at Mortemart. It had a sweet flavour, which reminded him of flowers and summer fruits. Aimery could drink it all day long, and he almost had to if he wanted to instil some warmth into his poor, frozen limbs.

The ancient castle was built high up on a rock. Winds whipped it from all directions, whilst drafts haunted its corridors day and night. The great hall in particular, where they were forced to have their meals, was ghastly cold even at that time of the year. Spring had yet to come to that God-forsaken place.

His cousins, Gabrielle and Madeleine, were playing with their dolls, supervised by a nurse, at the back of the room. The lady of the castle sat in an armchair, not far away from Aimery's, seemingly absorbed by her needlework. It was beyond understanding how women folk could entertain themselves with such a tedious endeavour. Embroidery seemed to be the most futile and redundant of pastimes. One did nothing but pierce a small piece of cloth back and forth all day...

It suddenly occurred to him that his aunt was still expecting an answer from him.

"Yes, alas, she did, dear aunt. And I cannot, for the life of me, understand her reasons!" he said with a sigh.

Aimery took another sip of wine, and his expression sulked, having been reminded of the terrible disgrace that had befallen him.

Chapter Twenty Three

Madame de Mortemart

U nseen by Aimery, for a fleeting moment, a knowing smile passed upon his aunt's lips. She caught, from the corner of her eye, a long glance at her nephew. He was, without a doubt, the most handsome of his parents' sons. Renée de Rochechouart had not met either of her other nephews in a long time. But she remembered that Aimery had stood out from his brothers even when they were little, the taciturn, long-chinned Armand and the forbidding, big-eyed Antoine. Aimery had grown up into a very good-looking young man, with his de Mortemart golden hair falling in long locks on his slim, elegant shoulders and the deep blue eyes of the de Ségurs. His face was shapely, with harmonious features, and he had a pleasing, carefree demeanour. It was no wonder that his mother treasured him above all her other children... He had the most pleasing features, and he carried, as it happened, the name of Madame de Montazeau's father, the late Baronet Aimery III de Mortemart, and Renée's father-in-law...

"Well, I cannot say that I regret it, my dear nephew. For now, we have the pleasure of counting you among us here at Mortemart. And I must say that I have grown quite fond of your company!" she said, sending him her sweetest smile.

"Yes. The feeling is, of course, mutual, chere tante[1]!" Aimery hurried to respond, though his words sounded half-hearted.

It was a detail that did not escape his aunt's astute scrutiny.

"But you would naturally have preferred to join your father and brother at the banquet in Bordeaux..."

She kept her eyes trained intently on the embroidery in her hands. Her fingers were moving with speed and precision as the needle in her hand was sewing an intricate wreath of lilies.

"Oh non, chere tante..." Aimery started to protest, but was soon interrupted:

"No need to excuse yourself, dear nephew. I, too, was young once. Back then, I would not have wanted to miss such a magnificent banquet for anything in the world! It would have felt like pure torture to instead be sent to visit some uncle, who lived far away, whilst my brother and father revelled in these spectacular, or so I heard, medieval games..." she said, carefully laying down her embroidery.

Madame de Mortemart looked her nephew in the eye to show how much she meant what she had said.

"You... you understand, ma tante?" Aimery asked, putting down his goblet in a hurry. He turned and inclined his head towards her in a gesture of confidence.

"More than you can imagine, cher neueu[2]," she admitted with a reassuring smile, reclining, in her turn, towards her handsome and impetuous nephew. "Most of all, I would have been furious with my mother for having arranged it all..."

"Well, yes, to be sure..." he agreed and then asked: "Excuse my surprise, dear aunt, but then you also know about the banquet and the medieval games?"

Aimery's face was shining like an Italian painting. His voice was most eager. She understood that she could not have wished for a more willing accomplice.

"Oh yes, my dear Aimery. I am afraid you judge us too harshly! We live secluded lives here at Mortemart, but we are not without ties to the fine societies of Bordeaux or Paris. I do have friends, you know, and they write to me often..."

"Oh yes, of course. I did not mean to imply otherwise!" her nephew hurried to state. "And what do they write of these medieval games?"

Aimery was sitting very straight, his bottom barely perched on the edge of his armchair. He seemed ready to jump to his feet at any moment.

"Well... I did hear a tournament being mentioned... and a medieval fair with mummers, acrobats and such... Oh, and, if I am not mistaken, an exclusive, secret game of fin'amor..." Renée made sure she spoke those words very slowly as if she was taking her time to remember all the details.

"Fin'amor? Does that not mean... courtly love?" Aimery asked, jumping to his feet.

"Maman, Maman, look what a pretty dress we made for my doll!" Her youngest daughter, Madeleine, came running from the back of the room, where she had been playing with her sister.

"Very pretty, my dear," she said, patting the girl on her head, then turned to the nurse and told her: "Babette, please take the girls upstairs. It is time they went to bed!"

The girls protested, but Madame de Mortemart did not need any more interruptions. Her nephew was in an agitated state of mind, walking back and forth in front of the fireplace, just as she had hoped he would be. She kissed her daughters on their foreheads, as she did every evening, and wished them good night.

"This sounds most intriguing indeed..." Aimery added after the girls and their nurse had left.

"What does, my dear?"

Madame de Mortemart feigned ignorance. She did not look at him as she spoke, keeping her eyes trained on the embroidery in her hands instead.

"This secret game you named... of courtly love..."

"Oh, yes... Intriguing, isn't it? Delightful, even!" she said with an even voice, piercing the fabric with her sharp needle.

"Delightful?" her silly nephew asked, coming to a halt.

It took all her self-control to prevent her lips from curling into a smile. The quizzical look on Aimery's face was absolutely precious!

"Yes, my dear, I should think so! Especially since there will be plenty of lovely young ladies willing to demonstrate their love to any young gentleman interested in receiving it..."

"Oh, that would be most delightful, indeed!" he said, resuming his agitated walk. "Oh, my dear aunt... To think that I shall miss it all while that bore of Armand will be there!"

"Oh, my poor, dear Aimery!" she said, putting down her needle to look at him, eager to see what he was going to do next.

"If you agree, then... will you help me, dear aunt?" her nephew asked, kneeling by her armchair with a sudden movement and taking her hand in his.

It was an exaggerated gesture of dramatic supplication. Renée knew that her prowess in the art of conversation would not fail her. Aimery had swallowed the bait.

"Help you with what, my dear?" she wondered.

But truth be told, she knew the answer to that question already.

Chapter Twenty Four
Alienor

Bordeaux, Easter Monday,
noon

"Éléonore, I have looked for you everywhere! Did you not watch the games of chivalry?"

Madalena de Lamothe could not hide her glee. She interlaced arms with her friend as they both walked below the tall arches of the amphitheatre's most impressive entrance, one of two to have survived the ruthless passage of time.

Once her uncle had been declared the winner of the joust, Alienor had rushed out of the seating area. Her heart had been beating very fast, and she had felt apprehensive about her daring behaviour as she had run down the worn stairs. It seemed unbelievable that she had had the audacity to flirt with and then tie her ribbon to an unknown gentleman's arm! It had been very childish of her to have run away from him in that manner, but she had dreaded having to explain her gesture to him. Taking part in the game of courtly love had been a good, and even necessary idea, but it was not exactly appropriate, all in all. Since neither Alienor

121

nor any of her sisters had a dowry to their name, that was the only way for them to secure a decent match.

Her conscience was clear. She had merely acted in accordance with the rules of the game, and she knew she had been the first to tie her ribbon to his arm. He had made quite sure of that. Yet, to think an embarrassing confrontation might ensue if they were to stumble upon each other too soon, a scandal for everyone around to witness, sent shivers down her spine. It was better to avoid that and let the facts sink in. Mademoiselle de Durfort had made her choice, however reckless. It was the gentleman's turn to weigh his options and come to a decision of his own. She resolved to wait until the banquet.

She had pondered about all that while hiding in an alcove by the monumental gates of the Galien Palace. Alienor had seen the mysterious gentleman in black attire pass her by, and she had blushed to see her red ribbon tied to his elbow.

After a while, she came out of her hiding place to join her parents and sisters as they were about to exit the amphitheatre, accompanied by the Lamothes.

"Yes, Alienor..." Elisea chimed in, turning her head to look at her. "Where have you been?"

She and Catarina were walking arm in arm ahead of her and Madalena. Her nosy eldest sister accompanied her words with a suggestive smile.

As she stepped outside, Alienor saw that her gentleman in black was far from being the only one to have received a token of fin'amor. There were young ladies and gentlemen with red and black ribbons on their sleeves everywhere in the open fields around the Galien Palace. She stifled a sigh. How she longed to have a black ribbon adorning her arm, too...

"Elisea, you are terrible!" Catarina exclaimed. "You know very well that she went to sit..."

"With our uncle Jacques de Durfort!" Alienor hurried to complete her brilliant elder sister's saving line.

"Uncle Jacques?" Elisea asked with enormous eyes. "Is he not in Paris?"

"Élisabeth, please look where you step!" Catarina warned, and her eldest sister turned her head away at last.

"Alienor, you did not mention that any uncle of yours was to attend the festivities today..." a suspicious Madalena asked.

"That is not true, Madalena, and you know it. Why, it was my uncle, the Lord of Monluc, who won the joust just now!"

"Well, yes, that uncle..." her friend exclaimed. "But I am sure you did not sit next to him, did you?"

Alienor thought she discerned a note of irritation in Mademoiselle de Lamothe's voice. She seemed displeased with the game's result.

"No, of course not, my dear. I ran into my uncle Jacques, the Lord of Castelbajac, while I was looking for my handkerchief. I had lost it, you see, upon entering the palace... It was a stroke of fortune really to bump into my uncle. He is part of the Count of Noailles' retinue, so it comes as no surprise that he should have followed him here. Although he had failed to inform us in advance, to be sure... He invited me to follow the games of chivalry in his company, and I am very glad I accepted, for he had been most helpful in explaining the tactics used by the knights who took part in the tournament... Speaking of which, did my eyes deceive me, or did you, daring friend, tie your silk ribbon to a certain knight's lance?"

Alienor was surprised at how good she was at making things up of thin air. But once she started talking, it had been hard to stop. Deflecting the conversation away from her had been a smart move, but then she found herself in equally unpleasant territory. Madalena's reckless deed had been weighing heavily on her mind...

"Shhh, dear friend... keep your voice down!" Mademoiselle de Lamothe admonished. "My mother does not approve of my actions, and she has already scolded me twice. Not a word of it anymore!"

"But Madalena, you know he did terrible things to... to my family. Things that I cannot speak to you about..." she protested.

"Whatever that was, fines, sanctions; I am sure all is well dead and buried now. It happened ten years ago, dear! And please make quite sure to call me Madeleine from now on, chere Éléonore!" her friend exclaimed loudly, making her elder sisters turn their heads again. "We are ladies now, my dear. French is the language we should use today of all days..."

"Oh, this nonsense of using only French again!" Elisea whispered in Occitan.

She and Catarina started to giggle, and Alienor could not contain a smile. She agreed with them. Occitan was a beautiful language, in no way inferior to French.

"Seven and a half years, dear. And it was not just sanctions, I assure you..."

"Have patience, my friend! You shall hear all about my mysterious knight. All in good time!" Madalena interrupted and whispered in her ear, choosing to ignore Elisea's, as well as Alienor's, words.

Alienor forced herself to smile, although deep down, her heart was filled with dread. For that particular knight held no mystery to her. And listening to her friend drone on about him was the last thing on her wish list that day. If only he had stayed in Spain...

They reached the chariottes of the de Lamothes. Alienor got to ride back to Bordeaux with Madalena and her parents in their spacious, fashionable carriage while the rest of her family rode in the Lamothes' spare carriage.

Upon their return to the city, the two families set out to explore the medieval fair, which dominated the grand square by Saint André's Cathedral. The merchant's tents were displaying a multitude of colourful merchandise, some of which Alienor had never seen before. There were minstrels playing old music, jongleurs and acrobats performing daring tricks, and even a puppet theatre, where the mummers made the children laugh... Alienor had found it all tremendously entertaining.

"Wasn't the Count of Monluc's victory utterly glorious?" Alienor asked as she and Madalena walked arm in arm around the marketplace.

Although she dreaded the subject, she had to come to the bottom of her friend's unexpected choice in the game of fin'amor.

"Well, yes... But let us not get ahead of ourselves, my dear! He won the joust game, not the tournament..." Madalena allowed.

"My dear Madeleine, you surprise me... He made all of Aquitaine proud with his performance today!" Alienor exclaimed.

"Well... Yes, of course. I know your uncle is a skilled warrior. Your mother would speak of nothing else since she arrived at our house!" Mademoiselle de Lamothe said in a rather malicious tone of voice. "But I found it very gallant and honourable that the Chevalier de Montmorency decided to step down. Although he had not been defeated, in deference to his opponent's advanced age..."

Alienor felt like a great weight was slammed into her belly, and she came to a halt, dragging Madalena with her. She could do nothing else but stare at her beautiful, reckless friend. As she had feared, the girl had feelings for that dreadful man, François de Montmorency.

"Éléonore, why are you stopping?" Madalena asked.

"But, chere amye... Can it be true that you gave this chevalier your token? Him, of all men? You do remember that he has caused my family a lot of harm! If we are unable to afford a carriage or attend banquets every month as you do, it is because of him..."

"Yes, I have heard this story before, Éléonore... But quite frankly, I am tired of it. What happened, happened. And the chevalier is not his father! He was but a boy at the time... And you do not know him like I do!" Madalena declared, starting to walk again and pulling Alienor with her.

She followed her friend in silence until they reached a food stand where they were roasting a piglet over an open fire. Declaring that she was hungry, Madalena ordered two pieces of meat for them. Alienor received the food but felt unable to eat it. Hearing her friend talk with such praise and affection of the despicable man who had ruined her and her siblings' lives had chased away her appetite.

"How well do you know this chevalier then, chere Madeleine?" Pushing the words out of her mouth came as a struggle. To cover her emotions, she bit into the pork meat. She forced her teeth to chew it and her tongue to swallow it as she waited for an answer.

"Not that well yet, my dear. But we have been acquainted with one another for a while now..." her friend answered with a tale-tell smile.

Alienor was reminded that Madalena's father, François de Lamothe, had become the mayor of Bordeaux precisely after the de Montmorencys had plunged the entire Aquitaine into a bath of blood. So, the same events that had led to her family's ruin had, in fact, provided a golden opportunity for the Lamothes to rise to wealth and status in Bordeaux.

Her friend's words implied that the rumours they had heard were true, and the de Montmorencys had something to do with her family's sudden climb to fame. Madalena and her family had denied it over the years, but it all made sense at that moment. Whatever the nature of the bargain they stroked with the constable of Montmorency eight years ago, the Lamothes owed him everything. It was no wonder that they had chosen to keep their true allegiance a secret, not only in order to cultivate a close relation with the Durforts de Civrac, but with every other honourable family in Bordeaux. But the truth threatened to come out at last, thanks to Madalena's impetuous gesture at the tournament. It was understandable that Madame de Lamothe had chastised her daughter.

Alienor was growing more and more suspicious of her friend. She did not know who she was anymore...

"Oh, ma chere Éléonore, I quite forgot to inquire. Do you

still have your silk ribbon?" Mademoiselle de Lamothe asked after a while when they had finished eating.

There was a certain snobbish inflexion in the voice of her friend, if she could still call her that. She knew that tone well. It was the one Madalena used to adopt when speaking to certain young ladies of her acquaintance that she disliked.

"No, dear friend," she answered with her best mysterious smile.

"Oh no, did you lose it? I hope it did not fall in the filthy mud outside the Roman theatre! Think if it got trampled upon by hundreds and hundreds of feet..." Madalena exclaimed with affection.

Alienor had a difficult time interpreting her friend's remarks as heartfelt and friendly. She saw her in a whole new light all of a sudden, and perhaps the feeling was mutual, for Mademoiselle de Lamothe seemed to treat her differently. It was strange to be at the receiving end of Madalena's chicanery, but she was not going to allow her to win the upper hand.

"Oh, ma chere Madeleine. Not at all!" Alienor said with a smile, then freed her arm from her friend's grasp and went to examine a roll of emerald-coloured brocade that was on display in a merchant's tent nearby.

The fabric was stunning. It had an intense and luscious shade of green and a fashionable pattern of golden flowers. Alienor passed her fingers over it to feel how soft and smooth it was. With a fabric like that, she would be able to sew herself a gorgeous banquet gown... Sewing was her favourite pastime. After she had had to alter her mother's old gown for the Easter celebrations, she had discovered a new passion for creating her own gowns. But, alas, her family had no money for such expensive luxuries.

"Then you have given away your token, too, dear friend?" Madalena interrupted her thoughts, following her inside the tent.

Instead of answering, Alienor flashed a smile and then grabbed a piece of blue silk: "Oh, look at this fabric, Madeleine! Wouldn't it look divine on you? It certainly brings out the beautiful blue colour of your eyes!" she exclaimed, unrolling the fabric and pressing one of its corners to her friend's shoulder.

"Oh, it most certainly does, mademoiselle!" the fabric merchant chimed in, appearing by their side with a wide smile. "It is the purest silk, arrived all the way from China! Please feel it. You cannot find this high-quality silk anywhere else in Bordeaux, I assure you!"

He had a foreign accent and a very large nose. Alienor listened to him with a smile, inserting words of encouragement and praise into the conversation now and then. It was a smart move, for Madalena's attention was immediately drawn to the fabric, having forgotten all about Alienor's ribbon. If there was one thing her friend adored just as much as idle gossip, it was to adorn herself with beautiful gowns made from the most expensive fabrics, after the latest fashion. And, unlike Alienor and her sisters, she could afford all that.

After a while, Mademoiselle de Lamothe made up her mind and signalled for her lady's maid, who had been shadowing them all along, to step forth and negotiate the price and delivery details with the merchant. As they left the tent, Madalena almost bumped into Elisea, who was passing by, with Catarina at her side.

"Do not tell me that you bought some new fabric, dear Madeleine! Please, you have to show it to me at once," her eldest sister exclaimed, noticing that they were coming out of a silk merchant's tent, and then dragged Madalena de Lamothe back inside with her.

Alienor could not have prayed for better timing. She and Catarina smiled at each other, then entwined their arms and walked away. After some consideration, she decided to not talk to her sister about the Chevalier de Montmorency's presence and Madalena's thoughtless gesture of offering him her token. Catarina and the rest of her family deserved to enjoy themselves at the fair. There will be time to discuss all that later...

Alienor looked around and saw her mother and father

standing by a table filled to the brim with sweetmeats. Her mother was a tall and corpulent lady, impossible to miss in a crowd. Her red arcelet[1] also stood out, as there were only a couple of other ladies wearing it that day. They were all older ladies and must have arrived, just like them, from the province. None of the fashionable ladies of Bordeaux wore those hoods anymore, having replaced them with hairnets and veils woven into their elaborate coiffures.

The two sisters exchange a quick look. Reading each other's minds, as they so often did, they both dashed at the same time towards their father to beg him to buy them some of the delicious sweetmeats on display.

Chapter Twenty Five
Marguerite

Saint Puy, late March

M arguerite de Monluc had been very surprised to receive a letter from her distant cousin. Though they were related and they had met on a couple of family occasions when they were children, they had lost contact with each other in more recent years. Perhaps it was because of her father's surge to glory during the wars in Italy and, as a result, their family's improved circumstances. But in her heart, Marguerite did not entirely approve of her family's new ways. Deep down, she missed the days when they had led a simpler life, devoid of fame and riches, just like any other family that made up the small gentry of Gascony... She envied Cousin Alienor in that regard, truth be told. It was a blessing to be anonymous and to devote one's life to spiritual, not earthly, concerns.

Alienor de Durfort's letter had arrived out of nowhere, containing a very peculiar request and bringing news of the lavish Easter celebrations in Bordeaux. Marguerite, or Mademoiselle de Monluc, as she was known outside her family, had made up her mind to leave the vanity of the aristocratic life behind her. Banquets and tournaments held no interest to her anymore. She was, in fact, preparing to say farewell to her family and everything that she had been familiar with so far and join the holy mothers at the Saint Quiriace monastery in Provins. Monastic life appealed to her tenfold more than superficial social pursuits of the kind her cousin described in her letter. But she also had a good heart and saw it as her calling to help those less fortunate, especially when they wrote and asked for her help and guidance. Although she no longer entertained such worldly thoughts herself, she understood her cousin's unenviable circumstances. The Durforts de Civrac were still poor. Alienor had, in all likelihood, no dowry to her name. She and her sisters were sure to fret over their prospects.

As for Marguerite, she felt quite glad that, by devoting her life to God, she was to avoid the misery, the powerlessness and the vacillation that were a woman's lot in life. Ladies were expected to wait and obey. They were, for the most, unable to forge their own path in life. Pain and suffering were the lot of all the daughters of Eve, the Holy Scriptures taught her. But by joining the orders, Mademoiselle de Monluc could, at least, ensure that she was spared all the unnecessary heartache brought about by romance and matrimony. And it allowed her to choose her own path.

With a sigh, she folded the letter over and over until only a very small and thick square of paper remained. She then got up from the window seat in her father's study room. Marguerite decided that it was a good deed, an act of Christian charity, to help her cousin. It was not so much that was required of her, after all. But she wondered whose support she ought to enlist in order to find out the names of all the knights and gentlemen who were to attend the Easter Banquet in Bordeaux...

She knew she could not ask her father. She cast a look at the Lord of Monluc, who was standing in the middle of the room, bent over some maps he had unfolded on the worktable in front of him. He would be most suspicious that his eldest daughter, who had decided to dedicate her life to Christ, would take an interest in such matters.

"Il fait fort froit, monsieur!"[1] she exclaimed as she passed him by on her way to the fireplace.

Her father mumbled something in reply without lifting his eyes from the papers he was studying.

Reaching the fireplace, Marguerite crouched as if to inspect the fire and then added, as she stood up: "I will ask the maid to come and put some more wood on the fire!"

Unseen by her father, she had thrown the small square of folded paper into the fire. She knew that neither of her parents, least of all her mother, would approve of Marguerite getting involved in such frivolous matters. She had to be stealthy if she was to escape her mother's scrutiny.

She left the study and looked for the maid. After telling her to tend to the fire in the study, Marguerite descended the stairs leading to the lower floor and went to the castle's chapel to pray to the Lord for His counsel. With His blessing, she might succeed in coming to Alienor de Durfort's aid.

She thought of her brothers, who were, like their father, seasoned men of arms. They would know all about the family crests of the knights attending the tournament in Bordeaux. She knew it for a fact because the Lord of Monluc had been elated to receive an invitation and had wasted no time in sharing with his family all the details enclosed in the Lord of Montaigne's letter. That had been a couple of weeks ago, and Marguerite had not retained a word of it. But Marc-Antoine and Pierre-Bertrand must have paid great attention to it.

She remembered that, for the first time in months, her eldest brother's face had lit up, and he had asked their father several questions about the tournament. It was the most interest he had shown since his return from Sienna half a year ago. Marc-Antoine's spirit appeared to have continued to ail long after his body had recovered from the ravages of famine and disease. Although his wounds had healed, and the doctors who had seen him confirmed one after another that her brother was in perfect health, he was not his old self. There were days when he did not leave his room, and he hardly ever spoke to any of them. He just gazed out of the window all day long.

But Marguerite thought it wise to not disturb Marc-Antoine's peace with unnecessary concerns like the future of their distant cousins from Rauzan. At the same time, if she were to include him in her scheme, she might be able to shoot two birds with the same stone. Being within earshot of a conversation about the Easter tournament might wake up her eldest brother from his lethargy again. That left her with only one option. She had to enlist Pierre-Bertrand's aid. He had the knowledge and the inclination. She knew he was unable to resist an opportunity to assist a damsel in distress. But whether he could keep their cousin's secret was an altogether different matter...

"Do you know where my dear brother Marc-Antoine is, madame?" Marguerite asked as she entered the hall where her mother and sisters were seated, engaged in needlework, a while later.

"Why, in his room, as usual, sister. What a strange question!" Marie exclaimed and then exchanged a look with Françoise, who started to giggle.

The Lady of Monluc admonished them for their silliness, reminding everyone that only the village idiots giggled out of the blue.

Her youngest sisters were quite silly. It was impossible to imagine Marie as a nun. She was way too young, although she insisted that she wanted to walk in her sister's footsteps and join the orders.

Marguerite felt gratified by their mother's intervention, but her scrutiny targeted her next.

"Why do you ask, Marguerite? Come here and pick up your needlework. You have neglected it for too long today already!"

"Yes, Mother," she said, taking a seat by her mother's side.

It was best to do as she was told for the moment. Marguerite bent down over the needlework basket and picked up the cushion case of yellow velvet, which she had already half adorned with red and white flowers.

After a while, she let out a sigh and said: "Oh, Mother... I have to confess that I worry for my dear brother Marc-Antoine's health..."

"As do we all, my dear. As do we all..." Madame de Monluc echoed, without as much as lifting her eyes from her needlework.

All four of them were working on identical cushion cases. Her mother had decided to create new ones for one of the guest rooms.

Marguerite pushed the needle through the thick velvet.

"Poor Marc-Antoine... There must be something we can do to help him regain his forces..."

"Marguerite, you know what the doctors said. We need to let him rest. There is nothing else left for us to do than to show patience and pray for him to get well!" Marie preached, as was her habit.

"Well, yes... That was precisely what I did, dear sister. But, as I was praying in the chapel this morning, kneeling before the statue of Saint Michel, the Lord sent me the good thought that perhaps a walk in the gardens might do my poor eldest brother some good..." Marguerite began.

She did her best to speak without passion and to explain, with patience, her plan.

"Very well. I do not see any harm in it, dear daughter. If your brothers agree to it, you may all go for a walk in the garden. But only after you have finished that red flower you are embroidering," Madame de Monluc agreed after what felt like a very long time, and it took all of Marguerite's restraint to keep her composure and not break into a smile.

She thanked her mother and set to work. It was already noon when she left the parlour. Mademoiselle de Monluc had to find her brother and enlist his aid in convincing Marc-Antoine to go for a walk. She murmured a prayer as she rushed to the stables.

Her elder brother liked to ride every morning, and she was sure to find him there.

"Dear brother, how are you today?" Marguerite asked once she caught sight of Pierre-Bertrand de Monluc coming out of the stable just as she was about to step in.

"I am well, dear sister. And you?" he replied, without stopping, marching with his decided, forceful steps towards the castle.

"Very well, now that I found you. I have an interesting proposition to make you!" she said, running to keep up with him.

"A proposition? From you? Dear Marguerite, that is a most intriguing notion!" he exclaimed, coming to a halt and turning to look at her.

"Oh, I am glad you agree, brother!" Marguerite said with a smile. "I am afraid a damsel in distress needs your help!"

"A damsel in distress? Surely, you do not mean yourself..."

"No, no, a distant cousin of ours!"

"Interesting, indeed... And who might she be?" he asked, and she knew that she had his undivided attention.

"I will tell you all in good time. But first, I need your help to convince our brother Marc-Antoine to go for a stroll in the gardens!"

"The gardens!" Pierre-Bertrand laughed. "He will never agree!"

"Oh yes, he will, if we both put our minds to it. He will not be able to fight us for long. And I actually believe the fresh air might do his ailing health some good. As for our cousin's secret request... that stroll will give us the perfect opportunity to talk, away from prying ears..."

"A secret request, you said? Nothing too dangerous or immoral, I hope, dear sister?"

"Nothing of the sort, dear brother," Marguerite hurried to explain, seeing the naughty smile that had bloomed on her brother's face. "It is about the Easter tournament in Bordeaux. I am sure you will want to hear a valuable piece of information that she gracefully sent us in repayment for our aid... a little known detail which might help our father win the games. And if you decide to accompany him to Bordeaux in a few weeks' time, dear brother, you are sure to meet the young lady in question and ask her all the questions you may have in person. But for now, I need your help to get Marc-Antoine out of his lair!"

With that, she started to walk towards the castle. After three more heartbeats, she heard Pierre-Bertrand's footsteps behind her as they bit into the gravel that paved their courtyard.

She smiled. The Lord was on Alienor de Durfort's side. Marguerite will be able to help her, after all, and so will Pierre-Bertrand. She will make sure to save a prayer for her cousin every evening. For, inconstant as her brother was, there was no telling what he might say or do should he run into the poor girl in Bordeaux.

Chapter Twenty Six
Catarina

Bordeaux, Tuesday after Easter

"Cara Alienor, it is of the utmost importance that I tell you what I saw last night when we were in the stone courtyard with that gentleman. After you turned and rushed away from him, I saw the Chevalier de Ségur..." Catarina tried to whisper to her younger sister, who sat next to her in the carriage that the Lamothes had lent them.

It was the day after the Easter festivities, and she and her family were travelling back to Rauzan.

"Please, Catarina. Do not utter that name to me now. The very sound of it hurts..." Alienor interrupted her, in a tone of voice devoid of all emotion, raising her hand to massage her temple.

"But, you know, Alienor, I think that maybe if you had waited a little longer and listened to what he had to say..." she tried once more.

"Please, Catarina. I beg you!" her sister raised her voice and alerted their mother to their teste a teste[1].

"Catherine, please, leave your sister in peace. I know you must be utterly disappointed by how the banquet unfolded for you, as am I! But your sister had, at least, tried her best... You see that she is tired!" Madame de Civrac intervened, glaring at Catarina from her place on the opposite side of the carriage.

"Mays, chere mere..."[2] Catarina tried to protest, turning almost red with embarrassment and indignation. "I am not talking about myself..."

"Yes, of course, you are not. What is there to talk about, after all? What had you been doing the whole day yesterday, I pray to ask?" Her mother's temper was starting to rise.

"Chere mere, ie vous en pry, trancquillisez vous!"[3] Elisea interceded and bent forward to take her mother's hand in hers.

"Ma chere fille[4]. One is grateful for you... and very happy for your engagement!"

Catarina knew that the baroness of Civrac did not wholeheartedly approve of Elisea's engagement to Louis de Rémy. But she was the only one of her daughters to have secured a match at the Easter festivities, and she, therefore, lavished her motherly affections on her, even more than usual.

Catarina decided to swallow her embarrassment and keep silent for now. She felt her face still warm and her heart wounded. But her mother's displeasure was to be expected, after all.

She looked at her family as they all sat rather uncomfortably in the small carriage. To her right, Alienor had turned her back towards her, staring at the patch of sky visible through the carriage's small window. Across from her, their father had already fallen asleep in his corner with his head tilted to the side. He had started to snore ever so lightly next to their mother, who had also closed her eyes, having released Elisea's hand from hers. Elisea, seated to her left, was humming a melody and played distractedly with her hair, a smile of contentment on her rosy lips. She had must have missed the reticent tone in her mother's congratulations.

"Cara Elisea," Catherine whispered in her eldest sister's ear in

Occitan, the language that the sisters used when speaking to each other. "I am very happy for you. I hold no bitterness or envy in my heart...."

For a long moment, her sister looked at her from under her eyelashes, with her head tilted, as if to appraise the sincerity of her words.

"I know, Catarina..." she nodded.

"But forgive me... I have to ask you, just this once and then never again," she took a deep breath and continued: "Do you think you can make peace with being Louis de Rémy's wife?"

Elisea gave her a startled look. Then, the beautiful alabaster skin on her forehead lost its creases, and she smiled at her. "Cara sor, of course I can. And I shall!" A frown clouded her forehead as she uttered the last words. There was a dark determination in her voice.

Catarina knew that Elisea was stubborn and ambitious. Whatever path she chose in life, she was sure to pursue it with passion until its bitter end. But Catarina was not convinced that the Chevalier de Rémy was a good match for her when it came to character. He was kind and gullible, but also boring and unlikely to keep his future wife's interest kindled for a long time.

"I know, Maman, and some of you look down on the de Rémy family and their rather... recent noble history. But I, for myself, agree with our father. And I intend to be very happy with Louis de Rémy. And very rich!" she declared in a playful tone of voice, with a wink, elbowing her.

Elisea had a reassuring smile on her pretty face, and her sister found herself smiling back at her. It was impossible to resist her.

"And you, Catarina, you can also make peace with being someone's wife. And be happy... if you can put aside your huge pride and be... accommodating."

Her sister was right. She could be accommodating. Everyone could, and should... at least up to a certain point. In any event, if anyone could be accommodating and make the most of the opportunities she was served in life, it was Elisea! She will marry, move to Bordeaux and become vastly rich. And that will make her very happy... for a while, at least. Moreover, her marriage to Louis de Rémy will provide much-needed support for their entire family.

Catarina had been raised, like a proper young lady of rank, to turn a blind eye to matters of coins and trade, which were considered to be the artefacts of a lower social class. But, since her family had fallen on harder times, they had all been constantly concerned with those notions, trying their very best to live up to their noble rank without the financial means to support them. Her, Elisea's and Alienor's gowns for the banquet had all been whisked together by altering several of their mother's old dresses, after all...

Catarina felt a rumble in her belly and was reminded that she had hardly touched any food at all since she had left Rauzan, except for the occasional fruit. Her belly hurt. It was not because they were poor or because she was fasting. The Easter Lent had ended days ago, and she was, in any case, not bound to keep it, for she was a devout Protestant, just like her father. But Catarina had vowed a long time ago to never put salt on her tongue again. The food served at the banquet, at the medieval fair and even at the de Lamothe residence had plenty of salt in it.

She was aware that others could not be expected to cater to her preferences. But she would rather starve than break her oath, taken to honour the memory of her beloved ones. For if it hadn't been for the people's greed to put more and more salt into their food, the salt tax need not have been increased. And then the miners and the common folk would not have had to rebel and demand justice... So she knew that salt, such a common, everyday commodity, one that none of her peers of noble rank would even spend a moment to ponder about, had been, in fact, the root of her family's undoing. And she had vowed to never again feel its treacherous taste on her tongue.

But, when all was said and done, Catarina had to admit that she had enjoyed herself at the banquet, despite her mother's harsh words and her constant prompting, even despite that horrid encounter, which she did not wish to dwell upon... Although the sharp exchange with that dreadful chevalier had led, indirectly, to one surprising revelation.

"Chere Catherine, I must confess I have been in awe of you the entire evening!" The gentleman's words still lingered in her ears. As did his scent and his touch.

How truly unexpected! she thought.

Alienor shifted her body in the silence that had settled upon the carriage. Catarina turned to have a better look at her. Her younger sister had closed her eyes and was about to fall asleep. Her head rested on a shawl, which she had crumpled into a ball and pushed against the sidewall of the Lamothe's chariotte. A strand of black hair had become undone from her hairnet and lay plastered to her wet cheek. She could see that Alienor was aching, feeling crushed by that gentleman's spurn. But it was possible that she was mistaken. Catarina had to tell her sister about that peculiar gesture she had witnessed while they were leaving the Ombriere Palace's stone courtyard the night before. She had seen the Chevalier de Ségur let go of something that he had been holding in his hand, something that looked very much like a long ribbon... But she guessed her confession could wait another day...

Chapter Twenty Seven
Armand

Montazeau, late April

"Do you mean to tell me they...? And that he got engaged to...? And that he..."

The countess of Montazeau suddenly sprung to her feet. Her needlework tumbled to the ground, and her voice echoed through the great hall of their ancestral castle.

Armand's family had gathered there after supper. His father had just announced to everyone what had come to pass at the Easter banquet in Bordeaux. He had never seen his mother so flustered that she was unable to find her words. And the words she did find seemed to die on her lips, time and again. It did not escape him that she had refused to even say name her, the name of her son's intended.

"Mother, allow me to explain..." Armand began, but then stopped short when he saw her raise a hand in his direction.

"Not a word! I do not wish to speak to you, ungrateful child. Monsieur, how could you allow this to happen?"

The countess looked at her husband, who was seated on an

armchair on the opposite side of the fireplace. Armand noticed that she had hurled those words from between clenched teeth. It was not unlike the hiss of a viper.

"Madame, please sit... you look unwell!" his sister, Anne, tried to intercede, jumping to her feet to offer their mother her support.

Madame de Montazeau, who did not look well, as she always did when being disobeyed, ignored her daughter and fixed a blade-sharp glare on her husband.

"Yes, madame. Do gather yourself!" his father exclaimed, jumping to his feet.

He must have anticipated his wife's displeasure at hearing the news, yet he seemed astonished by her overly dramatic response.

Armand, on the other hand, was not surprised. He knew what was most likely to happen once Madame de Montazeau had made up her mind that her honour had been hurt. Ever since he could remember, he had been the favourite object of his mother's disdain. Stonewalling was her strategy of choice, but she did not shy away from using strong, cutting words either. He knew the signs well. Whatever they said or did from that moment onwards, there was nothing any of them could do to avoid the storm that was coming...

"This is quite enough, mes seigneurs[1]. I do not wish to speak to any of you anymore!" she said in a low and steady tone of voice.

But Armand was not fooled. He knew that there was an ocean of anger simmering inside his mother's head. Her nostrils flared as she struggled to keep it bottled inside. Armand knew from experience that it never worked. She was bound to spit out her wrath on the three of them, like a fire-breathing dragon of yore.

"Do not start with your exaggerations now, madame! It could not be helped, and that is that," their lord father declared, with a deep frown, turning his back on her.

He walked towards the small table where Antoine, his eldest brother, and his wife were playing a card game, seemingly unbothered by the tense conversation taking place right beside them.

He sat with them at the table and watched their game. Armand took a big gulp of red wine and then crossed his arms. His father's words and gestures could not have been more badly timed. The glare the countess shot her husband in response looked downright murderous. Armand wished he was anywhere else in the world at that moment than in his family castle's main hall to witness his mother's ill-temper. He would have given anything to find himself on a battlefield with a long sword in his hand. At least, those were enemies he knew how to fight and slay...

"Please, Mother. If you would just listen... This engagement is far from being as bad as it sounds!" his younger brother opened his mouth, at last, sitting on the very edge of the sofa. He extended his arms towards the countess in a gesture of supplication.

Armand knew that Aimery should have abstained from saying the word "engagement" or anything at all. He should have kept quiet, just like him. Thus aggravated, Madame de Montazeau was sure to resort to her hurtful accusation of choice. And sure enough, after an uncomfortable moment of silence, she shouted out the ultimate injury.

"Blood traitors! You have betrayed me... betrayed this family, polluted our noble lineage..." she launched, her words dripping with loath.

"Madame mere..." Anne began, but was cut short by their mother.

She pushed Anne aside and made for the stairs. The crestfallen expression on his sister's face would have made anyone feel sorry for her. But she was their mother's favourite child and hardly ever had to endure her wrath. Armand, on the other hand, was sure to become, one more time, the preferred target of the countess' displeasure. It was just a matter of time before she hurled some more injuries at him.

Madame de Montazeau started to climb the monumental staircase, which led to the upper floors.

Aimery turned around and exchanged a meaningful look with Armand, but none of them dared break the silence that reined once more over the hall. Even his reckless younger brother had understood that their mother's mood was sure to sour even further if they did. Aimery clasped a hand over his mouth to prevent himself from giggling. He was the silliest of brothers, prone to getting into trouble in the blink of an eye. But, as luck had it, and luck seemed to favour his younger brother, time and again, he was seated with his back towards the stairs, so the countess could not see his buffoonery.

Armand, on the other hand, had a good view of the wooden staircase, which spiralled upwards around a sturdy pillar and followed his mother's advance from the corner of his eye. Having climbed a full circle of steps, Madame de Montazeau stopped and perched over the wooden rail. She glared once more at them from the height of her position, like a priest from his pulpit. Armand knew she was sure to reserve the last whipping words for him. He braced himself. With the tip of his boot, he kicked Aimery in the shin to warn him. The last thing anyone needed was for his younger brother to burst out in uncontrollable laughter. His brother swirled around, his hand still covering his mouth.

"You ungrateful son..." their mother's voice thundered as she looked her son in the eye. "You have disappointed me most of all! May the Lord give me the strength to forgive you... one day..."

And having said that, she gathered once more the ornate skirts of her burgundy red gown and climbed, with poise, the stairs towards her apartments. She must have stomped her feet as hard as she could against the wooden steps, for the spiral staircase screeched, and the countess' dramatic footsteps echoed throughout the hall in the silence that followed.

After a moment's hesitation, Anne darted after her. Armand knew that Madame de Montazeau was bound to spend the next weeks locked in her chamber, as was her habit after a great confrontation. She would show the full force of her stubbornness by refusing to get out of bed or allow anyone, with the exception of her lady's maid and perhaps Anne, in her vicinity. As for the men of the family, they were sure to be given the cold shoulder for a long time to come.

Aimery had sobered up and sat with a crestfallen expression on the sofa, nursing his goblet of wine. The others carried on with their game in silence. Once the doors to the countess' chambers closed with a thud behind her and Anne, the rest of them looked at each other without saying a word.

Henriette de Ségur started to cough all of a sudden. Antoine called for the footman to come to his wife's aid. It appeared that the lady had choked on her wine, judging by the spillage that stained the front of her yellow gown and the carpet beneath her feet. She kept coughing, her face buried in her handkerchief. Armand could have been mistaken, but the coughs sounded more and more like muffled bouts of laughter.

"Please excuse me..." Henriette said as she got up, right before a loud snort escaped her lips.

The Count of Montazeau and Antoine clicked their tongues in displeasure at the same time. One footman accompanied the lady out of the hall. The other kept filling a sulking Aimery's goblet with wine. Armand looked at the ceiling and thanked the Lord that it was all over.

But then the count turned towards his sons. "Well now, this time, you surpassed yourselves. This will take weeks, maybe months, to repair. And in the meantime, this castle will turn into a living purgatory for us all!"

And with that, the Lord of Montazeau threw his cards on the table, stood up, and retired to the library. Armand cast his younger brother a long look. Aimery shot him a sheepish smile in return. Antoine got up and walked towards them with a goblet in hand, in that provocative, arrogant manner of his.

"I must say I did not see this one coming, brother," he said with one of his insipid courtier smiles.

Armand felt like choking. He couldn't bear to spend one more moment in that damned house. He jumped to his feet, gave his goblet to the footman, and left the hall without another word. After receiving his black cape and his hat, he put them on and rushed out of the door. He crossed the stone courtyard in a hurry, reached the stables, saddled his black steed, and rode through the massive gates, leaving the castle behind. He did not stop until he reached the nearest village and its tavern.

Chapter Twenty Eight
Alienor

"A response from Cousin Marguerite! And a letter from Pierre-Bertrand de Monluc!"

Alienor could hardly contain her joy at the arrival of those long-awaited letters, which had been delivered to her that morning at breakfast by Maria. She was their former nurse, her mother's lady's maid and the most reliable and kind woman in the world.

By the time she joined her mother and eldest sister in the ladies' parlour, she had already read and re-read each letter several times.

Elisea looked up from her needlework. She was working on a beautiful banquet gown made of green brocade, adjusting its sleeves to match the latest fashion. The trumpet sleeve was no longer in fashion in Paris and Bordeaux, having been replaced by sleeves that closely fitted the arms. Their mother's old dresses were in excellent condition, yet rather old-fashioned when it came to style. So she,

148

Catarina and Elisea had spent the past couple of weeks working on making them more fashionable and up to the high standard of la société bourdeloyse[1]. They all wanted to make sure they looked their best at the long awaited-Easter celebrations. But Elisea's progress has been very slow. Needlework required a lot of patience, and that was far from being her eldest sister's strongest virtue.

Elisea appeared glad of the interruption and put away her gown at once. She lay it next to her on the couch, careful to cover the part she had been working on. Those details did not escape Alienor. Her elder sister was not exactly the most skilled embroiderer in the de Durfort de Civrac family. She tried every trick in the book in order to avoid their mother's reprimands.

"Dear sister, tell us of the news you received. Is Pierre-Bertrand de Monluc related to the famous man of arms, le Seigneur de Monluc?" Elisea asked, feigning interest in her sister's letter.

"Yes. And to us!" came her mother's rather dry reply.

"Is that so? I was not aware, Maman..." Elisea said. "How is it we have not met them then?"

"We have, Élisabeth. You, of all my children, should remember that. You were ten years of age when we visited your grandparents' castle in Gascogne..." Madame de Civrac started in a slightly irritated tone of voice. "When my dear mother departed from our midst..." Her voice started to tremble, and Alienor saw tears gathering at the corners of her eyes.

Elisea knew all that already. She was just pretending she didn't to waste time. And she had managed to get their mother in a sad mood.

"In any event, I did not expect such a swift reply from Cousin Marguerite..." Alienor hurried to shift the focus of the conversation.

Her mother, Elisea and Elina had spent almost a year at Chasteau de Sérillac while her maternal grandmother lay on her deathbed. That was the reason why they had not been there all those years ago, when tragedy had knocked at their ancient castle gates.

Although, in truth, it did not knock, Alienor thought with a bitter smile. *It had barged in, blowing the gates out of their hinges with the force of a hundred cannons. And it left them forever changed, forever haunted, forever un-whole...*

"Cousin Marguerite? I am confused! Did you not just say that Pierre-Bertrand de Monluc has written to you?" Elisea asked in a high-pitched voice. "And, in any case, I find it highly inappropriate that you should receive letters from young gentlemen and not me. I am, after all, the eldest daughter of our parents and the one to marry first!"

Alienor was stunned but also flattered. It was not every day that her sister was envious of her. She stole a glance at her mother. She appeared to have recovered from her moment of weakness and kept her eyes trained on the piece of white fabric she was trimming. The fabric was to be attached to Madame de Civrac's banquet gown as a partlet to cover her neckline and shoulders. But Alienor was not fooled. She knew that, despite her detached air, her mother was following her and Elisea's conversation with interest. Talking about her family's connection to the Monlucs of Saint Puy was one of the subjects closest to the baroness' heart. She was utterly proud that her own departed mother, Alienor's grandmother, had been born Anne de Lasseran de Monluc. Ever since her cousin, Blaise, had risen to fame about a year ago, thanks to his legendary defence of Sienna against the Spanish, Madame de Civrac was known to show a personal interest in any news concerning him and his family. When he was awarded the order of Saint Michel by the king, her mother spoke of nothing else for weeks on end, regaling every guest who happened to pass their threshold with exaggerated accounts of his heroic deeds at Sienna and his triumphant return to France, taking special pride in it all, as if they were her own accomplishments.

"Alienor, you must tell me all about these letters!" her sister exclaimed, inviting her to take a seat by her side.

Alienor could not tell whether Elisea was genuinely interested in her letters or if she was just eager to seize any opportunity to delay resuming her needlework. She might have been curious to hear what Pierre-Bertrand de Monluc had written.

Alienor sat on the empty chair between her mother and elder sister, making sure to fold and cover the letter with her hand lest her sister might be tempted to take a peek.

"Éléonore, not Alienor!" her mother admonished, as was her habit. "You are both young ladies now, old enough to give up speaking the tongue of the servant folk. Most of all, you, Élisabeth! Remember that we are to use the correct form of our names and only the French language when we are out in society. No daughter of mine shall be embarrassing herself by using the peasant's tongue at the mayor's banquet!"

In preparation for their visit to Bordeaux, their mother had been making all of them use their French names even when at home. But behind her back, the girls continued to use the endearing Occitan names they have called each other since they were little girls. It had been established at a secret meeting that none of them intended to cease whispering their secrets in the local tongue.

"Yes, of course, Maman... Éléonore, please tell me all about these letters!" her sister obliged, although her eye-rolling did not escape Alienor's attention. "Please!" she added after a while, noting that her sister was in no hurry to answer her request.

"Very well... Élisabeth... But first, Pierre-Bertrand de Monluc is our second cousin, not any young gentleman. And he is most definitely not writing me fanciful letters of the sort you imply! Perhaps it might help you understand if I were to explain how we are related."

Here she paused and looked at Madame de Civrac, who nodded in encouragement. Alienor noticed that she had laid down the needlework.

"Our cousins, Marguerite and Pierre-Bertrand, are the children of the Seigneur de Monluc. His full name is Blaise de

Lasseran de Massencosme de Monluc, and you might remember that he was made a knight of France last year. Well, his father was François de Monluc, whose younger sister was our own grandmother, Anne de Sérillac, née de Monluc. May the Lord rest her soul. Our mother and the Seigneur de Monluc are, therefore, first cousins, while we and Marguerite, Pierre-Bertrand and their other siblings are second cousins."

Her mother nodded in approval.

"Is Pierre-Bertrand de Monluc to inherit his father's titles and land?" Elisea asked with sudden interest.

"I highly doubt it, my dear, given that he is his second son!" Madame de Civrac remarked, resuming her embroidery.

"Very well," Elisea said, sounding rather disappointed. "But why are they writing to you all of a sudden, Alienor... Éléonore?"

"I wrote to our cousin Marguerite some weeks ago. I wanted to know if the Lord of Monluc or any of them were attending the Easter festivities in Bordeaux. I thought that it would be wonderful to meet them there! I also inquired whether they had any knowledge of the valiant knights partaking in the tournament and their coats of arms..."

Elisea stifled a most unbecoming surge of laughter.

"Since when are you interested in tournaments and coats of arms?"

"Élisabeth, please mind your manners. That lack of control is most unbecoming for a refined young lady. And please resume your needlework at once. You still have much to do if you plan to have those new sleeves in place before Easter!" Madame de Civrac objected, raising her tone of voice in alarm. "Chere Éléonore, are my cousin and his family travelling to Bordeaux for Easter? I do so long to see him..."

"Yes, dear mother. My uncle is to fight in the tournament."

"Oh, like a true knight of the kingdom!" her mother exclaimed, taking a hand to her bosom.

"In any case, I just wanted to be well-informed, Élisabeth. Marguerite has not only been kind and obliging to write back but has also enlisted the support of her brother. Pierre-Bertrand de Monluc sent me a list of the participants' names and their colours. I must say it has been a most unexpected surprise! When I resolved to write to my cousin, I did not even dare hope for such an elaborate reply. That the Captain of Monluc would go through the trouble of sending me the lists himself had never crossed my mind..." Alienor explained.

Elisea scoffed in reply.

"The family of Monluc has ancient, noble origins. It comes as no surprise that your cousins should carry themselves with such grace and solicitude as it becomes their rank and upbringing. As to your cousin Pierre-Bertrand's advice, you must consider yourself very fortunate indeed! His knowledge of the subject is vastly superior to his sister's... Indeed, I dare say, to any one of our immediate acquaintance!" Madame de Civrac declared, looking at Alienor with pride. "Please make sure to send them a very effusive reply to express your utmost gratitude for their aid. And do cultivate this illustrious family connection, dear Alienor!"

"Yes, dear mother, I most certainly will."

"What else did your cousins say, Éléonore?" her mother asked.

"Well, in her letter, Cousin Marguerite had some news of her own..." Alienor answered.

She was unsure whether her cousin had meant for her to share that piece of information with the rest of her family. Unfolding one of the letters in her lap, she glanced through its contents, but could not find any mention of secrecy.

"Ah bon? Vn marriage?"[2] her mother asked, raising her eyes from her needlework in eager expectation.

Alienor folded the letters and placed them in the purse tied to her belt.

"On the contrary, chere mere. She is preparing to take the veil and join in monastic life. Come summer, she will start for Provins to take up residence with the sisters at the Couvent des Cordelieres[3]," she revealed, picking up her own banquet gown.

Being more resourceful and diligent than her elder sister, she had already completed most of the adjustments she had planned for it. She had taken away from the old gown the long, hanging edge of the trumpet sleeves and the fake sleeves beneath. She kept only the pieces of fabric fitted to the upper arms, which were dark blue to match the colour of the over gown. And she was almost done attaching the new sleeves for the forearms, made of light grey brocade embroidered with silver thread. The underskirt she planned to wear at the banquet was made of the same luxurious fabric, and stemmed from the same old gown her grandmother, the Dowager Baroness of Civrac, had worn in her youth at the Court of Navarre. The edges of the front opening of the dark blue over gown had also been trimmed with an elaborate pattern of entwined silver lilies. Pulling out the silver thread from the unused fabric of her grandmother's old gown and softening it with emulsions to embroider her own pattern with it, had been a painstaking endeavour that had taken her several days. Alienor could not have been prouder of her craft. The colours and the fabrics of her dress were carefully chosen to match those of her family's coat of arms, like in the olden days.

She still had to find a way to add the colour red to her attire. Perhaps a red hairnet or red ribbons woven in her braided chignon would do... She was disappointed that her mother had refused to give her the ruby necklace, which would have been the perfect accessory to complete her look. But Madame de Civrac wanted to wear that necklace herself since it matched the colour of the deep red gown she was to wear at the banquet. Alienor had to make do with the pearl necklace that had belonged to her other grandmother, Anne de Sérillac. She was not going to be wearing it around her neck, though. Her neckline was to be covered by a gauze partlet, which she had already attached to the décolletage of her mother's old dress. The pearl necklace was to be pinned to the bodice of her gown, draped in two rows across her chest to achieve a garland-like effect.

Needlework was Alienor's safe haven. When she had a needle and some thread in her hands, she felt she had a purpose, and she could forget all the horrors of the past. It was her way of turning pain into a thing of beauty, just like Catarina when she played the lute or like Ferran Barjac, the painter, who had immortalised her parents and grandparents in his portraits many years ago. She was determined to put all her skills to good use in reviving her mother's old gown. So far, the results of her hard work pleased her, and she looked forward to wearing the dress on Easter Monday. She had no dowry to speak of, but she could, at least, showcase her talent and ensure that she was dressed as befitted the scion of one of the oldest noble families of Aquitaine.

Alienor stole a glance at her sister's gown and realised that her mother had been right. Unless she got some help, it was not going to be ready on time for Easter.

"To have a daughter taking the veil!" Madame de Civrac exclaimed after a while.

Alienor was not sure if her mother was shocked or pleasantly surprised. She secretly hoped that neither she nor her sisters would be forced to take that step. They had already spent most of their childhood locked away in a castle...

She thought of Marguerite, who was the eldest daughter of one of the kingdom's most celebrated men of arms. But both Marguerite and her younger sister, Marie, were over twenty years of age and still unmarried. And it appeared that both of them had decided to spend the remainder of their days serving the Lord. Her parents must have been delighted, and they had probably encouraged them down that path. They were, after all, known for their devotion, and having two daughters take the veil was a sure way to demonstrate their religious allegiance to the Catholic Valois dynasty in a time when the Reform was gaining more and more ground, particularly in the south of France.

"I cannot imagine how anyone could wish to join in monastic life! The thought of renouncing all joy in life and spending one's days between the grey, boring walls of a monastery frightens me... I could never live like that, huddled together with strange, embittered old women, praying and suffering deprivation after deprivation..." Elisea commented, lowering the dress in her lap once more and looking out of the window.

Alienor could not help but agree, but she knew better than to voice her thoughts out loud. She kept her eyes trained on her needle instead.

As if to confirm her apprehensions, Madame de Civrac shot her eldest daughter a look full of indignation, and Alienor was sure that reprimanding words would have followed had not Catarina and Elina entered their mother's parlour at that very moment. They had their arms full of beautiful spring flowers: hyacinths, violets and daffodils. While everyone else hurried to admire the flowers, Alienor stole one look at her eldest sister. Elisea, too, was turning twenty in the fall. It was no wonder she wanted to marry as soon as possible...

Chapter Twenty Nine
Aimery

Mortemart, Good Friday

Aimery de Ségur had spent several days fretting over the success of his daring escape plan. It was imperious that nothing should raise the suspicions of his uncle and cousin. If everything could be taken care of in good time, as his aunt had promised, then he would be able to leave the castle of Mortemart in peace and luxury, in the same way that he had arrived there.

If they rode without too many stops and accidents, he was sure to reach Libourne on Easter Day. From there, he would have to ride a horse to Bordeaux. It was a loathsome business, but it could not be avoided if he were to arrive on time for the festivities on Easter Monday. A smile replaced the earlier grimace on Aimery's lips as he tried to imagine the astonished expressions on his father and his brothers' faces upon seeing him make his entrance at the banquet...

That morning, he had had a very hard time swallowing his frugal morning meal of eggs and hard bread. He had barely touched the freshly churned butter, although it had looked quite appetising. He hoped that his lack of appetite would go unnoticed. He was, after all, known to relish a good meal and a generous goblet of wine... But it was Long Friday after all, and the day was supposed to be spent in prayer and deprivation. Only a meagre bean soup was to be served for dinner that day. Aimery knew it for a fact, for he had misheard Madame de Mortemart give the orders to the housekeeper right before breakfast. He hoped that his fasting would not go unnoticed by the Lord Almighty and that He would thus ensure the success of his daring plans.

After the morning meal, Aimery had hurried to join his uncle in the library under the pretence of searching the shelves for a book on the history of the Rochechouarts de Mortemart and the Limosin. As his aunt had explained, it was important that he should receive the letter in the presence of the Baronet of Mortemart. His aunt had explained the reason, but Aimery could not be bothered to remember it. Suffice to say that he had gone out of his way to show an interest in the history of the early lords of Mortemart. It had been amusing to see his uncle's eyebrows rising in wonder when he had explained to him the nature of his errand in the library that morning. But he was determined not to allow anything to come in the way of his speedy departure from that God-forsaken place. He had to watch himself and make sure he kept a sober attitude while playing that farce on his uncle.

Having been allowed into the library, Aimery was skimming the shelves in search of a relevant book that could serve his purpose. It was hard to keep the pretence, truth be told, when his heart was pounding in his chest with anticipation, and he could hardly think of anything else than the letter. Time stretched slowly in the silent, dusty library, and Aimery started to doubt the letter's arrival. Had it been sent on time? Had it not met with some mishap on its way to the castle? Had his aunt remembered to pay the forger?

A knock on the door made him jolt in surprise.

"Bonne iournée, monsieur,"[1] said the butler with a bow after obtaining permission to come forth.

The old man walked with slow, ceremonious steps towards the desk where his uncle had been sitting together with his secretary, going through some papers.

Aimery froze to the spot by a row of bookshelves. He felt a chill rise up his spine. At long last!

"Your correspondence, my lord," the butler announced as he reached the side of the desk, stretching out the arm holding the silver tray.

Aimery prayed that the forger's letter was on that tray.

Is the letter amongst them? Oh Lord, I beg you, make my uncle look through his correspondence at once and put an end to these trepidations! he prayed.

His eyes had been following the advance of the butler with growing anticipation. He reminded himself to act naturally and not betray any previous knowledge of the existence of a letter addressed to him.

Aimery picked up a book from the nearest shelf and opened it. His index finger sprung to trace the words on a row, and he tried his best to appear captivated by that particular passage, even bending his figure over the tome.

'The pheasant cock is typically surrounded by several hens, whom he woos, one by one, with an elaborate mating dance. Standing tall and straight, the cock struts around the hen in circles, feathers fluffed and wattle puffed...' That was certainly not a book about the history of the Rochechouarts de Mortemart! He stopped reading and trained his ears on the conversation taking place behind him.

"Fort bien, monsieur," he heard the butler say, and he stole a quick glance towards his uncle's desk.

Aimery saw the servant leave the letters on a corner of the baronet's desk. His heart sank. There was no telling when his uncle would decide to look at them.

He felt his mood dampen as the baron dismissed the butler

with a mere flutter of his hand, keeping his attention trained on the paper that his secretary was holding in front of his eyes. He did not as much as glance at the letters.

Aimery was not a patient man, neither by inclination nor through experience. As the favourite son of a countess, he had been accustomed to have his wishes fulfilled all his life. He started to wonder what he could possibly do to draw his uncle's attention to the letters without giving himself away.

The minutes passed. His uncle and his secretary were still in close conversation, heads bent together over the heavy oak desk, consulting one document after the other.

Aimery started to sweat. It was a most uncomfortable feeling! But right when he had decided he could not wait any longer and had closed the book in his hands, intending to make his way over to his uncle's desk, the study's doors opened, and the valet announced: "La baronne de Mortemart et mademoiselle Gabrielle."[2]

Aimery stopped in mid-stride.

"Papa, papa!" exclaimed Gabrielle de Rochechouart, coming forth and offering her father a bouquet of flowers. "Elles sont pur vous!"[3]

Aimery thought that, in any other circumstances, the Seigneur de Mortemart would have reprimanded the intruder for interrupting his important work. But Gabrielle was his petite faiblesse[4], and he could not bring himself to be crossed with her for bringing him flowers.

While the baron was thus engaged in conversation with his daughter, the baroness threw an inquisitive glance at her nephew. At first, he did not understand its meaning, surprised and fearful as he was for the whole plan to go amiss. But after he caught the meaning of his aunt's innuendos, he gave her a nod, and then his eyes darted twice in the direction of the pile of letters stacked on the corner of his uncle's desk. Madame de Mortemart followed his gaze. Aimery hoped she had noticed the letter bearing the seal of the house of Ségur amongst the others.

"Gabrielle, allayons!"[5] she said, taking a step forward. "We must leave your father to his important responsibilities."

And with that, she bent forward as if to take hold of her daughter's hand, touching with her long trumpet sleeve the corner of her husband's desk. The correspondence left there by the butler fell to the ground.

"Mays ma petite Gabrielle![6] Look what you have done now! We should not be disturbing your father's work like this..." Madame de Mortemart exclaimed, taking hold of her daughter's hand, half dragging her towards the door.

"Mays, chere mere..." his cousin Gabrielle tried to protest.

"Vous auez ryen a croyndre, mon ange,"[7] the baron placated her. "Henri, what are you waiting for? Pick up the letters from the floor," he ordered his secretary, who rushed to comply.

The baroness had almost reached the study's wooden doors, already opened by the solicitous valet, when she turned around as if she had just remembered something of importance.

"Any correspondence for me this morning, cher mary?"

Hearing his wife's question, François de Rochechouart felt obliged to receive the correspondence from his secretary's hands and look through the letters.

Aimery, lingering by the bookshelves, followed his aunt's efficient manoeuvres with increasing admiration, and held his breath. He felt extremely fortunate to have been able to enlist that brilliant lady's support. He would not have succeeded on his own. His aunt was not only a kind and generous spirit but also a very astute ally. He was glad she appreciated him so much that she had taken it upon herself to ensure his happiness in that matter.

"Non, mays voicy vne carte adroyssée au Cheualier de Ségur..."[8] Aimery heard his uncle say, and he fought a smile.

The baronet turned around in his chair to face his nephew and hand him the letter. He accepted it with a "thank you".

"Ah, look, it is indeed the seal of the house of Ségur!" exclaimed his aunt from where she stood by the door. She turned to her daughter. "Allayons, Gabrielle, vostre professor de danse nous attend!"[9]

And then they both left the library. The doors were shut closed in their wake. Aimery continued to stare at the intricate wooden carvings on the doors, lost in thought, holding the unopened letter in his hand.

The Lord of Mortemart cleared his throat. "Mon neueu, are you not curious to open the letter? It might be from your father!"

"Ah, bien cert. Escusez moy, mon oncle."[10]

Aimery was suddenly at a loss as to what to do with the heavy tome he was still holding in his other hand. He needed both hands to break open the seal, did he not? He hurried to discard the book on a nearby shelf and then proceeded, with trembling fingers, to open the letter.

"Oh, non..." he exclaimed, after a moment, raising a hand to cover his mouth in awe.

"I hope there is no bad news from your parents..." He saw his uncle put down the letter he was reading at that moment and he turned around once more to face Aimery with a disquieted expression on his face.

"Bad news, indeed, dear uncle, I am afraid... my brother Armand has written to me. Ma chere mere, vostre seur,[11] has been taken ill! And my brother says she specifically asked for me to be by her side..." Aimery tried to sound as sincere and surprised as possible whilst repeating the words he had rehearsed in his room last night: "Mon cher oncle, I entreat you! You must allow me to return to Montazeau at once!" he supplicated, offering the baron the letter.

His uncle took the piece of paper and started to read it. Aimery held his breath again. Will the forgery pass his scrutiny? Did the man paid by his aunt manage to forge the seal well enough? Was his uncle truly unfamiliar with Armand's handwriting, as his aunt had assured him? And had he sounded grief stricken enough to convince his uncle of his sincerity?

"I must leave at once, Uncle! I must let my valet know that he is to start packing immediately... I will never forgive myself if I am not by my poor mother's side to offer her my comforting attention in her hour of need..." he added as the minutes dragged, accompanying his words with a nervous walk between the desk and the bookshelves.

"Yes, naturally..." he heard his uncle say at last. "Though one might wonder why..." he added, and then let his words trail away.

What could the baron possibly wonder about? Aimery chose to ignore his uncle's last words. Instead, he focused on the Lord of Mortemart's approval of his departure, which signalled the success of his and the baroness' plan.

"Ie vous remercy, cher oncle. Ie n'oublieroy iamais ce que vous venez de faire pour moy!" [12]

And with that, he took the Baron de Mortemart's hand in his and kissed it. Then he froze in place. The kiss on the hand might have been too much. He had to control his excitement.

"Forgive me, Uncle, but I am overcome with emotion. The thought that my dear mother... But I do not wish to say another word for fear of attracting some terrible bad luck..." he added.

And with that, Aimery hurried to leave the room before he said or did something else that might endanger his and his aunt's brilliant plan. He prayed to God Almighty to chase away any doubt from his uncle's mind and allow him to make a smooth escape from that dreadful place. If all went according to plan, he could be on his way to Bordeaux before nightfall.

Chapter Thirty
Armand

Bordeaux, Easter Monday,
noon

"L'Isle, you fought bravely!" Armand de Ségur entered the tent of his friend and companion in arms to congratulate him for his performance in the game of joust.

"Remercyements.[1] Although I wish I would have gone further..." Philippe de l'Isle replied.

Armand smiled broadly at the sight of his friend, as he was standing in the middle of his small tent with his arms and legs sprawled, to allow his squire to take off his heavy armour and chain mail.

"Yes. But still, a very commendable achievement considering that this was your very first tournament, my friend," Armand insisted.

"It was a pity you could not be a part of it, Ségur. It would have been much more interesting, to be sure. You know how I long to defeat you, Captain," Philippe said.

"I highly doubt you would, but you are welcome to try, l'Isle!"

he answered. "But perhaps the opportunity will arise soon. It is said that the king is very fond of these old-fashioned games…"

"You do not approve of them, Captain?" the Chevalier de l'Isle laughed once the squire took off his chain mail shirt.

His friend looked rather relieved to be able to slip out of it. He then walked to the small table by the side of the tent, picked up his goblet and drank with thirst. Once he was done, he instructed the squire: "Wine for the Chevalier de Ségur!"

Armand accepted the silver cup and then raised it with the words: "To many more deeds of valour!"

"Hear, hear!" the chevalier chimed in, and they drank in silence.

Then the squire rushed to help his master down into a chair. The grimace that his friend made when his body touched the cushions of the chair did not escape Armand.

"Nothing serious, I hope," he said.

"Oh, nothing but a mere bruise from the fall. The Count of Candale spared no effort in making sure he sent me flying from my horse!" Philippe de l'Isle answered, a bitter smile hanging from the corners of his mouth.

They continued to drink in silence for a while as the squire adorned his master in an elegant attire made of dark red velvet.

"I bet you are hungry, Captain! Let us eat. The joust has made me ravenous. Squire, go and fetch us some good pieces of meat and some fresh bread for our meal. And more wine."

With that, the chevalier gave his squire some coins. "Allow me to pay for today's meal, l'Isle…" he offered.

"Nonsense, Ségur. There will be other occasions for that. Today we celebrate my first game of chivalry! You cannot refuse me…"

Armand acquiesced with a nod and watched the page leave the tent.

"But I see congratulations are in order for you too, mon cappitaine!"[2] the chevalier exclaimed.

"For me?" he asked, not catching the meaning of his words.

Then he noticed his friend had been staring at the piece of red silk that the young lady had fastened to his arm in the tribunes. He blushed, despite himself. He had forgotten all about it...

"I was not aware that you were taking part in another game altogether," the Chevalier de l'Isle said with a teasing smile on his face. "You never cease to surprise, my friend! As I gather, the game of fin'amor had barely begun, and yet, here you are, a red ribbon on your arm already! Who would have thought, eh? So tell me, who is she?"

His friend's curiosity in regards to any subject involving the fair sex was legendary. And he was obviously in a teasing mood after several goblets of wine.

"Well, there is not much to tell... This... development has been as surprising for me, I assure you..."

Armand hoped Philippe de l'Isle might lose interest if he was vague enough. But he was not in luck.

"Well, what about your ribbon, then? Did you give yours away to the same young lady? Are we to hear the bans called for you, Captain?" The chevalier's smug smile was quite irritating.

"Please, do not make me laugh, l'Isle! I do not have a ribbon to begin with. I did not intend to partake in this... whatever one might call it..." Armand answered evasively.

"A game of courtly love?" his friend offered.

It was clear that he was relishing making his captain uncomfortable.

"But enough about me! Are you not partaking in this game, too, l'Isle? Sounds exactly like the sort of stuff to titillate your interest..."

"I am way too young for such an endeavour, Captain," he laughed again. "Oh no, no young lady, however charming and eager, is going to take away my freedom anytime soon, Captain. But I am sure as Hell not going to say no to one or two embraces at the banquet tonight! I will have to keep an eye on my elbows, of course... Young ladies can be cunning, devilish creatures. They can distract you with the most sensual of kisses whilst their fingers are busy at work, fastening an unwelcome ribbon to your sleeve!"

Armand had not thought of that. They were indeed cunning... The ladies in his family were always engaged in some scheme or another to outsmart each other.

"But you seem to have found yourself in quite a situation, Captain. What are you going to do about it?" his friend asked.

That, Armand thought, was a very good question. He raised his shoulders dismissively and changed the subject.

"What did you think of Montmorency's performance in the joust game today? Did you foresee him losing to our Lord Commander?"

Chapter Thirty One
Madame de Mortemart

Mortemart, Good Friday

"**A**nd you say your lady mother does not approve of the Madame de Montaigne, despite the close acquaintance of their husbands?" Renée de Rochechouart asked her nephew.

She had come to Aimery de Ségur's room in order to supervise the servants, who were busy packing his belongings. Her nephew was standing by the window, and he seemed unable to contain his glee at the thought of leaving Mortemart. She suppressed a smile. He was so vain and gullible.

"Yes. Who knows why my mother does not approve of other ladies? I have stopped trying to make sense of my mother's whims a long time ago... How can she, for instance, not approve of you? When you are clearly the kindest, most helpful aunt in the entire world!" he said, leaving his place by the window to take her hand in his. "I will never forget what you have done for me, dear aunt!"

Renée smiled. One could not help but wonder how such an exquisitely handsome head could be, at the same time, so slow. But it was only fitting that, of all her sons, that vain woman,

Claude de Ségur, would prefer the good-looking Aimery over the dutiful Antoine and the brave Armand...

As for the baroness of Mortemart, it was no secret to her that her sister-in-law's disapproval of her was rooted in that lady's distaste for anyone who did not belong to the oldest and most noble families of France. She had been born Renée de Taveau de Mortemer, but her family was far from boasting about the noble heritage of the Rochechouarts or the Ségurs. Her father had been born without a noble particle, as Pierre Taveau, and so did her mother. The family had been able to join the ranks of nobility thanks to the foresight of her paternal grandfather, a successful merchant from Paris who used his life's savings to acquire the estate at Mortemer outside Rouen. And although her sizeable dowry had saved the Rochechouart family from certain ruin, there were many among her husband's relations who still did not accept her, even after all those years. But none of them displayed their contempt of her as plainly as Madame de Montazeau, her husband's younger sister, who missed no opportunity to remind her of her humble origins...

"You are so very welcome, dear nephew. But it is unfortunate that your dear mother does not approve... For I have only heard the greatest praise for this lady, who is, after all, the wife of the mayor of Bordeaux. Indeed, I heard that her family is vastly rich, and it was thanks to her fortune that the de Montaignes succeeded to rise to the heights of their present glory," she told him, taking away her hand to adjust the snow-white collar of his shirt.

"Be careful! If you break anything, I will personally see to it that it is deducted from your wages!" Madame de Mortemart scolded a maid who almost dropped her nephew's heavy travel chest. She and another maid were taking it over the threshold and out of the room.

"Well, and you said the mayor's wife would be introducing her nieces at the banquet?" she continued, turning to face Aimery once the servant girls disappeared through the door.

He gave her a brief shrug. The carefree gesture confirmed her suspicions.

"You do not seem interested in this banquet as much as I thought..." she said in a lower tone of voice and then moved away to give an instruction to another maid, who was packing Aimery's hats.

Seemingly alerted by the baroness' last words, her nephew hurried after her.

"Ah, non, non. It is indeed of vital importance that I attend the banquet! Why would you think otherwise, dear aunt?"

"Well, I had assumed that you wanted to attend the banquet first and foremost because you were planning to partake in the court games planned by Madame de Montaigne and make your family proud!"

"Me? Partake in court games? Well, I do relish a good pastime... But how could that possibly make my family proud?"

Aimery's deep blue eyes were big with wonder. It was his aunt's turn to take his hand in hers and lead him back towards the window, away from the servants' prying ears.

"Mon cher, Aimery, you know that I want nothing more than for you to succeed and make your fortune in this world. We are so closely related and, after all, nothing is more important than family! We have worked hard, you and I, so that you may attend this banquet. I entreat you, dear nephew, let it not be all in vain! Surely, you must see that there is more for you to gain than your mere enjoyment, important as that may well be to you. The very success of the house of Ségur and, indeed, the making of your own fortune will be within reach at this banquet, dearest Aimery. All you will have to do is stretch out your hand and grab this golden opportunity..." she whispered in his ear.

Aimery held his aunt's hand in his but kept staring at her as if he still did not understand the meaning of her words. But Renée noticed that his eyes shone brighter when she had mentioned the making of his fortune, so she knew she was on the right path...

She smiled sweetly at him and, considering a new course of

action, said: "You have done well, my nephew! This morning in the library, I was most impressed with your flawless performance..."

"Do you think so, dear aunt? I did try my very best..."

Aimery looked more eager than a hungry dog under a lord's dinner table. He was so endearing, bless him. But he was not one to catch the meaning of a mere suggestion. She will have to lay it all out for him...

"My dearest Aimery, it saddens me to no end to have to remind you of this painful, unfair fact but... You are the third son of your father, who, although in possession of the noblest mind and lineage, is in no way owning as much land as his elder brothers. Pierre de Ségur, as the firstborn, is Lord of Sainte-Aulaye, Bridoire, Pontchapt and some other estates that escape me at the moment. Your other uncle Bertrand de Ségur is Lord of la Moliere, l'Estang and Parsac. He moreover manages his wife's vast estate at Pitray. In comparison, your esteemed father only has the grand estate at Montazeau and some more lands at Montravel and Castillon. But you must know all this already, dear Aimery. Please excuse your old aunt for not thinking clearly..."

"Yes... Of course, I knew, dear aunt!" her nephew hurried to confirm. "But I am most surprised that you, my lady, would know such details..."

"Well, yes, it is surprising. I am, but a lady, and I normally take no interest in such tedious matters, but... I have to confess that ever since you came to visit, I could not stop thinking about you, dear nephew, and your precarious situation in life. Please excuse me for intruding on your personal matters. I cannot help but worry about your future..."

"Not at all, dear aunt. I appreciate the interest you take in my well-being and your help in arranging my escape..." Aimery responded.

He got a bit too emotional and raised his voice. The last thing Madame de Mortemart needed was for the servants to hear that she had helped her nephew with his silly plans.

"Nonsense, my dear! You are being forced to leave us due to your mother's illness. The castle at Mortemart is an ancient fortress but is far from a prison which you need to escape from, dear Aimery!" she hurried to say in a loud tone of voice.

"No, no, far from it!" her nephew exclaimed, understanding his blunder. "I apologise for having offended you, dear aunt... My uncle's castle is mighty and full of history... I am, but a fickle-minded boy, and I get bored too easily..."

"No apologies needed, Nephew. I am not so easily offended!" Renée de Rochechouart said aloud, then lowered her voice: "We need to be careful, my dear. The servants talk. Now, back to our previous discussion. Do you not sometimes wonder whether your family's fortunes might be too small for you to inherit any of it? Surely you must know that most, if not all, of the estates will go to your eldest brother Antoine! Any leftovers will be due to Armand and his future heirs since he is the second son. And then there is your sister's dowry to consider... Oh, I do worry so for you, dear Aimery! Blessed with all the desirable qualities of a young lord and yet destined to the injustice of poverty! I am afraid you have no choice but to be smart and daring and make your fortune through other means..."

Her nephew opened his mouth and forgot to close it. He did not appear capable of uttering a sound.

"Come, my dear, let us go downstairs. Your valet can finish supervising the packing. You look like you could use a cup of sweet wine. You have such a long journey ahead of you!" Madame de Mortemart said, enlacing her arm through Aimery's and leading him towards the door.

"Oh, I meant to ask you, dear nephew... Am I mistook, or did the Lord of Montaigne's ancestors buy their estate from your family some hundred years ago? I cannot quite remember... In any case, I heard that they are vastly rich now. It occurs to me that there might be a way to rectify this historical mishap and see some of that fortune returned to its legitimate owners..."

Chapter Thirty Two
Alienor

Bordeaux, Easter Monday,
after sunset

"Mother, Élisabeth, have you seen Madeleine de Lamothe? I have looked for her everywhere..." Alienor asked, glad to have found them at last in the midst of the tightly woven crowd assembled in the great hall of the Ombriere Palace.

"No, Éléonore. Though there are so many people here. I can hardly breathe..." her mother answered.

"I cannot be entirely sure, but I think I might have seen Madeleine de Lamothe hiding in a corner of the stone courtyard... With a gentleman!" Elisea said in her contented, languorous tone of voice, ending her reply with a meaningful glance at her sister.

"With a gentleman?" Madame de Civrac asked, her voice choking for a moment. "In any case, that can be hardly surprising, given the circumstances..."

"Well, I am not mistaken..." Elisea started, ignoring her mother's last remark and relishing, as usual, her role as storyteller and secret-holder. "...he is that knight who took part in the joust game earlier today. I cannot believe what a display Madeleine made of herself, offering him her ribbon like that for everyone to see!"

"Élisabeth, stop it!" Alienor whispered in her sister's ear, taking hold of her arm.

She cast a concerned look at their mother, who seemed to have been struck by thunder. Madame de Civrac's face had turned white, her smile frozen in a rictus.

"De Montmorency! Oh, mon Deu..." Madame de Civrac let out under her breath, and Alienor rushed to offer her mother her support, just in time to catch her before she collapsed in dismay. "My poor boys..."

"Maman, are you not feeling well?" Elisea asked, holding their mother by the shoulder. "I am sorry, I did not know it was him..."

It was beyond Alienor's understanding how her sister could be so ignorant and tactless.

"How could you forget, Elisea?" she hissed under her breath.

"Oh my... I just..." came her stumbled reply.

"Help me find a seat for our mother. She is not feeling well. Let us try the hallway," Alienor interrupted.

They each took hold of one of their mother's arms and carried her out of the banquet hall. It was not an easy endeavour, given that Madame de Civrac was a corpulent lady and she had almost lost consciousness. Her daughters struggled to walk under the weight of her body, which hung limply from their shoulders.

"Mes dames, permettez moy de venir a vostre socors!"[1] A manly voice was heard all of a sudden while they struggled to lift her over the high threshold of the banquet hall.

"A la bonne hor, monsieur. Vous estes nostre héros!"[2] Elisea exclaimed with enthusiasm.

A tall gentleman in an elegant yellow outfit pushed Alienor aside and threw their mother's arm over his large shoulders. He lifted her limp body in his arms and stepped over the threshold. Alienor noticed that he grit his teeth as he did it. She also caught sight, from the corner of her eye, of the coat of arms embroidered on his sleeve.

Stunned for a moment, she stopped in her tracks. "Vens, cara sor,"[3] Elisea whispered and dragged her out into the cold and almost empty hallway.

The gentleman rushed to take Madame de Civrac to an empty stone bench hidden within a niche in the wall. The two sisters hurried in his wake. Once he put their mother down, Alienor took a seat next to her on the bench, and together, they gently placed the lady's head in her lap.

"Mother, do you hear me?" she asked.

"Élisabeth, my dear, is it you?" she asked, covering her face with her hand.

"No, it is me, Éléonore!" she answered, staring at the gentleman who had helped them, in an attempt to confirm her suspicions.

"I am here, Maman!" Elisea exclaimed, taking out her handkerchief and throwing herself on her knees by the bench, in that dramatic manner of hers.

"Help me up, my dear girls! I cannot be seen in such an embarrassing state by the whole of Bordeaux!"

The girls hurried to lift her up to a sitting position, but she was too dizzy. Her head slouched on Alienor's shoulder.

"How could we thank you, my lord? We would not have been able to do it without your gracious aid..." Elisea exclaimed, lifting her eyes to look at the stranger.

To her sister's dismay, Elisea was smiling unabashedly at the gentleman in yellow while she shook with ample gestures the handkerchief in front of her mother's face, almost slapping her with it. Leave it to her sister to start flirting while their mother lay almost unconscious next to her.

"There is no need to thank me, my lady. I am glad to have been of help," the gentleman answered with a smile. "But how is your mother? She does not look very well..."

"Indeed not! Chere seur, please go and find some refreshment for our dear mother!" Alienor asked with a glare, while shooting out a hand to grab the handkerchief out of her sister's hand.

"Allow me, mademoiselle or madame... It is the least I can do!" the gentleman offered.

"Mademoiselle!" Elisea hurried to correct, beaming.

"But you have done so much already, monsieur. I do not wish to abuse your kindness!" Alienor replied, searching for the small pocket she had sewn between her gown and her underskirt.

"Not at all, my lady. I will be back in a moment!" he said and darted back into the banquet hall.

At least he was gone, putting an end to those unsuitable flirtations. Alienor dug her hand deeper into her pocket.

"Oh, my dears, was that a gentleman's voice I heard? I shudder to think he has seen me in such dishevelment!" the baroness moaned, covering her face with her hands.

Having, at last, found what she was looking for, Alienor opened the vial of smelling salts and passed it under her mother's nose. They had the desired effect, and Madame de Civrac seemed to recover, to a certain degree, her composure. She raised her head and looked around. Elisea hurried to take her hand in hers.

"You fainted, dear mother. But never fear! A dashing young gentleman came to your aid and carried you outside the stuffy hall..." she said, relishing every single word.

"Élisabeth, surely, not that dreadful man, that criminal!" Madame de Civrac exclaimed, in a state of agitation, then whispered under her breath: "May he perish in the fires of Hell!"

Elisea flinched. She did not understand. But Alienor did. Madame de Civrac was speaking of the Chevalier de Montmorency, who had been the cause of her fainting. Their mother stifled a sob.

"No, Mother, not him! Of course not... Now, please calm yourself. He is nowhere around here. There is no reason to be alarmed..." Alienor comforted her, then whispered to her sister: "Dear sister, please go and find our father!"

It was clear to her that their mother had a better chance of coming back to her senses without Elisea around. As usual, her eldest sister was oblivious to the effect her words had on everyone around her.

"Yes," Elisea exclaimed, jumping to her feet. "He will know what to do!"

But Alienor knew what she had to do, too. She had sent her sister away. Her insensitive remarks kept bringing their mother to tears.

"Oh, that dreadful, terrible man! Are we to never be free of his nefarious influence?" Madame de Civrac exclaimed. "And Madeleine de Lamothe, that stupid girl! Daughter, please tell me that my eyes deceived me, and she had not given her token away to that murderer..." The baroness of Civrac accompanied her words with a sudden gesture, taking hold of her daughter's arm.

"I regret to say it is true, dear mother. I did not expect this of my friend, either, but she is fickle and likes to make a spectacle of herself. Madeleine must have seen some of her friends give their tokens away to the knights partaking in the tournament and then hurried to give away hers to the next man that trotted on a horse without thinking of who he was," Alienor said, patting her mother's arm. "But let me assure you that the chevalier is not wearing any red ribbon on his sleeve tonight!"

It was the one thing that gave her hope. Her friend must have come to her senses after their conversation at the fair, and had asked him to give back her ribbon. To distract her mother, she started to straighten her appearance, tucking away two locks of hair which had become undone.

"Praised be the Lord!" her mother whispered.

"But did you see how valiantly the Lord of Monluc carried himself during the tournament? I was so proud to call him my uncle!" she started, bending to smooth away the creases of her mother's over gown.

"Oh, yes. He crushed that horrid chevalier in the arena! Oh, I knew I could rely on my brave kin to serve justice. The Lasseran blood is thick and fearless, and it runs through your veins, too, my daughter. Do not forget!" Madame de Civrac's voice was exalted and proud.

Alienor lowered her head even further to re-arrange the hem of her mother's gown and smiled. She knew that mentioning her uncle's victory in the arena was sure to help her find her strength. And she was going to be even more pleased when she told her who her rescuer was.

"Of course not, Mother, I remember. But speaking of the valiant Lasseran blood... I believe the brave gentleman who helped carry you outside the banquet hall is none other than your nephew..."

"He is, indeed! Pierre-Bertrand de Monluc, a vostre seruice!"[4] a jovial voice exclaimed, and both ladies hurried to regain their dignified postures.

Her mother sat upright on the stone bench, and Alienor stood to her full height. Standing before them was none other than the tall gentleman dressed in yellow. He had a smile at the corner of his mouth, and he looked her up and down. She put her hands together, one on top of the other, in front of her chest, and held his gaze. Her heart was beating very fast. There was no telling how much of their conversation he had heard.

Alienor curtsied, as required by protocol, in response to the stylish lord's bow.

"Chere tante, vous voicy en meilheur estat!"[5] he continued, turning his attention to her mother. "For, if I am not mistaken, you must be Madame de Civrac, my father's beloved cousin and my esteemed aunt? But where are my manners? Here is your drink, madame. Please drink it to restore your forces..."

"Yes, it is me. What a wonderful surprise, my dear chevalier!" her mother exclaimed with impeccable composure, taking the goblet of wine he was offering. "Although I have to confess that to me, you will always be le petit Peyrot..."[6]

"You are most welcome to do so, dear aunt. I am used to it, for my father is just like you! He keeps calling me 'le cappitaine Peyrot'..."[7]

Alienor bit her lip to stifle a giggle. Looking at that tall, broad-shouldered man of arms, no one would have possibly expected him to be called 'petit Peyrot'.

Her cousin planted a brief kiss on top of his aunt's hand. "I am glad to see you once again, dear aunt, after all these years... And glad that you seem to be feeling better. I must say that you gave us quite a scare before, madame, didn't she?"

He turned towards Alienor in expectation. She smiled and nodded.

"The Lord must have sent you to my rescue, dear Peyrot. You are a true Lasseran, reliable and brave! But allow me to introduce my daughter, your cousin, Éléonore."

"Cusine Éléonore, quel plaisir de faire vostre cognoyssance!"[8]

Pierre-Bertrand de Monluc took her hand in his, planting a rather long kiss on top of it. There was something that she did not quite like about him. It must have been that sarcastic smile he had on his lips at all times.

Alienor retracted her hand. "The pleasure is all mine, dear cousin."

When he rose back to his full height, the captain stared down at her unabashedly. She wondered whether Marguerite de Monluc had kept to herself the secrets that Alienor had shared in her letter. There was no way to tell how much 'petit Peyrot' knew about her intentions. Her cheeks must have been burning, for she felt very hot all of a sudden.

"I am sorry, dear mother, I could not find father!" Elisea said, stopping to catch her breath.

Her sister could not have chosen a better moment to come back. Their cousin took away his amused gaze from Alienor, at long last. And the moment it landed on Elisea, his entire face lit up. Her eldest sister's beauty had on him the immediate effect it usually had on all men. Truth be told, she had never looked more beautiful. The colour of her eyes was put to a great advantage that evening by the luscious dark green velvet of her gown and the glorious emerald necklace she wore around her neck.

"Dear nephew, allow me to introduce my eldest daughter, Élisabeth!" their mother said, and they both curtsied to each other. "This is your cousin, Pierre-Bertrand de Monluc."

"Oh, Cusine Élisabeth... I thought you looked familiar! Did you not, by any chance, attend your grandmother's funeral at Sérillac a long time ago?"

"Yes, my lord. You have a very good memory!" Her eldest sister could flatter like no other.

"I assure you, mademoiselle, it would not have been possible for me to forget you, even if I were reckless enough to wish it..." Pierre-Bertrand replied, casting a meaningful look towards her sister and taking his time to bow and plant a kiss on the back of her hand.

Her mother seemed to have completely, and almost miraculously, recovered from her moment of weakness. She seemed to thrive in the company of her nephew. His solicitous attention must have felt like a balm on her heart.

When Alienor turned her attention back to the conversation, she heard her cousin say: "And are my lovely cousins to partake in the game of fin'amor this evening, dear aunt?"

"Yes, indeed. Both Élisabeth and Éléonore. And my second eldest daughter, Catherine. I wonder where she might be... Élisabeth, my dear, you said you could not find her?"

Alienor felt her face burn again. She wished her mother would have shown a little more tact. Having three daughters of a marriageable age participating in the game that evening was hardly something to be boastful about...

"Is that so?" she heard Pierre-Bertrand whisper, looking from her to her elder sister, who was talking to their mother. He had that detestable, ironic smile on his face again.

"And you, dear cousin? Are you also to partake in the game of courtly love this evening?" she asked.

She held his amused gaze with composure and dignity, or at least, she hoped she did, with all her heart. Despite his impeccable manners, 'petit Peyrot' was not all kindness. But she was not going to let him have the upper hand.

"Non, chere cusine. Alas, I am a man of war! And I am yet to prove myself a hero in battle. Until that day comes, I have, alas, little interest or time at my disposal to pursue the enticements of courtly love," he replied, with a tad too much dramatic flair in his voice.

"You are very young, nephew. I am sure time will show us all that you were born to achieve glorious deeds on this earth, following in the footsteps of your father and elder brother. How is le Chevalier de Monluc faring, dear Peyrot?" her mother interceded.

Alienor noticed a note of disappointment in her mother's voice. If she knew her well, Madame de Civrac must have entertained the notion that one of her daughters might catch his eye. She stole a side glance at Elisea, who was obliviously passing her long, elegant fingers through the ribbon of black silk fastened to her sleeve while laughing at everything 'petit Peyrot' said. Alienor blushed for her sister. She was as good as betrothed to Louis de Rémy, and yet there she was, flirting with another gentleman. Although, she had to concede that the captain was not bad looking and had an inexplicable charm about his person...

"My daughters are excellent dancers, dear nephew."

Alienor was startled to hear what her mother said. She looked at her in disbelief, rather self-conscious of her cousin's presence and the conclusions he was sure to draw regarding her and her family's character. But she did not say a word.

"Is that so?" Pierre-Bertrand de Monluc said, letting his eyes linger over her eldest sister.

Alienor almost let out a sigh of relief. He was not going to ask her out to dance. Her cousin had been charmed by Elisea's pretty face, like many gentlemen before him.

And sure enough, she saw the two of them head back to the banquet hall, hand in hand.

Her mother stood up from the stone bench and whispered in

her ear: "Do not tell a thing to your father about this... this business with Madeleine de Lamothe and... well, you know what I mean!"

"Of course, dear mother," Alienor replied, holding Madame de Civrac's arm. "Are you feeling better?"

"As much as one can expect, given these unpleasant circumstances..." came her mother's dramatic reply while they both walked arm in arm back into the hall.

Alienor's relief at the sight of her cousin and Elisea walking towards the dance floor together was, however, short-lived. Later that evening, whilst she was sharing a laugh with Catarina and her father, she saw the lean silhouette of Captain Peyrot headed their way from the corner of her eye. Elisea was nowhere in sight. Perhaps she was dancing with Louis de Rémy.

Oh, no... she thought to herself, almost choking on the sweet mead she was sipping.

"Catarina, quickly..." She took hold of her sister's arm with urgency and pushed her in the opposite direction.

But their way was blocked, and they only succeeded in making a couple of steps before the voice of her cousin thundered behind them: "Cusine Éléonore, would you do me the honour of the next dance?"

Alienor cast a tale-telling glance at Catarina, who looked confused. She turned around to face him and replied: "Yes, I will, Cousin Peyrot. But allow me to first introduce you to my sister, Catherine de Durfort."

After the introductions were made and the usual pleasantries exchanged, she was obliged to follow her cousin to the dance floor. Catarina hurried after them.

"Cusin Peyrot?" she asked, whispering into Alienor's ear.

They leaned into each other and giggled. The Captain of Monluc turned around to look at them and cocked an eyebrow. They sobered up. Her sister broke away, her shoulders still shaking from another fit of giggles. Alienor bit her lip and gave her hand to her cousin, who led her to the middle of the dance floor. Madame de Civrac all but elbowed her way to the front of the watching crowd, beaming with pride. Subtle she was not, but at least, her mother seemed to be in better spirits. As for her, she dreaded a 'teste a teste'[9] with the irreverent Pierre-Bertrand de Monluc, which had become unavoidable at that point since they were going to dance together. Alienor let out a long breath. He was sure to mention the letters, for one, and then tease her about her interest in heraldry, for second. Comments about the inappropriate behaviour of her mother and sisters were a possibility, too.

They took their place at the end of the long row of couples holding hands. The allemande was about to begin.

She looked at her cousin, and he held her gaze with his bright brown eyes and that same smile at the corner of his mouth. Alienor could not decide if it was an insufferable or a becoming smile on him. Perhaps, instead of fleeing his company, she ought to be grateful for his presence at the banquet. Captain Peyrot was talkative and gallant and could even lead her to his father, who was her mysterious gentleman's lord commander. He had come to her aid before, so he might be persuaded to do so again... But she had to be careful.

Third Part

Wheel of Fortune

Chapter Thirty Three
Alienor

Rauzan, mid May

Several weeks had passed since that fateful Easter Monday. They had been slow and not without pain for Alienor. Everyone at Rauzan was busy preparing for Elisea's wedding. One week after Easter, Louis de Rémy and his parents had paid them a visit to make the engagement official.

That morning, Alienor had received a letter from Madalena de Lamothe. They had not been able to talk to each other in private at the banquet, and they had not done so the morning after either. She had a vague memory of the two of them locking eyes and smiling at each other across the banquet hall shortly before the lists were to be read.

Reminiscing was difficult. She had been wrong about so many things, so many people that day... And Madalena was one of them. Alienor's head spun every time she thought of her friend and François de Montmorency together. Neither she nor Catarina believed it possible for their names to have been read out that evening. Madalena and her mother would have made sure to boast about forging such a powerful alliance at breakfast the next day. The letter made no mention of it, either. It was a relief that they were not engaged, but the fact remained that her best friend had offered her token, perhaps even her heart, to the Chevalier de Montmorency, the man who had ruined her and her siblings' lives.

It unnerved Alienor to even hear him being called a chevalier. The man was not a knight, not if being a knight had anything to do with the code of chivalry. And yet, if the rumours were true... He was to be knighted soon with the order of Saint Michel.

She curled her hands into fists to prevent them from trembling with indignation. But she felt appeased by the memory of their confrontation at the Easter banquet. She smiled and stretched her fingers. At least she and her sister had put that man in his rightful place in front of all the noble guests present at the Ombriere Palace that evening.

Alienor let out a sigh and looked up at the clear sky that stretched above the ravine neighbouring their castle. It was a warm afternoon in spring, and she was sitting on a bench in her family's small garden. Situated in the lower courtyard, outside the castle walls, by the side of the ravine, it was so small and wild it could hardly be called a garden. In truth, it was more like a square patch of overgrown grass surrounded by a thicket of wild bushes and four trees with two stone benches covered in moss and the ruins of a dried water fountain in the middle. The once elegant stone fence, which separated that place from the ravine's steep slope, had crumbled in places. Its colour had once been white but had become a rotten grey. The small pillars made to resemble Roman urns were barely visible under the weight of the overgrown vegetation, which spread its tentacles up from the depths of the ravine like a giant squid from the tales of yore. But it was a peaceful little corner, and Alienor liked to visit it, sometimes accompanied by Catarina or her grandmother, but for the most, alone. There she could reflect or read her letters in peace, away from her mother and sisters' prying eyes.

That day, like so many others during the past month, she thought of Catarina's misapprehensions. Her sister thought that the Chevalier de Ségur's intention had been to offer Alienor his token that last time they had spoken in the courtyard, after the announcements. She asked herself again whether that evening might have ended differently had she shown more patience and poise... But she did not dare hope, and there was no way to know for sure. However, Alienor found in retrospect that her own manners had been lacking. Perhaps she should have allowed Armand de Ségur more time to explain himself. Or perhaps she should have explored other possible matches. Instead, she had rushed to offer her ribbon to the first gentleman whom fate had placed in her path! For example, her mother had wished for her to form an alliance with her cousin, Pierre-Bertrand de Monluc... But that was just a silly thought because the gentleman in question had been clear that he was not interested in romantic pursuits. Although, truth be told, he had spent most of his evening flirting with Alienor and her sisters. 'Petit Peyrot' had been nothing but a nuisance, spending the entire evening trying to catch her on the wrong foot, in the hope of stirring up some mischief...

She smiled. But, in truth, she knew that there was no one else to blame. Alienor had been reckless. That day, she had been certain that the Chevalier de Ségur was interested in entering an alliance with her. She had thought that after all the dances they had danced together, their animated discussions, their walk on the palace's ramparts, their confidences had meant as much for him as they had for her. But, in truth, she had simply taken it for granted that he was going to return the favour and offer her his ribbon.

Charmed and blind, Alienor had forgotten that there had been much better matches to be made at that banquet than her, the mayor's nieces amongst them... She kept telling herself that there was no reason to feel disappointed. She had, after all, only known that gentleman for one day. And, when all was said and done, Alienor had played a risky game and lost. It was fated, and there was nothing she could do about it. But she had to be strong and not lose faith. Like the wheel of the goddess Fortuna, her family's luck would also turn. They had been on the bottom for such a long time... one way or the other, the wheel would lift them up again. All they had to do was to make sure they clung to it for dear life and continued to have faith.

She picked up the letter cradled in her hands. Alienor read it again in an attempt to make some sense of the sparse words contained therein. It was strange. Madalena had never written such a short letter before. After the usual pleasantries, it said that her friend had important news to share with her but that they were of a secretive nature and, therefore, better discussed in confidence. The letter also contained the usual invitation from the Lamothes for her family to join them for a week at their summer residence in Cambes. That used to be the most anticipated event of the year for Alienor, yet all she had felt upon reading it that time was dread... dread at the possibility that her friend's secret had something to do with... did she dare utter the name... François de Montmorency. How could she ever bear it if Madalena were to pester her with unsolicited confidences? Alienor wanted to know nothing of her feelings for that terrible man. Even though it was a warm spring day, she felt a cold shiver crawl up her back, and she wrapped the silk shawl tighter around her shoulders. Then she closed her eyes and lifted her face upwards to feel the warmth of the sun's rays playing hide and seek amongst the leaves. The smell of acacia flowers filled her nostrils. Alienor wondered at how bland and boring the smell of early summer felt to her that year.

She needed to make up her mind about that visit and send an answer to her friend's invitation... Cambes was a mere day's journey away from her family's ancestral castle at Rauzan. But, truth be told, she did not want to go. In addition to fretting over what Madalena's confidences might reveal, Alienor dreaded receiving the latest gossip on life in Bordeaux in the aftermath of the Easter banquet. She did not want to hear about all those lucky young ladies and gentlemen who, unlike her, had forged advanta-geous alliances that evening. It was painful enough that she had to hear her mother and Elisea speak of little else besides her sister's upcoming nuptials all day long.

She let out a heavy sigh. On the other hand, Mademoiselle de Lamothe was sure to know the exact content of the engagement lists. And she would be able to dispel any lingering doubt she had that Armand de Ségur had wanted to marry her and not the mayor's niece.

The noise of steps awoke her from her thoughts, and Alienor turned her head towards the garden alley. She saw her grand-mother make her way, one step at a time, on the gravel path. She was supported by Yolanda de Castelbajac, who was her compan-ion, as well as the housekeeper at Rauzan. Alienor was very fond of her grandmother, her only surviving grandparent.

Both her grandfathers had died before she was born, and she had only met her other grandmother, her mother's mother, once, before she, too, had died eight years ago. Her paternal grand-mother had been born Louise de Castelbajac and had been, in her youth, a lady-in-waiting for Queen Marguerite of Navarre. Alienor and her sisters had grown up listening to her and Yolan-da's enthralling stories about life at the Court in Béarn. She loved it when her grandmother recited by heart her sonnets or read to her the beautiful novellas written by the Queen, which the Dowager Baroness of Civrac claimed to have helped write down and compile into what was meant to be known as the new Decameron[1]. These novellas, only seventy or so, were never published, but her grandmother had brought a copy of the hand-written text back with her. It was kept safe in a drawer in her room at Rauzan.

But the baroness had grown old. She was over fifty, ridden with gout, and often kept to her chambers. Yolanda was not much younger than her but carried herself better and capably managed the family's household affairs. The two of them had grown up together at Castelbajac, and her grandmother took

Yolanda with her to Rauzan as her companion upon her marriage to the Baronet Jean de Durfort. She was, in fact, the dowager baroness' younger sister from her father's side, born out of wedlock but recognised by her father. As a family member, she dined together with the Durforts de Civrac and took no wages. Yolanda de Castelbajac had not married. Instead, she had devoted her life to the service of her older sister and her family.

"Bonjorn, cara avia.[2] Why don't you come and sit with me? And you, too, miss. The weather is so pleasant." Alienor spoke to them in the language of the south. Her grandmother wouldn't have it any other way.

"It is, indeed," the dowager baroness said as she reached the bench.

Her sister helped her onto the bench.

"Thank you, Miss Alienor, but I am afraid my responsibilities do not allow me a moment of peace. The tailor is to arrive soon to discuss your sister's wedding gown, and I must prepare for his arrival. If it is not too much trouble for you, miss, could you please do me a favour and escort the dowager baroness back inside in my stead whenever she wishes to return? I would do it myself, of course, was I not needed to negotiate the tailor's... compensation."

The old lady spoke very fast, as was her habit. Alienor could see that she had a lot to do. She gladly agreed, and Miss Yolanda, as they all called her, almost sprang back to the castle. Alienor thought she looked fitter and younger than her mother, Madame de Civrac, who was several years her junior.

"Joyful news, I hope," her grandmother said after a while, gesturing towards the letter resting in her lap.

"Oc, cara avia. It is a letter from Madalena de Lamothe. She extends the annual invitation for us to join her and her family at their summer house in Cambes."

Alienor knew that she needn't use the French version of her friend's name in her grandmother's presence. Louise de Durfort de Civrac was a stern promoter of the Occitan language and traditions. She would often remind her and her sisters that the Occitan language was the most poetic language on the face of the earth, the language of courtly love itself.

"Our culture has given the world the poetry of the 'troubadours' and the ideals of 'fin'amor'!" she liked to say.

In her old age, her grandmother had come to refuse to utter a word of French at home or elsewhere. Needless to say, that was another point on which she clashed with her daughter-in-law, Alienor's mother, besides religion and a myriad of other issues, which ensured that nobody had a dull moment at Rauzan.

"I wonder if your parents will think that is a good idea this year, what with... all the febrile preparations going on at the moment..." her grandmother said after a while.

Alienor had not considered that. In truth, her sister's wedding preparations were the perfect excuse to turn down the invitation...

"But I think you should go, Alienor," her grandmother added with a knowing smile.

"You mean for me to go alone? I should not think it wise, cara avia..."

Alienor had never travelled alone before. The thought alarmed and thrilled her at the same time...

"Oh, but it is, cara Alienor. Wouldn't you like to go away for a short while from all this talk of weddings and engagements? I know I would!" came the Dowager Baroness of Civrac's answer.

Alienor looked at her grandmother and saw her close her eyes, tilt her head backwards and smile. She smiled and closed her eyes, too. Her grandmother was wise and astute. Perhaps going away from Elisea and their mother was not a bad idea. But she doubted she would escape all talk of weddings and engagements at Madalena's house. If anything, the prospect of losing her best friend to that dreadful man who had already taken her brothers away from her was sure to make any talk of engagements ten times more painful.

"Dear grandmother, I have been meaning to ask you..." she started.

"Oh, yes... I have been wondering when you would come to me with your questions, child," the dowager baroness interrupted.

Alienor opened her eyes in surprise and saw that her grandmother had that knowing smile on her lips again.

"You have, dear grandmother?"

"I most certainly did, dear granddaughter. Do not think for a moment that your brave attitude has fooled your old grandmother... You have been pinning, and you are feeling lost," she said and then continued, after waving away Alienor's attempt to interrupt her: "A grandmother knows her granddaughters. I assure you, it is quite futile to attempt to persuade me of the contrary, dear. I have a nose like no other for the troubles of fin'amor. Queen Marguerite herself commended me for it, once upon a time..."

"Eh ben, cara avia...[3] It is obviously impossible to keep a secret from you..." Alienor allowed. "You seem aware of my predicament, so I will spare you the details. What do you think I should do?"

Her grandmother took her time to reply. Alienor looked at her and envied her serenity. She lay with her eyes still closed, listening to the wind blowing through the foliage of the old oak tree beneath which they sat. Louise de Durfort de Civrac had also had her share of miseries and heartaches in life. She had had to see her husband, her daughters and her grandchildren to their early graves. And she had to live her remaining years in a home where she was not always made to feel welcome.

"Shall I tell you what I think? I think you should accept Mademoiselle de Lamothe's invitation and go to Cambes. Perhaps your father should accompany you, dear. The Lamothes are sending over their carriage as usual, are they not? It does seem like a waste of space if you were to occupy it alone. Moreover, the roads are as uncertain as ever, and my son needs a break from all the scolding... Your mother and the rest of us can carry on with the arrangements for Elisea's wedding splendidly without the two of you. And then, well... who knows what you might find out in Cambes? The Lamothes are well connected, and they like to talk a lot... But, when all is said and done, my dearest Alienor, you can only put your trust in the Lord Almighty!" she said.

"Oc, cara avia..."[4] she hurried to reassure her grandmother, though at the same time she wondered, like so many times before, which Lord she should trust.

At times, it seemed like her grandmother and father believed in one God, while her mother prayed to another.

"I mean it, dear Alienor. Trust that the Lord always takes care of everything, and rest assured that what is meant to pass shall pass. Put an end to this struggle inside of you and concern yourself with the future. You think too much of that which cannot be changed."

"It sounds easy when you say it, cara avia..."

"It is not easy, my love. Nothing about the tribulations of fin'amor is! But if one is to believe the troubadours, a lady needs to stay virtuous and patient. If the knight truly sees her as the lady of his heart, he will have to prove his allegiance through an extraordinary deed of valour. I am not in your place, of course, but if I were cara Alienor, I would strive to acquire a better understanding of what had passed that evening at the banquet. Most of all, I would endeavour to keep an open and inquisitive mind..."

The Dowager Baroness of Civrac looked her granddaughter in the eye while she spoke, allowing her words to sink in. Alienor nodded. The sunbeams were playing on her beloved grandmother's ageing features. They looked like flakes of gold against the whiteness of her hair.

"I have faith in you, my granddaughter. You are a de Durfort. Remember who you are! Remember our family's motto!" she heard her say.

"Si ell dur, yo fort!" Alienor enunciated.

"Yes. You are Jeanne Angevin's great-granddaughter. The blood of the Angevins' flows through your veins. You are stronger than you think!"

"The blood of kings..." she whispered.

The dowager baroness nodded in approval, and they smiled at each other. She took courage from her grandmother's words. Alienor decided to talk to her father as soon as they returned to the castle. She would then write to Madalena de Lamothe that they accepted her family's invitation. And once at Cambes, she would find a way to uncover the truth. It had to be done. Come what may, she would be strong, strong like a fortress, strong like her ancestors, strong like Alienor of Aquitaine, her namesake...

Chapter Thirty Four
Aimery

Bordeaux, Easter Monday,
early evening

The torches were being lit on the streets of Bordeaux when Aimery de Ségur arrived at the Montaigne residence. He had arrived in Bordeaux the night before and had slept at an inn near Porte Cailhau. He had thought it wise to not alert his father and brother of his presence. They were capable of forcing him to return to Montazeau before the banquet even started. Free to enjoy himself, he had spent a delightful morning and afternoon watching the games and roaming the city's streets at leisure, unbeknownst to his family. Aimery would have loved to attend the banquet incognito, too, but he needed to change his outfit, and he had spent the last of his pocket money on a delicious meal of roasted piglet at the fair. So, he had no choice but to enter the Montaigne residence unless he wanted to appear sweaty and underdressed at the festivities.

After making sure that his father and brother had already left for the banquet, Aimery made his entrance in style, accompanied by his trusted valet, Amanieu.

In the main hall, he met the Chevalier de Montaigne, the mayor's eldest son. After the required exchange of surprised greetings, Aimery's attention was instantly drawn towards a beautiful young lady dressed in a bright red gown. She was standing by the window, so he could only see her profile from where he stood, in the middle of the hall, but she looked exquisite. The lady appeared to be lost in reflection and did not react to his entrance. He was irked and intrigued at the same time.

"I am afraid we were not expecting you, chevalier!" Michel de Montaigne said, leading him to the windows.

"Oh, I am sorry to hear that, chevalier!" Aimery replied, feigning surprise. "If I am to be entirely honest with you, I do not know if I should be upset... My father was expecting me today. Hasn't he or my brother mentioned it, mon chevalier?"

"I am afraid not, chevalier..." came the reply. "But allow me to introduce you to my cousin, Mademoiselle Jeanne de Louppes. This is Chevalier Aimery de Ségur, the third son of the Seigneur de Montazeau, who is staying with us and whom you have already met."

Aimery welcomed the opportunity to change the subject of the conversation and have a closer look at Michel's beautiful cousin. She tore away her melancholic gaze from the scenery beyond the windows and settled her deep, black eyes on him. At first, Aimery wondered if she had seen him at all. She appeared to be absorbed by other thoughts. But then, a smile bloomed on Mademoiselle de Louppes' rosy lips. Aimery could swear he saw a dimple appear on her cheek as she lowered herself into a curtsy.

"Inchantée de foire vostre cognoyssance, monsieur."[1]

Aimery, for his part, could hardly tear his eyes away from that single, charming dimple. It looked like a tiny line in the middle of her round cheek. She had ebony black hair, held in place at the back of her head by a hairnet, and small, delicate ears. He was thrilled to meet one of Madame de Montaigne's nieces. His aunt had spoken of them to him. It was a delight to discover that in addition to being vastly rich, Jeanne de Louppes was also very, very pretty.

"I am afraid you have just missed your father and brother, chevalier. They are already on their way to the banquet together with the Lord and Lady of Montaigne," Michel de Montaigne said, tearing Aimery away from his reverie.

"Oh, what a stroke of bad luck!" he exclaimed, making sure to sound dramatic.

"But if you make haste, my lord, perhaps you can ride in the carriage with us!" said Mademoiselle de Louppes, with that inebriating smile of hers.

"What a splendid thought! Thank you, my lady," Aimery hurried to reply. "If you may instruct the lackey to show me and my valet to my quarters first, chevalier..."

He could not prevent a smile flowering on his lips at the thought of riding in the de Montaignes' second, narrower carriage in the company of the Chevalier de Montaigne's lovely cousin. One way or the other, he had to ensure he grabbed the seat next to her as he climbed into the carriage.

"Very well, chevalier," his host said, but Aimery had a hard time taking his eyes off his fair cousin.

"I will see you later, monsieur," Jeanne de Louppes said, in a languorous tone of voice, looking Aimery in the eye.

He could not help but feel flattered. The evening could not have started under better auspices. There he was, flirting already with a good-looking young lady before he even set foot at the Palais de l'Ombriere. More young ladies were bound to follow in her footsteps and succumb to his charms... To think that, were it not for his generous, brilliant aunt, Aimery would have missed all that!

"I am afraid we are rather crowded at the moment, cher chevalier. But you may share a room with your brother," said his host, then turned to instruct the lackey: "Show the Chevalier de

Ségur and his valet to the other Chevalier de Ségur's room, and see to it that they have everything they need…"

"Yes, of course, my lord," came the reply.

Aimery excused himself and headed for the door. He cast one last glance over his shoulder at the beautiful young lady before he left the hall. He was rewarded with another smile and the view of another dimple. Mademoiselle de Louppes appeared to be already besotted with him. She couldn't help staring at him, even when he was not looking. The thought pleased Aimery, and he felt that all his efforts to ensure his presence at the Easter festivities in Bordeaux had been well worth his while.

Chapter Thirty Five
Armand

Bordeaux, Easter Monday,
early evening

Armand de Ségur had yet to make a decision, and he knew
he had but little time left. He had had no interest in
attending the Easter festivities, least of all in being a part of that
farce of fin'amor. Not because he was against that rekindling of
medieval entertainments of which King Henri and Queen
Catherine had become fond in recent years. It was because it had
never even crossed his mind that, if he were to participate in some
sort of game of chivalry, it would be anything else than a tournament. In truth, he wished he could have joined the Chevalier de
l'Isle in the joust game that morning. But his body was still weak
and useless. It was ridiculous the amount of time it needed to
recover from the wounds, the fever and the hunger he had
endured at Sienna. Unexpected bouts of dizziness still plagued
him, most of all, in the evening. He prayed to the Lord to spare
him such an embarrassment at the banquet.

The news that Armand was to accompany his father and

represent their family at the Easter festivities, for the sake of their relation to the Montaignes, had come as a shock. His mother had not even bothered to prohibit his involvement in the game of courtly love. Although she had gone to great lengths to take that trouble with his younger brother, Aimery. She had sent him away to visit their uncle and aunt in Mortemart for the duration of the holidays in order to ensure his absence from the Easter games. Madame de Montazeau had taken that precautionary measure due to Aimery's notorious penchant for wine, banquets, and mischief. To think that he was the son his mother preferred above Armand, and even Antoine, the family heir!

The injustice of it had irked him since he was a child, as it did his eldest brother. In that, they were united. Armand did not understand what lay at the root of her coldness. Some mothers were that way, incapable of showing affection to their offspring. But Madame de Montazeau doted on her two youngest children, lavishing them, and only them, with her maternal affections... to the very detriment of their characters. His sister Anne's haughtiness and Aimery's unchecked manners came to mind...

In any event, Armand knew that his mother had not seen it fit to forbid him from taking part in the game of fin'amor because he was disfigured, and that made him ineligible in the eyes of most young ladies. He had never been of a flamboyant disposition or a charmer with words. The ladies had hardly paid him any attention, even before he got his cheek cut open at Sienna... And yet, a young lady did find him eligible enough to bestow her token on him!

Armand felt a smile pulling at the corner of his mouth, and he passed his fingers again through the silk ribbon adorning his sleeve.

He knew that if he were to enter the game and forge an alliance, his mother would be beyond furious. She would take it as a personal slight if a son of hers, even one as disliked as him, would strike a match without her consent, and even more so, if he would arrive at it by playing Antoinette de Montaigne's game of fin'amor. His mother made no secret of her disdain for anyone who could not trace their origins back to the times of Charlemagne. That included her sister-in-law, Madame de Mortemart, and her neighbour, Madame de Montaigne. The thought of crossing her had a certain appeal. For once, she would be the one to boil with helpless anger... But he was better than that. And he found it unsound, ridiculous even, that anyone should enter matrimony for the sole purpose of aggravating one's parents.

Armand stood in a corner of the Ombriere Palace's courtyard, staring at the contents of his goblet. Without realising it, he had started to play with the wine, tilting his goblet leftwards and rightwards. He noticed how its deep red colour shifted in nuance and gleamed under the dim light of the torches. Minstrels were playing the lute and singing in the langue d'oc[1], while in another corner, the jongleurs were entertaining the noble audience with their tricks.

Darkness was falling. He raised his right arm to take another look at the young lady's ribbon... It was a token of fin'amor, and the code of chivalry demanded for him to return the gesture. Even though, to his knowledge, the tales of yore did not speak of ladies who cast their favours first. One thing was certain, the knight had to declare his allegiance, provided that the lady was worthy, in other words, virtuous, fair and noble... And Armand had to admit that, in his eyes, the young lady who had given him her token was all that and more. It was true that he knew very little about her. He did not even know her name. But he did not know of any reason why she would be unworthy of his allegiance, either...

He let out a deep sigh. That was a difficult decision. His future hung in the balance. The more he thought about it, the more his head hurt. The conundrum was, however, the lady's resolution to offer him her token... A lively, instructed, fascinating, and, by all signs, noble lady like her could have chosen any of the other eligible gentlemen present at the festivities that day. There were so many who were more suitable than him, more charming, more good-looking, more... wholesome. And yet, somehow, she had chosen him...

All of a sudden, he felt a tightening in his chest, and he had the strange suspicion that someone was watching him from afar. A lady's cry pierced the air. Armand turned his head and was stunned to chance upon the very lady who had been in his thoughts all afternoon. Her beautiful brown eyes were not following the jongleurs' daring acts, but were fixed on him. To his dismay, he noticed that her body was turned towards him and that her upper arm was being held by another young lady, who was also staring at him... There was no way to know for sure, but it looked as if the lady who had given him her token of fin'amor had been headed in his direction but had come to a halt due to the other lady's interference.

Alarm washed over him at the thought that she was there to demand an answer. He had no answer at the ready. He needed more time. Embarrassed, he looked away. Once the lady had turned her back on him and engaged in conversation with her companion, it felt safe to steal another glance from the corner of his eye to make sure that the young lady's elbow was still unadorned by a black-coloured ribbon... To his relief, it was. The feeling took Armand by surprise. He had no cause to feel relieved. And it was downright ridiculous that he should feel alarmed at the thought that some other, more suitable gentleman might have fastened his token to her arm!

When he looked in their direction again, the ladies were gone. Armand craned his neck and saw that they were headed for the doors. He let out a breath he did not know he had been holding. At least he had some more time on his hands to make up his mind. In the meantime, it would be wise to try to find out more about his lovely lady.

Chapter Thirty Six
Madame de Civrac

Bordeaux, Easter Monday,
after sunset

Madame de Civrac felt utterly exhausted. But she had enjoyed herself to no end that day. It has been many years since she had attended such splendid festivities. She thought of her youth when she was but a young girl in her parents' house. She remembered the splendour of the banquets that her father, le Baron de Sérillac, used to host at his chasteau in Gascogne. If she closed her eyes, she could still see it all again... the hundreds of candles casting a magnificent golden glow on all the elegant ladies and lords dancing together in the castle's grand hall... the excellent music of the Italian minstrels, who her father had brought with him from Genoa... the fond attention she had enjoyed as an eligible young lady and her parents' only daughter, born to them in old age. Her parents, most of all her father, had allowed her every whim. Her only surviving sibling, the Chevalier Jean de Sérillac, was twenty years her senior, and he was more like an uncle than a brother to her.

By the time she had grown into a young lady, he had already married and had children.

Élisabeth de Sérillac had had several suitors vying for her hand. A smile flowered on her face as she reminisced how, after one lavish banquet, her husband, then titled le Chevalier de Civrac, had ended up fighting in a duel with another of her suitors, le Chevalier de Lary, the younger brother of her sister-in-law, Anne. Although younger and less experienced with a sword, the Chevalier of Civrac had impressed everyone present with his faultless technique and grace. He won the duel and her heart, and the two of them were married within the year. But those days were long gone. Her husband had become a very different man with time. She cast a furtive glance at him as he stood with his back to her, talking with another gentleman. She still respected and was fond of him, as was her place and duty, and she had forgiven him a long time ago. Although, deep inside, she knew that his leniency and lack of character had played a crucial part in bringing about the catastrophe that engulfed their family once the revolt reached their gates.

A sigh escaped her lips, as it always did when her thoughts took her back to the darkest moments of her life, to the deepest pain and despair that may befall a woman...

La iacquerie[1]... Vens, Elise, do not allow yourself to think of all that now, she thought and tried to return to fonder memories. *Oh, yes... Pierre-Bertrand, mon cousin Blaise...* she thought and was thus reminded of those occasions when her mother had taken her to family celebrations at the Chasteau de Saint Puy, where her cousin Blaise lived with his parents and his numerous siblings.

She had, from a young age, enjoyed spending time with her cousins. Though, in all honesty, their celebrations looked nothing like the elaborate festivities her father used to arrange at Sérillac. Her mother's family had always been more on the ascetic side of life, being particularly preoccupied with living a sparse lifestyle in conformity with the scriptures. Her father, on the other hand, had been a lover of music and the arts in general and had been of the opinion that life had to be not only lived but also enjoyed. Her parents had not always seen eye to eye, due to their different upbringing and values in life. As a girl, Élisabeth de Sérillac had been particularly close to her father, who had spared no expense when it came to her education. He had encouraged her to become an accomplished lute player and to learn to dance from several prestigious Italian teachers.

The banquet in Bordeaux brought back fond recollections of her father and her girlhood. Madame de Civrac looked at her daughters and saw herself in them. She was well aware that her daughters were nowhere near spending the same carefree, resplendent girlhood as she had. That was their first grand banquet. She saw Éléonore amongst the dancers at the centre of the hall, dancing with Pierre-Bertrand de Monluc.

A smile flowered on the baroness' lips, for the two of them made such an elegant, distinguished pair! It was a pity that her nephew had declared himself uninterested in matrimony. He would be a perfect match for her daughter... and not that disfigured gentleman who wore a hat indoors, to whom Éléonore seemed to have taken a liking. She was certain that her daughter would not have considered striking an acquaintance with such a bad-looking man of dubious manners had their family fortune remained intact, her future secured.

Madame de Civrac had to admit, however, that Éléonore had appeared to be enjoying herself in that gentleman's company, against all odds. She had seen her daughter smile more than once, in her usual, restrained manner, while they had danced together earlier that evening. It was an auspicious omen, to be sure, as was the gentleman-in-question's rank. After making some discrete inquiries, she had been able to ascertain that the gentleman was one of the sons of the Count of Montazeau. And since the man was from a respectable family, and by all accounts, their superior in rank, if her daughter could find it in her heart to make peace with living in his company for the rest of her days, then neither she nor her husband ought to interfere with the Lord's plans. But, as any mother, she would have hoped for her daughter to marry someone with a more... wholesome appearance, someone like Pierre-Bertrand de Monluc...

The Baroness of Civrac took a sip of sweet wine to prevent another sigh. She turned to smile at her husband, who had come to stand next to her, engaged in yet another frivolous conversation with the Rémys. What he had to talk to them about for so long was a complete mystery to her. She could not help but wonder whether she and her husband would have even entertained the notion of spending so much time in the company of that kind of newly enriched people had it not been for the wretched state of their coffers.

Her thoughts slipped once more towards the treacherous slope of painful memories. She thought of the Chevalier de Montmorency. It was the mentioning of that terrible man's name that had almost caused her to faint. He was the man she hoped to never be forced to set eyes upon again, the man who had ruined, in the blink of an eye, her family's future. And to think that Madeleine de Lamothe would willingly give away her token to such a man!

She became aware that Madame Rémy was inquiring about her health. The baroness felt almost grateful for the interruption and hurried to reassure the lady of her improving condition. Henriette Rémy could be tolerable when she was at her best. She was a kind woman, after all. But her less than refined upbringing shone through the more time one spent in her company. A lady, she was not. And Madame de Civrac could not think of her and her husband as the "de Rémys" as others did. To her, they were simply the Rémys, enriched merchants from Bordeaux.

Alas, the Baroness of Civrac thought, stealing a glance at her eldest daughter Élisabeth, named after her. *It seems I will be spending far more time than I would ever care for in these common folk's company in the years to come...*

Her eldest daughter was laughing rather indecorously, her hand resting on her stomach, most likely at some remark Louis

Rémy had made... a remark that would undoubtedly not make her laugh. But the baroness had to admit that that daughter, too, seemed to be enjoying herself, despite all odds, in the company of an unlikely suitor. She had dreamed of a more distinguished match for her eldest child, given that she was to inherit Rauzan one day and all of her father's lands. But the tokens had been exchanged. The dices had been cast. "Iacta alea est!"[2] Madame de Civrac felt grateful once more to her enlightened father, who had ensured that she had a classical education.

She took another sip of wine. In all fairness, the match will prove to be their salvation. What the Rémy family lacked in noble lineage, they, more than enough, compensated in coin. They had already waved the issue of the dowry, the de Durfort de Civrac noble name having been, no doubt, considered dowry enough, especially since it will cast newfound legitimacy to the "de" recently added to their own surname. In addition, she knew from her husband that Master Rémy had already agreed to pay off their sizeable debts. As much as it pained her to admit, the alliance shall prove beneficial to them. And Élisabeth seemed happy enough with it, at least, for the moment.

The Baroness of Civrac watched her daughter take Louis Rémy by the hand and lead him towards the middle of the banquet hall for yet another dance...

Well... that leaves Catherine... she thought, her eyes searching for her second eldest daughter through the multitude of colourful apparels and shining faces.

It was unbearably warm inside the hall, and the rancid smell of sweat was overwhelming. There were too many souls crammed in one place. And they were constantly moving, dancing or coming and going as they pleased.

Madame de Civrac raised her lace handkerchief, which had been doused with lavender water, to her nose. It was a habit she had acquired as a child from her beloved father, who had embraced with glee every new Italian custom. She remembered the words of Erasmus of Rotterdam, a favourite of her father's, despite him not being Italian, and a stern advocate of normalising the usage of handkerchiefs to delicately take care of one's nose droppings.

Thoughts of her late father always made her eyes tear up. But it was a blessing that the Good Lord had decided, in his infinite wisdom, to take away the Baron de Sérillac long before he could witness the penury in which his daughter and granddaughters had been forced to live in recent years.

The baroness dabbed at her eyes with her mouchoir. The scent of lavender invaded her nostrils. She had brought some plants with her from Sérillac and tended to them together with her loyal, trusted maid, Maria, who had learned to distil perfume out of their purple flowers. But she could do nothing to fight the intolerable heat. Madame de Civrac was reminded of her dislike of big cities. There was no fresh air like in the country, only the foul smells of the open gutters and the body odours of thousands of men and women forced to live too close to one another.

"Are you hungry, dear mother? I brought you some oranges!"

Catherine's solicitous voice startled Madame de Civrac. She thanked her and took some slices of the sweet fruit.

They really have everything in Bordeaux! she wondered.

She took a closer look at Catherine. Though neither as beautiful as Élisabeth nor as resourceful as Éléonore, she was decidedly kind and well-mannered. A wonderful daughter to her parents, to be sure, yet shy and reclusive beyond understanding. Those traits made her extremely ill-equipped for the joys of a banquet in general and for those of a game of fin'amor in particular. Catherine lacked the skills and perhaps even the inclination to catch the interest of a suitable gentleman. As a mother, Madame de Civrac worried about all of her daughters' futures. But she worried most of all about Catherine. If left to her own devices, she had all the prospects of becoming an old maid...

Chapter Thirty Seven
Armand

Bordeaux, Easter Monday,
after sunset

"Ie vous remercy pur cete danse, mademoiselle!"[1] said Armand de Ségur with a gallant bow.

"Auec ploisir, monsieur,"[2] the lovely young lady he had met that morning at the Roman ruins replied.

She spoke with grace, and taking hold of her long skirts, she curtsied, as the etiquette required at the end of a minuet.

"One more dance, perhaps, mademoiselle?" he felt emboldened enough to ask.

In truth, the two of them had already danced together many times that evening. Armand had lost count, but he had to admit that he had enjoyed their dances and the conversations that had come with them.

"Ie vous pry de voloir m'escuser, monsieur.[3] I think I need to catch my breath. I should probably look for my sisters..." she said, resting, for a fleeting moment, her hand on his forearm.

"Bien cert, mademoiselle."[4]

Armand bowed, and she left. He retired to a corner of the hall. He had still not been able to learn her name, although they had danced together for a long time. The etiquette required them to be properly introduced by a third party, but he had not yet managed to steal a private moment with his lord commander, who was the ideal candidate for the task. Even though the peculiar circumstances of Madame de Montaigne's courtly game might give them license to abate themselves from the usual etiquette requirements that evening, Armand still had a hard time coming up with a suitable way to ask the lady for her name. He never quite knew how to speak to the ladies. But he felt he was ready to come to a decision. While he hadn't learnt her name, he did gather from their time dancing together that she must have been a lady from a noble family. Her attire, her language, her graceful dance movements, her manners and her knowledge of the strengths and weaknesses of the most celebrated knights of France, as well as of their family crests, all spoke towards it. He was determined to seek out the Lord of de Monluc and enlist his aid.

Armand made his way towards the table of honour where his lord commander was seated, among other notable guests, his own father, the Count of Montazeau included. He looked at the other ladies around him, dancing, talking, drinking, laughing... He had to concede that there were many other ladies there that evening who surpassed that mysterious young girl in both beauty and grace. And who probably had more wealth to their name. He knew that the game of fin'amor arranged by Madame de Montaigne was enticing for most young ladies and gentlemen because it was waving away the promise of any monetary compensation or exchange. The unions were to be based on mutual respect and admiration, and nothing else, just like in the tales of yore.

Madame de Montaigne had chosen well her words in mapping the day's celebrations, lending them imagined legitimacy by tying them to the myths and literary traditions of the langue d'oc, and even to Queen Alienor herself. Games of fin'amor... They were sure to awaken not just the guests' longing for chivalry and romance, but even their dreams of a fierce and independent Aquitaine. But those days were gone, and the stories of fin'amor were excessively idealised. A tryst of fin'amor in the poems of the troubadours was not just a chaste exchange of ribbons, after all. It was something much more carnal, even sinful, since the lady involved was usually married to another. Armand found himself blushing. There was no point in dwelling on such thoughts. They were not going to take him closer to a resolution.

He reached the long table where his lord commander was seated next to his father. The best course of action open to him was to gather more information about that young lady. Regardless of her motives, she had bestowed her token on him. And she was by no means ugly or unrefined. Armand had to admit he had been rather taken with her deep brown eyes and her milk-white skin, her lovely smile and her slender neck. And it was obvious that she belonged to a noble, even though not wealthy, family of Aquitaine, perhaps one with a long military tradition, too. Most of all, she was kind, very lively, and astute beyond her years. If he were to marry, she had all the premises of making a good wife for him, as good as any other...

"Ah, Armand. Here you are!" the Count of Montazeau called out and waved him over to his seat, then whispered in his ear: "I am afraid I have rather bad news..."

But before he could continue, le Seigneur de Montaigne turned around in his seat and exclaimed: "Chevalier de Ségur, you are just in time! The Seigneur de Monluc here was praising your acts of courage at Sienna..."

His commander turned around as well, as did several other ladies and lords seated at the table.

Armand straightened his posture and said: "My Lord de Montaigne, you flatter me excessively with your praise. I did only what any honourable man of arms would have done in those circumstances..."

"The Chevalier de Ségur is being excessively modest. He saved my life! Do you know what he did? Let me tell you the story. It is quite impressive! In the early days of the siege of Sienna, when we still had strength on our side, I got caught up, together with the Chevalier de Ségur, in a fight right before the city gates..."

Armand stifled a sigh. His lord commander relished playing the storyteller, and war stories were his favourites, especially if he was featured in them. He would have to wait a long time until he could exchange a word with him in private.

"... That formidable blow might just as well have sent me all the way to Heaven, to meet my Lord and Creator... and let me assure you that I was ready then as I am today! But the Chevalier de Ségur here ruined that filthy Spaniard's plans in the most heroic manner, protecting me with his own body. This, noble lords and ladies, is the scar to prove it!" the Lord of Monluc declared in that thundering voice of his, accompanying his words with an ample gesture towards the gash on Armand's left cheek.

"Oh, mon Deu, quel courage!"[5] he heard Madame de Montaigne exclaim.

"Congratulations, chevalier!" said Louis de Saint Gelais, the soon-to-be new mayor of Bordeaux, raising his goblet of wine towards him.

Armand felt the long line the Spanish sword had left upon his cheek throb and burn. To hide his embarrassment, he bowed his head and then turned to look for a page.

"My boy, fetch me a goblet of wine!" he asked when the servant arrived.

"To the Chevalier de Ségur! And to the health of le Seigneur de Monluc, may God protect him and give him the strength to win many more victories for the kingdom in the years to come!" Pierre Eyquem de Montaigne stood and raised his goblet in a toast. He was soon joined by all the other guests standing around the banquet table.

The page returned with a goblet filled to the brim with wine, right on time for Armand to join the toast. Once everyone had taken a drink from their goblets and the others returned to their previous conversations, the Count of Montazeau took hold of his son's arm. The contents of Armand's goblet spilt onto his velvet jacket and his leather shoes. He put his cup on the table and bent over to catch his father's words: "I am afraid that your brother Aimery..."

But he was not able to finish his thought. Blaise de Monluc thundered with his impressive voice, which could be heard on occasion even above the drumming of the harquebuses.

"Ségur, come! I need to speak to you."

The chevalier had to leave his father's side. He wondered what he had wanted to tell him. It appeared to have something to do with Aimery. But his younger brother was far away at their uncle's castle in Mortemart, so the matter could not have been too urgent. He, on the other hand, needed to talk to his lord commander about that lady, so he welcomed the opportunity to do so.

On his way over, Armand took out his handkerchief to dab at the wine stains on his jacket. To his surprise, the Lord of Monluc rose from his high chair and turned to face him. The two of them almost collided. The Chevalier de Ségur hurried to hide away the handkerchief.

"Let us go outside, Ségur. I have important news from Paris."

Armand replied with a nod and followed his commander into the dark courtyard. The sun had already set. The torches were the only source of light.

"I have spoken to the king while I was in Paris, Ségur. The Spanish are getting bold and greedy once more. There are rumours that, this time, they had set their ungodly eyes on nothing less than the Holy See itself! Nothing is certain as of yet, but the king has asked me personally to travel to Rome and lead the Royal Troops together with Strozzi, should the Holy Father call for our help." His commander continued to speak to him in a low tone of voice, which was unlike him.

"I understand, my lord," he replied.

"As I said, nothing is certain yet, but it will be sooner rather than later. And I know I can count on your silence, for none of this is to be repeated yet! But I wanted you to know all this, Ségur, because if you consider yourself well enough, I will want you by my side!" Blaise of Monluc said.

Armand was stunned into silence. He had hoped to be sent somewhere else, perhaps to Flanders or the Pyrenees. But it appeared that the Lord had ordained otherwise, and he was to travel once again to the ancient lands of Julius Caesar. Regardless, the chevalier knew what his answer was. Fully recovered or not, a true knight was always ready for war.

"I am well, my lord. Just send me the word, and I will follow you wherever you may lead!" he declared with a bow of his head.

"I knew I could count on you, Ségur!" the Seigneur de Monluc replied, putting his hand on Armand's shoulder.

"What else do we know about this mad plan of the Spaniards, my lord? Can we count on our allies?" Armand asked.

The Lord of Monluc answered his questions as best he could. The two of them walked around the palace courtyard several times, speaking in a low voice, discussing all the known details of the campaign. They paid little attention to the other few guests, who were laughing and talking loudly in the courtyard, though they made sure they were not overheard. Armand was not altogether thrilled to go back to Italy, but he was a captain in the Royal Army, a title he had earned through sweat and blood at Sienna, and as such, his fate was to serve the king and his interests.

After a while, they returned to the banquet hall, having drawn the general lines of a strategic plan.

As they reached the banquet table, his lord commander surprised him by saying: "If there is anything I can do for you, just say the word. I am forever in your debt for saving my life at Sienna!" and then he made as if to turn away.

Those were the exact words Armand had waited to hear. He could, at last, enlist his help in identifying the young lady who had offered him her token of fin'amor.

"My lord, there is something I would like to ask of you..." he said, but his words trailed off.

Armand felt his heart beat faster in his chest, as it often did before the onset of a battle. For standing before him was none other than the lovely young lady he was about to mention. She was walking towards him, her hand resting on the arm of none other than the Captain of Monluc, his lord commander's son. He swallowed hard. It became clear to him that she was a close acquaintance, perhaps even a relative of the Monlucs.

Chapter Thirty Eight
Alienor

Bordeaux, Easter Monday,
after sunset

D ancing with her cousin turned out to be more enjoyable than she had expected. Alienor took courage from the lively conversation she had exchanged with him in between dance moves. She resolved to enlist his aid in uncovering the identity of the gentleman to whom she had tied her fate.

As soon as she rose from the reverence that signalled the end of the allemande, she asked: "My dear cousin, I wonder if I might bother you with a request?"

"Pur vous? Quoy que ce soyt, chere cusine!"[1] Pierre-Bertrand de Monluc answered, taking her hand in his.

"I would very much like to see your father, Cappitaine. I want to convey to him in person my sincere felicitations for his victory in the game of chivalry!"

"But of course, my lady. My father is your uncle after all, and he will undoubtedly be very glad to see his niece again!" he said, still holding onto her hand and leading her towards the table of honour, where the mayors, their families and the most illustrious guests were seated.

Alienor smiled. She found her cousin to be a tad mischievous, but his manners were faultless. It had to be said that he was a good dancer and a master in the art of pleasant conversation. But her smile faded away when, coming forth from the crowd, she saw her uncle walking towards the long banquet table, in deep conversation with none other than the gentleman in black attire, the very man to whom she had given her token that morning. Her eyes darted to his elbow to make sure he still had it. The red ribbon was still fastened to his arm, its loose ends trailing behind him as he walked. The fact that the chevalier had not taken it off kept her hopes afloat, even though he had not offered her his ribbon.

The gentleman and her uncle came to a halt by the side of the table and carried on with their conversation. The long scar on his cheek was fully visible now as he stood with his left side towards her.

At that very moment, Alienor tripped on the hem of her long gown. Her cousin hurried to her assistance. One moment later, his hand held hers even tighter while his other arm shot forward and caught her by the shoulder, stopping her tilting body in mid-air. She realised at once that she must have dropped the skirts she had been holding in her right hand upon catching sight of her mysterious gentleman.

"Est ce que vous vous trouuez bien, chere cusine?"[2] Pierre-Bertrand asked, lowering his face uncomfortably close to hers.

She suspected that the purpose of the scrutiny was to find the source of her embarrassment and perhaps even make merry of it. It was, therefore, important that she got a grip on herself and stopped displaying her emotions.

"Bien certes, mon cusin,"[3] Alienor answered, taking one step back.

After one moment's hesitation, Cousin Peyrot let go of her arm, and she broke free of his embrace. The last thing she needed was to give the impression that they were sharing an intimate moment right in front of the illustrious guests seated at the banquet table.

"I am simply moved to see your father, the great hero of Sienna, after all these years..." she added, regaining her composure.

Alienor stood very straight and waited. Pierre-Bertrand de Monluc did not seem entirely persuaded by her explanation, but he took away his inquisitive gaze. Turning his head towards the table of honour, he, too, noticed his father and the gentleman in black standing next to him. Her cousin was perceptive, so she had to be careful.

To her mortification, she saw that her uncle's companion was also looking their way. Mademoiselle de Durfort hoped he had not seen her lose her footing earlier, nor the way Pierre-Bertrand had held her. The latter one, at least, proved to be a short-lived hope.

Her cousin once more took hold of her elbow and gently but determinedly pulled her towards him while whispering in her ear: "Oh my, dear cousin! Do I see a ribbon fastened to the sleeve of the Chevalier de Ségur? I wonder... Who could possibly have put it there? And chosen him? Fancy that... The man is rather unbecoming to look at, with that scar of his, don't you think?"

He accompanied his words with a snort. Alienor pulled her arm free of her cousin's grip once more. She felt her face burning. It was not because Petit Peyrot had been so close to uncovering her secret... or because the mysterious gentleman in black was still looking at them, and she was apprehensive of how that whole scene might have appeared in the eyes of an onlooker... but because she felt hurt by her cousin's arrogant, malicious words. He had been utterly inconsiderate to deride in that manner the scar of a man of arms, the scar that the gentleman-in-question had acquired fighting together with Peyrot's father in Italy. Moreover, he had indirectly questioned and even ridiculed her and her ribbon. But Alienor willed her racing heart to quiet down and not betray her. Ignoring her cousin's question, she took a deep breath and walked towards her uncle, who had his hand on the chevalier's shoulder.

Pierre-Bertrand, although obnoxious, had proved very useful. For he had at last revealed to her the gentleman's name. The Chevalier de Ségur! And from the obvious familiarity with which the Seigneur de Monluc was treating him, it appeared that her uncle must have had a high opinion of him.

As she approached them, it did not escape Alienor's attention that the chevalier, while still engaged in conversation with her uncle, seemed to be following her and Peyrot's advance with interest. She whispered over her shoulder: "Cher cusin, soyez gentil, présentez moy!"[4]

"But of course, my lady," her cousin whispered in return and hurried past her to reach his father's side. "Monsieur pere! Ie vays vous faire vn immense plaisir,"[5] the Captain of Monluc told his father once he reached his side.

He accompanied his ceremonious words with a stretch of his arm towards Alienor, who took two steps forth and joined the three gentlemen by the table. They all turned their heads to look at her.

"Voicy ma cusine, Éléonore de Durfort de Civrac,"[6] she heard her cousin make the introduction at last.

She fell into a deep reverence in front of her uncle.

"Ma niece!" the Lord of Monluc exclaimed with a loud voice, effusion in his voice. "I would have recognised you as Élisabeth de Sérillac's daughter anywhere. You look just like your mother when she was your age!"

"Thank you, my lord," she replied as he took her hand in his and planted a wet kiss on its back.

Madame de Montaigne and several other high-profile guests seated at the banquet table craned their necks in her direction. To Alienor's great relief, that dreadful Chevalier de Montmorency was not among them. Both his and the Lord of Lamothe's seats were empty. Madame de Lamothe smiled at her, and she forced a smile back.

"Mademoiselle, allow me to introduce you to the most loyal captain in the entire Royal Army, the Chevalier de Ségur!" her uncle added, and her heart skipped a beat.

They were, at last, properly introduced. And it was clear that he was a brave gentleman who had his lord commander's trust.

"Mademoiselle!" he said, taking a bow.

"Mon cheualier!" Alienor smiled with all her heart.

She curtsied, and he reached out his hand. She gladly gave him hers, and he planted a kiss on top of it. It was not the first time he had done so that evening, but she still found it delectable. His lips only grazed her skin, but Alienor felt shivers crawling up her back.

"Is it just my impression, Father, or do they seem to know each other?" her cousin asked.

Alienor found his manner impertinent. Petit Peyrot spoke as if the two of them were not there. But the Chevalier de Ségur's impeccably composed answer surprised her. "I have had the honour to make Mademoiselle de Durfort's acquaintance earlier, yes, but only in passing..."

"You know each other, Captains, don't you? You remember my son, Le Cappitaine Peyrot!" Blaise de Monluc remarked, looking from his son to the chevalier.

"Of course, my lord. Good evening, Captain."

"Good evening to you, too, Captain," Pierre-Bertrand said, his voice so cold that it took Alienor by surprise.

"Monsieur, allow me to congratulate you on your victory today," she said, turning to her uncle.

"Thank you, my niece. And not just for your felicitations. I believe it was you, was it not, who advised my daughter Marguerite regarding a certain chevalier's weakness in his left elbow?" the Seigneur de Monluc lowered his voice to a mere whisper.

Alienor stole a glance at the Chevalier de Ségur. She wondered if he remembered that detail she had shared with him earlier at the Roman amphitheatre. But he was not looking at either of them. He appeared to have shifted his attention to the couples dancing in the middle of the hall, his face devoid of any expression.

"I am merely glad to have been of help, dear uncle. Your performance in the tournament was indeed commendable, and I cannot think of anyone more deserving of the title of champion!" she replied with a smile.

"Is your lady mother here with you?" her uncle inquired.

"Yes, indeed she is, my lord. Together, with my father and elder sisters..."

"Isn't it remarkable, Captain?" He turned towards his son, who smiled back at him.

Alienor did not quite catch her uncle's meaning. But she hoped he was not alluding to the fact that so many of the de Durfort de Civrac family's daughters seemed to be participating in the medieval games that day in search of husbands.

Her neck started to burn, and she did not even dare look at the Chevalier de Ségur. Even though his eyes were looking elsewhere, his ears might catch everything that was being said. And it appeared that both her cousin and her uncle were intent on embarrassing her that evening.

"My mother has not been feeling well," she hurried to say, in the awkwardness of the moment.

"Oh, yes, indeed. She almost fainted, Father. Were it not for me, she might have injured herself!" Petit Peyrot exclaimed, eager to sing his own praises.

"Yes, but I assure you, Uncle, she had more than recovered since..." Alienor added, and saw the Chevalier de Ségur turn and crane his neck with a sudden movement, as if something of importance had caught his attention.

Curiosity got the better of her, and she tried to crane her neck as well. She saw nothing of note, only two young guests clad in bright red and blue attires dart out of the banquet hall holding hands. The chevalier appeared to be crestfallen, as if he had seen a spectre.

"Then you must take me to your lady mother at once! I must

make sure she is doing well or send for a physician," the Seigneur de Monluc declared.

Alienor looked back at him and agreed. She had to leave the chevalier and show her uncle the way. Pierre-Bertrand was following her every move with that sarcastic smile of his. But she could not allow one gentleman's irreverent gaze to deter her from succeeding that evening.

"Cappitaine, volez bien nous escuser!"[7] Blaise de Monluc said, turning towards the Chevalier de Ségur.

Then the chevalier looked at her, and Alienor asked: "Are you quite well, chevalier?"

"Yes, of course, mademoiselle. It was a pleasure meeting you!" he hurried to say, although his face was whiter than a piece of parchment.

"The pleasure was all mine, my lord," she said, offering him her hand to kiss again.

Alienor fought away an army of butterflies spreading their wings inside of her.

"Venez me chercher apres, mon cheualier. Nous deuerions parler..."[8] she bent her head towards his and whispered.

"Certes, mademoiselle," the Chevalier de Ségur whispered back.

Alienor led her uncle and cousin towards the other side of the banquet hall where she had last seen her mother. Her cousin laid a hand on her shoulder and smirked.

"Say what you might, dear cousin, but I do suspect you and the Chevalier de Ségur are rather closely acquainted!"

She smirked back and freed her shoulder from his grasp. Pierre-Bertrand de Monluc's reasons for teasing her in that manner were anyone's guess, but he was proving to be more and more tedious as the evening progressed.

During their crossing of the hall, Alienor's mind was busy at work. She did not wish to make any more inquiries about the Chevalier de Ségur in her cousin's presence. But if Petit Peyrot were to leave her and her uncle alone for some moments, she could ask him more questions. Blaise de Monluc was, after all, the chevalier's lord commander, so he was sure to know everything there was to know about him and his family. But first, she had to find a way to get rid of that nosy cousin of hers. If only one of her sisters was in their mother's vicinity... then Alienor could suggest to Pierre-Bertrand to invite her to dance in a way that he could not refuse.

A triumphant smile crossed her lips as she caught, at last, the sight of her mother. Her sister Catarina was by her side.

Chapter Thirty Nine
Armand

Bordeaux, Easter Monday,
after sunset

The young lady's name was Éléonore de Durfort, and she was the daughter of the Baron de Civrac. She was also a niece of the Lord of Monluc, which explained why she was so well-informed in matters of war. More specifically, in his and his lord commander's military exploits in Italy. That all bode well. She was, in all appearances, a worthy match.

Armand was left alone with his thoughts again once the lady, her uncle, and cousin had excused themselves. He looked around, searching for his father, but the Count of Montazeau was nowhere in sight. His father had wanted to talk to him. Aimery's name had been mentioned and, in his experience, that seldom bode well.

A certain sighting of a gentleman in a fancy light blue coat leaving the banquet hall at the arm of a beautiful lady in a bright red gown had further confirmed his apprehensions. If he had not been mistaken, the lady in question was none other than Jeanne de Louppes. The gentleman accompanying her reminded him of his brother. But it seemed like a very far-fetched notion, given that Aimery was far away in the Limosin. Mortemart Castle was, at least, a three days carriage drive away. There was no way his younger brother ran away and travelled all the way to Bordeaux without them knowing it. His uncle was a man of honour, entrusted with the guardianship of the young boy, and it was unthinkable that he would not send as much as a word of warning to his family should he have escaped. It would take only one night and day for a messenger to ride to Bordeaux, after all.

Armand chased away those silly thoughts. He had more pressing matters to attend to than to ponder on the meaning of his father's words or the whims of his younger brother. His thoughts returned, inevitably, to the lovely Éléonore de Durfort. He could not help but feel rewarded by his assumptions regarding her noble lineage. And he noticed that a certain feeling of warmth tended to seize him whenever he thought of her. She was not only a lady of beauty and noble breeding. She had a kind heart as well. She had been, after all, the only person willing to sit next to him in the gallery of the Galien Palace earlier that day. Far from being taken aback by his appearance, Mademoiselle de Durfort had even acknowledged his scar, in a most gracious way, while they had watched the tournament.

"And she has shown great honesty. And that, surely, must be one an essential quality in a future companion, was it not?" the Chevalier de Ségur asked himself.

Armand considered the alternatives before him. The lady had given him her ribbon, the token of her affection. He had to let her know if he accepted or rejected her offer. It was such an unusual position for a gentleman. Truth be told, he had no idea how he had managed to get himself dragged into that game of fin'amor. But to not return the gesture would be a slight. That lovely young lady did not deserve that...

Catching sight of Madame de Montaigne rising from her seat at the banquet table, he decided to approach her and request a ribbon of black silk. He told himself that it was the only honourable thing to do. He took a deep breath to still his racing thoughts. That might, after all, be one of the most important decisions of his life, one that was sure to create dissension in the midst of his family... His mother was sure to object to any union forged without her consent, and the fact that the Durforts were known Calvinists would only aggravate her all the more. But Armand trusted Mademoiselle de Durfort's character, regardless of her religious allegiance... although it might be worthwhile to ask her views on that matter when he saw her next. The two of them needed to talk. It could no longer be postponed.

"Come and find me later, chevalier. We should talk," she had whispered to him before she left.

He had to concede that he had felt flattered, especially since le Cappitaine Peyrot had cast such a half-shocked, half-envious glance their way. The lady was daring, and she seemed steadfast. Come to think of it, it was all a man of arms could wish for in a life companion. And an alliance with the family of his lord commander could only bode well for his career.

Full of resolve, he made his way towards the mayor's wife. "Madame de Montaigne, may I compliment you on the exquisite banquet?"

"Oh, thank you, Captain. You are enjoying yourself, I hope?" she replied, a bit surprised.

"Yes, indeed. I came to you, my lady, because I wanted to inquire about the game of courtly love and..." he started, feeling self-conscious and unsure on how to put forward his request.

"Oh, my dear captain!" she exclaimed, stunning him with her delighted tone. "Do you want to partake in the game yourself? This is indeed a most wondrous surprise! First of all...." she started and made a quick sign to her lady's maid, who was standing nearby.

While Antoinette de Montaigne was busy explaining the rules of the game, her maid came forth and took out from her reticule a ribbon of black silk.

"...You must take the token, mon cappitaine," she continued and made a wide gesture towards the ribbon in the maid's outstretched hand. "And be sure to fasten it tightly yet delicately to a young lady's upper arm. We would not want it to fall and get lost now, would we? But at the same time, remember that this is a young lady's arm we are talking about, not a harquebus, so I will be counting on you, Captain, to not be too harsh when tying it, either!" she added with a smile.

Armand was so surprised by Madame de Montaigne's quick spoken tirade, of which he had hardly understood a word. It took him several moments to understand that she was done, and she waited for him to pick up the token from the maid's hand.

Springing into action, he thanked the mayor's wife and grabbed the sleek piece of ribbon. The fabric felt warm and smooth to the touch. He was about to turn around and look for Mademoiselle de Durfort when he heard Madame de Montaigne call out to her niece, Mademoiselle Marie de Louppes. And before he knew what was happening, he had Marie's hand in his, and he was leading her to the middle of the banquet hall.

Chapter Forty

Catarina

"Chere cusine, quelle mereuillioze soirée, vous ne trouez pas?"[1] Pierre-Bertrand de Monluc asked his cousin as they were waiting for the page boy to fill their silver goblets with more sweet wine.

"Yes, my lord," Catarina answered.

After two dances, basses and an allemande, she had grown quite tired of her cousin's incessant talking.

But, having no doubt been disappointed in her short answer, he pursued to subject her to more inquiries.

"Oh, but let us not stand on formality, dear cousin. We are family, after all. You can call me Cousin Peyrot, like your sisters..."

Catarina hurried to take a generous gulp of wine to hide her giggles.

"Are you enjoying yourself, dear cousin? Is the wine to your liking?" he asked with a sarcastic smile. "Shall I call for the page again?"

She felt her cheeks burn. Cousin Peyrot was even more annoying and arrogant than she had expected. Every single word or gesture of hers seemed to prompt some new remark, heavy with double entendres. On second thought, the nickname of "little Peyrot" suited his silly attitude very well.

"That will not be necessary, Cousin Peyrot. I am not extremely fond of wine," she replied in her driest tone of voice.

He seemed to enjoy teasing her. Catarina looked around, rather self-conscious, lest someone of her acquaintance may be privy to that increasingly uncomfortable conversation.

"Let us converse about the music then, mademoiselle. I do hope it is up to your standards?"

The gentleman was relentless. She wanted nothing more than to wipe that unbearable smile from his face or to get as far away from him as possible.

"The music is enchanting, to be sure..." she allowed, her mind busy at work to find a suitable pretext to leave her cousin's side.

"Enchanting!" he exclaimed, accompanying his words with an indecorous burst of laughter. "Though, if I am not mistaken, you have not enjoyed yourself on the dance floor too frequently tonight, dear cousin... Well then... that leaves the company. I sincerely do hope that many a noble lords present at the banquet this evening have bestowed their attention on you, Cusine Catherine?"

He was openly mocking her and relishing every single moment of it. She wished she could just turn around and run away from this tedious cousin.

What if I pretend to trip and spill the contents of my goblet on his elegant coat? Catarina wondered.

A smile flowered on her face, as it often did when she imagined what people might say or do if she were to truly follow her thoughts and be bolder.

"Oh, I see you are smiling... So you did enjoy the attention of noble lords tonight. Perhaps, of one noble lord, in particular, dear cousin?"

He had lowered his voice and almost whispered the last words in her ear. Catarina flinched at the unwelcome familiarity of his gesture and took a step back. Then her smile spread and reached her eyes. If only he knew what was the true cause of her smile! But his narrow-minded interpretation was God sent.

She found the perfect reply to his irreverent insinuations. She could be a bit bolder if she so wanted. "Oh, dear cousin, you have no idea!" she said, taking a sip of the wine and offering him a long glance from the corner of her eye. "Now, if you will be so kind as to excuse me, Cousin Peyrot, my mother is sure to wonder where I am..." And with that, she turned around and started to make her way towards the other end of the hall.

"Chere cusine," Pierre-Bertrand exclaimed, running after her. "I see that my words must have displeased you. Pray, excuse my forwardness. I did not mean to cause insult..."

Catarina was forced to turn around and face him once more, although she had no wish to further engage in meaningless pleasantries with that insufferable bore. She took a deep breath and said: "Not at all, dear cousin. I am not so easily vexed! But I must find my mother..."

She resumed her walking, hoping he would take the cue and make himself scarce.

"Yes, of course. Let us search for her together," he offered, following in her footsteps.

It was beyond Catarina's comprehension why Pierre-Bertrand de Monluc insisted on accompanying her. She had done nothing to encourage his attentions, and she had no use for them, either. Alienor was sure to have a piece of her mind when she saw her again. That uncomfortable situation was her doing. Eager to get rid of their nosy cousin, she had forced him upon Catarina, who, taken by surprise, had found no reason to refuse his invitation to dance. She regretted her naivety, but she had to behave with composure, like a true lady, and not betray her growing impatience.

Nothing could have readied her, however, for what her cousin said next.

"Chere Catherine, I must confess that I have been in awe of you the entire evening!"

"Whatever might you mean, Cousin?" she asked, taken aback. She stopped in her tracks for a moment and turned to look at him.

"Ever since I witnessed your grit and courage in confronting, alongside your sister, the Chevalier de Montmorency," Pierre-Bertrand de Monluc carried on, unperturbed.

He took a sip of his wine and looked at her with intent. No doubt, in order to have a closer look at the effect that his words had on her.

Catarina felt a blush coming and looked away. She took a long sip from her goblet to bid her time.

"And I must confess that I felt quite proud to call myself your relation, dear cousin, when I later discovered your identity. Think of it: a room full of grown men, war heroes, noblemen of the highest rank from all the four corners of Aquitaine... and yet, the only persons brave enough to throw in Montmorency's face the words that were on everyone else's mind, were two young, and may I add lovely, noble ladies. From my own family, nevertheless..."

Catarina found herself at a loss for words. She resumed her walk through the crowd gathered in the banquet hall. It was impossible to make sense of her cousin's intentions. First he mocked her, and then, without as much as a warning, he started to praise her.

"Allow me to reassure you, dear cousin," she heard Pierre-Bertrand de Monluc whisper in her ear whilst she felt his strong fingers encircle her upper arm. "My words are coming from the heart. I have no intention of speaking to you in mere jest."

She was forced to come to a halt once more. "I do thank you for your praise, Cousin Peyrot," she said, at last, unable to restrain her thoughts any longer. "But I would have had much more use of your encouraging words, my lord, when I stood there, alone but for my sister, facing the man responsible for our family's ruin!"

Her face felt even warmer than before. She had spoken in a low voice without turning to face him.

"You are right, my lady," her cousin agreed and released her arm.

They continued to brave in silence the multitude of noble guests in attendance. Mademoiselle de Durfort knew that her cousin was still following her. She felt his hot breath on the back of her neck. It dawned on Catarina that his tone of voice had changed. It was grave, even apologetic, and did not sound sarcastic or haughty anymore. And somewhere along the way, he had started to call her "my lady".

A rather peculiar man, this cousin Peyrot, she thought.

"Allow me, mademoiselle," Pierre-Bertrand de Monluc added, putting a large and heavy hand on Catarina's slim shoulder. His fingers grazed the sensitive skin at the base of her neck.

His unexpected touch sent shivers down her spine, and she came to a halt. Her cousin pushed his way past her. Crammed between the other guests gathered in the banquet hall, their bodies brushed against each other for a fleeting moment along their entire length. Catarina had not been so close to a gentleman's body before and could not help a gasp. The Captain of Monluc turned to look at her, and their eyes met. He was taller than her, so she had to tilt her head to hold his gaze. It felt strange and novel, for she had never had to do that before. Mademoiselle de Durfort was taller than most ladies and as tall as most gentlemen. Their thighs were still pressed against each other.

Embarrassed, she tried to take a step back but stepped on someone's foot. The body of the guest behind her pushed back in response, and she lost her balance. Without warning, her hands shot forth and landed on her cousin's chest. Pierre-Bertrand caught her by the shoulders. They stood liked that for a long moment, as if frozen to the spot, in the midst of the other noble ladies and gentlemen passing them by. Their faces were so close to each other that she could feel his breath on her lips. He held her tight. Catarina could feel his fingers pressing through the thick fabric of her velvet gown.

To her surprise, he was not smiling with that irreverent smile of his. Instead, there was a strange and alarming intensity in his gaze that made her heart beat even faster. Through the tips of her fingers, she could feel his heart beat just as fast. She retracted her hands in a panic as if she had burned herself.

"Are you unharmed, my lady?" her cousin asked, releasing her from his arms.

Catarina nodded and looked away. Her cheeks burned, and she prayed, against all odds, that no one had noticed their intimate embrace.

To her relief, Pierre-Bertrand de Monluc stepped away without another word. He turned around and started to walk again, opening with a broad gesture of his arm a path for them to advance through the crowd. Catarina followed close behind, more confused than ever.

Chapter Forty One
Armand

Bordeaux, Easter Monday,
after sunset

Marriage was, after all, an agreement and not a dream of doves and flowers, as the poets and the troubadours would have one believe. It was, most often, a contract between two families, where fortune was sometimes of the utmost importance, as it had been for his brother, Antoine, and his wife, Henriette de Rieumes. Theirs was a match that his parents, especially his mother, had taken great pains to orchestrate to the Ségurs' advantage.

Yet Armand was but a second son. Destined to inherit very little, perhaps nothing at all, if his mother had a say on the matter, since she clearly favoured his younger siblings. He had, therefore, sought to make his own fortune as a man of arms. And in that, he had succeeded already. The Chevalier de Ségur had acquired a small fortune in the last war with Spain. But it had come at a price. The war had left him scarred, and that, in turn, had made it more difficult for him to find a bride. He had come to understand that no lovely young lady of equal birth and fortune was inclined to marry a man with a deformed face... But somehow, all of a sudden, a suitable match was within his reach... with the daughter of a baronet and a niece of the Lord of Monluc. Armand came to understand that regardless of where he was or what he was doing that evening, his thoughts were inevitably drawn, over and over again, to Éléonore de Durfort and to the decision he had to act upon. He had to offer her his ribbon, and soon. He heard the resounding calling of the bells over the music of the minstrels. Time was, alas, not on his side.

Armand had succeeded in securing a ribbon of black silk, but only to be trapped in dancing with Madame de Montaigne's niece. He stole a glance at her while he reclined his body backwards, as required by the dance steps. Marie de Louppes held no interest in him, and the feeling was mutual.

They were both guests of the de Montaigne family while in Bordeaux, and he had been seated next to her at dinner the previous evening. He had, therefore, been forced to exchange the required pleasantries with her, but beyond those, the girl endeavoured to ignore him and had even smirked at his words on more than one occasion. It had become quite clear that she had only a rudimentary understanding of the manner in which a lady should express and carry herself in a distinguished society. Mademoiselle de Louppes' language and manners reminded him of the servant folk at Montazeau. To be fair, her elder sister made more of an effort, and her beauty and charm more than compensated for her lack of lustre.

All in all, as much as Armand was fond of his friend Michel and his family, he had a hard time feeling flattered that Madame de Montaigne had appeared to suggest a match between him and the simple-minded Marie. But he might have given Mademoiselle de Louppes a fair chance, if her shortcomings had stopped there. It was, after all, not more her fault to have been born into an impoverished merchant's family than it was his fault that his face was forever ruined by a hideous scar. But the way she had treated him because of his disfigured appearance was the very reason he could not wait to be rid of her. He had not missed the disgusted glances that the Chevalier de Montaigne's cousin had cast towards his scarred cheek both at dinner the day before and that evening as they danced together. Neither did he miss the disappointed expression on Marie's face when she had been summoned forth to dance with him. Her concerted efforts to avoid conversing or even looking directly at him had been hard to swallow.

As the minstrels' last accords faded away, both of them must have felt equally relieved to curtsy and then take their leave from each other. Armand touched his purse to reassure himself. It contained the black ribbon, his token of fin'amor. It was time to go and find Mademoiselle de Durfort...

"Captain!" he heard a voice call out.

He turned and saw Michel de Montaigne, the mayor's eldest son and his childhood friend, approach.

Once by his side, he took hold of his arm and whispered in his ear: "You did not tell me that your brother was to join us tonight at the banquet!"

Armand was determined to seek his lady out, at last, and did not welcome yet another interruption. He freed himself from his friend's arm. Then the full meaning of his friend's words dawned on him.

"Chevalier, what do you mean?" he whispered back.

"Your younger brother, the Chevalier de Ségur. He had arrived at our house this afternoon! Didn't you say he was visiting your uncle in the Limosin?"

"You mean to say Aimery is here? At the banquet? In Bordeaux?"

A sense of foreboding washed over Armand, and he grabbed Michel de Montaigne's upper arm. He wondered if that was what his father had tried to warn him about earlier.

"Yes... where else?" his friend replied, clearly surprised by Armand's reaction.

"Are you sure? How is this possible?"

The image of that young gentleman in sky blue apparel running out of the banquet hall in the company of a lady clad in red flashed before his eyes.

"I saw him arrive at our residence earlier this evening. We were naturally surprised at his arrival, of course..."

"Does my father know already?" Armand interrupted him.

That nagging sense of foreboding was growing more ominous by the moment. If Aimery was indeed at the banquet, trouble was sure to follow in his footsteps.

"Yes, I have already informed the Count of Montazeau. And he has been searching for your brother without success. Where he might be, we do not know. But this is as much a surprise for you and your father as it has been for the rest of us, I take, mon cappi-taine?" asked the mayor's son.

"Indeed, my friend. There is no time to waste! Let us search for him and hope we can find him before he does something we might all come to regret... I will search outside. You look for him inside the castle, chevalier. And not just in the banquet hall! He could be anywhere..." Armand whispered the final instructions in his friend's ear before letting go of his upper arm and disap-pearing into the multitude of guests.

If that gentleman in blue was Aimery, there was a high chance he was somewhere in the courtyard. He remembered seeing him exit the hall through its large oak doors. And if his younger brother was indeed there, Armand wanted to be the first to grab him by the shoulders and give him a good shake. Aimery was known to disobey their parents when it served his interests, but he had not thought him capable of the elaborate and careful plan-ning that was needed to achieve such a daring escape from their uncle's castle. And if he was capable of such ruthlessness and deceit, there was no telling what he was planning to do next.

Armand wished his brother had, at least that once, done as he had been told. The more he thought about it, the angrier he felt.

He dashed towards the exit. But once he reached it, Armand came to an abrupt halt just in time to avoid colliding with none other than Éléonore de Durfort. They had both tried to step through the doors at the same time.

Chapter Forty Two
Alienor

Cambes, mid May

It was already late when Alienor and her father arrived in Cambes. The sun was about to set, casting its last rays over the lush green fields that ran along the shores of the Garonne. From the height of the carriage steps, she craned her neck and caught a glance of the peaceful waters. They were but a shimmer of light in the distance beyond the Lamothes' manor. She stepped down from the carriage. Her father was already exchanging greetings with his old friend.

"Monsieur le Baron!" François de Lamothe, Madalena's father, exclaimed.

"Cher amy!" her father said in return, and the two of them embraced, like two friends who had known each other since childhood. "Ma belle dame!"[1] he added, with a bow, upon catching sight of Madame de Lamothe. "Ah, before I forget! My beloved wife, Madame de Civrac, sends her regards and her deepest regrets for being unable to join us. The wedding preparations are taking up all her time, you see..."

"Soyez bien venus a Cambes, monsieur, mademoiselle![2] We are so glad to have you here," said Marguerite de Lamothe with a curtsy while the Baronet of Civrac planted a kiss on her outstretched hand. "Madame de Civrac's presence shall be sorely missed, to be sure, but we do understand. Such joyous news! Perhaps, God willing, we shall find ourselves in a similar situation..." she added, casting a furtive glance at her husband, who glowered back at her and interrupted:

"Permettez nous, mon seigneur, mademoiselle, de vous présenter nostres félicitations pur les fiansailles!"[3]

"Thank you, my lord, my lady," Alienor and her father replied almost at once.

To give herself time to regain composure and hide her apprehensions, she curtsied low to each of them. The lady's words and the haste with which her husband had changed the conversation shocked her and all but confirmed her worst suspicions. They had congratulated them for Elisea and Louis de Rémy's engagement, whose wedding was to take place in a month's time. But Madame de Lamothe had also insinuated that a similar event might soon take place in their family. Madalena was the eldest child and her siblings were much younger than her, so there was no doubt that they had meant her.

"Éléonore, I am so glad you are here. How I feared you might not come!" Madalena's high-pitched voice interrupted her thoughts.

Alienor turned to see her come out of the manor with outstretched arms. She swallowed hard, trying to find her words. Paralysed by the knowledge that her best friend was to marry the man who had brought about her ruin, she just stared. Her friend had a genuine smile on her lips and looked radiant in her pale blue dress. The shifting nuances of the silk fabric shone brightly under the warm light of the setting sun, at times blue, at times purple. As she allowed Madalena to embrace her and then forced herself to throw her hands around her in response, Alienor recognised the fabric. At last, a useful piece of information to help her phrase her response! It was too early to question her friend about an engagement. She had to bid her time. And flattery was a sure way to make Madalena open up.

"My dear Madeleine, you look so beautiful! Do not tell me this is the fabric you bought that day in Bordeaux, the one we found together at the medieval fair?"

"Oh, yes, yes it is! I wondered if you would recognise it. You and your sister helped me choose it, after all... So do tell me, does it indeed bring out the beautiful colour of my eyes?" she replied with an even broader smile, entwining her arm with Alienor's and leading her towards the entrance of the Lamothes' summer residence.

At dinner, several dishes of pork, fowl and fish were served. Alienor found the partridges exquisite. They had been stuffed with sweet raisins and basted in a generous sauce made of red wine. Her father had been very talkative throughout the dinner, and he and the Lord of Lamothe reminisced about the years they had spent together at the Court in Paris in their youth. They always did when they met. It was there that her friend's parents had met and became engaged. Alienor and Madalena mostly listened, exchanging knowing smiles now and then, just like in the olden days when they were little girls and used to sneak out of the nursery to eavesdrop on their parents' conversations late at night.

The de Lamothe family was very particular about using only French at all times. And that included always using the French form of their names. They were just like her mother... But Alienor had known her friend since childhood as Madalena, and she could not think of her as Madeleine or Marie-Madeleine, like Madame de Lamothe liked to call her. She felt the same about her sisters' and her own name...

She carried the beautiful name of the legendary Queen Alienor of Aquitaine, whose blood might very well run through her veins. Her ancestors were Angevins, as was the Queen's second husband, the King of England, and her sons, the kings: Richard the Lionheart and John Lackland, whose descendants had ruled Aquitaine for centuries. But Alienor's great-grand-mother, Jeanne Angevin, stemmed from a minor branch, and it was unclear whether she was descended from Queen Alienor herself. In her heart, she wished for it to be true. It was a thought that gave her strength and comfort.

Regardless, being called Éléonore felt strange, and she did not like it. Upon her friend's insistence, she had started to call her Madeleine in recent months. For Mademoiselle de Lamothe, Madalena and Alienor were names for silly little girls who knew nothing about the world and played with dolls. Her friend felt that only a French name was suitable for a young lady aspiring to join the Court, a name fit for rubbing shoulders with the Royal family itself.

Alienor let out a sigh. Things were changing more and more in Aquitaine. It was frowned upon in recent times if a noble lady spoke a word in Occitan or referred to herself as Alienor instead of Éléonore... or if she thought that Catholics and Protestants were not so different after all and believed in the same God...

Much had changed between her and Madalena, too. The events which had unfolded in Bordeaux on Easter Monday had brought about a rift between them, and they seemed to be growing more and more apart with time. Alienor no longer felt comfortable sharing her true thoughts and opinions with her friend. It was a very sad feeling. On her first evening in Cambes, the two of them retired early to their rooms. Mademoiselle de Durfort was very tired after the long ride, but she was alone with her friend at last, and they had to talk.

"I must confess, I was very intrigued by your letter, dear Madeleine. You said you had news of a most gladdening nature!" she whispered in Mademoiselle de Lamothe's ear while they were climbing the stairs to the upper floor.

"Shhh... not here!" Madalena hastened to reply, putting a finger to her lips and making a quick gesture towards the maid, who was showing them the way. "And not tonight... Join me for a stroll tomorrow after church. You will be joining us there, won't you?"

"Yes, of course," Alienor replied, wondering why Madalena seemed to doubt that.

"Very well. You will see that Cambes is a quaint little town. This is your chamber, my dear Éléonore! Mine is further down the corridor. I will send the maid to help you get ready for the night just as soon as she is done helping me. I hope you will enjoy your stay in Cambes."

"Thank you, dear Madeleine. I am sure I will. Bonne nuict."

"Bonne nuict!"

Alienor took one of the candleholders from the maid and entered the guest chamber. It was a quaint room, as far as she could tell. She took in the bed, the little night table next to it, her travel chest by the wall, and then another table and a chair next to the window... It was not big, but she was glad to have it all to herself.

She sat on the edge of the bed and started to unpin the hairnet that kept her braids in place at the back of her head. Knowing her friend, the maid was unlikely to be done with her evening toilette anytime soon. Madalena put much importance upon appearance, hers, as well as that of others, which is why she was so entertaining when conveying hearsay about all the gentlemen and ladies from the noble society of Bordeaux.

But that evening, Alienor did not feel any excitement or anticipation in regards to her friend's news. Not if, God forbid, it had anything to do with that monster, François de Montmorency!

She felt her body tremble as a cold shiver climbed up her spine. She saw before her eyes an arm covered in armour, holding the shining blade of a sword coloured crimson with blood. Behind it, in the background, she saw Montmorency's face, purple with rage, streaked with blood and mud... And then she heard the screams...

"Go away! Go away!" she whispered as she clenched her fists and forced her eyes open.

Alienor willed them to focus on the candle's flame as it flick-ered on the night table beside her. It was a trick she had learned long ago while she was still in mourning. It helped her keep the horrid memories at bay and bring her thoughts back to the present day, away from the shadows of her haunting past. After a while, the images faded away, and she felt a shooting pain in her palm. She unclenched her fist, and a hairpin fell to the floor, smudged with blood. Her palm was bleeding, but the wound was not deep. She let out a deep breath and stared at the red gash. It was strange how the Chevalier de Montmorency could still hurt her, across time and space. Mademoiselle de Durfort rose and went to the window table, where she found a towel to press against her palm.

She thought about her friend and the stroll they were to take together after church. Perhaps her best strategy was to delay Madalena's confession as much as possible, yet, at the same time, try to have her own suspicions concerning the Chevalier de Ségur's intentions put at ease. Either way, she had to seek clarifica-tion on what had come to pass at the end of the Easter banquet.

While her mind was thus engaged, Alienor kept walking back and forth in her room. Once she reached a decision, she came back to her bed and took off her shoes. She struggled to loosen her skirts with just one hand, but then gave up and threw herself on the bed. She would have to wait for the maid. Like her sisters, Mademoiselle de Durfort was used to taking care of her own preparations for the night. Her family could not afford many servants like the Lamothes. Maria cooked and tended to the lady of the house. Yolanda de Castelbajac helped care for her elder sister, the Dowager Baroness of Civrac. The girls had to count on each other to dress, undress, and style their hair. But that evening, there was no way Alienor could take off her gown or unlace her stays by herself.

After a while, Alienor stood up and went back to the toiletry table. The bleeding had stopped, and she washed her wound with water from a jug. She then wrapped it in a clean towel, throwing the old one to the floor. She looked at the other toiletry items spread on the table. Opening a small tin box she had found by the water jug, she discovered cloves. Mademoiselle de Durfort took some in her hand and rubbed them against each other. Their inebriating scent filled her nostrils. Madalena had once told her that it had become fashionable amongst nobles to chew those strong-scented sticks after a mealtime to improve the smell of one's breath. In truth, Alienor's family could not even afford such expensive spices to flavour their food. Yet the Lamothes were so wealthy, they could offer them to the guests visiting their summer house to chew upon at night... She popped one in her mouth and felt the flavour burn into her tongue and gums. It almost brought tears to her eyes, but she did not want to spit it out. If all the nobles in Bordeaux were doing it, then she could do it, too.

Chapter Forty Three
Armand

Bordeaux, Easter Monday,
after sunset

"Please excuse my frank manners, my lady. I am, after all, a man of arms, unaccustomed to the intricacies of courtly love. But I will endeavour to speak from the heart, as the poets say..." Armand started, but his voice failed him.

He was standing next to Mademoiselle de Durfort, on the roof of the Ombriere Palace's fortified tower. He held her hand in his. It was a bold gesture, but the extraordinary circumstances of their courtship demanded it. Much time had already been wasted, and he had to give her his answer.

The Chevalier de Ségur swallowed hard. "I want to thank you, my lady, for having bestowed your token on my insignificant person."

Emboldened by the encouragement he seemed to discern in the lady's eyes and her expectant stillness, Armand lifted her hand to his lips.

"I cannot begin to understand why you have chosen me, my

lady. I am a man of few words, a man of arms, a man scarred by war. I am, moreover, a second son and do not stand to inherit my father's titles. There are, without a doubt, many others here tonight who are more worthy of your favour..."

He was struggling to find his words. Mademoiselle de Durfort's fingers gave his hand a gentle squeeze. The chevalier's stomach tightened in apprehension as he looked down at their entwined hands.

"But you have chosen me, my lady, and I am grateful," Armand said, then paused again and swallowed hard. "In my turn, I, Armand de Ségur de Montazeau, captain in His Majesty King Henri II's army, chose you, Mademoiselle Éléonore de Durfort de Civrac..."

As he spoke, the chevalier let go of the lady's hand and began to pull out the silk ribbon from his purse.

"Cappitaine! Deu soyt bénit. Vous voicy en fin..."[1]

The Chevalier de Montaigne emerged from the stairs leading up to the tower's roof and stopped to catch his breath. Armand almost dropped his ribbon.

"Escusez moy, mademoiselle," his friend said, acknowledging the lady's presence, before addressing Armand: "I regret the interruption, but the Count of Montazeau requires your presence urgently, Captain."

"The Count of Montazeau? Can it not wait, chevalier?"

"I am afraid not, regrettably..." Michel de Montaigne answered, then took a step closer and whispered in his ear: "We are still to find your brother. And what is more, my cousin, Jeanne, seems to have gone missing, too."

Then he had not been mistaken. The gentleman and the lady he had chanced upon earlier were indeed Aimery and Mademoiselle de Louppes.

Armand whispered back through clenched teeth: "If I just get my hands on him! Today of all days..."

An overpowering feeling of dread washed over him. He had to find his brother in time and prevent a scandal! Otherwise, it was sure as hell that Mademoiselle de Durfort would never agree to marry him. The Chevalier de Ségur turned towards the young lady, who stared back at him in confusion.

"Please excuse me, my lady. Urgent matters that I am unable to disclose to you at the moment are calling me elsewhere," he said with a heavy heart.

Armand had been so close to giving Mademoiselle Éléonore his ribbon! It was nothing but bad luck that the Chevalier de Montaigne had found him when he did. Noticing the disheartened look on the lady's face, he took a step forth and whispered so only she might hear him: "I regret this interruption terribly, mademoiselle. I promise to come back and finish our... conversation."

"Yes, of course..." she said.

"But where are my manners?" he exclaimed and gestured for his friend to step forth. "My lady, let me introduce the Chevalier de Montaigne. Chevalier, the Lady Éléonore de Durfort de Civrac."

Michel de Montaigne bowed and Mademoiselle de Durfort curtsied.

"A bientost, mademoiselle,"[2] Armand said, and then they both hurried away.

"Have you searched the courtyard, Captain?" his friend asked once they were out of the lady's earshot.

"No, chevalier. I had... other matters to attend," he answered, unwilling to disclose more than was needed.

"Well, then let us search the inner courtyard..."

If the Chevalier de Montaigne wondered about the "matters" that had kept his friend busy, he did not betray it in any way. He dashed for the stairs, and Armand followed.

"Chevalier, you say that Mademoiselle de Louppes is missing, too," the Chevalier de Ségur asked, with a pounding heart, while he climbed down the steep steps.

"Yes, indeed. I dare say it might not be a coincidence, Captain!" came the reply.

"This does not bode well at all…"

"Let us hope it is all a simple misunderstanding…" said Michel de Montaigne, right before they reached the end of the steps and emerged into the palace's courtyard.

Armand wanted to hope, too, but he knew his younger brother's character.

They kept looking for Aimery and Jeanne in the palace's various courtyards. Together, they left no bush, alley, alcove or corner unexplored. The Chevalier de Montaigne even went to search for them in the crowd, gathered to watch the jongleurs' acrobatics in the square outside the palace's gates.

As the minutes went by with no trace of Aimery in sight, Armand started to become more hopeful. He told himself that perhaps his friend had been mistaken. It was possible that he confused Aimery with their elder brother, the Chevalier de Montazeau. He had not seen any of Armand's brothers in a long time, and the two of them looked quite alike. They had the Rochechouarts' golden locks and a predilection for colourful apparel, feasts and wine. The gentleman in a sky-blue coat, of whom he had caught but a fleeting glimpse from behind, could very well have been Antoine, not Aimery. It was the most probable explanation, since it had been agreed at first that Antoine and his wife would attend the banquet, whereas Aimery had been sent to Mortemart. The plans were changed when Antoine's wife, Henriette, had become indisposed, as was her habit, and Antoine had decided to remain at home with her, which was surprising, given how much he loved banquets. But his elder brother might have changed his mind. He attended festivities unaccompanied all the time since he spent all his summers at Court, away from his wife.

In any case, Aimery was nowhere in sight, and the Chevalier de Montaigne could have mistaken one brother for the other. Antoine's presence at the banquet was, after all, a much less alarming thought, even if he did leave the hall accompanied by Jeanne de Louppes. Unlike Aimery, he was a quiet and dignified gentleman, uninterested in the frivolities of the flesh. And, as the heir to their family fortune, he could be counted upon to do everything in his power to avoid tarnishing their good name.

After a while, reassured by those thoughts, Armand decided to abandon the search and return to Mademoiselle de Durfort. He had to give her his token. He turned and sprang towards the tower. With a bit of luck, she was still there, waiting for him.

Just then, Michel de Montaigne called out his name from across the courtyard. The Chevalier de Ségur swore under his breath and came to a halt, casting a longing glance at the stairs leading to the lady he had chosen as his life companion.

"No sign of them, mon amy.[3] I dread to think that they may have... that they may be hiding somewhere together..." his friend said, catching his breath.

"Chevalier, are you quite sure it was Aimery and not my elder brother, Antoine? You have not seen either of them in a while and they do look so alike..."

"No, I am quite certain, dear friend. Just as certain as I am that my cousin Jeanne disappearing at the same time is bad news..."

He cursed his brothers and their troublemaking. All Armand wanted was to make haste and find Mademoiselle de Durfort. He and Michel de Montaigne were among a handful of guests to still find themselves outside in the courtyard. All the others had already entered the banquet hall or were lingering around the entrance, waiting to make their way inside. Armand was well aware that it could only mean the announcements were about to start. And he had yet to fasten his silk ribbon around Éléonore de Durfort's arm... He took two more steps towards the tower stairs.

"We need to go back inside, mon amy," the Chevalier de Montaigne said, putting a hand on his shoulder. "We have to find them before the announcements, in case...."

"I don't know, chevalier..."

"Well, we looked everywhere outside. They are not here,

neither one of them. And they are certainly not in that tower you are eyeing, Captain. Let us search inside."

Armand was forced to leave the tower behind and accompany his friend inside. He cursed Aimery under his breath over and over.

"You search the hallways again, my captain. Perhaps I have overlooked some nook, some narrow corridor... I will speak to my parents. They must be informed of this disquieting development..." Michel de Montaigne said.

Armand was running out of time. He needed to speak to Mademoiselle de Durfort without delay to make his intentions known and secure her agreement. Monsieur de Montaigne needed to be informed of it, too, if their names were to be added to the engagement list. Yet, at the same time, it was paramount that he found his brother to prevent a disgrace. He felt a headache coming.

Chapter Forty Four
Catarina

Bordeaux, Easter Monday,
late in the evening

"Alienor! The announcements are about to start..." Catarina said, but her sister paid her no attention.

She had been sent to bring Alienor back to the banquet hall. After having searched for her in every corner of the palace's hallways and courtyards, Catarina had been on the verge of abandoning her quest when her sister had called to her from the height of one of the palace's towers. She had swallowed her surprise and climbed the stairs to join her there.

In all the years she had known her, she had never seen Alienor so restless, so distraught. It had been difficult to understand why she was there, all alone. Her sister had only told her that she had to wait for the Chevalier de Ségur. That mysterious gentleman of hers was apparently called, and she refused to leave the tower's rooftop.

"Where is he? He promised me..." she mumbled.

Catarina took her hand in hers and forced Alienor to stop for a moment. "Come down with me, cara sor. Whoever you are looking for is not up here..."

"I am not going anywhere," Alienor exclaimed, drawing back her hand. "The chevalier might come back here, and then he would not find me!"

Catarina's eyes darted to her sister's elbow and saw no trace of a black ribbon fastened to the dark blue fabric of her sleeve. She let out a heavy sigh. Alienor started pacing back and forth again. Catarina had to think of a way to calm her down.

"Come, Alienor. We can look for him from here," she said, going to the crenellated edge of the parapet. "I can see all the guests in the courtyard. The torches cast a steady glow on their faces..."

Her sister rushed to her side, and they both bent to watch from the height of the fortified tower, the guests moving in the stone courtyard below. They looked like ants, distant, small, insignificant... as did the antiquated game of fin'amor, and every other fairy tale. In reality, they were vain and meaningless.

Elisea would have wedded Louis de Rémy regardless, and Alienor was about to have her heart crossed by some good-for-nothing chevalier who could not even claim himself charming or good looking. Pierre-Bertrand de Monluc, on the other hand... Catarina's heart skipped a beat when she remembered his scent, his breath grazing her lips, his strong arms around her... Surprised by her own thoughts and feelings, she rebuked herself. That was not the time to be silly.

She stole a look at Alienor, who was glued to the edge of the wall, perched almost dangerously low. Her eyes were moist from all the squinting.

"Cara Alienor, let's climb down the stairs and look for this chevalier in the courtyard instead..."

The guests in the courtyard were heading towards the banquet hall, and there was already a crowd waiting for their turn around the entrance. She was, truth be told, quite eager to get back. She did not want to miss the announcements.

The evening breeze was ruthless that high up, biting her through the fabric of her banquet gown. She braced herself to keep warm. But her sister did not seem disturbed by the cold. Indeed, Catarina wondered if she had heard her at all. Alienor was not looking at her. She was still bent over the edge of the parapet, and her eyes were searching for that chevalier of hers.

"Alienor!" she pressed again. "It is time to get back inside. Our mother is sure to be waiting for our return. The announcements..."

"He must come. He said he had chosen me..." her sister whispered, her voice so faint that Catarina could not make out the words at first.

Then she understood. The gentleman had promised her his token and then disappeared.

She took hold of her sister's hand. "Oh, cara Alienor..." she started but then stopped, emotion choking in her throat, not knowing what to say next.

The two of them held each other's gaze for a moment. Catarina could see determination mixed with fear in her sister's eyes. She feared for her, too, for she had placed her trust in an undeserving gentleman who did not intend to keep his word and offer her his token.

In truth, Catarina was persuaded that her approach had proved the wisest. For wasn't it better to have not hoped at all than to have hoped, only to have one's hopes crushed in utter disappointment? She had known from the very beginning that she would not succeed in the game of fin'amor. So there had been no point in even trying. She had only come along for the sake of her mother and sisters and for enjoying a trip to Bordeaux. It was, after all, a most wondrous gift from God to have even been able to spend Easter somewhere else that year and to see the mighty city of Bordeaux. That day had been the happiest of her life, and Catarina had enjoyed every single moment of it... the exciting tournament, the lively fair, the delicious seafood and the exotic fruits, the divine music of the minstrels, the spectacle offered by the mummers and the jongleurs, even the occasional dance she had joined in together with Louis de Rémy or Cousin Peyrot... those were all treasured memories that no one could ever take away from her.

Unlike her sisters, she had taken the ribbon of red silk in her hand that morning only to put it away in her reticule and not look at it even once since. Truth be told, Catarina was not certain she wanted to marry or that she would find happiness by doing so. She was not as ready to agree with her mother as her sisters were, when she kept telling them that a husband and children were a blessing or a woman's only purpose in life. She had come to understand, by observing the lives of others, that while some seemed to find a sense of accomplishment and peace in family life, some did not. Husbands could be weak and simple-minded, or furious and unforgiving. Many women died in childbed, regardless of their rank, her aunt Françoise among them... There was no telling what dangers awaited a young lady after marriage. And it was impossible to ascertain a gentleman's true colours within a day's time. The entire concept of that game made no sense to her. It was built, like her mother's reasoning, on the assumption that a husband, any husband at all, however flawed, was better than none. Catarina did not share that view...

All in all, she felt content and at peace. She had enjoyed every single moment of the Easter celebrations, and she had no regrets at all. The Lord was good and merciful to have spared her all the fretting and the ache which appeared to plague her sister.

"I will help you look for him, cara sor. But we will not find him if we remain here," Catarina said, and her sister, at long last, let out a long sigh and nodded in agreement.

Alienor turned away from the parapet and started to walk towards the steep staircase that led back into the courtyard. Catarina hurried after her, glad that her sister had seen reason at last.

"I hope you are right, cara sor... I hope we find him..." her sister whispered before putting her foot on the first step.

Alienor's words felt like small arrows piercing her chest.

Seeing her beloved sister suffer was more painful than any sorrow she might have felt herself.

Catarina climbed down the spiral staircase, stepping in her sister's tracks. Once in the courtyard, she took Alienor by the hand so that they might not lose each other in the crowd waiting to enter the hall. She stole a look at her headstrong sister. Her jaw was set, and there was a certain decisiveness in her steps. Catarina understood that her sister, unlike her, was far from feeling content. She was not ready to let go of her hopes of securing a suitable alliance that evening... an alliance that Alienor believed would be, like Elisea's, the key to a better future for them all... Catarina, on the other hand, knew that things were not that simple.

Chapter Forty Five
Alienor

Cambes, mid May

"Madeleine, you cannot possibly mean it! Please, tell me it is all in jest..." Alienor exclaimed, coming to a halt.

It was a gut response, and she could not bridle it. Her friend's revelation had stunned her.

The two of them were walking back from church. Alienor and her father had attended the Sunday mass together with the de Lamothes. Hers and Madalena's arms were entwined in affectionate companionship, as they always were when they walked together side by side. They strolled along the narrow streets of Cambes. They were followed, at a respectful distance, by the same maid who had helped Alienor with her preparations the night before. Under the pretext of showing her the beauties of Cambes, Madalena had taken her on a private detour on their way home. She had, at last, opened up about her liaison with the Chevalier de Montmorency.

Alienor had been expecting her friend's confession ever since she had received her letter some weeks ago. The image of

Madalena offering her token of fin'amor to that dreadful man before the joust game in Bordeaux had been haunting her. But to have it confirmed that she and him... Suddenly, the images she longed to forget flashed in front of her eyes. François de Montmorency and his cavalry in full, heavy armours, covered in mud and blood, striking right and left from the height of his black steed... She could still hear her own screams, Catarina's voice trying to lead her away from there, and Lois' sobs... She remembered the rain... the relentless, merciless, cold rain that had poured and poured down from the heavy, grey sky and washed away her tears...

"Éléonore, I assure you, this is not in jest. The chevalier and I exchanged tokens at the banquet, and we are engaged to be married!" Madalena de Lamothe whispered.

Startled by her friend's words, Alienor remembered where she was. She willed the images to fade away, back to the shadows where they belonged... The suspicion that there was a strong connection between her closest friend and that man, nay, that murderer, had grown over the past weeks, turning into certitude. And she had braced herself for her friend's confession for a while. Yet, Alienor had not expected their liaison to acquire such depth in such a short time.

It was happening all too fast. Madalena was slipping through her fingers, gliding down a dangerous slope, and she had no chance to warn her. Like in a scary dream, her movements were stifled, her voice choking. Alienor could not lose her best friend, too, to the man who had already taken her fortune, her dreams and her beloved ones from her.

The magnificent games in Bordeaux were to blame. The Easter celebrations had been like a total inebriation of the senses, a masterful plan to make young lords and ladies lose their heads... enthralled by the resuscitation of a bygone era and its ideals, the lure of a tryst of fin'amor, the splendour of the games of chivalry, the enchanting music of the minstrels, the dancing and the spinning, the mead and the wine...

Alienor let out a deep sigh as her thoughts were pulled once more towards Armand de Ségur and the time they had spent together that day. She looked at her friend and reminded herself that she needed to tread with care...

"Oh, Madeleine... Mais pur quoy? Pur quoy luy?[1] Don't you know who he is, what he has done?" she asked, suppressing her desire to take away her arm from her friend's grasp.

She felt hurt and betrayed. Madalena was her closest friend, her confidante. They had been inseparable ever since she could remember. And yet, she had pursued a relation with that terrible man, knowing full well that he had played a major part in bringing about the ruin of the Durforts de Civrac.

"I knew you wouldn't understand, Éléonore... I know your family has always been... indisposed towards the de Montmorencys. And I know that François has done terrible deeds in his youth..." she heard Mademoiselle de Lamothe say.

Alienor flinched to hear her friend use that man's Christian name. It made her head reel to think that they were already on such intimate terms...

"But, Madeleine, you do not understand. He..." Alienor tried to intercede but was interrupted by her friend's determined voice.

"But you are my closest friend, Éléonore! And I want you to share in my joy. For you see, me and François, we are in love! Ie suis amoreuze... Can you believe it, chere Éléonore? I, for one, never dared hope this would happen to me one day... The taste of love, like... like sweet liquor on my unknowing lips... Oh, Éléonore... All that the troubadours write about in their poems, all that the minstrels sing of in their songs... you see, it is all true!" Madalena accompanied her elated yet whispered discourse with an effusion of gestures with both her hands, and Alienor was glad to have her arm released at last.

She saw it on her friend's radiant face, in her hopeful, shining eyes and in the transposed smile on her lips that her friend had developed very strong feelings for that... entire situation and that she felt very, very happy. Even though it hurt Alienor deeply, it was undeniable that Mademoiselle de Lamothe felt content and joyful at the moment. But she knew that it was just a matter of time before her smiles turned into tears. That man was sure to sow sorrow and destruction in his wake wherever he went...

Mademoiselle de Durfort felt at a loss for words. She was torn between the honesty she owed her friend, her duty to warn her of that man's true character, and the temptation to let Madalena to her own devices so that she may have a taste of the Chevalier de Montmorency's cruelty and deceit, and suffer the rightful consequence of her poor judgment...

"Madeleine, I am truly glad for your sake! I, myself, can only imagine how divine it must feel to have your heart moved by love, feeling the ecstatic sweetness described by Pierre de Ronsard in his sonnets..." she started, but her friend interrupted her again.

"Then you will keep silent and refrain from dampening my happiness, dear friend! And you will be wise to not repeat my greatest secret to anyone, either. Do not make me regret that I have put my trust in you, Éléonore!" Madalena said with a cutting voice, no longer whispering.

Her friend stopped and turned to face her, a deep frown between her thin, blonde eyebrows. Alienor was taken aback by her friend's sudden change of mood and stung by her sharp words.

Casting an apprehensive glance at the surrounding townsfolk, she took hold of Mademoiselle de Lamothe's arm, and they resumed their walk.

"Your engagement with the chevalier is a secret, then?" Alienor whispered.

"Yes, my friend. Promise me that you will keep it so!" Madalena demanded with a stern look on her face.

"I promise, Madeleine... But don't you find all this secrecy odd? Why not announce the engagement at the banquet, like everyone else?"

Alienor knew that she had to be careful. But she had to learn more about their liaison and how it came to pass if she was to succeed in exposing the Chevalier de Montmorency. The fact that their engagement was being kept a secret gave her hope.

"No, it is not odd. We have our reasons. But I do not owe you any explanations, Éléonore! I know very well your bias against my François..." came the sharp reply.

"No, no explanations are needed, dear friend," she hurried to reassure her friend. "My family and the Montmorencys have a history, that is true, but you are my dearest friend. Your joy is my joy, and your sorrow is mine, too! All I need is for you to help me understand so that I may full-heartedly rejoice in your fortune... so that I may see him through your eyes..."

"Oh, if you could only do that, then you would understand how mistaken you and your family are about him and his father!"

The words hurt, but she did not flinch. Her friend was opening up at last, so it was not the time to be petty and proud and cross her.

"But then, please, tell me more about you and the chevalier, Madeleine. How did the two of you meet?" Alienor whispered and stilled her fast-beating heart for the confidences that were to follow.

Her friend looked at her with narrowed eyes and pursed lips for a moment, as if to ascertain the honesty of her request. But then she smiled and started to talk.

There was excitement in her voice, and she struggled to keep it down. Alienor smiled back and listened. If there was something Madalena could not resist, it was to talk about herself and her achievements. And it did not take a scholar to understand that to her, an engagement to the Chevalier de Montmorency was the most brilliant of matches, the crowning achievement coveted by any young lady of marriageable age.

"I first met François quite a long time ago, when he first came to Bordeaux with his father. I was but a little girl then, but he was handsome and dashing in his gilded armour, and he stole my heart at once! He and his father visited us often during their stay in Bordeaux. The Lord of Montmorency and my father worked hard together to restore peace to the devastated city..."

Alienor questioned that notion. She knew that the city had been devastated as a result of the long and bloody siege inflicted by the royal armies led by Anne de Montmorency and the Duke of Guise, who at the time was titled the Duke of Aumale. But she bit her tongue and did not say a word.

"My father's wisdom and talents highly recommended him, and soon, the Lord of Montmorency understood that he was the ideal candidate for the available position of mayor of Bordeaux..."

Alienor fixed her gaze on the path they were walking, lest her face might betray her thoughts. She had heard a different version of the events. The city had no mayor because Anne de Montmorency had executed the previous one — him and about a hundred and forty powerful gentlemen who had protested against the harsh measures inflicted on the city by the king. And Bordeaux had been in shatters, having lost all its privileges, burdened by heavy penalties for having sided with the revolted peasants.

In the beginning, Madalena's father had been one of the members of the council that the constable of France had put together to replace the position of mayor. All of them were men loyal to him and the king, willing to implement their policies of humiliating Bordeaux and Aquitaine. Even the city hall had not escaped the royal wrath. Anne de Montmorency demolished it, as he would have done with most of the city, had it not been for the intervention of one enlightened magistrate by the name of Guillaume le Blanc.

After a couple of years, when the situation had stabilised, François de Lamothe was elected as the new mayor of the city. Thanks to her friend's unintentional confession, Alienor found out the truth at last. The Lamothes owed their fortune to the Montmorencys, as her parents had longed suspected. She understood that it was impossible for her and Madalena to see eye to eye when it came to the bloody events of 1548 and the part played therein by her fiancé and his father. Moreover, it became clear that her friend had been infatuated with the Chevalier de Montmorency for years and had kept it a secret from her all that time.

To slow down the beatings of her racing heart, Alienor looked away and sought solace in admiring the passing of the clouds in the light blue sky. She had to find a way to let her friend know the extent of de Montmorency's crimes. But she knew that Madalena was in no mood to listen to her that day. Her warnings were sure to fall on deaf ears.

Chapter Forty Six
Madame de Montaigne

Bordeaux, Easter Monday,
late in the evening

"Cecy est vn désastre![1] Everything is completely meaningless if..."

Madame de Montaigne was sobbing in an alcove of the dark grey corridor of the palais de l'Ombriere.

"Not only have neither of you received a suitor's token of love, and your sister Jeanne is nowhere to be found!" she told a bewildered and teary Marie de Louppes.

"Ma bien aymée,[2] are you alright? What is the matter?" her husband asked, appearing by her side, together with their eldest son, Michel.

"All this... the banquet, the games of courtly love, everything... has just been in vain. It has led to nothing... Marie is here crying, and Jeanne... well, I do not know where she could possibly be. She has gone missing!"

Once she was done speaking, she sobbed even harder.

"Your niece, Jeanne de Louppes? How can this be? Perhaps

she is outside in the courtyard. There are so many people here tonight, after all... Have you looked for her?" Pierre de Montaigne was starting to get more and more annoyed by the unwelcome interruption. It was time for the official announcement of the new mayor, and his presence was required in the banquet hall.

"I have looked for her everywhere, Father. Together with the Captain of Ségur..." Michel interjected.

"De Ségur?" his father turned to face him in surprise. "What does he have to do with all this?"

"Well... it so happens that his brother Aimery, the Chevalier de Ségur, is also missing..."

"What do you mean the Chevalier de Ségur is missing?" Madame de Montaigne inquired.

A suspicion started to take root. The Count of Montazeau's youngest son was known for his lax behaviour. Her niece was not to be trusted, either.

"Aimery de Ségur? Par Deu, est il icy ce soir mesme?"[3] the Lord of Montaigne wondered and turned towards his wife.

She shook her head in disbelief. "I know nothing of this, mon seigneur..." she said while getting up from the bench with unsteady movements.

Marie rushed to hold her by the arm. Antoinette de Montaigne was all ears. Having spent two weeks observing her nieces from Tholoze[4], she had arrived at the conclusion that Jeanne was not only a great beauty but also a shrewd and ambitious young lady. Her younger sister, on the other hand, was conceited and simple-minded, and had no striking looks to mitigate for those shortcomings either. There was indeed nothing more she could do to find Marie a suitor. She had even chased away the bad-looking Armand de Ségur with her cold snobbery. But perhaps there was still hope for Jeanne...

"It is a long story, monsieur, but he arrived at our house just as we were getting ready to leave for the banquet, taking all of us by surprise. We took him with us in the carriage, so he is here. I told the servants to put his things in the same room with his brother's..." Michel started but was interrupted by his mother, who let out a small cry.

"Oh! You do not suppose that my dearest Jeanne and Aimery de Ségur...?" she said, and then let her words linger, looking Marie de Louppes in the eye.

The image of the handsome Aimery de Ségur and the beautiful Jeanne crammed together in their small carriage had been enough to confirm her apprehensions. Knowing them both, and the irresistible call of youthful passions, Madame de Montaigne did not doubt for a moment that the two of them had become infatuated with each other and had stolen away to some alcove, away from prying eyes. All the possible implications of that unexpected development had to be weighed with care. It was not impossible that something good might yet come out of the entanglement, should there indeed be one. The Ségurs were an excellent family, of impeccable birth and reputation, and with their wealth intact...

"Oh non... Tuct cecy est cert de nous a porter des annuis..."[5] she heard her husband say under his breath, making as if to turn back to the banquet hall.

"Chere tante, please take a seat." Marie tried to coax her into sitting on the stone bench again. But Antoinette de Montaigne waved her away and was, in two steps, by the side of her husband. Taking hold of his arm, she whispered in his ear: "Be careful, dear husband! The last thing we want tonight is a scandal. We need to find them, immediately. Let me take care of it. I will have the Chevalier de Montaigne assist me. You take your place in the great hall by Monsieur de Saint Gelais' side, where you belong."

Her husband made as if to protest, but Madame de Montaigne silenced him. That was not the time for endless negotiations. It was paramount that appearances be kept and that he allowed her to take care of things her own way.

She hissed under her breath: "The announcements must proceed as planned. Do not worry! This whole situation might yet be salvaged, even played to our advantage... If you do not get word from us in time, try to stall the closing of the announcements as much as you can."

"Fort bien.[6] But tread carefully, ma bien aymée. The Count of Montazeau is our neighbour and my old friend, and we will need him by our side, especially in the days to come..." he said, and then hurried back into the banquet hall.

Her husband was right. She had to be very careful. Much was at stake, to be won or to be lost...

"Chevalier," she turned to her eldest son. "Make haste and bring the Captain of Ségur here. We have no time to waste!"

Madame de Montaigne waited until her son had left and then turned towards her niece.

"Marie, venez, chere niece.[7] I am quite shaken. Imagine, your sister Jeanne might be in danger, alone with this gentleman, the Chevalier de Ségur..."

She was startled to hear the youngest Mademoiselle de Louppes burst into laughter, her voice loud and shrill. "I bet the one in danger is this poor fool of a chevalier!"

"Marie, stop this vulgar deportment at once! How can you say such things?" Madame de Montaigne was quick to censure her niece's coarse manners, lest someone else might be watching or listening.

She took a quick glance around to reassure herself. They seemed to be alone in the hallway, except for the guards by the entrance. All the other guests were probably inside the hall, eager to hear the announcement of the new mayor of Bordeaux and of the names written down on the engagement list. They were, after all, the highlight of the Easter festivities.

Through the open doors, she heard the Lord of Montaigne's voice addressing the audience. And to think that she was not even there by her husband's side! Bringing those young ladies and gentlemen together through the game of fin'amor had been her initiative, after all. She should have been in there to enjoy the fruits of her hard labour. Instead, she had to search for her scheming niece and that up-to-no-good chevalier!

But all was not yet lost... If she could turn around that nuisance to work to their advantage and ensure her niece's future, it was well worth missing her husband's speech... At the end of the day, finding suitable husbands for her two nieces from Tholoze was the underlying purpose of those festivities. She took note of Marie's knowing smirk, and a suspicion darted forward.

"My dear Marie?" Madame de Montaigne asked and looked her youngest niece in the eye.

"Yes, dear aunt?" the girl answered, but hurried to look away.

"You know exactly where your sister is, don't you?" Antoinette de Montaigne clasped her fingers around her niece's arm to press her point. She will not be trifled with, not one moment longer... "You are to lead me to them at once!"

Chapter Forty Seven
Alienor

Cambes, mid May

"Chere Madeleine... I have been meaning to ask you something..." Alienor said.

Her voice sounded less confident than she would have wished. It was time to utter the question that she had wanted to ask her friend ever since she had arrived in Cambes. And yet, somehow, almost a week had passed since she and her father had joined the Lamothes at their summer estate. Contrary to her expectations, besides their little detour after church on Sunday, she and Madalena had had very little time to speak in private. Indoors, they found themselves constantly in the company of Madame de Lamothe, or Madalena's little sister Anne, whom everyone still affectionately called Anaïs. And while outside, they kept bumping into their fathers, who spent their days in the gardens, making plans, since the Lamothes had hired a Piedmontese architect to come and lay out their plants and bushes in the Italian style. So Alienor had had no opportunity yet to discuss the delicate subject of the Chevalier de Ségur's engagement. And then there was, of course, the weight of Madalena's own confession, which still hung heavy between them.

She was left with the impression that her friend was almost avoiding her. But then, one afternoon, while they were all seated at the dinner table, in silence, Alienor felt filled with resolution and spoke up. After some general comment on the pleasant weather, she had requested for she and Madalena to be allowed to take an evening stroll by the banks of the Garonne on the pretext that she looked forward to the opportunity to admire them from up close. Neither her father nor Madalena's parents had seen any harm in granting her that innocent request, provided they returned to the manor before nightfall. Madalena, most likely taken by surprise and unable to come up with a good excuse, was obliged to smile and declare that it was a wonderful idea.

After dinner, they had put on their capes and hoods and left the manor. Madalena's maid followed them at a distance. They walked on a narrow path that ran along the river bank. Tall, lush grass and bushes in full bloom surrounded them on both sides. Alienor stole a quick look at her friend. She saw her frown in apprehension when she heard her request.

"Madeleine, I assure you, this is not regarding your secret engagement," she hurried to put her apprehensions at ease. "It is rather concerning me and, well, the connection that I had hoped to form..." she allowed her words to trail off, hoping her friend would catch her meaning.

She had planned that moment for many days, yet she seemed unable to gather herself enough to say the words out loud without blushing.

"What could you possibly mean, dear Éléonore?" Madalena asked.

"What I meant to say, Madeleine, was that I wondered if you have learned all the names written down on the engagement list, the one that was read at the Easter banquet in Bordeaux?"

To that, Madalena answered with enthusiasm. She relished being consulted on such matters. "Yes, of course. The whole of

Bordeaux talked about nothing else for weeks on end! Everyone was eager to discuss the interesting alliances forged by Madame de Montaigne's game of fin'amor... Why, even the servants..."

"Yes, of course. But you see... word has not reached us at Rauzan yet, and... that evening at the banquet, during the announcements themselves... well... there were so many guests in the hall and the air was so warm. So we had to accompany my mother outside for a breath of fresh air, and we missed the last couple of announcements..." Alienor hurried to explain.

She knew she was distorting the truth, and that it was a sin. But her mother and the Lord were sure to forgive her, given the circumstances. And truth be told, she had no wish to disclose too much of what had happened that night to Madalena de Lamothe, who was the biggest gossip she had ever met.

"I understand. Rauzan is so dreadfully far away in the countryside... But then you must have missed the most interesting announcements of them all!" she heard her friend exclaim, obviously elated by the opportunity to reveal important information to her unknowing friend. "One of the names on the announcements list was that of Jeanne de Louppes, none other than Madame de Montaigne's niece! Everyone we know in Bordeaux was quite in agreement that the former lady mayor's main purpose in organising that game of courtly love was to marry off her penniless nieces, so you can imagine how delighted the lady was when that announcement was made!"

"And what was the name of her suitor?" Alienor asked, at long last, her question. She fought to push out every single word. Her throat ached and her mouth seemed to be filled with pebbles. The weight of every syllable felt painful on her tongue.

"Oh, yes. It came as a great surprise to all of us, I can assure you! My dear Éléonore, you will never guess who..." Madalena started as if reciting a poem learned by heart, but then stopped.

Alienor knew her friend well enough to understand that it was a rehearsed discourse that Mademoiselle de Lamothe had delivered countless times before, when telling and retelling the events of that day to her friends and acquaintances in Bordeaux. It was obvious that she enjoyed uttering every single snippet of it, despite the repetition.

"But wait, of course, you must already know this…" Madalena said all of a sudden.

Alienor was surprised to see her friend stop in her tracks and stare at her as if seeing her for the first time. Forced to come to a halt by their joined arms, Mademoiselle de Durfort closed her eyes for a fleeting moment. She felt the kind sun of May on her face, and she prayed the Lord to give her the strength to bear the final confirmation of her worst fears.

"Why would I know, dear Madeleine? As I said, I had to accompany my mother outside, and we missed the last announcements…"

"But surely, you must have learned of this later on, from your… Wait! You do not mean to tell me you even missed the…"

"Please, Madeleine, just tell me. We all missed the announce-ments…" Alienor urged, feeling that she was about to lose her patience and willing her voice to remain calm and not betray her turmoil. "Who is the man who asked for the hand of Jeanne de Louppes?" she asked, facing her friend.

Madalena looked as if she had been turned to stone on the spot, her fingers clasped around Alienor's lower arm, holding her tightly.

For a few more moments, she seemed unable to either take another step forward or utter a sound. Alienor stared at her in sheer incomprehension. They stood in the middle of the green pasture covering the riverbanks, looking at each other, eyes wide open, as they both struggled to grasp the meaning behind each other's words. The maid, whose name was Manon, had also stopped in her tracks. Alienor saw, from the corner of her eye, that she had started to pick wildflowers while casting a curious glance at them now and then.

At last, Mademoiselle de Lamothe answered: "It was the Chevalier de Ségur. The third son of the Count of Montazeau…"

The third son? Was Armand de Ségur not the second son? Had her uncle been mistaken when he had told her about him and his family? Well, the second son, the third son, what difference did it make in the end? It was a minor detail and an easy enough mistake to make, especially for a brilliant man of arms, who must have had much more important matters on his mind. And Alienor knew that sons, even children in general, were only separated into the eldest and then the rest of them. It made no difference whether one was the second or the third son. They were not going to inherit their father's lands or title, regardless. It all fell to the eldest son. For those who had no surviving sons, a daughter could inherit. And then again, it was the eldest daughter who inherited everything. That was the case with Alienor and her sisters. Since their brothers were long dead, Elisea was to inherit one day all of their father's lands, whilst she, Catarina and Elina were to be left with nothing. Other second or third daughters could, at least, count on receiving a dowry when they married. They did not. The truth was that Alienor had nothing to her name. And it could very well be that Madame de Montaigne's game of fin'amor had been hers and Catarina's only chance at finding suitable husbands...

"Are you sure it was the third son and not the second? And do you know his Christian name?" Alienor asked, swallowing hard.

She had thought of the chevalier's name. If her friend knew the chevalier's Christian name, that could cast an unequivocal light on the matter. After all, Catarina thought that if Alienor had waited a little longer for the Chevalier de Ségur to speak his mind, he might have revealed his intentions more clearly and even offered her his token the last time they had exchanged words in the stone courtyard of the Ombriere Palace. And then she remembered, of course, Armand de Ségur's own words. He had, in fact, declared that he had chosen her, high up on the tower's rooftop, right before the Chevalier de Montaigne had interrupted them...

"But, my dear Éléonore, the second son... You must be saying this in jest, surely?" Madalena exclaimed and then burst into laughter.

Alienor stared at her friend, bewildered, not knowing what to say. She was hurt that her friend made merry of her misfortune. She cast an apprehensive glance at the maidservant and started to walk once more, hoping that her friend would follow and stop laughing.

"Oh no, Madeleine, I assure you... There is no jest! Do you know the Christian name of this Chevalier de Ségur, who is to marry Mademoiselle de Louppes?" she said, once her friend had caught up with her.

"No, but you must know it!" Mademoiselle de Lamothe laughed even harder.

Alienor hurried to put a finger to her lips and cast a suggestive glance at Manon, who was trailing behind them. At the same time, she felt her heart sink. Did Madalena know about her and the Chevalier de Ségur? And even if she did, why was her friend laughing at her like that? She was feeling more and more uncomfortable. It had decidedly not been the best course of action. She had allowed her curiosity to expose her to ridicule. Her friend's merriment hurt. But she had to admit that she did know his Christian name, after all...

"Yes..." she whispered with tears pooling at the corners of her eyes. "Armand..." His name burned her lips, and she felt a shot of pain pierce her chest.

Alienor turned around and started to walk back towards the Lamothes' manor.

Chapter Forty Eight
Armand

Bordeaux, Easter Monday,
late in the evening

"Mademoiselle de Durfort, I have been looking for you. The announcements..."

Armand had found her at last in the stone courtyard of the palace. She had two ladies with her, and he assumed they must have been her mother and sister.

"Madame, mademoiselle," he said and bowed before them.

"Monsieur, as you must be aware, we have not been introduced yet..." he heard the older lady interject.

He was not sure why, but she sounded offended. Éléonore de Durfort stepped forward and made the requested introductions. Her sister and her mother curtsied, and he bowed to them in deference, as the etiquette required.

"Madame, I know this will sound like a very surprising request, given the fact that we have just met, but may I be allowed to talk to your daughter in confidence for a moment? We will be just a few steps away, within sight..." he said.

"Chevalier, this is a most peculiar request. I cannot possibly..." Madame de Civrac replied.

Armand was stunned. He could not understand their reserved, almost hostile attitude. Not knowing what else to do, he kept looking from mother to daughter and back in an attempt to decipher the cause of that unexpected change of heart.

"Madame, mademoiselle, I see you are not pleased with the announcements... I should have... Of course, I should have spoken to you, mademoiselle, beforehand, but circumstances beyond my power prevented me from it. I most humbly request just a few moments of your time now, so we may talk alone," he pressed on, turning towards the young lady whom he had intended to marry.

In truth, Armand felt he was about to lose his patience. Nothing seemed to proceed as planned that evening. And what a bewildering, long day it had been! He could not understand why Mademoiselle de Durfort had not hurried to agree to his suggestion so that they might talk undisturbed, at last. She stared at him in silence. And to think that it had been impossible to stop her from talking during the entire duration of the medieval games that very morning...

"Very well, monsieur, I will listen to you. But only for a moment," she said and then reassured her mother before she started walking towards a corner of the stone courtyard.

Armand hurried after her. He did not know what to make of that sudden change of heart. He looked at her and saw that her hands, folded neatly in front of her, were slightly trembling.

"Are you feeling well, my lady?" he asked.

"Yes, my lord," came her curt reply.

Mademoiselle de Durfort's attitude and sharp words did not bode well. She was not the lively, candid young girl whom he got to know earlier that day. Her silence and glares were disconcerting, and everything pointed towards the fact that she did not want to talk to him anymore. Indeed, she seemed upset. The lady's response was the exact opposite of what he had expected. Armand felt at a loss for words. Perhaps he had been utterly mistaken about her true intentions...

He looked at her transfixed, noticing her lovely neck and cheeks had a deep, rosy hue. There was defiance, even a hint of hostility in her lifted chin and frowning eyebrows. All of a sudden, a tear shimmered from the corner of her eye. And then it dawned on him. Some misunderstanding must have come between them... something to do, no doubt, with that buffoon, Aimery's meddling! Armand did not even know where to begin...

"Mademoiselle Éléonore... it is true that I did not give you my ribbon before the announcements, but please believe that my intentions..." he said and reached out his hand.

He moved without thinking, as if his hand sprung forward of its own volition. His limbs sometimes did that when he was at an utter loss for words, and he was not quite sure what to do with them. Though, truth be told, before that day, his hands had never been so bold as to reach out towards a lady in that manner...

Mademoiselle de Durfort took a step back, out of his reach. Then, with quick movements, she curtsied. "A Deu, monsieur," she said in a low voice, and hurried towards the hall's entrance.

He caught a fleeting glimpse of a single tear falling down her cheek as she passed him by.

Armand flinched. He could not understand why she was rejecting him in such a rude manner after having encouraged him all day long. He thought that he had done the right thing, but neither the lady nor her mother had seemed pleased with the announcements. It was all very confusing...

From the corner of his eye, he saw Madame de Civrac and her other daughter send a hurried curtsy in his direction before following in Éléonore de Durfort's footsteps. Together, the ladies rushed towards the banquet hall.

A thought crossed Armand's mind that he ought to spring into action, run after the lady, and seek clarification before it was too late. Yet he was rooted to the pavement he was standing on, unable to say a word or move a limb... That fact baffled him even more. He was, after all, a man of arms, a captain in the king's army, a knight of swift and deadly actions on the battlefield.

As if through a curtain of mist, the scenes they had shared during the course of the day played before his eyes. He watched them as if from a distance, like when he was a boy, and he would sneak away to catch a glimpse of the gipsies' puppet show at the fair in Montazeau. Armand had been persuaded that Mademoiselle de Durfort had taken a genuine interest in his person and that she had wanted to tie her destiny to his in that game of Madame de Montaigne's... Otherwise, he would not have asked Monsieur de Montaigne to put their names down on the engagement list, right below those of Aimery and Jeanne de Louppes!

He squeezed his hands into fists as he thought of the momentous debacle his younger brother had created that evening. Not only had he crossed their parents' wishes, running away from Mortemart to attend the banquet unannounced, but he had managed to get himself entangled with Madame de Montaigne's niece. The memory of the compromising situation in which he had found them, embraced in a secluded alcove of the palace, flashed before his eyes. As luck had it, they had managed to make themselves presentable again by the time Madame de Montaigne and the Count of Montazeau arrived at the scene. Jeanne de Louppes had already fastened her red token to his brother's arm and maintained that he had asked for her hand in marriage first. Despite Aimery's protests, their father had to agree to an engagement. It had been, after all, the only honourable thing to do under those circumstances...

But Armand had to concede that Éléonore de Durfort had never agreed to marry him. He had been hindered in his plans to discuss his intentions with her in private by the Chevalier de Montaigne's interruptions and Aimery's foolish behaviour. Pressed for time, he had had to take that decision by himself and announce it to the Lord and Lady of Montaigne at the last moment. He remembered locking eyes with Mademoiselle de Durfort across the hall right before he had done so, and he thought he had discerned a sign of consent in the way she had looked back at him, in her nod. But it turned out he had been wrong all along. However hurtful to his feelings and self-worth, Armand had to admit that the most plausible explanation was that Mademoiselle de Durfort had changed her mind about their engagement. Perhaps, having hurried to give away her token all too early that morning, she had later in the evening secured the affections of a more dashing and well-connected gentleman. Images of her and the Captain of Monluc dancing together and moving through the hall arm in arm came to his mind...

The Chevalier de Ségur cast one last, dejected glance towards the three ladies, who had by then reached the palace doors. The lady he had hoped to make his wife stepped inside without as much as throwing a final glance in his direction. The lady's sister, on the other hand, turned and stared at him in a most peculiar manner.

Just then, Armand noticed that the object previously secured in his fist had vanished. He must have dropped it when he had relaxed his fists again, but the ribbon was nowhere to be seen on the dirty stones of the courtyard. He tilted his head back and looked at the sky above him. The moon cast but a dim light at that late hour, and the flames of the torches in the courtyard made it hard for him to see. But it appeared that a gust of wind had blown away the long piece of fabric from his grip, which he had intended to tie to Mademoiselle de Durfort's arm. It was almost imperceptible against the darkness of the night sky, and he had to squint to follow its elegant flight... over the rooftops of the palace... over its high walls... over the houses of the hundreds of people calling Bordeaux their home... far away towards the river... far away from them both... forever lost.

Chapter Forty Nine
Alienor

Cambes, mid May

"No, but you must know it!" Madalena de Lamothe exclaimed, referring to the Chevalier de Ségur who had become engaged to the mayor's niece.

"Yes..." Alienor whispered with tears pooling at the corners of her eyes. "Armand..."

She turned around and started to walk back towards the manor.

"Armand? No, I don't think so..." she heard Madalena say after a while, catching up with her.

There was still a tint of merriment to her friend's voice. Alienor resented Mademoiselle de Lamothe for making fun of her and continued to walk away from her.

"Manon, please go ahead and inform my mother that we are on our way back and will join her shortly!" Mademoiselle de Lamothe said.

The maid cast a long, inquisitive glance as she ran past

Alienor. There was concern, even unbridled curiosity in it. Alienor turned away to hide her tears.

"Éléonore, wait!" Madalena cried.

She ran after Alienor and took hold of her hand. She was out of breath but kept a firm grip of her friend's arm despite the latter's attempts to free her arm. Once Manon was out of earshot, Mademoiselle de Lamothe said: "Dear friend, I am now persuaded you are not talking in jest. But why are you crying?"

Mademoiselle de Durfort could no longer keep the pretence. "Well... remember when I told you at the banquet in Bordeaux that I had given away my token? As it turned out, I had given it to the Chevalier de Ségur..."

"Yes. To Armand, the Chevalier de Ségur, is it not so?" Madalena asked, with an emphasis on the word "Armand".

"Yes," came her whispered reply. "But you see... he never gave me his token! Although we danced and we talked, and we took a stroll together high up on the fortress' tower... Most of all, he had promised me... You see, Madeleine, he told me that he had chosen me!"

Alienor stifled a sob. She tried to free her hand, but her friend's grasp was strong.

Tears were streaming down her cheeks. She did not know how to stop them from falling. They felt wet and cold. The breeze blowing from the Garonne was growing stronger and stronger.

"He did not... give you his token?" she asked, taken aback, letting go of Alienor's arm. "I don't understand..."

"Well, what is there to understand, after all? Other than that he gave me false promises, which he had no intention to keep! In the end, he did not choose me. He chose Mademoiselle de Louppes... And now, they are engaged to be married..."

"But, my dear friend... You are mistaken. He did choose you! Oh dear, this is all so confusing... But please, Éléonore, stop crying. And please, listen to me!"

Madalena took a step closer and slowly wiped away the tears from her friend's face as she spoke.

"Jeanne de Louppes is engaged to be married with the Chevalier de Ségur, the third son of the Count de Ségur! His Christian name escapes me now... it started with an 'A'..."

"Armand! Armand de Ségur..." Alienor persisted, pushing away her friend's hand.

She felt a new wave of tears coming. Madalena was just repeating herself, and her words made no sense. In truth, Alienor did not recognise her childhood friend anymore. Given the strained conversation they had had last Sunday, the cat-and-mouse game she had played with her all week and the strange manner in which she was reacting to her questions that evening, it was impossible to deny that Mademoiselle de Lamothe was a changed person. She was cold and distant, like a stranger who appeared to rejoice in Alienor's misfortune.

"No, no, no... Listen to me!" she heard Madalena protest. "His name was not Armand, of that I am sure!"

"What do you mean his name was not Armand?"

"Aimery! The other chevalier de Ségur's name was Aimery. The one who is engaged to Mademoiselle de Louppes..."

"Aimery? You must be mistaken!" Alienor exclaimed, stunned.

"No, not at all! Because you see... there were two chevaliers de Ségur at the Easter banquet, and both their names stood on the engagement list! You truly did not know of this, my friend?"

Alienor felt her heart beat faster and faster. When she spoke, her voice was a mere whisper, choked with emotion: "Deux... cheualiers de Ségur? Non, ie ne le sauois poinct..."[1]

Was it possible that it all had been a simple misunderstanding? Like Catarina had suspected all along? Was it possible that Armand de Ségur had a brother with him at the banquet? And that it was his brother, that Aimery de Ségur's name had been written on the list next to that of Mademoiselle de Louppes? But then that would mean that...

"Éléonore, this is bewildering... almost impossible to believe! That you would not know of your own... But are you quite certain, dear friend, that this is not a trick you are playing on me for a good laugh?" Madalena accompanied her words with an even more intense stare.

"Madeleine, I assure you! I would never make merry of such a grave and painful subject... Do not keep me in suspense. I entreat you! If you know something more about Armand de Ségur, please say it..."

Her friend spoke slowly and clearly, almost as if she was talking to a child.

"It was the third son of the Count of Montazeau, Aimery de Ségur, who got engaged to the niece of Madame de Montaigne! The count's second son, Armand de Ségur, also got engaged that evening. His name was on the list next to... well..." she paused as if she was afraid to proceed with her revelation.

Alienor pressed her hands to her chest in an attempt to quiet down the palpitations of her heart. She held her breath as she expected her friend to say that he, too, had entered an engagement with the other niece of Madame de Montaigne. If she was not mistaken, there had been two of them present that evening. Well, two brothers and two sisters... it was not unheard of, after all. And it did not make any difference to her, one way or the other. She let out the breath she had been holding. Mademoiselle de Durfort realised her friend looked at her as though she were waiting for her to fill in the name of the lady...

"The name of Mademoiselle de Louppes, the mayor's other niece..." Alienor said.

"No!" her friend exclaimed, cutting her short, with an angry tone of voice. "To the name Éléonore de Durfort de Civrac!"

Alienor stared at her friend, unable to believe her ears.

"Your name!" Madalena said, more gently.

Alienor knew that was her name, but she could not understand why Mademoiselle de Lamothe was repeating it. What did she have to do with it all? But after thinking it over, a suspicion arose.

"Madeleine," she said, almost collapsing in her friend's arms. "What did you just say?"

"But, my dear Éléonore, Armand de Ségur is engaged to you! Your name was read out loud at the Easter banquet by the Lord of Montaigne... I heard it with my own ears. And then I saw it, too, when I came in possession of a copy of the engagement list that had been circulated in Bordeaux after the banquet. You are engaged! How can you not know it? All this time... How is it possible?"

"I am engaged?" Alienor said, at last.

"Yes, Éléonore. And I congratulated you, and my parents did too, the morning after the banquet, remember? And then upon your arrival in Cambes last week..."

"Oh, Madeleine... I thought you were congratulating us for Elisea's sake, for her engagement with the Chevalier de Rémy..." she tried to offer an explanation.

"Well, but regardless, your names stood on the list. You are engaged to be married, just like me!"

Alienor laughed out loud in disbelief. Madalena's face was grave, and she appeared to tell the truth. Alienor felt her stomach jolt into a knot as she thought of the Chevalier de Ségur... He had put their names on the list, after all! He had chosen her... All that while, she had suffered in vain when Armand de Ségur's intentions had, in fact, been honourable, and he had truly wanted to marry her...

Mademoiselle de Durfort turned her head and stared at the horizon. Somewhere far away, to the north, over the green pastures of the land between two rivers, on the opposite shore of the Dordogne River, at Montazeau, Armand de Ségur was waiting for a sign from her...

"He did not give me his ribbon at the banquet, you see... and I assumed... Then I left the hall in a hurry with my family... so we did not hear the last announcements. I find it hard to believe... But then everyone else knew! Oh, and all this time, we thought that the congratulations which had poured in from friends and family, congratulations which mentioned the 'daughters' of my parents were just simple slips of the hand or of the tongue... Oh, the Chevalier de Ségur did try to tell me, didn't he? Catarina thought as much... But he was behaving so strangely when we last spoke, and I just assumed he wanted to take his farewell. And I was... I was absolutely cruel and terrible to him! Oh, Madeleine, I must make amends..." Alienor spoke very fast; her words interrupted by sobs and bouts of nervous laughter. She realised she probably made no sense whatsoever to her friend, who stared at her in disbelief.

"Dearest Éléonore, we must take you home at once! You need to compose yourself. I admit this is most surprising, but I am sure it is nothing that cannot be set right in due time... The Chevalier Armand de Ségur chose you, and you chose him, didn't you? And you are now engaged! Even if you didn't know it, the whole of Aquitaine did. You should be glad and utterly happy!"

Alienor detected a hint of envious longing in her friend's voice. She straightened her body and stood on her own. The irony of their situations did not escape her. All that time, she had been publicly engaged, although she had not known it herself. Madalena, on the other hand, knew she was engaged but could not celebrate nor share that secret with the world. Knowing her friend, it must have felt like torture.

"Come along now, Éléonore! Let us go back. You need to talk to your father..." Mademoiselle de Lamothe said.

And right there and then, as she entwined her arm with her friend's and allowed her to drag her back towards the manor, Alienor knew what she had to do. She had to find a way to warn her friend about François de Montmorency's true character. Her friend had restored her happiness. She had to help protect hers... even if that meant revisiting the past and disclosing the painful truth behind her family's fall from grace. But first, she had to make sure that her name had indeed stood on Madame de Montaigne's engagement list. And she had to write to Armand de Ségur and apologise...

Oh, cheualier... Ound vous vous en trouuez... attendez moy![2] she thought as she cast a long glance to the north towards le pays de Peyragort.[3]

The sun was setting, and its gentle colours tainted the whiteness of the clouds. The two young ladies hurried to regain the manor. At their side, the placid waters of the Garonne were shimmering under the fading sunlight. The great river pursued its path unrushed, as was its nature, towards the vastness of the sea, oblivious to the joys and sorrows of the human heart.

Fourth Part

Seed of Revolt

A Letter from Éléonore de Durfort to Armand de Ségur

Rauzan, le 31 may de l'Année de Deu 1556[1]

Fort estimé Cheualier de Ségur,

I hope this letter finds you and your family in good health. It may seem too daring a venture to write to you, given the less than excellent terms on which we parted ways at the Easter Banquet in Bordeaux. But I am afraid a terrible misunderstanding occurred that evening and I do not wish to waste any more time in attempting to dispel it and explain myself. Please allow me, my lord, to atone for my brusque manners, for my impatience, for walking away from you that evening. I know it might prove difficult to believe, but I did not know until recently that you had written down our names on Madame de Montaigne's list of engagements. I am to blame. I was too hasty in my actions, too disappointed, too heartbroken to think clearly and to seek confirmation for my thoughtless assumption that you had become engaged to Mademoiselle de Louppes at the Easter banquet in Bordeaux. I know now that it was not you, my lord, but your brother, the chevalier Aimery de Ségur, who had written down his name next to that of Mademoiselle de Louppes on the engagement list. As embarrassing as that may be, I have no choice but to admit that I all but fainted and had to be carried out of the hall when their names were read out loud. I therefore missed the announcement that followed, which had my name next to yours, my lord. All I could think of was that you had not given your ribbon to me, but to another... I felt so hurt that I later denied you the chance to clarify your intentions.

How foolish you must think me! And with good reason. But I know better now. I know your intentions were true. As were mine. As they are still... The bans have never been read for us, so we are not truly engaged, as I am told. But perhaps there is still a chance to remedy that? Forgive me for being so forward, but I feel I must make up for lost time and avoid further confusion. I shall therefore speak plainly, my lord. I chose you in the game of fin'amor on Easter Monday, and I choose you still today. If you would still consider it, if my silence, my coldness, my foolishness have not entirely dissuaded you from it, I would very much like to tie my destiny to yours!

I include an invitation for you and your family to join us at Rauzan in a few weeks' time for my eldest sister, Mademoiselle de Civrac's wedding. I sincerely hope you will come, my lord, so that I may ask for your forgiveness and receive your answer in person.

May the Lord watch over you and your family. I remain yours faithfully,

Éléonore de Durfort de Civrac

A l'attention du

Seigneur de Ségur a Montazeau

Le Baron et la Baronne de Civrac

schaident que vous et vostre famille les honnorerez

a vec vostre présence a

Rauzan le 25 de iuine 1556.

pur fester en semble le mariage de leur fille aisnée.

Élisabeth de Durfort, Demoiselle de Civrac

et

Louis de Rémy, Cheualier de Rémy

To the attention of

the Lord of Ségur at Montazeau:

The Baronet and the Baroness of Civrac

wish for you and your family to honour them

with your presence at

Rauzan on the 25th of June 1556 to

celebrate the wedding of their eldest daughter,

Élisabeth de Durfort, Mademoiselle de Civrac

and

Louis de Rémy, Chevalier de Rémy

A Letter From Éléonore de Durfort
To Madeleine de Lamothe

Rauzan, le 3 iuine de l'Année de Deu 1556

Ma chere Madeleine,

Many days have passed since I took my farewells from you and your family in Cambes. Yet, it seems like it was only yesterday that we walked together by the Garonne River and I, at long last, uncovered the truth about what had come to pass at the Easter Banquet in Bordeaux. I know I promised to write soon, but there has been so much to do since my return. As you might imagine, dear friend, we all had to come to terms with the surprising revelation of my engagement. Needless to say, it was soon established that none of us had been in the hall during that fateful last announcement. This explains why our entire family has been oblivious to the truth until you were so kind as to point it out during my last visit. My dear mother was quite beside herself when it was revealed that we had to thank my sister Élisabeth's penchant for mischief for her, my father's and the entire de Rémy family's absence. Having decided that it was the right place and time to play a game of hide and seek with her betrothed Louis de Rémy, she had succeeded in getting herself locked up in the wine cellar. It had all turned out well in the end, when the Rémys alerted the servants and Élisabeth was freed from her brief, self-induced captivity. But this distraction ensured that none of them were present in the great hall of the Ombriere Palace when my name was read out loud that evening.

I am therefore ever so grateful to you, dear Madeleine, and to your family. Without your help, there is no telling how long it would have taken me to learn that the Chevalier de Ségur had written down our names on the engagement list at Madame de Montaigne's magnificent banquet! I might have wasted even more precious time and delayed, perhaps even crushed, the possibility of rectifying this misunderstanding. In truth, I cannot help but feel sorry for the poor chevalier. He must think that I rejected his proposal. Oh, my dear, if you only had an inkling of the rebukes I torture myself with, over and over again, most of all on the subject of the dismissive manner in which I took my farewell from him!

I also keep asking myself whether I am truly engaged to the Chevalier de Ségur... You understand, no doubt, how all this fails to ring true to me on most days, despite having conducted thorough inquiries into the matter since we last met. The engagement was announced with due pomp at the banquet. This much has been established. Yet, at the same time, the church has not been informed of our engagement and the bans are not being read for us, as is customary! My dear Madeleine, I pray that you will not think ill of us for seeking confirmation of the news from other parties. We trust and cherish yours and your parents' testimony on the subject, but we had to cast an irrevocable light on the matter. My mother, therefore, wrote to the very lady who had orchestrated the game of courtly love, Madame de Montaigne, the safe-keeper of the list. How great must have been her surprise upon receiving my mother's unusual inquiry! But Madame de Montaigne was gracious enough to answer my mother's letter and confirm once and for all that my name was indeed on the engagement list, right next to that of the chevalier Armand de Ségur's. Her letter was amicable and dignified, and she was even so kind as to express her joy that our families will soon be related, since her niece, Jeanne de Louppes, is to marry the other son of the Count of Montazeau, the Chevalier Aimery de Ségur.

But, to return to my conundrum, there remains the question of the bans. Upon seeking the wise counsel of Father Arnaud Jaubert de Barrault, who is the shepherd of our Catholic parish at Rauzan, it has become apparent that we are not engaged in the eyes of Our Lord. No bans could have been read on our behalf either here or elsewhere since it appears that the spouses need to visit the priest of their choice together in order to confirm their intentions to marry. What the chevalier's intentions are at this point, I cannot possibly dare to speculate upon, not anymore...

Oh, dearest Madeleine, you cannot even begin to comprehend how deeply I regret my thoughtless behaviour at the banquet, and all the confusion that it has brought along with it! I find myself deeply ashamed of my conduct and my inability to overcome my emotions that night. If only I had shown more kindness and patience to the Chevalier de Ségur when I last saw him! Then he might have given me his token and I would have known, without a doubt, that his intentions were true... But in order to rectify my mistakes, I need to try to put the past behind. I must confess that I have spent many a sleepless night thinking of a way to meet with him as soon as possible, but we all failed to find an honourable excuse to do so. My parents were adamant that travelling to Montazeau uninvited, even in their company, would be an unthinkable faux pas. Since too much time had already been wasted, it was settled with my mother that sending a letter was the fastest way to seek reconciliation. I shudder to confess, dear Madeleine, how much paper and ink I have wasted in penning that letter! I could not stop thinking that those were to be the very first words written by my hand on which he will ever set eyes... But I had to make haste, and so I did my best to keep an elegant yet warm tone throughout the letter, reassuring him of my constancy. The letter left Rauzan some two days past and I dare say it must have already reached the chevalier by now, if he is at Montazeau. I do not even dare imagine what the chevalier might think upon receiving my apology! Will he be glad to hear from me and to know that my intentions remain unchanged, my apprehensions at the banquet misconstrued? Or had he already made peace with the fact that I had all but officially rejected his proposal, and he has, therefore, no intention of marrying me anymore? Waiting for his answer proves most unbearable, but I must brave the consequences of my impetuous deeds!

On a more joyful note, my family and I are in the midst of feverish preparations for my sister Élisabeth's wedding. The wedding is to take place in a couple of weeks' time, after the Feast of Saint John the Baptist. My mother reminds me to make quite sure that your family receives the invitation which I attach to this letter, and to convey our hopes that you shall join us at Rauzan for the wedding feast. If you come, you shall have the opportunity to bear witness to the Chevalier de Ségur's answer with your own eyes! After much vacillation, my parents agreed that, however extraordinary the circumstances of our engagement, it would be most indelicate to not invite the family of my potential suitor to the wedding. So I included an invitation in the letter I sent him. If he comes, his presence will be answer enough for me. I pray there will still be a future for us, but I am too afraid to hope anymore. So, whilst I am truly happy for my sister, who seems to be beside herself with joy and anticipation, I must confess, dear friend, that I dread the day of the wedding as much as I long for it. I shall have clarity. I shall have my answer. But there is no telling what that might turn out to be.

This letter has already become very long. And all I did was prattle incessantly about my own circumstances. How is your dear family? Please be sure to convey my deepest gratitude to your parents for making my and my father's stay at Cambes so pleasant and comfortable. We deeply regret the hasty manner of our departure! I do hope you all find yourself in good health and in good spirits.

I long to hear of your news! Have you heard from our... mutual acquaintance in Paris? I know that when we last spoke of this, you had been disappointed in my reaction. But I want to reassure you that you continue to be my dearest friend, and that I want nothing more than for you to be very, very happy. I know I have already briefly shared with you my concerns about this person's character, although they were not agreeable to you at the time. But I do hope that you will allow for a more detailed explanation, one that will shed better light on the character of those involved and the source of the enmity between our families.

I have asked my beloved sister, Catherine, to share with you her memories of the tragic events that came to pass eight years ago. I do this in the hope that Catherine's letter will show a more impartial and detailed recollection of the circumstances which led to the change in our family's fortunes. It is also my hope that you listen to her story with patience and a generous, open heart, however painful it will prove for you to read it. Dear Madeleine, you deserve to know the truth about the character of the person you have decided to entrust with your happiness! Truth be told, neither my sister nor I stand to gain anything by spreading unjust rumours about such illustrious and powerful members of the Court. We merely seek to relate, with honesty, the facts as we saw them happen. Please rest assured that this will be no easy task for my poor sister, for it will force her to face the ghosts from our past and the questionable choices we all made during the revolt! But we both felt you should know the truth, however unkind to our own family's reputation, because your very happiness may depend upon it. We trust you will draw your own conclusions and that your love for us will prove as strong as our love for you, so that you may keep our family secrets to yourself. You must understand, just like we do, that spreading them will most likely ruin mine and my sisters' future!

Ie reste iusques a mon dernier souspir la vostre amye la plus deuotée, quy ne désire rien de plus que vostre félicité,[1]

Éléonore de Durfort de Civrac

First Letter From Catherine de Durfort
To Madeleine de Lamothe

Rauzan, le 3 iuine de l'Année de Deu 1556

Chere Madeleine,

Ie vous pry d'escuser l'audace que ie prends en vous escrire cete longue lettre, gratie aux supplications de ma bien aymée seur, Éléonore, dont vous estes vne bonne et estimée amye. Vous serez sans doubte fort sorprise en la receuant et peut estre mesme escandalisée en la lisant. Nous n'auons iamais iuy ensemble du dous lien d'amytié que vous compartez a vec ma seur. A la mesme fois, nous nous cognoyssons dépuis l'infance et ie doys vous auouer que ie pense a vous comme on pense a vne seur. l'espere que vous aussy, vous purrez, en lisant cete lettere, penser a moy comme a vne grande seur quy ne veult que vostre bien. C'est pour cecy que ie me permets de vous offrire mon testmoignage de la tragique histoire de nostre famille, en confiant a vous et au Bon Deu le pouoir de passer iudgement sur la conduicte des illustres personnages qu'on y nomme.[1]

I beseech you to not think ill of my sister, dear Madeleine, for she has not broken your trust. Everything I know about your relation with this common acquaintance of ours is what I have seen with my own eyes. Like everyone else present at the Galien Palace that day, I, too, saw you attach your token of fin'amor to a certain chevalier's arm during the Easter tournament. Later that night, I

303

spotted you speaking to him in private, in a corner of the Ombriere Palace's courtyard, together with my sister, Élisabeth. So I cannot claim to know how deep or shallow your acquaintance with this person is, and I assure you that Éléonore refuses to shed any additional light on the matter. My sister is concerned for your wellbeing, as am I, and she asked me to write to you about our family's past and the part that our mutual acquaintance has played therein. After much consideration, I have agreed to be the one to do it, although I know this endeavour will be a strenuous one. But I share my sister's belief that by recounting the events that had changed our fortunes, the true nature of this person's character shall be revealed. And you, dear friend, deserve to know the whole truth, before it might be too late...

I imagine that you must be quite unfamiliar with the sad circumstances which had led to the enmity between our families. I will, therefore, endeavour to do my best to relate the facts as they happened or as I remember them to have happened. You will soon come to the realisation, dear friend, if I may be allowed to call you thus, that this is in no way an easy undertaking for me. But I shall try my best to strike a fair and unbiased tone.

It all started, as you may know, with the king's decree on increasing, yet again, the tax on salt in the year of the Lord 1541. As I understand it, in our province, discontentment had been brewing for a while, ever since Aquitaine had passed on to the Kingdom of France some hundred years ago, and had been burdened with several other tax increases throughout the years since. I was told that this new tax increase proved to be especially unbearable for, alas, the peasants and the poor, who already had very little to their names. The higher tax on salt was perhaps the last drop for many.

In any event, discontentment increased over the next months, fuelled by the general resentment towards the central government in Paris. Other political circumstances might have influenced these developments, but I am, as you know, merely the daughter of a country baronet, and I have little understanding of such matters. Suffice it to say that, by the beginning of the year of the Lord 1548, a revolt was underway in Engoulmoys[2], which is said to have originated in the vast salt mines of Xaintonge[3]. The revolt, which later came to be known as "la iacquerie des Pitauds"[4], soon spread towards Bordeaux on the one hand and towards the Peyragort on the other. It was not long before its first signs came to be felt in Bazadois and even at Rauzan...

You see, dear friend, salt was the root cause of the misfortunes that abated upon our family. If it hadn't been for the people's bottomless appetite for salt, and the powerful nobles' greed to make more and more money out of it through taxation, all that bloodshed and devastation might yet have been avoided. It is why, chere Madeleine, I have vowed a long time ago to never again feel the taste of salt on my tongue. And to this day, I have, to the best of my knowledge, remained true to my word. Salt is repugnant to me. It tastes of disaster. It tastes of blood.

I was only nine years old around the time when these events unfolded, Éléonore eight. Our family was, at the time, caught in the midst of other events, which perhaps played their part in the tragedy to come. Our maternal grandmother, the Baroness of Sérillac, née de Lasseran, blessed be her memory, had fallen ill earlier that year. My mother had travelled to Sérillac in Vasconie[5], together with my sisters, Élisabeth and Hélene, to see her mother one last time as she lay on her deathbed. The Dowager Baroness of Civrac, our other grandmother whom you know well, was also away at the time, staying with her friends in Béarn. Accompanying her were her younger sister, Mademoiselle de Castelbajac and her eldest daughter, my aunt Françoise, who was making her debut at the Court of Navarre. Our uncles, my father's younger brothers, were no longer living with us at the time. They had entered into military service, as was and still is expected of the second and third sons of a noble family. It was due to these circumstances that my beloved father, the baronet, found himself alone at Rauzan with us children at the time the revolt reached our gates. Besides me and Éléonore, the castle housed our brothers, Jean and Louis, and our beloved Aunt Isabeau, a young lady of sixteen.

I cannot help but wonder whether these past events would not have played themselves out in a less tragic manner, had only my mother or my grandmother been at home when disaster struck. But there is, as you well know, dear friend, little merit in dwelling on such thoughts, and we must let the bygones be bygone.

What I am about to tell you next, dear Madeleine, will probably surprise and even shock you. It is my deepest wish that you may keep the contents of this letter to yourself and never utter a word of it to a living soul! For this is a secret our family has strived to hide for many years, and spreading it might have dire consequences for my beloved sisters' futures and our family's respectability at large. In all honesty, I had quite made up my mind to omit this chapter from my letter to you, dear friend. But try it as I may, I cannot bring myself to keep silent any longer. The role this chapter played in the downfall of our family cannot be denied because, perhaps at long last, Aunt Isabeau's story demands to be told, and because it is of essence for you to read it, dear friend, if you are to reach a deeper understanding of the dangers one invites into her life, and those of their dear ones, when one allows one's soul to be consumed by burning passions.

My Aunt Isabeau, my father's youngest sister, was not much older than me and my siblings at the time. She was about as old as you and Éléonore are now. And she was, without a doubt, the favourite child of her mother, who had doted on her since childhood. She had instilled in her all the new and daring ideas of the Renaissance, ideas that my grandmother had learned of in her youth, during her tenure as a lady-in-waiting to the Queen Marguerite of Navarre. My beloved father, in his turn, had a very special place in his heart for his adorable little sister. He could hardly ever refuse a request, however whimsical, if it came from her. And Isabeau knew how to charm and persuade like no other! This sentiment of brotherly affection, though laudable, played its part in the drama which is yet to unfold, as you will soon come to see, dear friend. Because it was this unbridled affection that motivated my beloved father to act the way he did during the revolt and ultimately put us all in harm's way.

But Aunt Isabeau was less like an aunt and more like an elder sister to me and my siblings. She and my eldest brother Jean were almost of the same age. I shall therefore call her just by her Christian name henceforth, as I do with my siblings, not out of disrespect, but out of affection.

We had all grown up together in the same nursery, you see, and we all loved and admired her. How could we not, when Isabeau was so full of life, had such an adventurous spirit and her beauty took anyone's breath away the moment they saw her? Me and my siblings fought amongst each other for her favour. She had an inexplicable charm about herself, like a magical spell, for I remember that when she smiled at me, all I wanted was for her to love me and never leave my side. Isabeau was conscious of this powerful effect that her beauty had on everyone who happened to cross paths with her because she could make others, even adults, bend to her will with incredible ease. My sister and I were truly in awe of her powers and we longed for nothing more than to be like her one day. I did not know in those days how foolish my wish was. Nor that my aunt's character contained within itself the seeds of her own, and others', demise. In any event, I cannot bring myself to throw blame upon her for the destruction that she unwillingly brought upon our family. For in the end, dear friend, Isabeau and her secret lover paid with their lives for their passion and their mistakes...

It is growing late and I simply cannot bring myself to put quill to paper anymore. The shy first rays of dawn announce themselves on the horizon. I see myself forced to leave my story unfinished if this letter is to be sent together with my sister's this morning. Much remains to be revealed, but I promise to write again soon.

May the Lord keep you and your dear ones in good health!

Yours devotedly,

Catherine de Durfort de Civrac

Second Letter From Catherine de Durfort
To Madeleine de Lamothe

Rauzan, le 7 iuine de l'Année de Deu 1556

My dear Madeleine,

Several days have passed since I sent you my first letter. As promised, I shall continue to tell you of the painful and sometimes shameful secrets deeply buried in my family's past. This one is a tale of forbidden love, impossible dreams and unimaginable consequences. When Isabeau's fairy tale romance came to an end, her whole world came crumbling down, and it took us all with it...

The son of our housekeeper, mistress Barjac, had been allowed by my grandparents to be educated together with my uncles. They were animated, perhaps, by the humanist principles so potent at the Court of Navarre at that time and were, without a doubt, impressed by Ferran's artistic talent, which was apparent since a raw age. I still remember how steady and confident his hand was as he drew colourful strokes on the white canvas, how his magical touch seemed to instil life into the people and the animals he painted. Even after all these years, the vivid beauty of his paintings remains intact, unsullied by the passage of time. In truth, to an outsider, they might appear to be the work of an Italian artist. You have seen some of them, too, chere Madeleine. It is he who painted the family portraits that grace the cold walls of our great hall and even those of my aunts and brothers that hang in the hallways.

According to the tiny crumpets of conversations, whispers and hearsay, I have gathered throughout the years, Ferran Barjac had been an avid learner. Once the tutor of my uncles, Jean-Claude and Jacques de Durfort, was dismissed, and the two of them were sent to Court to start their military training, Ferran moved to Bordeaux to study the art of painting in the workshop of a Genovese master established there. You may wonder how the housekeeper's son could afford all that, but you have probably already guessed that it was my grandparents who made the necessary arrangements. They cared for Ferran, as they did for his widowed mother, and had been moved by his unmistakable talent, as were we all.

When he returned to Rauzan, several years later, Ferran was a young man of twenty and two, who had received laudable praise from not only his master painter but several well-connected citizens of Bordeaux whose portraits he had been commissioned to paint. Thus, it is perhaps not so astonishing, dear Madeleine, that upon his return, my grandmother had him paint the portraits of our entire family. A small portrait he painted of Aunt Françoise was sent to her betrothed, the Chevalier de Courros and it is rumoured that he found it so lifelike that he did nothing but stare at it day and night until they were at long last married. As for Isabeau, it was most likely during the long hours they had spent together in the same room, when she posed for her portrait while Ferran attempted to capture her proud beauty on the lifeless canvas, that their feelings for each other started to bloom.

They had known each other since they were children, and they were both handsome and daring. My elder siblings and I were more often than not their chaperones and my head still reels with memories of all the exciting escapades Ferran and Isabeau concocted when they had tired of the portrait. Isabeau, in particular, was easily bored and quick to become tired of anything that did not awaken her enthusiasm. Ferran resisted her at first, devoted to his art as he was and loyal to my grandparents, but in the end succumbed, like all the others, to her unearthly charm and wit. One day we would all ride through the dense forest all the way to Pujols and back, another we would build makeshift rafts to sail along the Dordogne River. On occasion, we used to dress ourselves in rags and sheets, pretending to be ghosts and monsters, scaring the villagers of Rauzan. Although only a child, I could see that while the rest of us revelled in the playfulness of these games, they made Ferran and Isabeau grow closer and closer. They would talk in whispers and laugh, and sometimes they disappeared for hours. I saw their admiration turn into attraction, a mere spark at first, which evolved gradually into a flame and then into a hungry wildfire that consumed them both in the end.

I know that you will think all this unlikely and unbecoming of the daughter of a baronet. You understand now why this is a secret my family has endeavoured to keep buried for years. My dear Madeleine, I beseech you once more to keep this secret in the name of the friendship that binds us and my dear sister Éléonore! Most of all for her sake, as she is soon to be engaged and her future happiness may be forever ruined should a word of this leave your lips or quill. Think that it was she who asked me to bring back to life these secrets in my letters, in order to assist you in your own quest for happiness by shedding light onto the dark and dangerous path that lies ahead of you!

I need no painted portrait to remember how good looking Ferran Barjac was. As a child, I kept sneaking into his workroom to just stare at him while he painted. What a dashing figure he made when he stood tall and mighty with a brush in hand, completely absorbed by his work! In my eyes, he looked like a saint receiving the Divine Revelation as he stood in the resplendent rays of light that filtered down through the many small pieces of glass that made up the large windows of his atelier. Or like a wizard, conjuring with his magic all sorts of beautiful images out of thin air and then laying them down in beautiful colours on the blank canvas. I remember he had strong arms, long, elegant fingers and dark, intelligent eyes. His long eyelashes made them appear even more striking as he fixed his dreamy gaze on you. Ferran carried his jet black hair in a fashionably round, short haircut. "Just like the Genovese painters do!" he would say, shaking his head from side to side, making it ripple, to our delight. A handsome smile was always at the corner of his lips, and though his origins were humble, he had refined manners and a kind word to say to everybody. We did not think of him as a servant. To us, Ferran was like a distant cousin who had fallen on a hard time and had come to live with us. I remember that my brothers, may they rest in peace, used to look up to Ferran, a dashing and learned young man of great talent, who had lived in the big city of Bordeaux. And, I blush to confess it now, I was charmed by him like everyone else, especially once Isabeau had made me her confidante, and I began to be directly involved in their forbidden romance.

Little did I know then that I would come to regret this for the rest of my days. With a foolish child's understanding, I saw the role of confidante, which my beautiful aunt bestowed on me, and not on any of my sisters, as a great honour. Oh yes, I had a role to play as well in the events that led to this tragedy! For, you see, dear Madeleine, it was Isabeau who persuaded our father to open the gates of our formidable castle for the revolted peasants to barge in. She did so, perhaps, animated by a noble desire to side with those less fortunate than her, hoping to help them. But she was, alas, unchecked in her intentions, animated by a passion so strong and so intense that it paid no heed to any warnings or to the destruction it was sowing in its wake. This passion, this fire burning between them, ultimately lit Isabeau's funeral pyre, as it did Ferran's. And I was the one who helped build it, one twig at a time.

Oh, but I fear that I am trying your patience unbearably, dear friend. You must wonder what any of this can possibly have to do with our common acquaintance. I ask you to have patience, for all will be revealed to you in due time. For, you see, Ferran was drawn from the very beginning into the jacquerie and its ideas. Perhaps it came from a desire to fight for a stronger Aquitaine, unbridled by the royal power in Paris, or from a sense of justice to defend the poor against higher taxes and further deprivation. In my humble opinion, his deepest wish was to upturn the social order, to change our world, so that he and Isabeau might be free to love each other openly and build a future together. What may come to appal you even more, dear friend, is that Isabeau de Durfort came to share, over time, his views... and I with her. In any event, Ferran had been secretly in touch with the leaders of the salt miners' revolt from Engoulmoys, and had been entrusted by them to sow and nourish the seeds of discord amongst the peasant folk of Rauzan. His reckless actions had, alas, the undesired effect of building a feeling of mistrust and hatred against our family. As for me, I do not seek redemption for my foolish demeanour, which led to the deaths of those I loved most. But I was a child. I could not have thought, at the time, that my lovely aunt and our dashing painter, whom I have both known since I was a baby, were bad or capable of harming me and my siblings. And, as I bare my memories and my soul in this letter to you, chere Madeleine, I have to admit that I still cannot bring myself to think of them as such. I believe that they were good of heart but unable to make the right choices. They were too young and reckless, too eager to rebel against a world that had no place for them and their dreams of a shared future. But by not tempering their passions, by throwing caution to the winds, they brought destruction to us all.

Let their tragic story be a word of caution to you, dear Madeleine! Do not allow your feelings of attraction for a certain powerful and skilled knight of France silence the voice of reason. Do not let his charming words blind you to the manner in which he treats you and others. I beseech you to not allow your passion to cloud your judgement when choosing the one to whom you entrust your dreams and your future! I have seen where this path leads with my own eyes. Neither I nor my sister could possibly bear to see you share the blood-curdling end my beloved aunt met...

With these words of warning, I must take my farewell from

313

you for now, dear friend. My grandmother summoned me to her chambers, as it is my turn to read to her from the Holy Bible. Sleep is sure to follow, deep and undisturbed, after these long lectures, so I doubt I shall have time to continue my letter afterwards. But do not fret, I will write again soon! The story is nowhere near its end and I am yet to reveal the nature of Isabeau and Ferran's early demise, and the role a certain knight of your liking played in the deaths of my brothers.

Until then, I remain your devoted friend,

Catherine de Durfort de Civrac

Third Letter From Catherine de Durfort To Madeleine de Lamothe

Rauzan, le 10 iuine de l'Année de Deu 1556

Chere amye,

Thank you for your letter, which you must have sent before you had a chance to read my last letter to you. I have to say that this is a most unusual correspondence! The story I have to tell you is long and complicated, impossible to contain in a few lines. And between caring for my aging grandmother and sewing my sister's wedding dress, I hardly ever find time to write during the day. So I stay up late into the night to pen my letters, sending them as soon as I am finished, without awaiting your reply. My hope is that you learn the truth about the Chevalier de Montmorency's wrongdoings before it is too late. You are right to wonder what the story that I have told you so far has to do with him. But I believe that before exposing the mistakes of others, we need to take a hard look at ourselves. My family does not stand blameless. In more ways than one, we have brought about our own ruin, as you will soon learn. And yet, my brothers were just children. Foolish, perhaps, but innocent, nonetheless. They were not to blame. They deserved better. They deserved to live!

But allow me to dwell deeper into the faults of my own family first. You have learnt of Isabeau and Ferran's forbidden passion, of their impossible dreams and of their changing allegiance. You know even the role I played in all this, with all the foolish blindness of my youth. But I have not mentioned so far a word about the only adult left in charge of us children in those days, the absolute lord and master of our castle, our head of family. My father, le Baron de Civrac, has always been of a kind yet withdrawn disposition. For as long as I have known him, he has been content to rely on his mother or his wife to take the needed decisions regarding our family and our estates. So you see, chere amye, it was indeed a misfortune for us all that my father found himself alone, without the sage counsel of either of the ladies in his life, when the rebels arrived at Rauzan.

By then, Isabeau had become obsessed with changing the world. Her own rebellion against the order of things grew stronger and stronger by the day, fuelled by dreams of impossible bliss at the side of the man she loved. And when the rebels rallied the peasant folk of Rauzan and they all came to our castle gates one night carrying pitchforks and scythes, ready to lay siege, Isabeau and Ferran were there to weaken our defences from the inside. They were not entirely alone. I was still their confidante. I knew all about their plans and I never said a word to anyone, not even to my father. I shall not shy away from admitting my own guilt. I believed they were doing what was right. I wanted the two of them to be together with all my heart. Little did I know that it was going to lead them to their deaths...

In any event, my clever, persuasive aunt succeeded in instilling in my father the conviction that the wisest course of action was not to meet the advancing army of discontented peasants with force or resistance, but with an offer of peace. She praised with eloquence the virtues of peaceful negotiations, of avoiding violence and sparing human lives. My father, taken entirely by surprise, shocked, paralysed by his indecisiveness, was all but too eager to avoid bloodshed and welcomed her and Ferran's plan. It pains me, my dear friend, to think of my father as weak. It is a most unfilial notion. I love him dearly now, as I did then. I know that all he did back then, he did it with the best of intentions. He wanted to protect us all, his children and his sister, as perhaps any gentleman would under such circumstances. Our castle is strong, as you well know, my friend, built in the old fashion, with sturdy high walls, a deep moat, a mobile bridge and a tall defensive tower. I believe to this day that the castle would have withstood a week's siege and the tragedy to come might have been thus avoided, if only we had kept the bridge raised and the iron gates closed. Even with only a dozen loyal guards to defend it, our fortress would have remained strong, impossible to breech. And all the Durforts within its walls would have endured, just like in our family motto. But, as it turned out later, not all our guards were loyal. Some of them supported the rebellion themselves. So perhaps the castle might have fallen apart from within in the end, regardless of my father's decisions that night. But we will never know for sure.

What is certain is that the Lord of Civrac ordered the bridge to be lowered and the gates to be raised. The crowd barged in and with them, a handful of inciters arrived from the Engoulmoys, armed with knives and swords. A dozen of them who called themselves the leaders of the rebellion were invited inside. After some hours of negotiations, to which my siblings and I were not privy, my father surrendered the castle to Ferran Barjac and the rebels. I remember sneaking up to the rooftop of our central tower with my eldest brother to watch the angry mob. It was late one night in early October, and I could see burning torches everywhere, like the entire village was on fire... on our bridge, in the lower court and even in the streets of Rauzan, all the way to the main square and the church. I knew they were peasant folk from Rauzan and Pujols, our family's estates. I even knew the names of the leaders arrived from Xaintonge. I knew a lot and yet did nothing. My silence had dire consequences. My regrets are my curse.

"They are attacking us. This is all that devil Ferran's doing!" I remember my brother Jean swearing between clenched teeth by my side.

But I still did not think that they were there to harm us. In my foolishness, I thought that they were there to ask my father to allow Isabeau and Ferran to marry and ensure their happiness.

As you might well imagine, esteemed friend, several days of terror and tragedy followed. The angry peasants were intent on looting the castle and did not pay any respect to us or to my father, their lord and master, who had shown them nothing but kindness in choosing to welcome them into our home. I remember the overwhelming feeling of fright that took possession of me when I looked at their faces, contorted by anger and hatred. Their eyes were shining with a raw hostility that made no distinction between children and adults. When their eyes fell on me, I saw that they did not wish me well, although I was but a little girl. I was unable to recognise the faces of our guards and our servants, the same people I had known since I was a little girl, who used to smile at me or offer me treats from the kitchen. I was scared, and I kept asking myself if I had wronged them in some way, trying to explain the shocking change in their manners towards me, their sheer hatred. Perhaps only they know the answer to that, but I do believe they did not see me anymore. They saw instead what I was, a rich and spoiled child, who had more the moment she was born than they could ever hope to gather in a lifetime. No one can choose the circumstances of their birth, dear friend. But we are fortunate, most people aren't. The world is unjust, built to serve our needs, the needs of the few. My aunt was right to wish to change it...

As for Ferran, the bold and striking Ferran, he was one of them. It was only upon seeing the sharp determination reflected in his eyes as he disclosed to the mob the places where we kept our valuables that I suspected, for the first time, that I may have lent a hand in bringing great misfortune upon those I loved. Isabeau took his side, speaking of justice, insisting that my father should not object to any of the rebels' demands. She, too, seemed changed, acting furious. I saw it all happen from the high gallery of the banquet hall, where Jean and I hid after leaving the tower to eavesdrop on their conversation.

"She sold us all to the traitors, to him. How could she?" my brother whispered in my ear.

There was no answer I could offer him, for I could make no sense of Ferran and Isabeau's actions either. But I remember feeling reassured by my father's presence, convinced that he would surely know what to do to keep us all safe. And yet, before I knew what was happening, an ugly looking man, speaking in a foreign accent, announced that the Baronet of Civrac and his family were the rebels' prisoners and that we were all to be thrown in the dungeons. My aunt protested, arguing that it was not part of their agreement. She appeared brave and undefeatable to me at that moment as she raised her voice to defend us and took a menacing step towards that ugly intruder. But she was silenced with a resounding slap that sent her reeling backwards into my father's arms. I gasped and fell into Jean's arms in shock. He let out a curse, writhing under my weight, trying to push me aside. I covered his mouth with my hands, begging him to not give away our position. Together, we followed in silence the events unfolding themselves in the great hall beneath.

Ferran stepped between her and the man who must have been the leader of the rebels from Engoulmoys. He drew out his sword. It surprised me to see that Ferran had a sword. I had never seen him carry one before, but at that moment, I felt grateful that he did. I hoped, against all odds, that he would make them leave us alone, that he would make them all get out of the hall. But, at a sign from their leader, the mob jumped with rehearsed precision to attack Ferran Barjac with their pitchforks. I cannot be sure, dear friend, so many years have passed since, but I believe he took two or perhaps three of them down before he fell. I remember Isabeau screaming and kicking in my father's arms. He, too, shouted at them to stop and promised to accept all their terms. But the blood-thirsty mob did not stop. My aunt and Ferran called out each other's names until his voice could no longer be heard. Their voices still haunt me at night sometimes. I cried in silence from my hiding place. Ferran was dead. And we were all in great danger.

The hall resounded with the rebels' cries of jubilation. I

looked at my father and saw nothing but a crestfallen expression on his face. The Baronet of Civrac had opened the gates of his fortress at Isabeau's entreaties. This welcome had been meant as a peace offering, a gesture of friendship. The rebels had promised that we were to receive kindness and mercy in return. Of that, we got but very little. It turned out it had been just a trap to lure us into giving up our castle without a fight.

After some men disposed of Ferran's corpse, their leader marched up to my father and snatched Isabeau from his arms, yanking her by the hair. Her cries filled the hall once more.

"No! Let go of her!" my brother shouted, giving away our hiding place.

He then darted to his feet and ran down the servants' stairs. I was too afraid to speak or move. Down in the hall, the Baronet of Civrac sprang into action at last and punched the nasty rebel in the face. My father looked livid with rage, like I had never seen him before. But the other men rushed forth and started to kick and punch him, making him crimp into a ball on the floor.

"Do not kill him. We need him alive!" said their leader, nursing his cheek, and his words gave me hope.

To make them stop, Isabeau declared that she would do everything they asked of her, if only no more harm was to come to her brother and his children. I heard my brother scream Isabeau's name and saw that the rebels had caught him as he had tried to burst into the hall. He struggled in their arms, and soon, a man smacked him unconscious.

I hugged myself and used all my strength to hold back my sobs. I was frightened, my friend, very, very frightened. I listened in a daze to the man from Engoulmoys agreeing to my aunt's terms and instructing the men to search every inch of the castle until they found us all. From the height of the gallery where I was hiding, I saw our former servants carry out of the hall the limp bodies of my father and brother. I swear that in those moments, dear friend, I thought that I shall lose them, too. I stood up and ran down the stairs to be by their side, and soon, the men caught me and threw me in a bad-smelling cell in the dungeon. The bodies of my father and brother were thrown into another cell. Soon, Louis, Éléonore and our nurse Maria joined us there. They had found them in the nursery. I remember how glad I was to see my other siblings unharmed and to feel Maria's loving arms around me after all the violence I had witnessed. We had no clue as to where they had taken Isabeau. I shudder even now, as I pen these lines, to think what those godless men did to her...

The night is growing late, dear friend. I must rest, although I shudder to think of the dreams that are likely to visit me tonight. But I am a lady of my word and you shall hear from me soon. The gruesome story of my aunt and brothers' last moments on this Earth waits to be told, and it involves the sinister arrival of the Chevalier de Montmorency at our gates.

Until then, I remain your faithful friend,

Catherine de Durfort de Civrac

Fourth Letter From Catherine de Durfort
To Madeleine de Lamothe

Rauzan, le 13 iuine de l'Année de Deu 1556

Dear Madeleine,

You must be growing very impatient with me. This is the fourth letter I pen to you and I do not know if it shall be my last. I must ask for your forgiveness for taking so long in finishing my story. I have to confess that I have delayed this moment on purpose. For, you see, this is one of the hardest stories to tell, a story that keeps haunting my dreaming and waking hours alike. It is a most painful memory for, as you will come to understand soon, my beloved aunt died in front of my very eyes. But I am getting ahead of myself. Let me tell you the story as it happened.

One morning, after we had spent yet another terrifying night in our cells, more awake than asleep, Aunt Isabeau was reunited with us. Several days, perhaps a week, had passed since our incarceration. Days faded into nights and nights into days. Time seemed to pass away differently in the dark, dirty cells... especially in the eyes of a frightened child of nine.

That morning, as I was saying, two men escorted my aunt back into the same prison cell I was kept in, together with Éléonore and Maria. Oh, my dear Madeleine, I say that they escorted back my aunt, but in fact, the lady who joined us that morning was someone we could hardly recognise. Her hair was hanging loose, in disarray, covering her face. Her lovely dress, the colour of vermillion, was torn in several places. And her face was bruised and stained with blood.

Upon seeing the state in which his beloved little sister was delivered back to us, my dear father let out a terrible scream, and he fell to his knees right where he stood, in the cell opposite ours. He stretched his arms upwards towards the stone ceiling, or perhaps towards Heaven... My brother Jean let out a cry as well, understanding better than I could at the time the gravity of the evils that had befallen our beloved aunt. He hurled himself against the bars of his cell in a feeble attempt to inflict some harm on the men who had brought her there. Jean only managed to pull at their clothes, accompanying his actions with angry, insulting words. In retaliation, the treacherous men thrust the handles of their swords with lightning-like speed through the bars and jammed them into my brother's face. They broke his brow, laughed, and left. I saw my brother fall with a stifled thud to the floor. All this happened very fast.

These men had once been our guards, sworn to protect us. Yet all they did in those days was to laugh and shout insults at us. As nourishment, they threw us bones and other remains from their meals. Some of them went as far as to relieve themselves on top of us as we were sleeping. I shall spare you the gory details of the indignities we all had to suffer during our captivity, dear Madeleine. But Jean and Maria got very sick, and my father was spitting blood. We found out later that the men had broken his ribs.

It struck me, even at the time, that they treated Maria just as bad, even though she was not of high birth. But she had refused to join them, preferring to remain by our side, and they called her a traitor. So she suffered at their hands just like the rest of us, and even more... For her devotion and courage, we see Maria as one of us now, shocking as that may seem to you or any other outsider. Only fifteen years old at the time, she cared for us like a sister, despite being ill, and she saved my life. For that, she paid a very high price. I realise now that she was to us everything Isabeau should have been but hadn't. Blinded by her passion, my aunt had not even spared us a thought when concocting her plans, instead using me and Jean for her selfish purposes. She had never cared for us the way Maria had, and our safety was never her concern. But I should not be ungenerous towards the dead. At the end of the day, Isabeau suffered greatly at the hands of the men who betrayed her trust.

I remember rushing to my aunt's side after the guards went away. I knelt down and held her hand in mine. I stared bewildered at the strange expression on her blood-streaked face. She just sat on the hard, filthy floor, where she had fallen after being pushed inside the room by the guards. And she stared in front of her without answering any of my questions or showing any sign that she understood where she was or who I was.

"They killed you!" she said, her voice raspy and unfamiliar.

I hugged her, trying to whisper comforting words in her ear.

"Why didn't they kill me, too?" she whispered, all of a sudden, taking hold of my arm and looking at me with glaring eyes.

Her haunted look sent chills down my spine. I freed myself from her grasp and ran to the cell bars, from where I called out to my father. But he seemed rooted to the floor, where he had fallen onto his knees. His eyes were fixed on the rotten ceiling as if he was waiting for Saint Michael the Archangel and his angels to come and save us. He did not even move to look at me, despite my pleading cries. A string of blood sipped out of the corner of his mouth. His loud and troubled breaths were the only sign that he was still alive. Louis, the kind, calm, practical Louis, struggled alone to help Jean stop the bleeding from his temple with a rag he had made by tearing away a long piece of his shirt. Maria asked me to come to her, and I obeyed, too scared to go near my aunt again. She was sitting in a corner, cradling a crying Éléonore in her arms. We were all frightened. We did not know if we were going to come out of those dungeons alive.

I know now that Isabeau must have suffered unspeakable

horrors for days on end... horrors so gruesome that she could not bear to live another day haunted by their memory. I know this because she seized the first opportunity to free herself from them. She never told us what those despicable men did to her. It is a secret she carried to her grave. It was probably for the best. In truth, I do not wish to know it, dear Madeleine, and I am sure, neither do you.

When news of the royal troops' advancement reached us some days later, most of the revolted peasants made themselves scarce. A guard threw a ring of keys in my father's cell before he disappeared. Perhaps he was a kind soul and wished to show us kindness. Perhaps he was aiming to put us in his debt and only guarded his own interest. In any event, he gave us the keys and freed us from our cells. But, dear friend, I must confess that whenever I am reminded of this fateful moment, I cannot help but wish that God had stricken that man on the very spot he was standing before he had had a chance to give us our freedom. I pray the Lord to give me strength and chase away from me such unchristian thoughts. And help me forgive this treacherous guard. Because if he had not thrown us the keys to the dungeons, perhaps my aunt and my brothers may yet be walking the Earth with us today.

But back then, we thought it a blessing. We all rushed out of the dungeons and into the then eerily quiet, deserted inner courtyard of our castle. My father and brothers vanished inside the castle in search of weapons. I saw Jean leaning into Louis at times, for he was weakened by the fever. My sister and I helped Maria climb the steep stairs out of the dungeon, and somehow, between the three of us, we managed to lower the inner gates of the castle halfway. We were all afraid, I think, and did not know what other dangers might yet await us. We wanted to close the gates to protect us, to protect our family. What we did not know was that the angel of death had already entered our home.

Out of nowhere, I saw a little kitten jump in the centre of the castle's outer courtyard. My sister must have seen it too, for she let out a cry and ran through the now half-closed gates. I had all but forgotten about these kittens she had been nurturing some weeks ago. It must have been some weeks, though at that moment, they seemed like years. For it felt like my whole life had changed in the blink of an eye, and I hardly knew what was real and what was not.

I followed Éléonore into the outer courtyard, admonishing her. Maria shouted for us to get back inside. I turned to look at Maria, who stood by the gates at the other end of the castle's bridge. Perhaps I had meant to answer her, but my words died on my lips. My eyes grew wide as I caught sight of a red silhouette at the very top of the great defence tower.

While we had all been engaged elsewhere, Isabeau de Durfort had climbed, unhindered, the stairs of the tower until there were none left to climb. It must have hurt her a great deal to do so. I had seen with my own eyes the extent of the wounds that those heartless men had inflicted on her legs and the rest of her broken body. I saw her stand there, at the top of the tower, a mere dot of red against the grey October skies. Before I could call out her name, she climbed the crenellated parapet of the tower, and without as much as taking a moment's pause, she hurled herself from its great height. It all happened so strangely fast. I had no time to move, no time to scream. Our castle's moat was devoid of water. It has always been. Instead, it was lined with sharp, thick stakes pointed upwards at a certain angle, meant to impale and instantly bring death upon any invader who might chance to fall therein. "Si ell dur, yo fort!" is the motto of our house. Our castle was very strong, and it was meant to protect us all. But we were not. When the hour came, we proved to be weak. The castle became our dungeon, and the stakes that were supposed to bring instant death to our enemies killed one of our own instead...

Sometimes, as I lay awake in my bed at night, I still hear her screaming. And her silhouette, clad in a red dress with long trumpet sleeves, flying through the evening sky, has haunted my sleeping hours since. Sometimes, in my dreams, her red dress blowing in the wind becomes a fire and her body turns into a living flame, and Isabeau becomes a Phoenix. But alas, my beloved aunt, unlike the bird of legend, did not rise again from her own ashes. Her body lay destroyed, impaled, with the bloodied sharp edges of two stakes protruding from her back. I was, as I said, in the outer courtyard, by the bridge's end, and saw it all happen. I was holding Éléonore by the hand. I remember as if it was yesterday, how first came the scream, then the fleeting vision of her fall, and then the crunching sound of my aunt's body being pierced by the stakes in the moat below us.

I will never forget, dear Madeleine, seeing the blood being pushed out of her body. The impact was so forceful that my aunt's blood flew all the way to the other side of the moat, tainting our castle walls in chaotic streaks of deep red. It spluttered on the other corpses, too. The sharp wooden stakes in our moat were full of them. Some were fresh, still oozing blood like my aunt's, others were already half-decayed. I recognised the dead bodies of some of our servants, those who had refused to betray us and had paid for their loyalty with their own lives. Amongst them were two young maids, not much older than me, with whom my sisters and I used to play in the gardens. I was too shocked to cry, but my heart ached for them all. I stared and stared at all the corpses, unable to look away. Our moat had been turned into a grotesque forest of the impaled.

Then I caught sight of Ferran Barjac's blue mantle hanging from the shoulders of one of the corpses and it all came crashing down on me, like a punch in the gut. I doubled over with pain and I became sick then and there. It was irrefutable proof that he, too, was dead and had been so for a while... I recognised his clothes and what was left of his face. He lay impaled face up on a wooden stake next to Isabeau. I could see other open wounds on his body, too, in all the places where the rebels' pitchforks had pierced him days ago. His mouth was agape. Black locks of hair hung wet with blood, and there were red trickles staining the one cheek that was visible from where I stood by the bridge. It was

Aunt Isabeau's fresh blood, raining on his white face from above...

I did not see it then, but I understood it later. Although their union had been doomed in this life, Ferran and Isabeau were united in death. They lay almost on top of each other, one impaled face down, the other face up on neighbouring stakes, although their corpses did not touch. I remember thinking that it was as if they still stared at each other, the way they had used to in his painter's workroom, when she had posed for her portrait...

As we both stood in full sight of this dreadful scene by the bridge, Éléonore started to sob. I took her in my arms, averting her eyes, and I remember we both held each other in a tight grip for a long time. I was unable to move or utter a word, as if I had been turned to stone on that very spot. I remember seeing Louis and Jean rush out through the gates and bend over the chain of the bridge to stare at the bodies. Strangely enough, Jean seemed to have recovered his strength, for he started to scream Isabeau's name with the fury of a wounded dragon. Tears were streaking his cheeks. For a moment, I thought that grief would overtake him. Alas, I could not have been more mistaken!

Before I could understand what was happening, Jean unsheathed his sword and took on running toward the village. Louis came and took me and my sister in his embrace without a word. He was like that, quiet and reliable. I remember clinging to him and Éléonore with all my might. I clutched my siblings to my bosom and felt determination sweep over me. Pass what may pass. I did not want to lose them, too! I soon realised we were all three crying silently, tears streaming down our cheeks.

My father's strenuous coughs grew louder and louder. I had become accustomed to them during our time in the dungeons. I turned and saw him double over the half closed gates, too weak to stand, his body shaking with every cough. Maria, on her knees, was trying to make her way to him, while shouting at us to get back inside. Thunders were heard in the distance. I raised my eyes for the first time to look at the sky. It had acquired a dark, and in my young eyes, menacing colour. It was a day in late October, and a storm was on its way. Dearest Madeleine, little did I know back then that before this ominous autumn storm would be over, more innocent lives would be lost forever...

You must surely wonder, dear friend, at the ink stains covering this paper. I pray you will excuse my clumsiness, for, you see, these are traces left by my tears. For me to remember these dark events is to relive them. It fills my soul with horror and unspeakable pain. The night is deep and an owl cries beneath my window, sending shivers down my spine. On nights like this, the ghosts of the dead refuse to remain silent. Or perhaps it is me who wakes them up, as I bring their story to life once more in my letters to you, dear friend. But rest assured, the role a certain chevalier of our mutual acquaintance played in this tragedy, and more specifically, in the deaths of my beloved brothers will be revealed to you in my next letter. For everything you have been told about the deaths of Jean and Louis de Durfort have been but a lie.

I pray the Lord to bestow His blessings on you and your family, and to keep you all in excellent health.

Your devoted friend,

Catherine de Durfort de Civrac

Fifth Letter From Catherine de Durfort
To Madeleine de Lamothe

Rauzan, le 15 iuine de l'Année de Deu 1556

Chere Madeleine,

I thank you for your letter and for your trust in me. Although I cannot claim surprise, I am thoroughly saddened by the news of your secret engagement. My dear Madeleine, I so wish to make you understand that you deserve so much more than being someone's secret! You are beautiful, lively and wonderful in every single way. Your family is rich and of noble ancestry. I believe you deserve an honourable suitor with nothing to hide, who courts you publicly, lavishes his attentions on you and sings your praises for everyone to hear! Forgive me for being so forward, my friend, but I must speak my mind. The Chevalier de Montmorency, alas, is not an honourable man. Not just because of committing the terrible deeds that I shall, at last, expose in this letter, but because of the lack of respect with which he treats you at present. But I shall continue my reminiscing, dear friend, and I entreat you to prepare yourself for the worst. Continue your lecture with a strong heart, for from now forth, the story is only shrouded in the dark veil of misery and death!

You must have heard before the stories of the ruthlessness with which the royal troops acted when smothering the revolt. By the time they arrived in Bazadois, they must have become, I imagine, hardened by all the brutality they had witnessed and imparted

on their way to us, in Engoulmoys and elsewhere... And somewhere along the way, they must have lost all trace of patience,
kindness and Christian mercy. Or perhaps, this is the way of the
men of arms, of which I know but too little. But what I do know
is that when they rushed from different directions towards
Bordeaux, at the helm of their armies, the two Montmorencys,
father and son, showed no mercy. "Montmorency without
mercy" should be their motto. They did not halt to consider who
they were striking when they imparted death, left and right, with
their mighty swords, from the height of their saddles. They spared
neither old men nor women carrying babies at their breast. And
they did not spare children. They did not spare us... But I am
allowing myself to be carried away by these dark memories, chere
amye. I shall continue my story from where I had last left it two
days ago.

As I continued to stare in painful disbelief at Isabeau and
Ferran's corpses reunited in death, I felt Louis untangle himself
from my arms. I tried to stop him, without success. He broke into
a run just like Jean, towards the village square. And before I had a
chance to say a word, my sister shoved me out of her way and ran
in our brothers' footsteps. If I close my eyes, I can still see my
siblings vanishing, one by one, behind the stables. I turned
towards my father in shock, crying out for help, only to see than
he was lying on the ground, right beneath the sharp stakes of the
iron gate. Forced into action by fear, I picked myself up and ran to
his side. He was alive, but unconscious. Maria asked me to help
her drag him away, to the safety of our inner yard. There was no
help to be expected from my father. But I was anxious to bring
back my siblings, so I begged Maria to come with me into the
village. She was whiter than linen and could hardly walk, but she
did it nonetheless. I was afraid and did not want to be alone. Arm
in arm, we headed deeper and deeper into the village. We did not
find my siblings, but some brutish royal soldiers found us.

I curse myself to this day for not being able to prevent my
siblings from running away and for asking Maria to follow me. To

protect me, she sacrificed herself. I escaped their lust only thanks to her quick thinking. Pulling out a pitchfork from beneath the corpse of a peasant, she told me to run faster than the wind and hide in a safe place. She then started to thrust it with unexpected strength towards each of the three soldiers, one at a time. I ran as fast as I could, praying they would leave her alone. They did not. Maria fought bravely, but soon they got hold of her pitchfork, punched her and kicked her, and dragged her into a ditch, where they took their turns to do unspeakable things to her. She was left for dead and came back to her senses only much later, when the battle was almost over. But I was spared and in turn, I was able to save my sister's life. If only I could have also impeded Louis' terrible, untimely death at the hands of François de Montmorency!

I know you might think that the eldest son of an admiral of France, a man of noble lineage, learned, cultured and a good Catholic, would never do such a thing. And yet he did. I know without the shadow of a doubt that it was none other than the Chevalier de Montmorency who slashed my brother Louis in half because I saw it with my own two eyes. It is a vision that I have endeavoured to forget, to no avail... the vision of the knight in black armour looming above the fleeing crowd from the height of his saddle, like a dark rider of the Apocalypse sowing death in his wake... the sight of the crest of the de Montmorency family, proudly displayed on his right arm... the vision of Louis running from his path, hand in hand with Éléonore... the muffled sound of my voice as I called out their names, drowned by the clamouring skies and the cries of the frightened crowd... the sight of Louis tripping and falling, some steps away from where I crouched, hiding under an upturned cart... of my sister Éléonore's hand slipping away from his... of her small body being pushed further away from him by the tide of desperate folk fleeing for their lives from the advancing knights... the faded memory of my own body moving as if governed by a higher force, dashing out of my hiding place... the vision of my fingers encircling my sister's wrist and dragging her back with me to safety, beneath the upturned cart... the force of my hand pressing hard on her mouth to stifle her screams, as I held her to my bosom... the cold wetness of our rain soaked-clothes... and then, the strongest vision of them all, that of Louis turning, with horror in his eyes, to watch de Montmorency's sword bearing down on him. It was a swift cut, from his left shoulder to the middle of his torso, a cowardly blow to a defenceless child of no more than ten springs.

This vision still haunts me, chere Madeleine. Try as I may, I cannot unsee it. And I cannot keep my tears from falling on this parchment as I write these words to you. Louis' eyes, the way they looked just before he died, are deeply etched in my memory... his wide-open, terrified eyes, looking up towards the angel of death rushing straight at him. I sometimes wonder what his last thoughts might have been, what passed through his mind at that moment. I also wonder if I could have saved him too, like I saved my sister. If only I had run out of my hiding place one more time...

You see, ma fort chere amye, this is the true face of François de Montmorency. He is a man capable of killing unarmed, innocent children in cold blood. You might still think, even after reading my testimony, that this must be a misunderstanding, that there must surely be some other, reasonable explanation as to why he acted in this cruel manner... that, perhaps, it might have been his father whose arm stroked my beloved brother down. But it was not Anne de Montmorency since he was not at Rauzan that day. As we later found out, he was at the helm of another contingent of the royal army, which made its way towards Bordeaux following the Garonne's valley, marching from the south. More-over, I saw the Chevalier de Montmorency's face that day, and I am sure to never forget it for as long as the Good Lord will allow me to walk upon this earth. Because, you see, as a result of that frightful blow, his sword got trapped inside Louis' dying body. The rider was, therefore, forced to come to a halt, ride back, and then dismount to retrieve his weapon. It is impossible to forget how he put his big, dirty boot on the side of Louis' neck and pulled at his sword with all his might. Once he freed it from my brother's flesh, he lifted the visiere of his helm and looked into the distance, without as much as casting a glance at the boy lying at his feet, drawing his last breath. I cannot help but find it strange that at a time like that, in the midst of battle, François de Montmorency found the leisure to just stand and gaze at the sky beyond as it rumbled, heavy with clouds and thunder. For it was him, dear Madeleine, beyond a doubt, no matter how much you would rather believe the contrary to be true. At that moment, I clearly saw his remorseless, hardened eyes through the heavy curtain of the falling rains. And they were not the blue eyes of Anne de Montmorency, le Grand Connétable de France[1]. They were the brown eyes of a cruel young man.

I am afraid this is the last piece of parchment I have left, dear friend. And I must end my painful reminiscence here. I did not witness my eldest brother's demise with my own eyes. I waited for the night to fall to make my way back to the castle, dragging Éléonore with me. There, we found my father barely conscious, coughing out blood. He had been found by our pastor and his wife, two brave and kind souls, who carried him to his bed and tended to his wounds. Our father praised the Lord for our return and seemed to regain his strength upon laying eyes on us, and neither of us had the heart to tell him about our brother's death. They offered us bread and cheese to eat, but none of us were hungry. As the pastor's wife was helping us take off our dirty clothes, we heard screams at the gate and I ran out in my shift dress to open it with the pastor, having recognised Maria's feeble voice. She had half crawled her way home and her face was so swollen I hardly recognised her. I was so overcome with joy to see that she was alive that I threw myself in her arms, almost toppling her over. I thanked her, over and over, for saving my life. We all soon went to sleep, exhausted and glad that it was over, praying that Jean, too, shall find his way back, like we did.

But, alas, it was not to be. The next day, the Chevalier de Montmorency appeared at our doorstep followed by his troops and presented us with Jean's corpse. His body was mangled due to a harquebus having been fired upon him, they said. But it was him beyond a doubt. We all recognised his favourite blue and silver tunic, which sported our family's colours and coat of arms. I remember that I started to cry again when I saw my eldest brother's corpse being laid on the cold floor of our once resplendent banquet hall, next to that of Louis'. At my father's request, the soldiers soon brought in even Isabeau's broken body. But we were not even allowed to mourn our dead. We had to hear instead from the chevalier's mouth the punishment the Crown had in store for us.

I remember my father sat, half slopping in his lord's chair at one end of our banquet hall. Both my sister and I were hid behind his chair upon catching sight of the Chevalier de Montmorency. His left elbow was heavily bandaged and there was a deep cut in his chain mail, which made it hang loose from the elbow down. I still remember the unchristian thought that crossed my mind at that moment... if only that blow had been better aimed... But I forget myself, dear friend. I am sure these words will displease you.

Having heard that my father had willingly opened the castle's gates to the revolted peasants, the chevalier declared our family guilty of siding with the rebels against His Majesty the King. There was no inquiry and my father, defeated, crushed and half unconscious, agreed to everything they said that day. He decided to impose heavy sanctions on our family, the payment of which took several years and put us into heavy debts, as you well know, dear Madeleine. I still shudder to think of the injustice of it all! It was as if the painful loss of my dear aunt and brothers' lives, as well as the general destruction of our estates, were not punishment enough...

As painful and sometimes discrediting to our good name as the secrets revealed within these letters are, I felt, along with my dear sister, that we owed you the truth about this gentleman and the suffering he has brought upon our family. I pray that you have found the strength to read all of my letters to the end. I must confess that my style was lacking at times, but I beg you to judge me kindly, for writing this story has been a most cumbersome and painful undertaking. I endeavoured to describe to you the tragic events of 1548 as they happened, or as I remember them, after all these years. Allow me to reassure you, chere amye, that I can see these visions before my eyes today with the same clarity that I did back then. I see them again and again in my dreams, and the pain caused by the untimely loss of my beloved brothers and aunt has never faded. I pray you will forgive my sentimentality and the occasionally inelegant appearance of my letters.

I entreat you to reconsider your choices and to be prudent in your actions. But most of all, I pray you to heed our words of warning and do not allow yourself to be compromised in the haste of the moment. Be wise and bid your time, chere Madeleine! I wish for nothing more than for you to be spared all and any heartaches at the hands of this chevalier. And please know that it is not too late to save yourself from a fate that you may come to regret for the remainder of your days!

Hoping you are well and that we shall see each other soon at my sister's wedding, I remain your devoted,

Catherine de Durfort de Civrac

The End

Family Trees

Family of Durfort de Civrac

Jean de Durfort de Civrac ~
Louise de Castelbajac

Isabeau de Durfort

Françoise de Durfort

François de Durfort, Lord of Civrac ~
Elisabeth de Sérillac

Jacques de Durfort

Jean-Claude de Durfort

Helene (Elina)

Eleonore (Altenor)

Catherine (Calarina)

Louis (Lois)

Elisabeth (Elisea)

Jean (Joan)

Family of Lasseran de Monluc

Amanieu de Lasseran ~ Marie de Pardaillan

François de Lasseran de Monluc ~ Françoise de Mondenard

Jean de Monluc

Marie

Blaise de Lasseran, Lord of Monluc ~ Antoinette d'Ysalguier

Marguerite

Pierre-Bertrand

Marc-Antoine

Elisabeth de Sérillac ~ François de Durfort de Civrac

Anne de Lasseran ~ Jean de Sérillac

Jean de Sérillac ~ Anne de Larty

Marguerite, Lady of Sérillac

Family of Lamothe de Cambes

François de Lamothe, Lord of Cambes =
Marguerite de Savigny

Nicolas

Anne (Anaïs)

Marie-Madeleine
(Madalena)

Family of Ségur de Montazeau

Bérard de Ségur =
Marguerite de Chassaignes

Bertrand de Ségur,
Lord of la Mollère and Pitray

Jean de Ségur,
Lord of Montazeau =
Claude de Rochechouart

Pierre de Ségur,
Lord of St. Aulaye and
Pontchapt

Antoine de Ségur =
Henriette de Rieumes

Armand

Aimery

Anne

Family of Rochechouart de Mortemart

Aimery III de Rochechouart de Mortemart – Jeanne de Pontville

Anne, Louis, Aubin, Aimery

Claude de Rochechouart – Jean de Ségur de Montazeau

François de Rochechouart, Lord of Mortemart – Renée de Taveau

René

Gabrielle

Madeleine

Family of Louppes and Montaigne

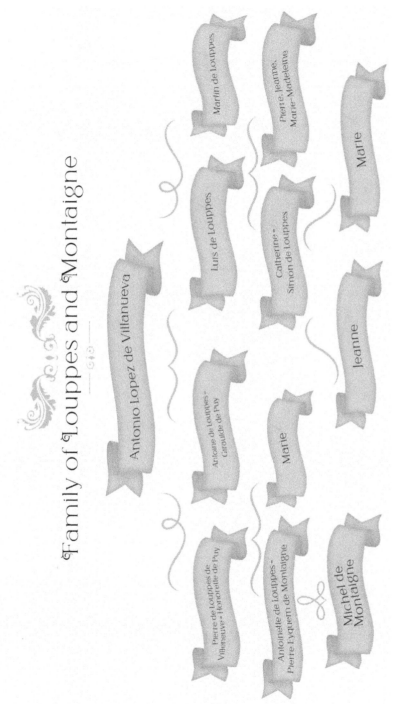

Antonio Lopez de Villanueva

Luis de Louppes

Martin de Louppes

Catherine - Simon de Louppes

Pierre, Jeanne, Marie-Madeleine

Antoine de Louppes - Giroalde de Puy

Marie

Marie

Jeanne

Pierre de Louppes de Villeneuve - Honorette de Puy

Antoinette de Louppes - Pierre Eyquem de Montaigne

Michel de Montaigne

Endnotes

CHAPTER ONE: ALIENOR

1. "I came here in search of some fresh air." (The French phrases included in this book are following the orthography and spelling of Middle French, as it was written in the 16th century, not of the modern French language.)

CHAPTER TWO: ARMAND

1. Catherine de' Medici (1519-1589), Queen Consort of France between 1547-1559 as the wife of King Henri II.

CHAPTER THREE: CATARINA

1. "Dear sister" (From Old Occitan, the vernacular language of Aquitaine in the 16th century.)
2. "My God...!" (Translated from Old Occitan.)
3. "My Lord de Montmorency!" (Translated from 16th century French.)
4. "If he (the castle) holds fast, I am strong." (Translated from Old Occitan.) This is the motto of the house of Durfort.

CHAPTER FOUR: ARMAND

1. "Miss, your veil!" (Translated from 16th century French.)
2. "I thank you, my lord!"

CHAPTER FIVE: ALIENOR

1. Lord of Civrac, Rauzan and Pujols. (Translated from 16th century French.)
2. "Dear mother"

CHAPTER SIX: CATARINA

1. Courtly love. (Translated from Old Occitan, the language thought to have originated the concept.)
2. "Élisabeth, I beg you..." (Translated from 16th century French.)

3. "With pleasure, sir."

CHAPTER SEVEN: ALIENOR

1. Wit, quick thinking. (Translated from 16th century French.)
2. "Dignity and patience are the foremost virtues of a noble young lady."
3. Silver. Argent is the term used in heraldry, where even in the English language, the words used to describe coats of arms are derived from the French language. The "bend azure" is a blue band, "lion rampant" is a standing lion, "gules" is crimson.
4. Pierre de Ronsard (1524-1585) is an important figure of the French Renaissance, and contributed to popularising the sonnet in France. He was a member of a prestigious group of writers called La Pléiade and he was sometimes called "the prince of poets" by his contemporaries. His second book of sonnets, "The Continuation of Love" or "The Second Book of Love" was published in 1555.
5. "Sonnet XXXVI" by Pierre de Ronsard. The author's translation from 16th century French into modern English:

    "My sighs, my friends, you please me
    More so since you are born of a worthy place:
    I carry in my heart incurable flames,
    But fire agrees with me, alas, and does me no harm.
    I am as pleased to feel the cold as I do heat;
    Pleasure and displeasure, I hold no faith in these.
    I am truly fortunate to be elevated to the realm of love,
    Although my fate puts me among the wretched.
    Among the wretched? No, among the blessed.
    "A man cannot, without falling in love, know
    That it is through pain that one can count their blessings.
    No, I would not want, for all the gold in the world,
    To not have suffered the pains which I had in loving,
    In the hope of a blessing that is worth a thousand tears."

CHAPTER NINE: MADAME DE MONTAZEAU

1. "Dear friend" (Translated from 16th century French.)
2. "But of course, my dear."
3. Shrovetide, Carnival, the days before the beginning of the Easter Lent.

CHAPTER ELEVEN: ELINA

1. "Elina, come!" (Translated from Old Occitan.)
2. "Good night" (Translated from Old Occitan.)
3. "Let us go!"

4. "Alienor, wait!"

CHAPTER TWELVE: ALIENOR

1. "Excuse me, madam" (Translated from 16th century French.)
2. "Oh, no"

CHAPTER THIRTEEN: MADAME DE CIVRAC

1. "Dear husband" (Translated from 16th century French.)
2. "Thank you"
3. "Good night"
4. "Elise, this is scandalous!"

CHAPTER FOURTEEN: ALIENOR

1. "Do not worry, dear mother."
2. "Goodbye, my lord."

CHAPTER SIXTEEN: ALIENOR

1. "Be careful, my daughter!" (Translated from 16th century French.)
2. "Be brave, Alienor. And dignified!"
3. "Please be seated, miss!"
4. Gentleman
5. "Oh, excuse me, my lord."

CHAPTER SEVENTEEN: ELISEA

1. "One more dance, miss?"
2. "It is I who should be excused, miss!"

CHAPTER EIGHTEEN: ALIENOR

1. A type of early crinoline, worn by the noble ladies of Western Europe in the 16th century.
2. Henri de Foix, the fifth count of Candale (?-1572), son of Frédéric de Foix (to be mentioned shortly) and Françoise de la Rochefoucauld (appears in Chapter 5).
3. "Shh... wait, my lord."

4. Louis Prévost de Sansac (1496-1576), also known as the Captain of Sansac.
5. "You are quite right, my lady."
6. "Some cider for my lord?"

CHAPTER NINETEEN: ARMAND

1. Antoine de Noailles (1504-1562), the first count of Noailles. He was made an admiral of France in 1559.
2. Frédéric de Foix, fourth count of Candale (?-1571), a famed military man and a fervent supporter of the Protestant cause, married to Françoise de Rochefoucauld (who appears in Chapter 5) and father to the Chevalier Henri de Foix (mentioned in Chapter 18).

CHAPTER TWENTY TWO: AIMERY

1. Castle. (Translated from 16th century French.)

CHAPTER TWENTY THREE: MADAME DE MORTEMART

1. "Dear aunt"
2. "Dear nephew"

CHAPTER TWENTY FOUR: ALIENOR

1. A type of headgear for noblewomen, similar to a thick, round tiara, which was very popular in the first half of the 16th century. In England, it was known as a French hood.

CHAPTER TWENTY FIVE: MARGUERITE

1. "It is very cold, my lord." (Translated from 16th century French.)

CHAPTER TWENTY SIX: CATARINA

1. Private conversation, tête-à-tête. (Translated from 16th century French.)
2. "But, dear mother..."
3. "Dear mother, calm down, I beg you!"
4. "My dear daughter"

CHAPTER TWENTY SEVEN: ARMAND

1. "My lords..." (Translated from 16th century French.)

CHAPTER TWENTY EIGHT: ALIENOR

1. High society of Bordeaux.
2. "Oh, well? A wedding?"
3. The monastery of the Cordelières.

CHAPTER TWENTY NINE: AIMERY

1. "Good day, my lord." (Translated from 16th century French.)
2. "The baroness and miss Gabrielle."
3. "These are for you."
4. Little weakness.
5. "Gabrielle, let us leave."
6. "My little Gabrielle."
7. "You have nothing to fear, my angel."
8. "No, but here is a letter addressed to my nephew..."
9. "Let us go, Gabrielle; your dance teacher is waiting for us."
10. "Oh, of course. Excuse me, my uncle."
11. "My dear mother, your sister."
12. "Thank you, dear uncle. I will never forget what you have just done for me!"

CHAPTER THIRTY: ARMAND

1. "Many thanks."
2. "My captain"

CHAPTER THIRTY TWO: ALIENOR

1. "My ladies, allow me to come to your aid!" (Translated from 16th century English.)
2. "You come at the right time, my lord. You are our hero!"
3. "Come, dear sister." (Translated from Old Occitan.)
4. "At your service!" (Translated from 16th century French.)
5. "Dear aunt, you are feeling better!"
6. "Little Peyrot". Peyrot is a diminutive from Pierre, commonly used in the south of France.
7. Pierre-Bertrand de Monluc was known as "Captain Peyrot" during his lifetime, according to his father's famous memoirs "Commentaires de messire Blaise de Monluc" (published posthumously in 1592).

8. "Cousin Éléonore, what a pleasure to meet you."
9. Private conversation, spelt as "tête-à-tête" in modern French.

CHAPTER THIRTY THREE: ALIENOR

1. Queen Marguerite de Navarre's (1492-1549) most praised work, "Le Heptaméron", was meant to contain 100 stories told over ten days of travel by different characters, much like Giovanni Boccaccio's *Decameron*. But the collection was left unfinished, the story ending on the seventh day, since the eight was left incomplete at the time of the Queen's death.
2. "Good day, dear grandmother." (Translated from Old Occitan.)
3. "Oh well, dear grandmother..."
4. "Yes, dear grandmother..."

CHAPTER THIRTY FOUR: AIMERY

1. "Delighted to make your acquaintance, my lord."

CHAPTER TWENTY FIVE: ARMAND

1. Another name for Old Occitan.

CHAPTER THIRTY SIX: MADAME DE CIVRAC

1. Revolt, rebellion. (Translated from 16th century French.)
2. "The dice is cast," the famous words attributed by Suetonius to Julius Caesar. Better known under another variation: "alea iacta est". (Translated from Latin, from "The Life of the Deified Julius".)

CHAPTER THIRTY SEVEN: ARMAND

1. "I thank you for this dance, my lady." (Translated from 16th century French.)
2. "With pleasure, my lord."
3. "I beg to be excused, my lord."
4. "Of course, my lady."
5. "Oh, dear Lord, what courage!"

CHAPTER THIRTY EIGHT: ALIENOR

1. "For you? Anything at all, dear cousin." (Translated from 16th century French.)
2. "Are you feeling quite well, dear cousin?"
3. "Of course, my cousin."
4. "Dear Cousin, please be so kind as to introduce me."
5. "My lord father! Allow me to bring you great joy."
6. "Here is my cousin, Éléonore de Durfort de Civrac."
7. "Captain, please excuse us."
8. "Come and find me later, chevalier. We should talk."

CHAPTER FORTY: CATARINA

1. "Dear cousin, what a delightful evening, isn't it?"

CHAPTER FORTY TWO: ALIENOR

1. "My beautiful lady." (translated from Middle French.)
2. "Welcome to Cambes, my lord, miss."
3. "Allow us, my lord, miss, to present you with our congratulations for the engagement." In the French language, the word for "engagement", in this case "les fiansailles", is always a plural, even in its modern form "les fiançailles". (A/N)

CHAPTER FORTY THREE: ARMAND

1. "Captain! Praised be the Lord. Here you are, at last."
2. "See you soon, my lady."
3. "My friend."

CHAPTER FORTY FIVE: ALIENOR

1. "Oh, Madeleine... But why? Why him?" (Translated from 16th century French.)

CHAPTER FORTY SIX: MADAME DE MONTAIGNE

1. "This is a disaster!" (Translated from 16th century French.)
2. "My beloved."

3. "In God's name, is he here this very evening?"
4. Toulouse, a major city in the South of France, capital of the region Languedoc. In Middle French, the language spoken in the 16th century; it was spelled Tholoze.
5. "Oh no... All this is sure to cause us problems..."
6. "Very well."
7. "Marie, come, dear niece."

CHAPTER FORTY NINE: ALIENOR

1. "Two... chevaliers de Ségur? No... I did not know of it!"
2. "Oh, chevalier... wherever you are, wait for me!"
3. A French historical province and the administrative name of the region situated north of the Dordogne River until the French Revolution. Spelt in modern French as "Périgord", the province was home to the estates of Montazeau and Montaigne.

ELEONORE'S LETTER ON 31ST OF MAY 1556

1. Rauzan, 31st of May of the Year of the Lord 1556.

ELEONORE'S LETTER ON 3RD OF JUNE 1556

1. "I remain your most devoted friend, who wishes for nothing more than for you to be happy,"

CATHERINE'S LETTER ON 3RD OF JUNE 1556

1. "I beg you to forgive my audacity in penning this long letter to you at the request of my beloved sister, Éléonore, whose dear and esteemed friend you are. You will be undoubtedly very surprised to receive it and perhaps even scandalised to read it. You and I have never enjoyed the sweet bond of friendship that you share with my sister. At the same time, we have known each other since childhood, and I have to confess that I think of you as a sister. I truly hope that you, too, can think of me as an elder sister who only wishes you well. This is, therefore, why I am taking the liberty of offering you my testimony of the tragic history of our family, leaving it to you, and to the Good Lord, to pass judgment on the conduct of the illustrious characters named therein." (Translated from 16th century French.)
2. Engoulmoys is the 16th century spelling for the region of Angoumois, a historical region of France, situated north-east of Bordeaux.

3. Xaintonge or Saintonge is a historical region of France, west of Angoumois, along the coast of the Atlantic Ocean. The seashore was covered, in the 16th century, by sea water marshes abundant in salt, and was a main centre of salt production in France.
4. The salt miners' revolt (translated from Middle French). Pitaud was the old name given to salt miners.
5. Vasconie is the old name of Gascogne or Gascony, as it is known in English. It is a region in the South West of France, between the Pyrenees to the south, the Atlantic Ocean to the west and the river Garonne to the north.

CATHERINE'S LETTER ON 15TH OF JUNE 1556

1. The Grand Constable of France was the First Officer of the Crown and Commander in Chief of the king's army.

Acknowledgements

I want to extend my gratitude to all those who inspired me to pursue my dream of publishing my first historical novel and helped me along the way:

Represent Publishing for believing in me and my mission to bring Alienor's story out into the world,

Chelsea Lauren, my fantastic editor, for all the great tips and ideas that helped develop my draft into the finished novel you hold in your hands or look at on your app today,

Brittany Evans, the talented designer, who used her art to turn my words into shapes and colours, and did an amazing job in designing the family trees and the cover of "Ribbons and Salt",

My beta reader and fan-in-chief Victoria Diaconasu who has read and re-read the novel countless times and provided me with valuable insights at every step along the way,

My husband Maarten, my son Mikael and my bonus daughter Matilda who have supported me in my writer's journey and constantly had to put up with my absence while I cocooned in my creative space to write, as well as with my habit of bringing around a notebook and pen wherever we went, even when we would go out for tea or dinner,

The helpful staff at the Mériadeck Library of Bordeaux (Bibliotèque Mériadeck de Bordeaux) and the Archives of the Museum of Aquitaine (Musée d'Aquitaine) who brought me pile after pile of centuries old books and documents to consult without complaining once, and the curators at the Castle of Rauzan (Château fort de Rauzan) and Montaigne Castle (Château de Montaigne) who thoroughly answered my questions and introduced me to the secrets of the castles where some of my characters, historical or not, lived their lives,

The inspiring and supportive NaNoWriMo community, without whose advice, support and brilliant goal-oriented system, I would have never managed to write the first draft of "Ribbons and Salt" in just a month,

My extended family and friends who have always believed in me and my art, and encouraged me to pursue my vocation and nurture my creativity.

About The Author

Klara considers herself a creator of worlds, a conjurer of the past. She started writing when she was eight years old and has tried her hand at several literary forms and genres. Most often, she writes historical novels imbued with mystery and suspense, and flavoured with a dash of romance. Klara holds a BA in Literature from The University of Tokyo, where she researched the literary traditions of courtly love in French and Japanese classical novels.

Her first book, a collection of haikus titled "Purely, Simply Haiku" came out to local literary acclaim when Klara was seventeen. More recently, she graduated from Margaret Atwood's Masterclass in Creative Writing. When she does not write, Klara attends historical reenactment events as a costumer, reads, travels and takes long walks in the forest. After living for many years in Japan, India, Romania, Hungary and France, she has grown roots in the Swedish countryside, where she lives with her family.

Website: www.klarawilde.com
Instagram: @klarawilde.writer

Lightning Source UK Ltd.
Milton Keynes UK
UKHW010722070223
416609UK00002B/746

9 798986 499529